MW00777206

Praise for Award-winning Author
C. Hope Clark

Hope Clark's books have been honored as winners of the Epic Award, Silver Falchion Award, and the Daphne du Maurier Award.

"Page-turning . . . [and] edge-of-your-seat action...crisp writing and compelling storytelling. This is one you don't want to miss!"
—Carolyn Haines, *USA Today* bestselling author

"Her beloved protagonist, Callie, continues to delight readers as a strong, savvy, and a wee-bit-snarky police chief."
—Julie Cantrell, *NY Times* and *USA Today* bestselling author

Murder on Edisto selected as a Route 1 Read by the South Carolina Center for the Book!

"Ms. Clark delivers a riveting ride, with her irrepressible characters set squarely in the driver's seat."
—Dish Magazine on *Echoes of Edisto*

"Award winning writer C. Hope Clark delivers another one-two punch of intrigue with *Edisto Stranger* . . . Clark really knows how to hook her readers with a fantastic story and characters that jump off the page with abandon. Un-put-downable from the get-go."
—All Booked Up Reviews on *Edisto Stranger*

The Novels of C. Hope Clark

The Carolina Slade Mysteries

Lowcountry Bribe

Tidewater Murder

Palmetto Poison

Newberry Sin

The Edisto Island Mysteries

Murder on Edisto

Edisto Jinx

Echoes of Edisto

Edisto Stranger

Dying on Edisto

Edisto Tidings

Edisto Tidings

The Edisto Island Mysteries
Book 6

by

C. Hope Clark

Bell Bridge Books

This is a work of fiction. Names, characters, places and incidents are either the products of the author's imagination or are used fictitiously. Any resemblance to actual persons (living or dead), events or locations is entirely coincidental.

Bell Bridge Books
PO BOX 300921
Memphis, TN 38130
Print ISBN: 978-1-61194-956-8

Bell Bridge Books is an Imprint of BelleBooks, Inc.

Copyright © 2019 by C. Hope Clark

Published in the United States of America.

All rights reserved. No part of this book may be reproduced in any form or by any electronic or mechanical means, including information storage and retrieval systems, without permission in writing from the publisher, except by a reviewer, who may quote brief passages in a review.

We at BelleBooks enjoy hearing from readers.
Visit our websites
BelleBooks.com
BellBridgeBooks.com
ImaJinnBooks.com

10 9 8 7 6 5 4 3 2 1

Cover design: Debra Dixon
Interior design: Hank Smith
Photo/Art credits:
Photo Credit (manipulated): C. Hope Clark

:Lted:01:

Dedication

To Night Harbor Book Club in Chapin, South Carolina, along with its illustrious leader Dee Stogdill, for discussing so many of my books. Love you, ladies.

Chapter 1

POLICE CHIEF MORGAN'S radio crackled. "Chief, you there?"

About to exit her patrol car, Callie stopped and freed her mic. "What is it, Marie?"

"A disturbance at the new Mexican restaurant. Thomas called it in."

This was Edisto Beach in December, three days before Christmas, and Callie'd just rolled up at an old friend's house on Pompano Drive to pick him up for a long lunch, because nothing happened this time of year. At least not until the small cadre of habitual visitors arrived for a brief Christmas.

Stan Waltham opened the passenger door and sat, silently waiting to see if his lunch date had to bow out of their meal plans. He knew the drill. He'd once walked in her shoes.

"Thomas can't manage it?" Callie pretended a grimace at Stan, rolling her eyes.

"Said to call you," Marie said.

"So why didn't *he* call me?"

"I'm just dispatch, Chief."

Marie was golden and way more than Edisto PD's admin. She wouldn't have called Callie unless necessary.

"On it, Marie. Out." She hung up and sighed. "Sorry, Stan."

He reached for the seatbelt. "Mexican's as good as anything else for lunch. I'll ride along."

Callie peeled out to make a short trip of the one-mile ride to Palmetto Plaza. A resident fresh to the community had leased the west end of the thirty-year-old store strip and outfitted an eatery called El Marko's. Last week's grand opening went moderately well, but the timing had most of the natives scratching their heads as to why Mexican cuisine, and why open in the off-season when most businesses shuttered windows or cut to minimal hours.

"Hopefully this is no more than customers skirting a tab," Stan said.

"Yeah. If the owner's so naïve to open during the off-season, someone might've pegged him for an easy mark."

"Maybe," he said. "I rather like the guy, though, and you would, too, if you gave him a chance."

"Quit matchmaking."

As her old captain when they both worked on the Boston police force, Stan had molded her professionally and nurtured her emotionally, even after she resigned from the force and relocated to Edisto following her hot mess of a meltdown. She'd been entitled. Her husband had been murdered.

But her old captain's advice to give the new guy in town a chance would have to be ignored right now. No one took crime as seriously as they should in Edisto, meaning she had to. Residents made excuses, and tourists looked the other way calling incidents spirits and accidents. Her job was to keep them safe and theirs to pretend nothing happened.

"You might wind up walking home if there's an issue," she said.

"It's a mile, tops. I can stand it."

They took Jungle Road with lights rolling. Stan rode laid-back, comfortable, like a training officer watching his rookie.

They approached the end of the mini-shopping center, with an unusual collection of cars for the middle of the day. Especially in December.

Thomas Gage's cruiser parked near the front, no lights. Thomas was her youngest yet favorite officer. Of an age to be eye candy, he volunteered for traffic stops, because it kept him perusing Palmetto Boulevard parallel to the sand, the road everyone had to cross to reach the water, especially tourists in bikinis.

He could handle most things on Edisto, so it surprised her that he'd called this one in. "On the scene, Marie," Callie radioed to dispatch, putting the car into park.

They approached, and though sensing no signs of threat, she did so cautiously, Stan a few feet behind her. Nobody outside. "Thomas?" she said into her mic. Only crackle.

"Thomas?"

"Inside, Chief," he replied, voice low.

The tinted storefront window obscured her vision with flurries and bursts of primary colors from the restaurant's Mexican theme and Christmas decorations. Less leery with Thomas sounding relaxed, she eased in and immediately stopped. Why were the lights off?

"Surprise!!!!!"

Lights flipped on and people popped out from everywhere.

Callie backed up a step into Stan, his barrel-chested form too heavy to budge. He belly-laughed and righted her.

"Happy birthday, Chief!" came at her from a dozen mouths, the laughter and cheers a cacophony of celebratory racket. Someone cranked up the music. *Feliz Navidad.*

Callie punched Stan. "You conned me, old man." Then she hugged him, his big long arms lifting her to her toes in a smother.

One by one people congratulated her.

"Which birthday is it?" Only Janet Wainwright, retired Marine real estate broker who reigned supreme on the beach, would ask that question. Her white, close-cropped hair took on an uncharacteristic pink tone in the lighting.

"None of your business," Callie said. "Your nephew arrive yet for Christmas?" A lot of residents took on relatives during the holidays.

Janet tipped her head toward a group of laughers. The college senior tailed Callie's neighbor Sophie like a dog in heat, ogling her for all to see. Both headed Callie's way.

Sophie thrust a margarita in her hand. Virgin from the smell of it. "Get this kid off me, Janet, before I hex him to kingdom come. Here, Callie. Drink up. Happy birthday."

One of her closest compatriots on the beach, Sophie Bianchi served as yoga mistress to the island . . . and the closest thing to an Alcoholics Anonymous sponsor one could have. She didn't come over without nosing through cabinets and closets when she thought Callie wasn't aware, hunting for the hidden bottles Callie used to strategically hide.

Callie finally registered the full view of her friend. "Good gracious, look at you."

Sophie twirled, her green, multi-striped skirt flaring, toes painted to match in golden sandals. Lemon yellow peasant blouse off those olive-tanned shoulders. A large rose over her left ear. "You like?"

"Come here. Open those eyes wide. What color contacts are you wearing?"

Sophie stopped, bent at the waist, and widened her eyes. "Green. What do you think?"

Callie laughed, then laughed again, feeling good. It had been a while. Even the crowd felt good. Before Callie knew it, she was engulfed by Stan again. "So damn glad to see you happy, Chicklet. Now go thank your host."

"Absolutely, where is he?" she asked, but a tender embrace caught her by surprise first. A woman in her mid-sixties beamed when Callie pulled back. "Sarah? Oh my gosh, you're early. I wasn't expecting you until Christmas Eve."

Sarah Rosewood. Her biological mother. The mother hidden from her knowledge for almost forty years by the political duo of parents Callie grew up with. Learning about her father's affair the same week of Mike Seabrook's murder, however, had been an unexpected blessing in a tragic time. It took the overwhelming love of both mothers to help Callie get past Seabrook's death.

Eyes moist, Sarah touched her daughter's cheek. "The first birthday I've been able to openly share with you. How could I not be here?"

Callie fought the threat of tears. "God, it's good to see you. Come over tonight. Please." She raised a brow." Is Ben . . . "

"I haven't even been home yet. Just got here." She patted Callie's arm. "He doesn't know I'm coming, but I'll explain about him later. You go have fun with your friends."

Someone raised the volume on the music as the crowd increased. Hors d'oeuvre platters began appearing on each table. The aromas of queso fundido, cilantro, mini tacos, and salsas tempted everyone to find a seat, or at least hover close by.

Word got around, because more bodies poured in. Callie pushed her way past back slaps and hugs over to Thomas.

She almost had to holler. "Who's working if everybody's here?"

"Ike," he said, bending to her ear. "He said he'll call if anything comes up. Marie, too." He held out a hand for a shake, the other hand occupied with a chicken flauta. "Happy birthday, Chief. Had my doubts about this place, but this new guy seems to be doing all right."

"So far," she said.

He shrugged. "Sophie ought to help. She's officially hostess for this joint."

With a smirk, Callie shook her head. "She campaigned hard enough for it."

Before the ink was dry on the lease, Sophie had schemed to land the job, a perfect match for a woman who craved people in her circle from sunup to sundown—making people spill their deepest secrets was her hobby, and she was masterful at it. A distinguishing quality Callie'd taken advantage of when the need arose at the station.

In the off-season the eatery didn't open until eleven, long after Sophie's yoga classes adjourned, and closed early. Summer, however, would be another story. Sophie flitted like a bee from one flower to another, and Callie expected her friend's interest to have moved on by then.

"Callie!" came Stan's voice from across the room. He was easy to locate. Her mentor had become an island fixture in his array of Hawaiian shirts that everyone on Edisto labeled *Stan shirts* and didn't dare wear. Even in December, he donned a long-sleeve tee with a floral shirt over it to preserve his image.

"Gotta go, Thomas," Callie said, swooping a chip through mango salsa en route back to Stan and the owner standing behind the bar.

She set down her empty glass and swallowed the chip before extending a hand. "How can I thank you for this splendid gala, Mark?"

"Already have," he said, returning the grip. "Not sure if it's the lure of free food or your influence on Edisto Beach, but either way, I'll take the attention." He rested on the bar. "Been meaning to come see you at the station, but this"—he motioned with a sweeping arm to the room—"has kept me sort of occupied."

"Good problem to have," she said.

He stood straight and took her glass. "Let me fill that margarita back up for you."

"Um . . . " Stan started.

Mark stopped, waiting for Stan to finish his sentence.

Callie smiled. "He's trying to discreetly tell you I'm on the wagon. Make it plain, please."

He winked. "You got it."

Mark had arrived on Edisto in late August, bought a small cottage two blocks from the strip mall, and optioned the restaurant's property in September the minute that sandwich shop vacated. Callie hadn't had a chance to say more than, "I'm the police chief. Call on me if we can help." And to give a nod in passing.

Everyone exceeded her five foot two, but she guessed Mark about an inch shy of six feet. He wasn't Hispanic, but his dark hair helped the image. If she picked any ethnicity, it'd be Cajun with a name like Dupree, but he came across as more All-American to her. He was well-muscled and fit.

Rumor had it he'd retired early from public service, but she didn't care to pry. Out here everyone had a past. When people moved to Edisto from across the Big Bridge, that past remained behind.

Besides, Edisto had Sophie Bianchi to dig up any details. Surprisingly, she hadn't come to Callie with the scoop on Mr. Dupree. Either there wasn't any intriguing intel or Sophie respected him enough not to pry. To Callie that sort of placed the man on a higher scale.

He placed the fresh drink on the bar with a dry napkin. "Can't say I've seen you smile like this before, Callie."

She liked how he didn't automatically call her Chief. "I'm not a crowd person, but these are good people," she said. "Took me a while to get to this place in my life."

"Sounds like a story," he said.

"A long and windy one," she said.

He smiled. "Wouldn't mind hearing it downstream."

Stan kicked her foot.

She forgot Stan was there. Then a twinge of a memory made her suddenly miss Seabrook.

Sophie showed. "Am I allowed to have a drink? I mean, I'm working, right?"

"I'll fix you one of Callie's," Mark said.

Scrunching her nose, she declined, stepped on the bar's foot rail, and leaned across the bar top, not caring who eyed that yoga backside. "Open your refrigerator down there. I stashed some carrot juice."

Chuckling, Mark did as told.

"He's learning," Callie said.

"Doesn't take long," Stan replied, laughing.

Sophie came back down and took her glass of thick orange drink, Mark having stuck a celery stick in it for fun. "I like this guy," she growled in Callie's ear.

"You like most guys who aren't in a nursing home or middle school."

Sophie batted her eyes in sultry acceptance, sipping on her drink.

"Wait, someone's missing," Callie said. "Where's Brice?"

"Oh darn, I must've forgotten his invitation," Sophie said, all innocent and coy.

Snickering, Callie took a sip of her fresh drink. "Better hope he doesn't find out you made the guest list."

"And I hope he doesn't think it was me," Mark added, spiritedly. "I can't afford to piss off a town councilman. I sank everything I own into this place."

Sophie stroked his arm. "We'll take care of you, Mr. Dupree."

"Yeah," he said, grinning. "No telling how that would go. Let me get back to work. And Sophie—"

"Get back to work, too," she said, and sashayed off, obviously loving the swish of that skirt on her hips.

Callie scanned the room for people she hadn't thanked yet. Real estate agents, business owners, retirees.

Stan leaned over. "Told you he was a good guy."

"What are you, my mother? Already have two of those. Don't need another."

An old-fashioned clapper bell overhead announced another arrival. Glancing up at the entrance, Stan's expression fell sour making Callie turn.

The man who entered shouted, "What, y'all started without me?" in a laughing pretense that he belonged. He waded into the room, toward Callie.

"Damn," she whispered under her breath. Brice LeGrand.

He reached the bar. "Beer," he barked at Mark, who only nodded to oblige.

Callie cringed at Brice's behavior, feeling the urge to apologize for this blight of a man.

"What the hell is all this?" Brice asked.

Stan answered first. "It's Callie's birthday, you idiot. And you better not ruin it."

Brice pivoted, giving his back to the bigger man, still intent on confronting his favorite adversary on Edisto Beach. "Mid-day, Chief? During duty hours? You realize how irresponsible this looks to visitors? Whose insane idea was this?"

"Mine," Sophie interrupted, and shoved a baby quesadilla at him. "She had nothing to do with this surprise party except unexpectedly become the guest of honor. Why didn't you RSVP if you wanted to come?"

Eying Sophie from the tips of her frosted pixie to her sparkle-painted toenails, Brice scoffed at her. "Never got an invitation."

She aimed at him with a napkin, then tucked it in his shirt pocket. "Talk to your wife, then, but don't come spoiling things here." She flippantly motioned him to scoot away. "Go on and eat. Mr. Dupree went through a lot of trouble for this shindig. And quit monopolizing Callie. She has guests."

Brice followed orders, scouting the tables for food options.

"You're welcome," Sophie said to the collective three and flitted off again.

Mark shook his head. "That woman can work people, can't she?"

"You have no idea," Callie said.

A buzzing sounded in her pocket. Halfway expecting her son or other mother to call and wish her happy birthday, she withdrew the phone. Caller ID showed Ike, one of her three most recent hires, though he'd worked the beach over a year now. A transfer from another city with a decade of policing under his belt. Easing to a back corner as best she could, Callie answered. "Why aren't you radioing me?"

"Sorry to interrupt, Chief, but the phone seemed best for this incident," he said.

She gave her back to the party, covering her other ear. "Talk to me."

"Tractor driver waved me down," he said. "Was clearing a vacant lot. I'm putting up yellow tape and securing the scene. Sent you pics."

Callie opened her messages. Three from Ike, three pics in each.

The driver stood next to his tractor in one, studying the ground. Other pictures moved in closer.

Face down lay a body mashed into the moist ground, half covered with poison ivy and greenbrier vines. No blood. "Jesus, Ike. Can you tell who it is?"

"Not really," he said. "Thought someone more native might be able to."

"Location?"

"Dolphin Road," he said. "First vacant lot down from the corner of Portia Street, behind a large two-story house with dark green shutters. Being this place is a lot, I'm not sure the number."

But Callie knew. Scanning the crowd, she located the lot's owner. "Be right there, Ike."

Both Thomas and Stan spotted her concern when she moved through the people with purpose. She waved to Thomas and motioned outside. By instinct, Stan would do his best to keep others from being nosy enough to tail them.

"Brice? Can we speak outside?" she asked, freeing two men shackled to one of the town councilman's political pontifications.

"Excuse me, gentlemen." Brice grabbed another taco and obliged the chief, following her out. Seeing Thomas already waiting gave the councilman pause. "What's the deal?"

"You own 617 Dolphin, right?" Callie asked.

"It and a few other lots," he said. "Why?"

"Come with me to that one, if you don't mind."

Brice's expression clouded, with Thomas taking a stiffer stance in defense of his chief. "What if I don't want to? And I won't until you tell me what this is about."

She tried to read him. "Something was discovered in clearing your lot a few minutes ago."

"What? I gave no approval to clear that lot." Up came a pointed finger, the one he'd shoved at Callie on more than enough occasions.

"Who's been on my property?"

"This man, for one," Callie said, showing him a picture. "And who-ever dumped him there."

Chapter 2

WITH CORONER AND county forensics already called en route to the scene, Callie drove to the Dolphin Road lot with Thomas behind her. An expected group of locals hovered, the temps in the low fifties making them huddle. Dolphin Road houses were mostly residences instead of rentals, and the few rentals on this road were probably empty.

The sight of three of Edisto police's four vehicles on this short, silt, two-block road would spread chatter fast. Thomas assumed his job without being asked, his priority on a crime scene always traffic control, humans, and vehicles. People got nosy over a grill catching fire, so crime scene tape would attract people from Scott's Creek to St. Helena Sound.

She hadn't waited for Brice. He knew the way.

His involvement would draw even more people, though. And fast. Brice was an accuser, never the accused. Callie almost couldn't help but relish his trouble.

The picture she hadn't shown Brice was that of Aberdeen, his wife, seated in Ike's patrol car with tears melting her heavy makeup. "She still in your car?" Callie asked, fast walking to her officer on the scene.

Ike tilted his head toward the vehicle.

Callie took a short detour to study the body. A quick glance. Nobody she immediately recognized. Then she strode to Ike's open car and, with her weight on the inside handle, squatted. "Hey, Aberdeen. How you doing?"

"I . . . don't know." A fresh sob then a snorted inhale. Bright red hair served as a trademark for Mrs. LeGrand, poised on top of her head in a bird-nest sort of way with one of her flamboyant scarves not quite wrestling it into place. Too cool for one of her flowing caftans, she wore jeans and a knee-length wool sweater which she gripped tight around her, shivering beneath the wide collar.

Callie patted her leg. "Tell me what happened."

"I was just standing there. Randy drove the tractor. He shouted, 'Whoa' and 'Damn.' When I ran over, there was this . . . person there.

Not moving." Tears gushed with another snort.

One of those ugly criers.

"Did he run over the body, Aberdeen?"

"I think so?"

A question. She had no clue and probably saw no more than Callie had.

Callie passed her some tissues she'd brought from her patrol car. Always paid to keep a couple boxes. A simple traffic ticket could flip someone into a sniveling mess.

"Why were you clearing the lot? Putting it up for sale?" Odd season for prepping property, but they could need the money. And doing it without Brice's knowledge seemed odd as well.

"I wanted to go to Paris in the spring. Brice said we didn't have the liquidity to justify it." Her expression morphed and the tears seemed to stop. "Liquidity. What does that even mean? So I decided to sell a lot. We have four we'll never use. Figured I could get a buyer before he noticed."

"I see," Callie said as Aberdeen validated her reputed lack of common sense. Like a real estate agent in this town wouldn't confirm first with Brice.

"Let me over there. She owes me an explanation," Brice yelled.

Callie peered up to see Ike holding him back, giving Callie her space with Aberdeen. From the red in his cheeks, Brice was volcanic. Callie waved for her officer to let the man loose.

"What the hell is wrong with you?" flew out of his mouth halfway to the car.

Expecting one of Brice's infamous confrontations with her, a scene witnessed by more than a few Edistonians, Callie rose in preparation for the wrath. Instead, he pushed past her to his wife.

"You moronic woman. I didn't order this lot cleared, so what gave you the right to take it upon yourself to hire a tractor?"

But Aberdeen didn't flinch. The previously cowering damsel shot out of the car and shoved her husband back. "You're the moron. And I own half of everything. If I want to sell a damn lot, I'll sell a damn lot."

Callie moved between them. "Not the place, y'all." She lowered her voice. "Agreed?"

While Aberdeen quietly sulked, Brice spat back a mumbled "Agreed."

Positioning herself between the couple and most of the gathering crowd, Callie brought up the obvious. "Brice, if your wife hadn't cleared this lot, imagine how long before we would've found this poor man.

Would you have preferred the stench attract wildlife first? Or that someone's kid found it?"

The color rushed out of Aberdeen's complexion.

"Sit back down in the car, Abby," Brice ordered, half-bark, half-concern.

Callie leaned one arm on the roof of the car as the wife lowered herself to the backseat again. "Aberdeen, do you know the man?"

"I couldn't look," she said, shaking her head.

Callie softened her tone. "Would you mind looking?"

Brice pushed himself into the small space, forcing Callie to step aside. "Woman, you do not have to see that, you hear?"

Ike started over, and Callie let him, not trusting Brice to behave without an audience.

"Settle down, Brice."

"Yeah," Aberdeen agreed. "You don't tell me what to do."

Callie couldn't imagine the clashes they had behind closed doors, and she had half a mind to tell them to duke it out in the middle of the road and get this yo-yo love-hate quarrel out of their system. But the Edisto Police Department had a reputation of handling matters in a more professional manner, regardless how many angry clowns walked the beach.

Assisting Aberdeen to her feet, Callie nudged Brice out of their way. "Let her go alone, Brice. We don't want y'all to start shouting again. I got her."

As had most untended land on Edisto, the lot had gone feral. Four live oaks shaded the lot from most sun, some of their Spanish moss tendrils draping fifteen feet long from the upper limbs, long enough to be brushed aside when walking past. And where sun pierced the oak canopy, a half dozen Palmetto trees grew, never pruned, giving them a wild, ragged appearance with half-dead fronds drooping down the trunks. Collections of them scattered beneath.

"Watch where you step," Callie warned, leading Aberdeen by the hand. Poison ivy thrived in the unmanicured dirt of this semi-tropical part of the state. Once she got home, she'd have to take soap and water to her boots, then spray them down with alcohol.

They reached the tape.

"Didn't mean to run over it," the tractor driver hollered from the silted road. "Was trying to get started moving the downed tree trunks first. Just didn't see . . . " he said.

"We appreciate the information, sir," Callie said, then with a swift wave beckoned Ike to see to the driver, maybe collect his thoughts more quietly so the whole beach didn't hear details of how bones had crunched.

But the damage didn't appear too gruesome. No doubt the tractor mashed the body, but thanks to the overly wet season they'd had, it had sunk into muck. A few bones no doubt broken from some of the angles, but less damage done than would've occurred in the drier days of summer when the damage would have exposed organs and gray matter.

He'd been a tall man, brown hair, if the mud hadn't camouflaged it too much. Oxford shirt on a caved-in back. Khakis. One loafer, the other probably claimed by the vegetation shifted by the tractor. He wore the uniform for casual Friday in Charleston. Nothing defining about him, at least to her.

As always, Callie prayed this wasn't a tourist for one set of reasons, then prayed again he wasn't a native for other reasons.

She watched the woman beside her. "Recognize him?" she asked Aberdeen, who dug nails into her arm, peering hard but pulling back.

"Not really."

"Try again, Aberdeen. If you aren't certain, we'll need you here when the coroner turns him over."

The woman slid her feet just inches forward, leaning more. "Something about the watch," she said.

Callie studied the left wrist nearest them, a yard away. "I'm not seeing a watch."

In a sudden shift, a shiver emanated from Aberdeen into Callie's arm, and Callie reached over to take a firmer grip on her. "The other wrist." Though muddy, his right wrist showed what seemed to be an expensive watch, the crystal on the inside of his wrist. "Oh God. Oh God," Aberdeen said

She wobbled, going weak in the knees. Despite Aberdeen having forty pounds on her, Callie kept her from sprawling. Ike rushed over, lowering the woman to a seated position. Brice ran to her as a sea of exclamations spanned the spectators. "Abby?" he scolded. "Don't you pass out on us, you hear?"

"Who is it, Aberdeen?" Callie asked, but Aberdeen had dissolved into despair.

Callie let the others care for the woman, and with different eyes, approached the body again. The watch indeed jarred a memory. A concrete memory, and she was surprised she hadn't recognized him sooner.

"Brice? Come over here," she said.

"I'm taking care of my wife," he snarled.

Gaze glued on the body, Callie repeated her order. "She's fine. Get your butt over here so I don't have to yell what I have to say. And trust me, you don't want everyone to hear."

He didn't seem to care about the murder in their midst. Another excuse to dislike the man, like she wanted to add to that list.

With effort created by a life of alcohol and fried food, he labored to his feet and walked like he had to work out the kinks. "What the hell is it?"

"Open your eyes, Brice. Who is that?"

He half-assed glanced then jerked his gaze away. Callie recognizing a weak stomach when she saw it. "Hell if I know," he said.

"Look harder, damn it," she said up close to his ear, tolerating the scent of old alcohol in his pores, the tacos on his breath.

So he studied harder . . . and paled.

"When was the last you were out here?" she asked, irritated.

He hesitated. "I, um, I . . . "

"It's not a trick question, Brice."

"Not sure," he said, staring at her, flummoxed. "A month ago? Two?"

"When was the last you saw *him*?"

"Um, yesterday? We met at SeaCow for a late breakfast."

The two men weren't bosom buddies, because neither was capable of a loyal relationship, but they'd lived on Edisto as long as Callie'd lived on the planet. Yes, they knew each other.

She wanted to move off from the scene, apart from other ears, but she'd rather he respond to her questions with that unforgettable vision laid out before him to emphasize the importance of his answers. "You seemed awful upset about this place being cleared. Why?"

He spun to her. "Why? Because I didn't want it cleared. I'm not selling. Didn't want to spend the money. Don't like things being done behind my back. How many damn reasons do you want?" Then the old Brice made an appearance. "Leave it to you to deflect blame when you can't solve your own problems." He started to leave.

"Don't you dare leave before I'm done, Brice."

She'd never used that tone with the town councilman before, usually saving it for the guilty, the arrested, the ones who resisted. This man ran roughshod over half the island, puffed with the pedigree of his Edisto lineage, but truth be told, his ancestors would be embarrassed beyond the grave at how he treated people in the name of leadership.

And the deceased, if her deduction proved her right, had a personality not too dissimilar from Brice LeGrand.

"I'm not your problem, Chief," Brice said. "Do your damn job and solve this."

She snagged his sleeve.

"Don't touch me," he started, so she met him halfway, only inches apart. Callie tried not to let him bug her, but this man felt impervious to the law or any other authority on the island, and this was the last place for him to feign regal.

"Shut up and listen. How many more bodies will I find out here?" she asked. "Or how many of your other lots should I inspect? Shouldn't be too difficult to find bodies since you can't dig six feet without hitting water. All we'll need to do is just move a few ferns aside."

"Dig all you damn well want," he said. "I didn't kill him. Or anyone else for that matter. My lots are clean."

She moved in tighter. "Like this one was clean, you jackass?"

"Chief?" Ike came up from behind. "County van just arrived. Want me to take statements from the LeGrands and let you deal with the coroner and his people?"

Recognizing the opening Ike gave her to back away from a potential mistake, Callie nodded. "Yeah, thanks."

As one of the upper echelon of Edisto, Brice would feel himself too superior to be questioned, much less to be a suspect, and she hated him bucking up at her and flashing that arrogance when someone they knew lay dead. *Questionably* dead.

Would Brice try to assist? No. He didn't help anyone or anything. His forte was to criticize, aggravate, and harass other people, most of all *her* people, who diligently did their jobs.

She surveyed the crew from the van. Of course. They would send Richard Smith from the coroner's office, too. The damned assistant coroner had challenged her ability to remain civil when she'd handled the body of a retired FBI agent found in Big Bay Creek this past spring. She inhaled, exhaled, and walked over to greet him cordially, informing him of all she'd discovered, and what she thought, not that Smith cared about the latter.

"Nobody touched him?" he asked.

"No, nobody," she replied. "Except for the tractor that uncovered him."

He nodded once in acceptance. "We'll be here a while."

"Then we will be, too," she said. "Tell us how we can help."

With Thomas entertaining the crowd, Ike controlling the LeGrands, and the coroner busy doing his thing, she went to sit inside her patrol car and took a long-held deep breath. Stan appeared and leaned on the car, back to the crowd.

"So much for the party," he said under his breath.

"Tell Mark I'm sorry," she replied.

He gave a soft *humph*. "Pretty sure he understands. He made Sophie stay, so count your blessings you didn't have her in the midst of all this."

No telling how Sophie would've reacted with her proclivity to tune in and get in touch with the spirit world.

"So what've you got?" he asked.

She blew out, thinking. "Coroner'll have to do his thing first, Stan. Can't see squat as to cause of death. No blood I could see, but then old blood would blend into the muck. Can't tell if he walked here and had a heart attack, or if he was brought here and dumped. Could've even been brought here alive and killed on the site."

"But you recognized him, didn't you?"

Her heart weighed suddenly heavy at the task before her. "Yeah. And I've got to go deliver the news to his widow."

"Want someone with you?" he asked, a pat on her shoulder.

She shook her head. "No, this one I want to do alone."

He moved aside to let her drive off. She appreciated Stan not pressing for a name. He'd been in her shoes often enough. He'd learn the "who" soon enough.

She drove Portia Street then took a right on Jungle Road. A block further was her own house, and two houses before hers stood the Rosewood residence.

Callie's birthday afternoon would entail asking her birth mother a lot of serious questions. Like why Sarah Rosewood had returned to Edisto three days early for Christmas, and how her return coincided with the death of her estranged husband.

Chapter 3

CALLIE WOULD'VE MUCH rather dealt with the body and Brice LeGrand—even *two* bodies *and* two Brices—than make this visit.

Pushing the speed limit, she passed Sarah Rosewood's and pulled into her own driveway two houses down so no one would question a cop car in Sarah's drive. Callie preferred not leaving the county forensics team, but she didn't want Sarah to hear about Ben from anyone else.

All the homes on the beach towered twelve to fourteen feet off the ground on the stilts, designed to allow waves to pass beneath during hurricane storm surges. The construction gave ample parking as well, and Callie drove completely underneath *Chelsea Morning*. Callie's other mother, the one who raised her, named *Chelsea Morning* because of her Neil Diamond fetish.

Sarah's home, a mere fifty yards away, was *Shore Thing*. A name that sounded more like a weekend rental than the permanent home of Ben and Sarah Rosewood. The house was cream and gold, leather and teak.

A home with no children, a husband who kept to himself when he wasn't on the road, and a wife who'd been treated wrong by every man in her life.

Callie trotted over. Ben's car was in the drive. Sarah's car had died after going off the road into Scott's Creek a year ago. The unrecognizable second vehicle Callie assumed was Sarah's replacement.

At the base of the stairs, she took a second then climbed the flight two risers at a step and pushed the bell. Callie could see the floorplan in her head, had memories of sharing conversations with Sarah at the kitchen table, both before and after their revealed familial relationship. She'd gravitated to the woman, felt a connection from the moment

Callie first met her about eighteen months ago. Sarah had kept an eye on Callie from afar from the day she was born. Though Callie's father brought his daughter home to be raised by his wife—both a political *and* a financial move—he'd kept visiting Sarah on Edisto, sometimes mentioning their daughter and updating Sarah on Callie's childhood. Other days he actually brought her along for a quick hello. Callie remembered little of those brief visits.

It had taken Callie a while to come to terms with having three parents who'd hidden her origins for forty years. Now, when everything seemed sorted, tension would rise again. Suspicious deaths tended to evaporate the calm of all involved.

The front door opened. Sarah must've been in the kitchen to answer so soon.

Her mother beamed at the surprise. "Well, hey, Callie." Instrumental Christmas music floated out the door. Sarah always liked to have the sounds of Christmas even if she couldn't have the snow. "What're you doing . . . thought we were meeting after your work? We all waited for you, but after an hour guessed you weren't coming back to the party."

Callie wished she could have. "Mind if I come in?"

"Of course. Go sit. I'll see what's in the refrigerator. Just got here not fifteen minutes before you did. We must be psychic . . . or related."

Sarah had relished coming out of the closet as Callie's real mom and an easiness existed between them, but now doubt and concern about the unexpected visit must've filtered into her thoughts. She opened one cabinet, then another. Sarah'd suddenly sensed the visit must be a formal duty call. Callie saw it in her movements like she'd seen the nervous, uncertain motions in many others when making calls just like this.

Callie waited at the kitchen table. "Sarah, come sit with me. Just grab a couple of glasses of water. That'll be fine."

Sarah did as asked, but the water in the glasses trembled a bit when placed on the table. When she sat, Sarah studied the bamboo placemat. "Why are you here, Callie?"

Callie remembered all too well the snobbery, the nastiness, the overbearing domination Ben displayed toward Sarah before she decided to leave. To the average islander, she left over the ordeal when she'd almost drowned, when her car was sabotaged over mistaken identity. One of Edisto's favorite sons drowned that day trying to save her after her car left the highway and sank into Scott's Creek. Some blamed her for the loss of that officer. Back then Callie had struggled herself not to blame the woman.

Ben had cut his wife no slack at all.

"Where's Ben?"

Sarah shrugged. "Honey, I haven't been in this house since October a year ago. Fourteen months. I arrived to find it empty and unlocked. Figured he'd be back any minute."

"What were you planning to do once you got home?" Via cell, Callie'd offered *Chelsea Morning* to Sarah as a more comfortable place to sleep, but Sarah had declined with mannerly comments like she couldn't be a burden. With the state's divorce law requiring a one-year separation, Sarah could finally file papers. Maybe she already had. They hadn't discussed the issue.

"His car's out front," Callie said.

Sarah's shoulders remained tense.

Callie hated this cat and mouse sort of thing. Regardless what the law said, cops interviewed most people from the perspective of possible guilt rather than innocence.

Sarah's brow furrowed. "His keys are hanging on the hook in the kitchen. When I came home, I had this sense he hadn't been gone long," she said. "Maybe he went for a walk. His phone was still here beside his recliner so he couldn't have gone far."

Who left without a phone these days? "Was he prone to walking?" He wasn't. He golfed, with a cart, and not often. Instead, he worked, fussed at the perceived incompetence of his wife, and then worked some more. Often out of town. A floating attorney with clients in multiple states.

"And you came home early for . . . "

Sarah almost sounded hurt. "For your birthday. I told you that. What's this about, Callie? So what if I came home three days early." Panic crept into the crow's feet of her eyes, and her blinking seemed almost manic.

As all fresh widows did, Sarah sensed the message a split-second before the delivery.

Callie took her mother's hands. "We found Ben's body about an hour ago."

Sarah's breathing hitched and caught. "Wh-what?"

"On a vacant lot on Dolphin. Have you seen him at all?" A trick question she hated to ask, to see if Sarah acknowledged returning sooner than she said.

"N-no."

"When did you last phone him?" Callie asked.

"Two months ago," she replied, a little shaky.

That long? "He didn't know you were coming?"

"I texted. Couldn't stand hearing his voice. He always became . . . condescending." But still no tears.

"When did he text back last?"

"Again, two months ago. One word. *Whatever.* I assumed he received his notice I'd filed for divorce."

Going into the kitchen, Callie found a box of tissues and set them before Sarah just in case. Maybe the woman hadn't come to grips yet.

Sounded like Ben hadn't changed. Big surprise. But even living two doors down, Callie hadn't seen Ben since Sarah left, a long stretch for neighbors to not even wave. He never involved himself in Edisto business or social functions. Before Sarah left or after. Didn't do the beach. Sarah's long ago involvement with Callie's father had anchored Sarah on Edisto for decades . . . and alienated Ben from it. One would've thought Ben would depart Edisto rather than Sarah, but he was the type to challenge, to dig in, and make you have to blink first.

After the Scott's Creek tragedy, Sarah had been too broken to deal with Ben any longer. She'd disappeared to family in Atlanta, taking a spell to sort her future, talking via email to Callie once or twice a month. Callie got it. Any communication to Edisto was painful for Sarah. It was where she'd lost her daughter to her lover's wife, where she watched her forever-love from afar as he raised her daughter, where she endured a gruesome marriage to a caustic spouse. Where she'd been scorned by Edisto residents for a fatal car accident.

Callie was surprised she'd come back at all rather than hire someone to pack up her life with Ben.

Taking a long drink of water, her mother remained introspective. Not quite the reaction Callie expected. As much as Sarah had been mistreated by Ben, she'd remained married to him for thirty-plus years. Callie expected *some* tears. The couple had a history, but still no questions from Sarah about what, when, or how.

"Sarah? Anything you'd like to ask me?"

"I'm not sure I want to hear this," she said.

Squinting a little, Callie delivered the facts anyway and ended by saying, "The coroner will inform us how he died. I doubt he'd been dead much more than twenty-four hours, but I could be wrong. They'll have to clean him up to tell what killed him." The delivery was blunt and a little raw around the edges, but Callie was seeking reaction.

Having lifted a tissue from the box earlier, Sarah only worried it into little balls. "Okay."

Callie couldn't see Sarah killing Ben, but it wasn't her place to make that call on gut alone . . . on love alone. Facts, interviews, witnesses, and forensics dictated how people died. While Ben could've dropped from natural causes, Callie couldn't waste thought assuming, even hoping, as in Sarah's case, that this wasn't a suspicious death. Maybe a murder. And Sarah wasn't helping. Didn't seem to care.

Her mother shook her head. "Like I said, I drove in early for your party, with luggage still in the car." She waved to the floor. "Go down and check my car. I've only brought up one of two bags."

"I will," Callie said. "But first, I have to say you're managing this calmer than expected."

Sarah's puzzled expression almost made Callie question her mother's mental state. "I'm as surprised as you, I think. I filed papers for divorce precisely at the one-year mark. Like I told you, that's when he quit texting. My main purpose for coming back was to determine if he'd left Edisto. The divorce settlement has me getting the house. Finding him gone, then dead, makes it almost anti-climactic."

Callie studied her. "A relief?"

"Yes. Much." Then Sarah noticed Callie's stare. "You're disappointed in me."

Shaking her head, Callie sat back in her chair. "No, I've seen people react all manner of ways hearing about death." She touched the tissue box. "You're stronger than I expected, though. Not the first tear."

"You didn't live with him," she said. "Am I a person of interest?"

Callie pinched her forefinger and thumb. "Maybe this much?"

Sarah's hand crawled up to her neck. "Oh my gracious, I'm a suspect?" Her eyes welled.

"To some you would be," Callie replied with pity, yet proud of her mother's unexpected strength. "While a lot of women are killed by their spouse, an extremely low number of men are murdered by wives. You've already filed papers, which means you were getting out. Why kill him when he's almost gone? Then there's the question of why kill him and dump him in that lot? It's not like you could move him. Ben was a big guy."

"Right." A few tears fell and Sarah brushed them off. "Why not hire someone to murder him weeks before instead of murdering him on the first day I arrive?"

Point taken, but they'd have a better timetable and cause of death soon. Any investigator would have to wonder if Sarah might've come in last night or this morning and lost her mind over decades of accumulated resentment. Brice certainly would. He'd blame his own mother to save his own ass, so why not blame Sarah to focus suspicion on someone who didn't *own* the murder lot?

If Ben and Brice shared anything in common, it was a deep distaste for Callie's father. Both had made their scorn apparent. And that scorn included both her mothers.

Callie's father had not only loved Sarah once upon a time, but he had also stolen Beverly, Callie's adopted mother, from Brice. Beverly and Lawton Cantrell, with Callie in tow, continued to vacation on Edisto throughout their marriage. A snub to Brice, at least from his perspective. And though Sarah's affair with Lawton preceded her union with Ben, he'd never felt chosen. More like second choice since she couldn't have Lawton.

Yep, the two men bonded by a united hate for Callie's father . . . and transferred that dislike to Callie.

Sarah reached for another tissue, using it properly this go around. "You . . . you of all people should see I don't have it in me to take another life. People already hold me responsible for Francis." Her cheeks flushed, tears rolling.

Callie reached over and stroked her mother's forearm, only to be knocked aside. Fists tight with damp tissues, Sarah thumped them before her on the placemat. "All right. I admit it."

Blood chilling, Callie reached to her phone to record, ruing she hadn't already. "Admit what?"

"Admit that I'm almost glad I don't have to go through the divorce. I've had nightmares about confronting Ben." Cheeks flushed, she stared hard at her daughter. "Yes, the ugliness of reality is that relief and security were the first thoughts through my mind."

Sitting forward, Callie lightly gripped each of Sarah's wrists. "Don't tell that to anyone, you hear me?" Then when Sarah didn't respond, Callie grasped tighter and shook them once. "Do you hear me?" Because Brice LeGrand could easily claim Sarah would love to inherit it all instead of fighting for half in divorce court. Ben had money.

Sarah sniffled once. "Yes, I hear you. But I can show my true feelings to you, Callie. You don't judge. And you understand what it was like for me for so long."

Callie did, but while she realized others would find it scary that

Sarah's first reflective thought upon hearing of her husband's death was relief, they wouldn't relate. Not many knew how bad it had been between them.

In serving divorce papers she professed to be acting sensibly. In reality, had she yearned to get even? That would be the question of the average person making up the average jury. Toss in a savvy attorney, maybe one of Ben's legal acquaintances . . .

Callie slid her chair up close to her mother. She was going to do her job and give Sarah advice all at the same time. "Get me gas tickets. Meal receipts. Names of people you spoke to while on the road, both on your phone and in person. Places you stopped. Names of people who can vouch for when you left Atlanta. Anything to show you weren't here when Ben died."

"But when did he die?" she asked.

"Not sure," Callie said, "but we must be prepared in case someone thinks it was you. Go back three days, okay? Just to be safe."

Marie called on her mic. "Chief?"

Callie stared again at Sarah. "Can you do that for me?"

Sarah nodded.

Callie left the room. "What is it, Marie?"

"You remember those two Christmas present thefts filed yester-day?"

"Yeah. Told the families to start locking up." Edisto's Chamber touted safe and crime-free living, and in Callie's opinion, too many people out here believed the hype and failed to lock their doors and windows. A crime-free place didn't exist, but she still aided the citizens in their quest to feel cocooned at the beach.

"Well, we just got calls from a couple more houses. Same complaint. One present opened at one house. Three at another."

"Over what time frame?"

"Between noon and now," Marie said.

"Noon?" Callie glanced at her watch. Four thirty in the afternoon. "What are the addresses?"

"Palmetto," she said. "Six hundred block. Both of them."

The others had been on Pompano, one block over from Dolphin. "Scan those reports and the ones from yesterday and send them to me. It's feeling like a long evening."

"Roger that. Marie out."

Her phone rang. As she lifted it to her ear, Callie peered around the bookshelf at Sarah who'd pulled a notepad onto the kitchen table and was writing and referring to her phone. *Good.*

"Hey, Ike. What's happening?"

"Coroner's asking for you," he said. "You want to see him move the body or not?"

"I'm just around the corner," she said. "Tell him to hold his horses for five minutes. He's not the only one missing supper this evening. And it's not his birthday."

Chapter 4

THE CROWD NUMBERING forty or more had grown since Callie left. As with any cluster around a crime scene, she studied the people. Nobody stuck out. Nobody shirked her eye contact. Everyone showed concern, shock, curiosity.

Both Thomas and Ike already snapped pictures and video to study later. Callie and the two officers, along with Marie, would identify every resident, then they might let Janet Wainwright, real estate broker extraordinaire, put names to the renters.

Ike was quick to approach when she arrived. "They didn't wait for you."

"As long as they're still here, that's fine," she said.

The body was being lifted into a bag, a gurney waiting, and she strode to it, holding up a hand for them to give her a second. Coroner Smith's flat-lined mouth indicated his inconvenience.

The aroma of Lowcountry muck mingled with the briny air blowing in from two blocks over. Partly overcast, the humidity ran thick, making the fifty-degree temperature chilly, especially under the oak canopy.

In spite of the mud, scratches, and dead plant matter, Callie easily confirmed Ben Rosewood. Funny. All she could think about was how Sarah would fare without her husband's income . . . and how the man who used to dress rather dapper would seethe at the messiness of his departure. "Any obvious wounds?" she asked.

Smith seemed almost bored. "Head trauma, but have to delve closer to determine whether from a fall or suspicious."

This guy didn't even want to guess. Colleton County employed one other assistant and the main coroner, yet she'd drawn Smith, again, and their working relationship was no better than the last time she'd worked a body with him. Chances were she was about to make it worse. "What'd you find on him?" she asked.

"We were hoping to wait until we got to Walterboro to scrutinize him in a much more sterile environment."

Callie caught his gaze and held it. "Sorry to dash those hopes, but could you go through his pockets, please?"

Last experience with this man, she'd delved into the dead man's pockets herself, on the spot, and it had paid off and expedited her investigation. This time, however, she'd give Smith the courtesy . . . first.

With a huff laced with arrogance, he motioned for one of his staff to assist.

"Wallet," he said. "Name Benjamin Emmett Rosewood. Address Twenty-Four Jungle Road, Edisto Beach. Age sixty-three." He named off the three credit cards and counted one hundred and ten dollars cash.

Smith hunted over others parts of the body. "Watch. Rolex. Still working. No wedding band, but he used to wear one per the indentation below his knuckle." He patted around more. "That's it. No keys, no papers."

"No phone?"

He showed surprise at the absence of a phone, too, and patted Ben down again. "No phone. You happy, Chief Morgan?"

"Ecstatically," she said. "Thanks for arriving so promptly. The minute you have an idea on cause of death, I'd appreciate a call."

"Like I'd do for anyone," he replied and left without a goodbye.

Stan appeared. "He loves the hell out of you. What's his beef?"

"If you hadn't been in Boston getting divorced this past spring when that FBI agent floated up, you'd have known," she said. "I slipped a wallet off a body without his permission."

"Hmmm." Then he laughed. "Coroners get rather territorial about their duties."

"So do police chiefs," she replied. The ambulance slowly drove out, Thomas having to wave the crowd aside.

Callie guessed death within the last twenty-four hours if not sooner. With no keys on him and Sarah mentioning his keys still on a hook at his home, Ben hadn't driven here.

"Care to go back and finish your party?" Stan asked.

"Right, like anyone's still there. Besides, we had two more gift thefts reported this afternoon. I've got to make a few house calls."

Stan frowned. "Two more? How many others are there?"

"Two yesterday," she said. "Or rather, that's when they were noticed. If the ones today are anything like those yesterday, someone goes in, opens a gift, discards the paper in the trash, and leaves with whatever he finds. Just that one gift."

"Forced entry?" he asked.

"No sign of it," she said. "Either the houses were unlocked or someone had a key. But then, a lot of these windows are never locked. Some can't be locked." She shook her head. "These people and their lack of security just slay me."

His big hand patted her on the back. "That's what they have you for, Chicklet."

"I feel so lucky," she said, and left to help Thomas and Ike interview the crowd before they dispersed.

Then she assigned the two officers to go house-to-house within a block radius of the Dolphin Road lot, knocking and asking if anyone saw or heard anything related to Ben. The houses on either side of the lot were empty. The vacant lot faced the back wall of a garage across the dirt road. Bisecting the rear of the lot was a heavily jungled creek with the house on the other side likewise vacant.

This locale was certainly safe from prying eyes. Strategic or by chance? Regardless, to dump a body here seemed naïve, or desperate. If it was a body dump. On this island, the best means to dispose a body was Mother Nature via the marsh or the ocean. Either decomposed a body faster than you could catch a tan. Creatures big and small, toothy and not, efficiently converted death into nothingness. Stupid not to utilize the opportunity presented by nature, which meant this death, if a homicide and not natural, was likely not premeditated . . . making finding the culprit that much harder.

But why would Ben be on that particular spot alone? And why walk into the middle of that poison ivy unless he were analyzing the lot prior to purchase? But Aberdeen hadn't placed a sign up yet.

Callie'd question Aberdeen again, just in case Ben had reached out to her. Still, Callie pictured him contacting Brice instead—the real estate version of the Bro Code.

And since Sophie was his immediate neighbor, Callie'd ask her if Ben had spoken to her recently. Welcomed guests. Acted differently.

Otherwise, she was stumped on this one. It'd be after dark before she and her two officers completed canvassing the area, and if nobody saw or heard a thing, which she would expect with no occupied houses nearby, she'd have little choice other than to wait for her favorite coroner to get back to her with his findings.

Callie volunteered to take the canvass of the Pompano Road homes. However, with the lagoon's tangled, overgrown creek obstructing their view of the backside of Dolphin Road properties, she didn't expect much. But two of those houses had reported the first two burglaries, and she wanted to get a grip on those cases while inquiring about Ben.

The surf sounded louder on this street, with the properties being the third row of houses back from the ocean. Tide coming in, from the sound of it, and with night falling, the rolling crashes always seemed more dramatic. Orange lit up the sky to the west, on the marsh side of the island. Sea birds called here and there, making their last feedings before roosting for the night.

From the street one could tell which houses had occupants. Christmas trees shone, and lights outlined windows, climbing and twisting around Palmetto trees in the yard in greens, reds, and the occasional renegade blue. At the next house, Callie climbed the stairs, hearing a television inside as she knocked.

While she waited, she recognized *Paradise Lost* next door. Vacant . . . for well over a year. Ever since she'd identified a six-year-old crime—a serial killer visiting every August to make another "accidental" victim— the cottage had been unrentable. Yet the ones around it filled, as if the drama served as an attraction. Close enough for fascination but far enough for safety.

The place would be a deal for somebody. Maybe she ought to buy it and renovate it, change the name.

The lit Christmas wreath swayed as the door opened to *Salty Dog.* "Hello?" said the man in sweat pants and Clemson t-shirt. Bumping fifty, she guessed from the sparse hair and paunch he quickly slid behind his elastic waistband.

"Hey, I'm Police Chief Callie Morgan. I understand you reported a burglary? A missing Christmas present?"

His eyes widened in recognition. "Yes, yes, come on in."

At his prompting, she sat on a sofa so typical of the average rental— the back and bottom cushions in a permanent state of sag, but the Christmas tree was anything but rental chic.

Someone had spent hours on the display. No overhead light or lamp was needed because the tree's glow filled the room. At least a dozen presents in gold and silver wrap hugged the base, the edges of an embroidered tree skirt peering from beneath them. A few gifts in red and green to the side. Crystal, brass, silver and gold balls reflected several hundred lights, which sparkled off beaded garland.

The happy homey scene was a contrast to the Law and Order rerun on the television.

"Sweetheart?" the man called toward the kitchen.

The wife appeared in jeans and a sweatshirt with rhinestones shaped into a reindeer, her gray and brown hair cut in a neat bob. "Oh, company." She wiped her hands on a dishtowel and scurried over to shake. "Mary," she said, tilting her head toward her husband then herself. "Greg and Mary. Our last name's Anders."

Callie rose and introduced herself, then sat, asking them to do the same. "I'm sure someone already spoke to you about your report, but I happened to be in the area on another issue and thought I'd drop in. Do you mind repeating some of the facts to me?"

Both strongly nodded, the picture of an innocent, old-fashioned couple aiming to assist. Greg peered at his wife who took the reins. "We come to Edisto almost every Christmas, especially since our son moved to California. We're from Simpsonville, in the upstate," she said.

"I can tell you love the holidays." Callie gave the tree another once over. "This is absolutely gorgeous."

"All her," Greg said. "Started off that this tree and the beach were our presents to each other. Then we started bringing gifts from family and friends with us. Then we gave each other gifts. This," he swept both arms wide at the tree, "is the result."

Callie had already donned her notepad. "What was stolen?"

Mary gave a sad smile. "One would think they'd go for the gold-wrapped packages because they appear more expensive, but they didn't. The gift was from my sister in Norway. Her husband is a doctor, and they usually send something unique, yet pricey. We called her last night to find out what it was. Hold on." Mary ran into the other room, soon back with her phone. She scrolled and scrolled then held it up for Callie to see.

"A sweater," Callie said.

"Oh, not just any sweater. It's a Dale of Norway sweater for Greg. Cost my sister almost four hundred dollars."

Wow, snowflake sweaters were pricey. "Is it this exact sweater?" Callie asked.

Mary nodded. "Black. With blue and white design."

"Did they open one present or more than one?"

"Just the one," she said. "Guess we can count ourselves lucky that they didn't take more."

Callie stopped her note-taking. "Count yourselves lucky you weren't here when they came in."

Mary's gasp drew Greg to her. "It's all right, hon."

"No, it's not," she said. "What if we had been here?"

Arm around her shoulder, he squeezed in reassurance. "But we weren't."

But she wasn't feeling the calm. "We could've been."

Indeed. "Were your doors locked?" Callie asked.

Greg gave a snap of a nod. "Oh, absolutely. Just like at home, you make it difficult for the burglar so he has to think twice."

Rising, Callie went to the door and opened it. Studying the bolt, the plate, the wood around it, the interior and exterior knobs. No sign of scratches, bent metal, or dug-out wood. "Mind if I check the other entrance and the windows?"

"Sure," Greg replied, standing to follow.

She found no signs of manipulation at the back. He raised blinds and held back curtains as they went room to room. One room away from the ocean side had windows painted shut, but those seaward had been replaced with vinyl. The locks worked and were engaged, except for one.

Mary eagerly waited, arms across her midsection. "So what's the verdict?"

"No sign of forced entry," Callie said. "But one window wasn't locked. Faces the back, away from the street, and while it wouldn't be the easiest window to breach, an agile person could. I locked it."

Mary teared up. "Being robbed hurts more than I imagined."

The term was burgled. A robbery involved person-on-person, but Callie understood nonetheless. Someone violated your world whether you were there or not, and that violation hung with you for a long, long spell. She'd been there. Back when someone from Boston had stalked her here. You don't have to see them take your things to be afraid.

Mary dabbed at her eyes once Greg gave her another tissue. Callie hated asking them the next set of questions. "On another subject, did y'all hear or see anything unusual back on Dolphin in the last day or two?"

"Like what?" Mary asked.

But Greg asked the better question. "Why, what happened on Dolphin?"

"A man died," she said. "In the last twenty-four hours."

Mary covered her mouth. "Oh! Was it the burglar?" She reached for her husband. "Are we okay here? Maybe we should leave."

Greg took her into his chest but kept his attention on Callie, waiting for her to answer the question.

"Ms. Anders," Callie said, the epitome of calm. "He was found on an empty lot that was going up for sale. No sign of a struggle. Could've been no more than a heart attack. Just wondered if you heard him call or anything."

Some of Mary's panic lessened, and the husband relaxed. "No, sorry," he said. "We'd have run to help the man if we had. Or called your people."

"I can tell you would," Callie said. "But for that family, I have to ask. For the report."

With a sharp inhale, Mary's empathy took over. "Goodness gracious, that poor family. Losing a family member practically on Christmas Eve." Then with a sudden thought, she said, "And I'm sorry you bear the burden of all these issues during the holidays, Chief Morgan. This has to be hard on you as well."

With a soft smile, Callie appreciated the remark. Unusual for any-one to realize the difficulty of Christmas on law enforcement. "Thanks. Well, I have all I came for." She gave the wife her card. "Do you mind emailing me that picture of the sweater? Might help my department keep a better eye out for it."

More nods from a couple whose experience with the criminal element apparently went no further than the Law and Order reruns Greg seemed to enjoy.

"Just a minute," Mary exclaimed, then scurried out of the room. She scurried back with a small sack. "Here, as a thank-you."

Touched, Callie hesitated then accepted the package no bigger than her palm, wrapped in a lace-like bag with a gold tie ribbon around the top. "I don't want to take someone's present," she said.

Arms crossed, smiling, Mary shrugged. "It's not much."

Greg chuckled, relief clear at the normalcy. "We make a dozen of those every year, for people who might drop in or those we happen to come across. Take it. Merry Christmas."

Lifting it up in acknowledgement, Callie offered her thanks and left the couple to their evening, hoping with each step down the stairs that she hadn't caused them nightmares. Seated in the patrol car, she called in to Thomas and said she'd finished with the couple in *Salty Dog* and was headed to the other just down the street. He'd been to a half dozen houses and Ike had covered eight. Nobody noticed a thing, so there was no telling who drove or walked by Ben and never noticed him dead.

She went to start the car, and stopped, lifting the gift back off the passenger seat. The lace bag had a heftiness to it for its size. Untying the ribbon with all the attention to detail that Ms. Anders had given to wrapping it, Callie widened the opening, lifting out one of four squares of fudge, and a small handwritten card with the recipe.

She took in the deep, sugary scent, keener than ever about finding the person or persons who'd rattle people like the Anders . . . criminals who if caught in the act, could overreact and become violent in the blink of an eye.

Chapter 5

AFTER PINCHING OFF a sample of the fudge, Callie drove down the next few houses to the *Purple Pelican*, the other residence that claimed a theft. At the driveway, she swallowed, then wondered if they'd smell chocolate on her. Whatever. There were worse odors.

She climbed stairs again. This time she found no wreath but lights on every opening on the house. Windows, doors, upstairs, even downstairs outlining the storage room all the beach houses had on ground level. And in the main window a vivid, multi-colored Christmas tree dominated the view.

Any other part of the year a thief would have to guess which house was occupied, or at least climb stairs to peer in windows, but Callie noted all too clearly that holiday decorations announced loudly that people were there . . . with presents to steal.

Upstairs, she crossed the deck and knocked. A kid's voice sounded inside, unintelligible. A girl about eight years old answered, freshly bathed and ready for bed in flannel pajamas, long dark hair slightly damp.

"Hello," Callie said, almost sing-song. "Is your mom home?"

"Mom!" hollered the child, running off, leaving the door wide open. "The police are here."

"What?" came an astonished voice from the back of the house. Her bewilderment was enough to give Callie a chuckle.

A woman seven or eight years younger than Callie arrived, slow and wary. "Is there something I can help you with, officer?"

Callie held out her hand to shake. "I'm Edisto Beach Police Chief Callie Morgan. Here to ask about your burglary?" The same script as with the Anders, only this woman wasn't so willing to invite a uniform in her home. She crossed her arms.

Callie took out her notepad. "I'm in the area on another case and wanted to check in, maybe hear the details about the burglary straight from you. Is that okay?"

"I guess," she said.

"May I come in?" Callie asked.

"Um, fine."

Callie stepped in. Standing, patiently allowing a whispering mother-daughter chat to conclude, Callie studied the blinking tree in front of the window. A severe contrast to the Anderses' decor. Red, blue, green, and every color one could imagine. A myriad of ornaments from homespun to a detailed glass manger, which Callie marveled at having lasted in the home of a child. A multi-colored light rotated inside the star on top.

"Eagerton, right?" Callie said.

"I'm Ingrid Eagerton. My husband Kyle is at the grocery store and ought to be home any moment."

Callie began her questions. "Can you describe your stolen property for me?"

Ingrid covered her daughter's ears. "It was a sterling silver birthstone bracelet for my daughter, and I'd rather not say her name."

"No need," Callie said. "Approximate value?"

"A hundred dollars."

Callie had a son, so she shouldn't judge someone with a daughter, but she marveled at dropping a hundred on a bracelet that was likely to get lost on the playground. "That helps, thanks. Was that the only item taken?"

"As far as we can tell."

"And how did you learn it was stolen?"

"Kyle found the paper in the trash."

Same as the other. The thief had cleaned up, or maybe bought time by stuffing the paper under other refuse so that nobody would notice the gift missing. Callie still struggled with the burglar taking the time to unwrap the gifts. Why bother with the wrap? Why not just grab an armful of gifts and run? "And you are sure the paper was just for one gift?"

"Yes," Ingrid said. "And you must find it."

Yep. This home was the polar opposite of the Anders. "We will do our best," Callie said. "Can you recall when it was stolen? I mean, did you immediately notice or are you unsure?"

"Of course we can say when. What kind of question is that?"

Letting out a soft breath, Callie let the rancor flash by and focused on the words. "I ask because the paper in the trash could've been two days old, one day old, an hour old, depending on what was disposed in the trash before and after it. Or depending on how often you take out the trash."

Surprisingly, that string of logic stopped Ingrid cold.

The report said they noticed the missing gift around noon. "When were you gone yesterday?" Callie asked.

Ingrid shook her head. "Someone was here all day. But we went out for dinner the afternoon before."

Edisto might have a culprit noting routines or simply watching a street for a car to leave.

Holding up her notepad, Callie thanked them. "This helps. Mind if I ask you about another situation? And you might tell your daughter to leave the room."

The mom whispered in the child's ear something to send her sock-covered feet padding down the hall to a bedroom. Callie heard the child close the door.

Callie held her phone out with the picture of Ben. "Do you recognize this man?"

Ms. Eagerton took the phone, even expanded the picture. "No, don't think so. You mean out here, right?"

"Yes, ma'am." Callie took back the phone. "He died on a lot one block behind you. During today or yesterday, did you hear anything unusual outside? Shouting, maybe?"

Blinking, as though the questions came at her too fast, Ms. Eagerton said, "No . . . " then halted and quickly lurched forward. "Just a second. That man died out here? Jesus, what's happening to this island?"

The problem with revealing the death to too many people was their burning desire to extrapolate how, when, where, and why things happened. The human condition craved drama . . . and blame and a reason. Like every criminal had it in for someone particular, or the dead had been stalked. Sometimes random was random, but with four burglaries and one questionable death on her plate, Callie had to admit that Edisto Beach wasn't being its usual hospitable self.

Callie pocketed the notepad. "That about wraps it up. We'll be in touch."

Talking en route to the door, Ingrid seemed eager to show Callie out. She gripped the knob. Again, door unlocked. "So what are we supposed to do about Christmas morning?"

Callie glanced back at the tree brimming with two dozen gifts. For three people. "I'll tell my officers to do their damnedest to find that bracelet so your daughter doesn't go without. Our apologies for your inconvenience."

Without another word, Ms. Eagerton let Callie out and shut the door followed by a fast click of the lock.

On her way down the stairs, Callie pondered the differences in people, and how the holidays probably made no difference in how these two houses normally behaved. Back in the patrol car, she reached for the fudge, and for a split second wondered if she ought to rewrap it and walk it back up to Ingrid, to make nice. Then she quickly dispelled the thought and bit off half a square, relishing the creamy meltaway sugar in her mouth.

Quarter to eight and dark. She messaged Thomas that she was done.

Then the unspoken thought she'd had sitting in the Eagerton living room popped up. How many other families were missing gifts they hadn't noticed? How many took out their trash without analyzing it? How many wouldn't even realize what was missing until Christmas morning?

CALLIE NUDGED HER patrol car up against the tail of her dated SUV, cautious about the unfamiliar vehicle parked on the street. She got out and approached her front stairs, guarding her side, motion sensors lighting her path.

She spent many a vacation on Edisto as a child, several visits a year, but her history with Boston PD and personal experience with a stalker made her house the anomaly on this beach. Cams inside and out. Security system. If a raccoon so much as knocked on the glass, she'd know it.

Anyone coming to her house was seen.

Halfway up the top flight of steps, she relaxed at the sight of the man resting in one of her rattan settees. If Stan put his stamp of approval on someone, they were golden. "Surprised to see you here," she said, no longer guarded.

Mark Dupree rose holding a plastic container. "You didn't get much chance to enjoy your party, and frankly, I've got a ton of leftovers that will spoil. Tacos and quesadillas don't freeze well."

Without a doubt, the surprise visit was flattering. "That's so thoughtful, Mark. Come on inside," she said, disarming the alarm.

"Fort Knox," he said.

She dropped keys in a bowl on the kitchen bar. "Allows me to sleep better. Mind if I change? This uniform . . .?"

He entered the kitchen like he owned it. "That utility belt gets heavy, I imagine. Especially on someone your size. Go ahead. Take your time. I'll warm this food up and have it waiting for you by when you're done."

Having a man in her house drew an odd feeling out of her. Odd but welcome. She wondered if Stan had put Mr. Dupree up to this. She sure as hell hoped not. That would be a disappointment. Her old boss meant well, but she preferred to manage her own social life. Had preferred not having one for over a year. But surprisingly she found herself almost welcoming this impromptu call.

Belt off. Shoes. Shirt, vest, etc., etc. What used to take twenty minutes to dress, and therefore, undress, had been replaced by a wham bam routine she had down pat. And nothing felt better than to trade the day's wardrobe for jeans or sweats. Both today as she went with her best casual jeans and a plain sweatshirt. Sneakers. Almost as good as going naked after a long day on the job.

The aroma of Mexican greeted her when she opened her bedroom door. "Geez, I hadn't realized how hungry I was until that smell." Then she paused. The gas log fireplace blazed, and he'd plugged in her Christmas tree lights on a five-foot fake green tree adorned with shells and starfish, the ornaments from when her mother decorated the cottage. Unlike the homes she'd interviewed today, only four gifts peeked out. Three for her son Jeb, not expected until Christmas Eve, and one for Stan. Sophie's present was hidden in a drawer, for fear that she'd snoop.

"I could get used to this." She approached the bar where a glass of Blenheim's ginger ale greeted her, over ice. A visiting investigator introduced her to the drink—made in South Carolina—back in August, when every hot, sweaty evening meant a tall gin and tonic, or two. Carolina Slade had known the drink might not replace the alcohol but hoped the ginger bite might substitute enough for Callie to climb back on the wagon. She'd grown rather fond of the taste, not to mention the memories that came with it.

"Thanks," she said, raising her glass. "This is quite the treat. Stan's idea?"

"You're welcome," he said, cautiously pushing hot quesadillas on the plate. "But no. Sophie asked me to do it. Said you tend to work through meals."

Callie took a drink. "Bet she said more than that."

"Maybe." He slid the plate before her. Refried beans and an assortment of hors d'oeuvres from the afternoon party. "Eat up." He already had a glass of ginger ale and leaned on the counter, watching her. "Can I pick your brain about something?"

"Something or someone?" she asked, mouth already full.

He grinned. "You got me. Someone."

"Sure."

"Sophie."

She should have known. Sophie was the most curious creature on the island, and Callie hadn't met a man yet who hadn't inquired about her. And she might even concede to a date with some of them, but to tie that woman down was like harnessing a hurricane.

"She teaches yoga, right? How often and where?" he asked.

Callie nodded. "At the bar behind Finn's. At least three classes a week. More in the summer with tourists. Are you a yoga man? She's always fussing about how men are too embarrassed to give it a try. I promise if you show up, she'll give you all the attention you want."

His mild grimace said he wouldn't be hitting a mat anytime soon. "Never been that much of a fan. Not sure I could bend into those crazy poses."

With a scoff, Callie jabbed an almost-eaten quesadilla at him. "Not the issue. She can. It's amazing how she rocks some of those moves. I would think more men would show up just to watch. That and she *helps* you," she said on the last bite, using air quotes. "Time for me to pick your brain."

"Shoot," he said.

"Do you recognize the name Ben Rosewood?"

He pondered the question. "Don't think so. Should I?"

She again showed Ben's picture. "Here. How about now?"

"Sure, I've seen him. Comes in with Brice LeGrand every so often. Is that . . ."

She nodded, mouth full. "Yep. That's him. Died on Brice's lot, thinking yesterday or last night. Still waiting for the coroner's take on things. Have you seen him other than in your restaurant?"

"No. Can't say I have."

A knock sounded, and Callie started to get up.

Mark held up a hand. "You eat. I'll get it. If it's the bogeyman, I'll beat him off."

With a spatula? Opening a taco to shovel beans into it, she kept one eye on the hallway. There was a self-assured air about that man, but like everyone out here, she'd bet a month's salary he had a past. But the rule was not to ask. Anyone willing to share their history did so on their own accord.

Callie heard Sophie before she rounded the corner alone. "I figured you'd be hungry," she said, then instantly checked the glass with a sniff. She tapped her girlfriend on the shoulder, in approval of the drink.

Wiping up the last of her beans with the remnants of a taco, Callie popped the wad in her mouth. "We were just talking about you. And thanks for giving Mark the idea to bring food. Appreciate it."

Sophie patted herself on the back. "Was hoping that was his car. Had to check."

"Of course you did," Callie said, pushing back the plate.

Mark had made his way back into the kitchen. "More?" he asked.

Callie shook her head. "I'm stuffed. Thanks so much."

He flashed a smile and took her plate. Sophie waltzed . . . because Sophie never just walked . . . to Mark and draped herself across his shoulder. "I'm really enjoying my job, boss. I sure hope you stick around."

"That's the plan," he said, washing the few dishes he'd dirtied, plus the couple of extra cups in the sink. "Sank my savings into that place, so it better work. Question is are you?" he said to his hostess.

"Am I what?" Sophie asked, her head comically tilted to the side, twice as far as anyone else could.

"Sticking around," he said. "Can I count on you, sweetheart, when the hordes start coming."

Sophie jerked around toward Callie and silently mouthed *sweetheart*, then gave a thumb motion back at Mark. "Are you listening to him? He thinks I'll jump ship on him." Then with just as quick a spin back, she ran fingertips down his muscled arm. "Why in the world would I leave a job with benefits like him?"

He winked down at Sophie. Callie liked that wink. Wished she didn't. Wished she hadn't misread his attentions.

"The meal was nice," she said to interrupt Sophie's cooing. "Soph, you did hear about today, didn't you? I wanted to ask you a couple questions."

She snapped around. "Well, glad you decided to ask in your house instead of mine. Don't want that damaging discussion poisoning my place. Was it Ben Rosewood?"

Callie nodded.

With a sarcastic scowl, she snapped back, "Somebody murder his sorry ass?"

"Coroner hasn't said yet."

Mark pivoted to study her dubiously over his shoulder. "A good friend, I take it?"

"He was down on women, Mark." Sophie motioned to Callie. "Her, me, not to mention Callie's birth momma, the new widow. I hope he left her loaded."

Mark's attention shifted to Callie. "Not your dad . . .?"

"No. Stepdad, but that's a long story for a longer evening," she said.

"And it's late, and we've all had a full day," Mark said. "Leftovers in the fridge, and I'll escort Sophie out."

Sophie's arm through his, Callie watched them take the stairs to the ground level, realizing she never got to ask all her questions. Sophie kissed Mark on the cheek. He laughed. Then both waved to Callie.

"Phone me tomorrow morning, Sophie," she called. "I want to talk to you about Ben."

Sophie giggled and waved again.

Back inside, Callie shut off the fireplace and settled into her empty house. Suddenly the empty bothered her. She'd misread Mark, his attention at the bar appeared to be nothing but birthday wishes. His coming over with dinner more an inquiry about Sophie. She gave a thought to that bottle of gin hidden in a suitcase wedged under the bed as she flicked the remote to an old Netflix movie.

Chapter 6

Two Days Before Christmas

SEVEN A.M. AND TINY blue holiday lights outlined the entrance to the police station, screaming *This is where the cops are.* Callie hated those lights, but the guys loved them. She walked through the blue aura and into the station, way earlier than she had before her ginger ale days. She hadn't been counting her days of abstinence, but last night had threatened to break her streak, and she couldn't pinpoint why. Mark coming in her house? His interest in Sophie? The rash of crimes, maybe.

Feeling foolish about feeling anything at all about the evening, she'd forced herself to do sit-ups until her muscles complained, then took a hot shower to relax, and slipped under the sheets. The gin had remained beneath her bed, the cap's seal intact, and she was early to work.

Ike, her most seasoned officer—even though he had only one year on the beach, and Thomas, her youngest, waited with coffee. Both were propped against Marie's desk where the admin queen already addressed her computer. *Jingle Bells* played in the background from one of her apps. She was glad to see them ready to get busy.

The Edisto PD had five officers in addition to the chief, plus a deputy on loan from Walterboro, the county seat. Her old boss Stan had even been coaxed to direct traffic during festivals, parades, and the fourth of July. Though the department was stretched thin during the summer peak, this part of year they could usually coast.

"Got two calls this morning about yesterday's reported thefts," Marie said. "Kyle Eagerton and Mr. Young on Palmetto. The Eagerton man was rather demanding. Mr. Young was nice enough, but nervous. I told them you'd be in touch."

Callie lifted her regular cup off the tray of their coffee table against the wall. "Met with Ingrid Eagerton, but Kyle wasn't there. I'll give him a call. I'm headed to Mr. Young and the other burglary on Palmetto later this morning."

"Marie opened up the pics from the Dolphin Road crowd," Thomas said. "We went through them once already and came up with about ten people we couldn't recognize."

Callie joined them, coat still on. The temperature outside had dropped to forty-five, and the warm cup rested toasty in her hands. After another run-through of the recorded people, she agreed with the identities made and missed. "Can you put that on a flash drive for me?" she asked to no one in particular, knowing Marie would do it. "I bet Janet can ID the others."

"No doubt," Thomas said. "I think she runs DNA tests on her renters."

Janet Wainwright had indeed mastered the real estate business on Edisto and controlled the majority of rentals. And if you *didn't* rent from her, she dropped strong enough hints in the form of brochures and limited-offer deals left inside screen doors and under windshield wipers that she made you want rent through her on the next go-around.

Callie blew across the top of her coffee. "Y'all finish canvassing houses last night?"

"Got two or three more," Ike said. "Then I think we've done all we can do. My money's on the guy just dropping dead. Nobody'd seen him anywhere the couple of days before and heard nothing anywhere around within the time frame he would've died."

"Why there, though?" she asked, her coffee finally cool enough to drink.

Thomas pushed off the desk. "Yeah, beats me why Ben Rosewood would be on an empty lot. Any empty lot. He's lived out here longer than I've been alive and never got involved with much, so I can't see him scouting out beach investments. Rather picture him finally dumping his wife and putting his place up for sale."

Marie backhanded the officer's sleeve. "Seriously, Thomas?"

"What?" Then, "Oh," at the realization of what he said. "Nothing against you, Chief."

Half grinning, Callie walked toward her office after patting the back of his arm. "Don't worry about it. You guys finish canvassing. Call me only if you learn something. Once it gets a little closer to ten, I'm headed to interview those new burglaries on Palmetto. Oh, and pay particular attention to the six-hundred blocks."

The two officers stared at each other.

"That's where all the thefts occurred so far, guys," she added.

"We always have a gift reported stolen, boss," Thomas said. "Happens every year."

"Four in two days, though?" Callie asked.

He shook his head slowly. "No. Not really."

"Not ever," Marie added. "With Ben's death, this holiday isn't quite so festive. Makes me want to lock my doors."

That's what Callie figured. These thefts had the potential of blighting the entire beach's holiday spirit and spill into spring business if word got out. People had spent good money to enjoy Christmas on the Atlantic with loved ones. Christmas morning was two days away.

"Breathing ought to make you lock your doors," Callie told her. "And you two guys remind people of that as you get the chance. Keep flashing Ben's picture as you make your rounds, and after I check those two Palmetto houses, I'll go see Janet about the gawkers from yesterday. Hopefully before the day's out we have a cause of death from the coroner." She held up crossed fingers. "Assuming nothing else happens."

"Speaking of problems, where's Brice?" Marie asked.

Thomas's face went blank. "Wow, yeah. He usually blows in here like a storm when we have a rash of anything on this beach. Like he has to supervise us."

"Or light a fire under our asses," Ike added.

They would be ordinarily right, but Callie wasn't surprised at the town councilman's absence. Ben's body was found on Brice's lot. He'd been ignorant of his wife's desire to sell the lot and her impromptu plan to clear the land. For him to show up in the station would open an embarrassing discussion about it all. Plus Callie hadn't exactly exonerated him standing on that silt road in front of the curious.

Thomas reached for his keys. "Gotta get back to it. See ya' later, Chief."

Ike gave a mild wave and headed out as well.

"Thomas," she said. "Hang back a second."

Question in his eyes, he stopped and let Ike leave. "What's up?"

"You got plans for Christmas?" she asked. He couldn't afford to live on the beach, so he lived further back on the island nearer the mainland bridge, renting a trailer, saving every dime he could for his dream boat. No parents.

"Maybe doing some fishing," he said. "Want me to work a longer shift? I don't mind."

More overtime dollars for that future boat.

Being single, he'd already volunteered for morning duty to let the older officers spend the holiday with their families and would get off around four. "You're doing enough that day, but if you find yourself in the mood for company, you're more than welcome to come by my place," she said. "No rigid schedule or anything. Drop in at your convenience."

His half-grin flashed sincere appreciation. "I might do that," he said. "Thanks."

After losing another young officer, Francis, last year in that car-in-the-marsh accident, Callie'd become rather protective of Thomas. When she'd arrived on the scene that autumn day, Francis was already in the water trying to free a panicky Sarah. Even with high tide the water hadn't covered the vehicle yet. He'd had time.

Francis slipped in the pluff mud at the same moment the car resettled, pinning him two feet under. Callie shed her belt and dove in, giving it her all to move the car, only to slip on the nasty bottom, pinning herself in the same predicament. Thomas arrived . . . and chose to save her first.

Francis had probably already drowned, everyone said. But both Callie and Thomas realized all too well that he had made a split-second choice to save at least one officer in lieu of losing two. They'd formed a bond from that horrible day, though that incident wasn't a topic they discussed.

Waiting for ten o'clock, she completed the little bit of paperwork left over from yesterday and made a few comments on the Edisto PD's Facebook page that people near and far tended to follow. She took a call from Kyle Eagerton, calmly addressing his not-so-calm demands to make the beach safer for his wife and daughter, attempting to soothe him, and enduring his threats to report her and her officers to somebody . . . he just wasn't sure who yet. Callie hung up, willing her frustration down, praying Kyle wasn't contagious to the other tourists, and counting her blessings that she wasn't dealing with Brice on top of everything else.

Yesterday had thrown the town councilman off-balance, left him unsure how to address a case in which the illustrious LeGrands were involved. As an elected official, he couldn't afford the scandal, and ignoring it might make it go away sooner. His about-face from the norm of lambasting appearances in the police offices was almost laughable if the case hadn't involved a death.

Admittedly, she enjoyed the peace and quiet from his gravelly, raucous voice.

THE TWO LATEST reported thefts were on the six-hundred block of Palmetto, the main drag that paralleled the beach. Crazy coincidental, but Callie hadn't been able to connect why that block. Coincidental in that Ben died on 617 Dolphin Road. The houses on Pompano were on the six-hundred block of their street, too.

Houses, like hers, Sophie's and Sarah's, had double-digit addresses, something to do with the origin of the beach in the forties. But for that quirk, they'd be on the five-hundred block. And that was too close to six-hundred for her comfort. Callie made a mental note to tell Sophie to lock up, too. Not that she would, not when Sophie believed, *To think negative is to invite negative.*

Sighing, Callie pulled into the driveway of *Sea Me*, a Palmetto Boulevard house on the water. *Good. Two cars.* Unless they'd left to enjoy some rather nippy beachcombing with the frisky morning wind, someone was home.

Sure enough, two young women answered. In their twenties, they appeared barely out of college, one with hair tight in a ponytail, the other in a pixie cut. No makeup but like most young girls, beautiful nonetheless. They stood motionless, silent, in awe at the uniform on their threshold.

Glancing inside, Callie spotted a three-foot tree sprinkled with inexpensive homemade ornaments on a kitchen table draped with a felt tree skirt, a hodgepodge of small gifts beneath it. No lights on this side of the house, but they could've decorated the back, where houses fronting the beach flaunted most of their personality. At night the tree would be visible through the front window.

"Hello." Callie introduced herself and delivered her card. "Someone report a theft?"

"Who is it?" hollered a young man from deeper inside.

"The police," the pixie shouted back.

"Shit," said another voice, and bare feet scrambled on the hardwood floor, the backdoor opening with a squeak.

The pixie stepped further out. "Um, no problem, officer. We appreciate your service."

Callie patiently waited for the boys to dispose of the pot she'd caught a whiff of when the girls greeted her. Not a heavy cloud. Too early for that kind of partying. She humorously imagined the scene if she'd dropped in last night. "As the chief, I wanted to address this personally since you're not the only incident."

"We had a theft?" Ponytail asked.

Pixie turned to her clueless friend and thumbed toward the back. "A mistake, Finley. I'll take care of it. Can you go deal with them?"

Ponytail left, and Pixie moved outside, closing the door behind her. "Listen, Officer."

"Chief is fine," Callie said.

"Oh, Chief. Right."

Rockers sat to the left, farther from the corner where the wind whipped around cool. "Go grab a jacket and come sit with me over here," Callie said. "And I'm not interested in your weed."

The girl ran inside and came back out with a hooded sweatshirt, a blanket, and gloves. Had to be Southern with blood that thin. "What's your name?" Callie asked.

"Taylor," she said, bundling up in a ball in one of the rockers. "My name's on the report. The guys weren't going to file anything, but the present was for Finley from Theo, one of the stupid degenerate morons you heard back there. Finley has no idea yet, and Theo's worried more about the cops coming here than how his girlfriend's gonna feel Christmas morning."

"You mind?" Callie said, again with her pad. She'd grabbed a clean one this morning expecting to fill the pages before the day was out.

Taylor shook her head.

"You're missing a watch?"

"An Apple watch. I mean, he went with a Series 3, so it's not the top of the line, but still nice."

"Value?"

"I think he spent four on it," she said.

"Four . . . hundred?" However, if kids could afford to rent this house on the water, the cost of a watch wasn't much of an issue.

Taylor's eyes were expressive, opening wide and narrowing with each word. "He didn't want to appear too serious. Like, no ring of any kind, so he went practical. No way he can get another one delivered all the way out here. How far is it to Charleston?"

"Forty-five miles to the Citadel Mall and fifty to downtown, but with two days to Christmas, expect the traffic to be brutal," Callie said. "Consider filing an insurance claim for that watch, though. Your police report will help along with the receipt."

The girl mashed her lips in a semi-smile in acceptance. "Someone else told us that, too. I'll make Theo do it."

Callie heard a bump inside and ignored the hustle taking place to clear the air. "When and how did you note the gift missing?"

"When? Yesterday morning, maybe eleven-ish? The others were sleeping in so I wrapped my gifts. But when I went to arrange them under the tree, I took count. There are four of us, and we agreed to give each other one gift. The number was off. At first I thought Theo just messed up, but when I got him alone, he swore he put his three under there. Finley's was the only one missing."

A different spin on this burglary. "The other two houses I spoke to discovered their presents missing when they found the wrappings in the trash. You were shrewd enough to miss the gift. Do you mind checking the garbage, or have you dumped it in the outside receptacle already?"

Taylor let out a guffaw, then covered her mouth with the hoodie sleeves running past her fingertips. "Sorry. But the thought of anyone in this group taking out the trash before it's spilling on the floor is comical. Come on in, and let me check."

Decent enough girl, and most likely the one who orchestrated this foursome's holiday getaway. When Callie entered, she found the two boys draped overly-relaxed on the decade-old, overused love seat and upholstered chair, Finley in the shower. A couple of lavender scented candles glowed on the coffee and end tables.

"Nice ambience for eleven o'clock on a Saturday morning," Callie said only for Taylor's ears. "Hey guys!"

Limp arms in short sleeves waved back, as if cable news held their attention like the final seconds of a national championship game . . . like the open back door airing out the place wasn't freezing their butts off.

Lifting the top off the trash can, Taylor scrunched her nose.

"Let me," Callie said, a pair of latex gloves snapping out of her pocket. "Got another trash bag?"

After disposing signs of a serious party into the bag Taylor held, Callie uncovered a small, beer-and-salsa-soaked wad of wrapping paper. "This it?"

"Oh, wow, yes! Is the present in there, too?"

Callie doubted it but better safe than sorry. Tenderly picking through the refuse, they reached the bottom and its utter dregs of ketchup, Dixie cups, soiled sandwich wrap, and potato chip bags dripping with Coke and again, beer. But no Apple watch.

"Sorry," Callie said, removing the gloves and dropping them in Taylor's bulging bag. "Tie that up and I'll put in the outside bin for you." But as Taylor bow-tied the top, Callie had to ask. "Do y'all lock up?"

"During the night?" Taylor asked.

"Day or night," Callie replied.

Taylor hoisted over the bag. "Why? It's dead. My parents always bragged that they never had to worry about that sort of thing out here."

"The missing watch ought to change your mind, I'd think. Edisto isn't the problem as much as the people who visit. Here today and gone tomorrow. Do me a favor and lock up."

Escorting Callie outside, Taylor wrapped her arms around herself. "Oh. Okay. Thanks."

Callie smiled and took the steps back down to ground level. Finding the bin hidden under the house where the kids had tucked their Lexus, she deposited the bag and secured the bin's top. Traipsing through the sandy drive to her car, she got in and glanced back up. Taylor had already gone inside, but Callie noted the house's carved and painted sign, *Sea Me*, then the sign next to it. A sign that appeared a couple hundred addresses up and down Edisto streets. Wainwright Realty.

The same sign as on the other two rentals, and when she glanced two houses down to the next address on her list, the big and bold red, gold, and black sign made it four.

Chapter 7

WHILE CALLIE'D BEEN in *Sea Me*, the sun had risen higher and decided to shine with vigor, rays bouncing off the cold, roiling water, so Callie put on her shades. She backed out of the driveway of *Sea Me*, then pulled into the driveway of *Palms Up*, just two addresses down. The house in between was a smaller, fish camp sort of two-bedroom shanty. Minimum upkeep. Wood rotted around the windows. Beach frontage was its only advantage, and Callie could see the next hurricane taking it off the market altogether.

In contrast, *Palms Up*—owned by a collective of FBI agents out of Columbia—was a coral-colored two-story house with five or more bedrooms, she guessed. Its rental income would be twice that of its neighbors, and the renters also usually consisted of a collective of families sharing the expense. Two cars parked beneath the structure and two behind them in the drive. Callie inched in leaving barely three feet behind her bumper and the occasional Palmetto traffic.

A squeal jerked her attention to beach level. A girl around ten dipped and dodged a lad about her age. The two pivoted and kicked up sand in chase around the house's pillars.

She trotted up the stairs but before Callie could knock, a man bumping forty darted out, barely missing a collision. He reached out to steady her briefly before stepping back. "Whoa, my apologies, Sergeant."

"Chief," she said, and held out a hand, rolling out her rank and name as before.

Sheepishly, he shook and held up a short and very familiar-shaped cigar. "Trying to slip out and taste at least one of these babies," he said. "My wife, hell, all the wives, hate cigars." He talked with it, diving it through the air. "Won't even let me sit on the back watching the water, a setting that we paid damn generously for. Says the smoke blows inside too bad." He ended on an exhale, then his expression shifted into something completely perplexed. "Um, something wrong?"

She pointed at the cigar, and he pulled it against his chest. "It's perfectly legal," he said.

"No," she laughed. "I have a friend who smokes a Short Story cigar. He's retired law enforcement, but I kid him that the stumpy smoke gives him a mob flare."

The man pivoted the cigar on the tips of his fingers. "Yeah, I can see that, but it smokes great. So, Chief, are you here about the presents?"

"I sure am. You want to talk out here so you can have your smoke or go inside . . . with all that herd of people I hear in there?"

He swept his arm toward the chairs. "No brainer. Move all the way to that end. It blows the smoke away."

Settling on two Adirondacks, Callie appreciated the heavier coat she'd put on that morning. She'd risen cold and couldn't get warm, and she thanked the heavens for prompting her to tug it from the back of her closet.

"Are you Mr. Young?" she said, pad and pen at the ready.

"Langston Young. I filed the report."

"Tell me about that burglary," she said for what felt like the umpteenth time . . . praying it was the last.

"We're missing three presents—"

"Three?" Marie had assumed Callie would read the report and didn't require briefing. Marie was right, Callie should have.

Young sucked in hard from a lighter to get the cigar going. The smoke covered his head for a second until a gust snatched it off. "Am I sure? No. Are the moms in there sure? Absolutely." A couple of hard, quick puffs, then he had the stogie sorted to his satisfaction. "We have four couples and nine children in this house for the holidays. Those women have been planning this escapade for a year. Who's getting which child what, comparing the money spent, the number of gifts per child. Hell, they even divided up the ornaments on the damn Christmas tree. The other husbands fish. Lucky them." He took another puff. "Leaves me to draw the short straw when it comes to errands, fixing this, carrying that. Next day those guys go out at dawn, I'm going with them just so I can smoke in peace."

"You don't seem that concerned," she said, wondering uneasily if he should be. There were too many people in this house to make it a prime target, meaning the thief had nerve.

"Have you seen that tree? Oh, of course you haven't. There must be sixty gifts in there." He started to take another puff and waved his cigar instead. "Color-coordinated. We're missing one each in the green, the red, and the gold categories. Apparently the silver-wrapped gifts are accounted for. I'm just not convinced that some miscalculations weren't made, but if I opened my mouth and said that? You'd find me in one of these creeks around here, trussed up and left for the crocodiles."

"Gators," Callie said.

"Regardless, I'd never be found."

She wrote about the colors, the number, his lack of concern. "Run down how you, or they, realized they went missing."

"I told you," he said. "The accounting under the tree. My wife noted one of ours missing. She spoke to the other wives, and they got out their little spreadsheets and went down the list. One green, one red, and one gold. The Youngs, the Hamptons, and the Williams. The silver Sayles lucked out. They sorted the details yesterday around three, and then I filed a report with you people."

The most recently reported theft, but not necessarily the most recent. With this many people, who knew when it really happened. "What about the trash? Another renter said they found the wrapping paper in the trash."

"Kids are told to take out the trash, and I seriously doubt they care what's in it."

"Think you could hunt through it for me?" she asked.

He loved leading with that cigar. "Nothing disrespectful, Chief, but would you mind making that request? To any wife? They're a network so doesn't matter which."

Callie snickered. "They'll stick you with it anyway."

"Yeah, but it won't be like it's my idea. What else can I help you with?"

She flipped a page. "When's the last all of you were out of the house?"

Young had to think about that one. "Not sure I can say."

"Can your wife answer that?" Callie asked.

"Maybe? With this many people, I'm not sure the house has been totally empty since we got here. There's always someone not wanting to go, and there's too many of us to go all at once. We'd fill half the restaurants around here. And when you gather the entire horde, invariably it gets too loud or someone gets miffed at something said. I'm telling you. If this house was empty, it was only because everyone happened to have gone out back to the beach, and even then, people would be in and out for something to drink or use the bathroom. That's why I think someone sneaked their gifts early, and the moms noticed before the presents could get slipped back."

"Do you keep the doors locked?"

He laughed. "You're joking." Then he laughed again. "You should see your expression."

Callie wanly smiled. "There's just me and my son. Hard to imagine . . . this." Hard to imagine *wanting* to do this was more like it. "Take me to your wife, Mr. Young, and I'll make the trash request."

He'd smoked the short cigar down to two inches. "Bless you, kind woman. I'll walk you inside."

Callie made the request of the all-too-eager-to-please wives in that huge living room. In front of the seven-foot artificial tree in the corner, she imagined a burglar's temptation, but worse, the unlikeliness the house would be empty long enough for a thief to be alone scared her to her core. This wasn't a dash and grab. The burglar could likely have entered when they slept, when the house was occupied. When any one of those seventeen people could've caught a bad guy in the act and paid a very nasty price for being thirsty for a midnight glass of water.

And so many kids in harm's way.

Three missing gifts. Should be four if the thief measured by family, but then, he could've been interrupted, or when confronted with the larger number of gifts, just raised his minimum from one to three. Only small gifts, too, making for a cleaner, simpler escape without the demands of any heavy, cumbersome loot.

But this location choice seemed awful bold compared to the others.

Callie followed the group outside. If they found paper in the trash, then this was the same guy. And she suspected he'd escalated.

Four wives and one husband were soon separating a bin of trash on a spread out array of plastic bags, several kids standing to the side scrunching their noses and making *Ewww* and *Ick* remarks. Finally, they hit pay dirt. One bag, its knot so tight they had no choice but to extend the bulging rip on one side, almost opened itself when they laid it out. There, amidst the empty milk jug, cereal box, coffee grounds, and chicken wing bones peeked a wad of red paper.

"Oh my goodness," exclaimed one wife, quickly scanning the other moms. "You don't think the kids . . ." and all four women laid gazes on the offspring.

"What?" squeaked a puberty-aged boy, the one Callie first saw upon her arrival. "Don't blame me!"

"Which one of you opened a present?" scolded mom number two.

"Not me" made the rounds like a stadium wave.

"Here's green paper. Jason? Was this you?"

"Honest, Mom. I didn't do anything."

In the end, they found the gold paper along with the others, with all children denying, the mothers not sure they believed them, and Mr. Young watching Callie with fresh fear in his eyes.

She nodded back, confirming his worry. He came over. "What does this mean?"

"It means lock up, and nobody leave the house empty," she said.

"But this is Edisto!"

She calmly nodded. "And it could be nothing more than some kid on holiday break. Nobody's been hurt, Mr. Young. They even disposed of their trash. Might only be a child not much older than one of yours." She smiled like they'd just discussed littering. "My apologies for disrupting your Christmas, and sorry you lost some gifts, but we'll do our best to nab this guy. Okay?"

"Okay," he said, not quite as tense, but not buying the incident as innocent.

"I'll be in touch." But then she remembered. "On another issue, have you seen this man lately?" she asked.

The shift in topic stunned Young for a few seconds. "He a suspect?"

"No," she said. "He's . . . um, missing."

He studied Ben's driver's license photo on her cell. "No. Nothing registers."

She could've queried the entire group of adults, but the rest were too stirred up in their own confusion.

She returned to her car and headed toward Jungle Road to visit Janet. On two counts. First, to see if she recognized the renters in the photos her officers took on Dolphin Road. Second, to see if she realized that at least four burglaries had occurred on the beach, with all four being her tenants.

EVEN WITH THE small surge of holiday visitors, the beach felt half deserted. Lights flashed in the occupied houses like motel marquees, dark windows indicating vacancies. Nobody out much. Only a few making short, symbolic strolls on the beach before disappearing inside, giving a desolate air to the streets.

Two days before Christmas. Didn't feel like it. Jeb and his steady honey had capitalized on their college break to enjoy each other in Charleston, without school obligations . . . and without mothers involved. After all, when your mothers were the police chief of Edisto Beach and the yoga mistress of the Edisto spirit world, you had to expect oversight, over-reaching, and overt attentiveness resulting in a probably justified feeling of being coddled.

Despite understanding, Callie sure missed her son. Her house never seemed to echo until she expected one of his visits. However, if he were home, she'd still be doing this—investigating. And he'd be frustrated at having to tease Sprite away from Sophie. It was much better that they could have this time in Charleston, and he'd be home tomorrow night for Christmas Eve.

She nosed the cruiser onto the gravel parking lot of the realty office, but waited before getting out, instead placing a call to the coroner's office. Voice mail. She left a message that she preferred to get the coroner's report *before* rather than after Christmas, then hung up and got out.

Only a gold Hummer and a small, sporty Ranger pickup joined her cruiser in the parking lot, meaning Janet Wainwright and her nephew Arthur. Like Callie, the young man had grown up vacationing on the beach his entire life. Since his aunt was childless and possessed ample funds, he'd taken up residence in her spare bedroom. Maybe hoping to inherit one day.

But the retired Marine had cut him little slack. He cleaned rentals until he reached eighteen, when Janet began grooming him for a career in real estate. Everyone assumed he'd take the reins one day. He had the people skills, and Janet hammered the business sense into him.

The realty office's porch stood naked without its warm-weather ferns. The signature lantana and roses usually lining the walkway lay dormant for the winter, depriving the place of their color, but the yellow and red lights draping the railing took their place.

Janet carried her beloved Marine Corps and its colors into retirement boldly. Even her clothes reflected the scheme, and her tight white hair gave the package a snappy pop. She'd given her office assistant two weeks off while Arthur acquired the management experience for his resume. Efficient nepotism.

"Janet?" Callie called, entering the lobby of the old beach house turned commercial. An eight-foot artificial tree rose tall in the corner, saluting with its yellow and red balls. She was surprised Arthur wasn't manning the front desk. "Arthur?"

"My office," Janet commanded as if ordering a fresh recruit to straighten up the line.

Callie made her way back to the inner sanctum, a large room of wood and leather, much like the retired Marine's home. Arthur lounged on the sofa off to the side, way more lax than Callie ever felt in this setting.

"Hey, Arthur," she said. "Janet, you got a moment?"

Janet waved Callie to a seat before her desk. "You see any clients lined up out there? Of course, I've got a moment. What's your boggle?"

Boggle? Arthur mouthed in jest.

With a smirk, Callie handed her the flash drive and took a seat. "Plug that in, please, ma'am. I'd like you to ID some people."

Peering over reading glasses, the older woman studied Callie, then the small computer stick passed to her. "What if I don't want to?"

"Oh, Janet, stop it. You heard why I left El Marko's yesterday."

Pausing, Janet slid the drive into her computer, and clicked open the file. "Sorry to hear about Ben Rosewood. Would appreciate intel that he just dropped dead from something natural instead of us having to worry about tourism taking a dive. But good it happened in December. Would've done more serious damage in the warmer months."

Nobody was more pragmatic than Janet Wainwright.

"These are the people who showed up to watch the scene," Callie said, crossing one boot over a knee. "Wanted you to tell me who the non-natives are since they are most likely yours. Marie, Thomas, and Ike already scanned them best they could."

Janet leaned closer to her screen, head tipped back to find the right focus on her glasses. Flip, flip. One photo to another. "Think he was murdered?" she asked in a calm few people could manage to carry off when talking loss of life.

"No clue yet," Callie said, then peered over at the sofa. "How're you doing, Arthur?" Callie hadn't had the chance to speak to him at the party. "Did I hear right? You're graduating this May?"

'Yes, ma'am," he said. "And it can't happen too soon. I'm ready to get out of the classroom and start making money."

With a nod toward Janet, she smiled. "She hiring you when you get out?"

He spoke behind his hand. "Why do you think I come here on my breaks and did my co-op semester with her? Volunteered for the Wainwright boot camp year after year. Yeah, there better be some kind of end game after dealing with this drill sergeant."

"You're not hired yet, nephew," Janet said. "Chief, I see a few of my tenants, but I'm not giving you their names. Not till I have to."

Nobody was more protective of their clients than Janet Wainwright, either.

"See anybody foreign?" Callie asked, reaching for the flash drive, hoping Janet wasn't computer savvy enough to have made a copy while they sat there.

Janet shook her head. Good. If the coroner deemed Ben's death suspicious, Callie'd be back. If natural causes, no issue.

Rising, she slipped the flash in her breast pocket.

Janet rose, too, chin cocked. "What're you doing about these stolen Christmas presents?"

"First, are you sensing more thefts this year than before?"

Rubbing her thin lips, Janet thought. "Yeah, have to admit so. What are you reading into all this?"

"Well, just got back from *Sea Me* and *Palms Up*. Janet, these people have got to secure their houses. Out of the four I've interviewed—"

"Four?"

"Yes, and that's all who've reported thus far. Yesterday I touched base with *Salty Dog* and *Purple Pelican*. All four thefts are from your tenants."

Janet shrugged. "I oversee ninety percent of the holiday traffic, so frankly, I'd be surprised if one of these incidents wasn't mine. But I'm telling all my people that you're all over this problem. Am I right?"

"Of course," Callie replied. "But your people aren't securing their houses. And *Salty Dog* has a window that won't lock, which is probably how he got inside."

Janet's attention snapped toward Arthur who sat backbone straight. "Yes, ma'am," he said without being asked.

"As for you, Chief," Janet began, and Callie waited for her own orders, the only way the Marine conversed. "Catch this person and find the loot before Brice jumps on your ass and word spreads we aren't safe around here. Our lives and livelihoods depend on it."

Janet played all ends against the middle. She could have lunch with Brice and five minutes later chat with Callie, fully aware of the clash between the two. She wouldn't quickly go against the police department, because she preferred them on her side, but she likewise worked the councilman. Her only allegiance, her only *oorah*, was to her beloved Corps and the success of Wainwright Realty. *Semper Fi.*

And she could always make Callie's day harder.

"It's the same culprit from the looks of things." Callie didn't tell Janet what *things*. At least not in front of Arthur. Janet could keep a secret, but Arthur was of an age when secrets had a way of slipping out. They didn't want the thief to change his MO or raise his game.

"Bummer getting cleaned out before Christmas," Arthur said.

"Nephew, don't you pay attention when these clients come in here?" Janet scolded. She held up a bony finger. "One gift," she said. "Guy's simply making a statement taking one gift from each residence."

"Or girl, Aunt Janet," Arthur said, but when Janet scowled at the correction, he stiffened again. "Not that it matters."

"Something to think about, Arthur." Callie prepared to leave, deciding not to correct them that *Palms Up* had lost three gifts. Need-to-know basis. "Anyway, I've got to go. Call me if you hear from any more of your houses."

"Who do you think's sending them to file a police report?" the drill sergeant said.

"And advising them to file insurance . . . and giving them a free beach towel plus a discount to come back," Arthur added. "But we'll talk to our people and insure their safety. I'll get Tate Jr. to drop by each house and check the locks and windows." Graduating to agent three years ago, albeit only during holidays, enabled Arthur to often delegate repair tasks to Wainwright's handyman. "Aunt Janet's all about her customers."

"*Our* customers. Get that into your head. But I gave Tate Jr. the week off. You visit each and every occupied rental and check those locks yourself. Hear me?"

Arthur's smugness dimmed a bit. "Yes, ma'am."

Callie slid on her shades. "Sounds like that job's practically got your name on it." Arthur would fit in nicely out here, assuming the youth didn't get bored with the laid-back air of the community. But then, summer always came 'round with its share of visual perks, too. Those perks rotated in and out of these houses each and every Sunday. Arthur had a front row seat.

She made for the front porch. Out of habit, she glanced up and down and across the street, always canvassing her turf. Her attention stopped on El Marko's, which was across the street and one building east. A small collection of people, maybe six, craned to see inside.

Another person ran out the door and huddled amongst the existing group. "Somebody call the cops," she shouted.

Callie took off running.

Chapter 8

CALLIE'S PHONE RANG in her pocket during her race from
Wainwright Realty to the restaurant, but she waited until she reached the
crowd collected outside El Marko's before glancing. Two voice
mails—Sophie and Stan, which she chose not to listen to . . . not that
she could with the drama-filled cluster of folks trying to tell her about
the commotion inside.

"Attacked the owner!"

"He feared for his life!"

"I thought he would kill somebody!"

She motioned them to stand back. "Off the sidewalk," she said.
"Go to the parking lot." But when they hesitated, eager to watch, she
barked. "Go! Do like I said."

She keyed her mic and called for Ike or Thomas, whoever was
closest. Then she chose to listen to Stan's voice mail before going in,
influenced by his friendship with Mark Dupree and the timing of his call.
"Get over to El Marko's, Callie. Mark's got a situation. I'm here.
Nothing life threatening, but it requires your attention."

She still unsnapped her holster, entering with hand on her weapon.

On the floor lay a man on his belly, maybe late forties, moaning,
drunk from the sound of him, his wrists cuffed behind. A lady friend,
maybe wife, knelt beside him, oscillating between cooing in his ear and
shooting curses toward Mark standing six feet off to the side.

Callie looked away from the scene, hunting for Stan, the only person she'd expect to carry cuffs.

Suddenly two vise grips took her arm, knocking her a step sideways.
Sophie crushed against her, chattering like a squirrel on caffeine. "Oh

my God, you should've seen it! Frightening. That man might've killed me!"

Stan reached her, way calmer. "Chief. Nobody hurt. You got officers coming?"

Callie nodded. "At least one, expect both." The place had emptied except for these three and the couple on the floor.

"Your cuffs?" Callie asked Stan.

He slowly shook his head, tilting it once toward the owner. "Mark's," he said.

That caught her attention. "Mark's? What kind of guy carries cuffs?"

"Callie, Callie, you should've seen it," Sophie spouted. "It was marvelous. That awful individual on the floor shoved me. Put his hands on me! When I told him to back off, he called me a slut. I mean, who does that? We can't tolerate that sort of person out here. What will people say? Maybe you could post a man at this shopping center . . . but then that might scare people away."

"Sophie, Sophie," Callie said. "Take it down a notch. Let Stan tell it, okay?"

"But it was about me!"

It's always about you, my friend. "I hear you. You'll get your chance. Hold on a sec. Stan?" She stared up past the foot difference in their height and waited for her old boss to give her the facts without the emotional embellishment.

"Sophie's right. The man was intoxicated. Should've stayed home. Something pissed him off with his meal, and he scared the waitress to death with his bluster. When Sophie stepped in, he grabbed her." Stan gently took Sophie's forearm in demonstration. "When she resisted, he yanked her."

Sophie retrieved her arm and rubbed it, her jade green contacts glistening with the threat of fresh tears. "That's right."

"Sorry you had to deal with that, Sophie," Callie said and waited for Stan to continue.

"Mark moved in quick," he said. "Asked the man to leave, but the guy picked up his knife, just a butter knife, but still . . . and Mark simply put him down. Slapped his wrists into cuffs mighty damn efficiently."

"Yeeees," Sophie said, dragging out the word. "Mark spun him around and *clink clink*, he was cuffed." An inhale. "Like, like . . . a Ginsu chef and kung fu all at once."

Callie took another glance at Mark, which only served to prompt Sophie. She dragged Callie by the sleeve toward the owner, whispering,

"He's friggin' hot, Callie. Damn, that stuff is a turn-on. Is that why you became a cop?"

"Go take a shower, Soph."

Enough of the soap opera from Sophie, and the minimalist version from Stan. Callie reached Mark, who didn't move from his lean against the bar.

"How's it going?" Callie asked.

"All good now," he replied.

"So you carry cuffs?"

"On occasion."

The wife staggered up with a lot of effort, using both table and chair to bear her weight as she rose from her husband's prone position. "What the hell happens now?" she demanded.

"He's going to jail," Callie said, catching Thomas's entrance from the corner of her eye. "And if you get too mouthy about it, you'll join him. You two have had a few and shouldn't be this intoxicated in public. Your husband crossed the line. You're walking it."

Thomas had been engulfed by Sophie who appeared to be delivering her rendition of the event again. No telling how that story would grow as she told it over the next few weeks.

The wife teetered enough to want to sit. "What are the charges?"

Callie turned to Mark. Certain her hunch was right. "Care to do the honors?"

Without missing a beat, he recited a list. "Drunk and disorderly. Assault and battery. Aggressive assault on me. Public endangerment. Depends on how high you want to stack it, Chief."

That about sized it up. "Thomas?" Time to save him from Sophie and help Mark salvage his business for the afternoon. "Escort this gentleman to the Colleton jail. Take the wife with him." Edisto had no lock up, unfortunately, and the county facility was forty miles away, but this fell on the side of fun for Thomas, and somewhere he'd probably place a tick mark to the number of arrests he'd made.

The crowd outside parted once Thomas perp-walked the man to the parking lot, the wife holding cupped hands to the sides of her face like blinders, with the occasional stumble, as a few of the bystanders clapped. The young deputy wore his stern, business-only persona when he left, but Callie bet the corner of his mouth slipped into a smile as he reached his car.

People filtered back inside, peering around as if there were some residual and infectious bad juju left behind. Sophie ushered them to their tables, and as the room began to thrum with chatter, strangers bonded over a shared experience. Mark drew Sophie aside for a word, and she gave him a thumbs-up before scurrying off, flitting table to table to make amends and apologies.

"Can we talk?" Callie asked Mark.

"Sure," he said, escorting her to the furthest table back, nearest to the kitchen, and the last place a guest would request to sit.

Without asking, he ordered a tray of nachos and two waters, and Stan chose to wave and leave. Callie reported to Marie that all was good and where she'd be.

With business settled, and customers enjoying free hors d'oeuvres, Mark leaned back in his chair and waited.

She watched him back, selectively choosing her questions. Not that she'd demand the man's life history, but she preferred to be familiar with the law enforcement types on her beach and have some sense as to who they were, why they chose Edisto, and if any of their baggage might arrive with them.

A straight ask was best. One LEO to another. "Federal, state, or local?" she asked.

"State," he said. "SLED."

She nodded. The South Carolina Law Enforcement Division. Reputable.

Mark was a few years older than she. Most people relocated to Edisto older, after retirement. Law enforcement officers could retire after twenty years, but most stuck with the job until they aged out in their mid-fifties. Any cops, agents, and troopers who made it past the first few years hung onto the badge as long as they could, which meant a story preceded this man's arrival.

But he wasn't volunteering.

"Are you retired?" she asked.

"Yes."

"Do you plan on policing my beach?"

"Nope," he said. "Just my restaurant, and only then if you can't do it first. Today was one of those times."

"At least call me next time."

"I was busy. Figured someone else would. Apparently they did."

His attitude slid into a mode she recognized. Answer the questions short and curt. No more than necessary, because to divulge too much could invite accusations. *Callie's daily mantra for living.*

"That man could sue you, Mark."

"Maybe," he said, eating a nacho. "Doubt it, but I'm insured. Enough witnesses."

Clipped phrasing. Such a different man from the one in her house last night. When this guy's guard went up, it stood concrete firm, tall, deep, and wide.

"What is this?" She leaned elbows on the table, not the least bit interested in snacks.

"This?" he asked.

"The resistance I'm feeling. You didn't do anything out of line. I'm just asking questions."

He didn't respond.

Jesus, her radar only pinged louder. Before the day was out, maybe she'd hunt down Stan and interrogate him about Mark Dupree, but at the moment, she just wanted answers to simple queries. Mark's demeanor only prompted more concerns. "Are you bringing baggage with you?" she finally asked.

That drew a frown. "What does that mean?"

"Most LEOs come with history."

"Everyone has history," he said.

"You get what I mean." She leaned in ever so little. "Anything that should concern me?"

He'd quit eating, his gaze boring into hers. "Did you bring baggage when you moved out here? I didn't realize the department required background checks on people before they moved to Edisto."

Truth be told, she'd brought enough baggage for ten people. People had died thanks to her baggage.

And Seabrook had brought baggage. An FBI agent died on the island and left baggage. Like Mark said, everyone had a history.

"We done here?" he asked, interrupting the silence.

"I'm just doing my job." She immediately hated the words. Such a thin reply.

His body language far from cordial, he slid his chair back. "Nobody ever said you weren't. If you need me to fill out a report or sign a statement, bring it to me. But I have damage control to tend to." He left her alone with the nachos.

A young man about twenty entered the place, waiting tentatively near the front. Wesley. A native of the island who worked at the Subway counter at the gas station. By winter most of the eating establishments shifted employees to part- or no-time. Not enough traffic to justify a full staff, so many of the blue-collar residents found themselves bouncing from restaurant to restaurant, in hope of being the one who arrived when a job came open, regardless the hours. The job search was a steady ritual until after college spring break when they might earn thirty- to forty-hour wages again with just one job.

Ordinarily, Callie wouldn't have paid him much attention, but one didn't see a blue Nordic sweater with black and white snowflakes very often on this sea island.

Callie rose and started over, but Sophie reached the kid first. If he'd had a hat, he'd have kneaded it in hopeful anticipation of a break. "Y'all hiring?"

"Awww, Wesley," Sophie said, taking him to the side. "I think we have all we can use." She rubbed his sweater. "You sure dressed up nice to come ask, though. Maybe I can ask Mark."

"Appreciate it, Miss Sophie." He turned to Callie. "You heard about anyone hiring, Chief?"

"No, but I need to ask you something," she said, escorting him farther from the nearest table. Of course Sophie followed, hovering to hear her question. "Where'd you get that sweater?"

Staring down at his chest, he replied, "Um, it was a gift."

"Who gave it to you?"

His expression changed to skepticism. "Why?"

"Just answer the question, Wesley," she said.

"Callie," Sophie said low, worried.

"I'm asking because it was reported stolen," Callie said, sorry to have to tell that to an unemployed man, so polite and eager to please.

A diner waved for Sophie's attention, but she'd taken up the torch for Wesley. "Who says it was stolen? How can you *possibly* tell that?"

"Yeah," the young man said. "Everybody wears sweaters around Christmas."

"Not a Dale Nordic four hundred dollar sweater," Callie replied. "Taken from under someone's Christmas tree day before yesterday."

Sophie skittered off, and Callie assumed she'd gone to retrieve Mark.

Desperation in his expression, Wesley watched Sophie leave like she was his last friend. "You've done made me look bad. They'll never hire me now. Ten hours per week. That's all I was gonna ask."

Callie doubted they'd let any of this cloud a decision about hiring the man, assuming El Marko's even had an opening. "I'm sorry," Callie said, "but you still have to tell me who gave you the gift." While the other family could well afford to do without the sweater, that wasn't how the law worked.

Mark strode up, Sophie in his wake. "Why are you conducting police business in front of my patrons?"

Oh God, Callie wasn't trying to step on toes, but damned if she hadn't stomped on every darn one in her path since she got here. "Not my intention, Mark . . . Mr. Dupree. Fact is—"

"Fact is you're insulting this man, my diners, my staff, and me," he said, then held out a hand to Wesley. "How do you do. I'm Mark Dupree, owner of El Marko's. Do you have experience prepping food?"

Wesley tipped his head. "Yes, sir. I've worked at every restaurant on this beach. It's just in the winter . . . "

"You're hired," Mark said. "When can you start?"

The man's eyes lit up like the colors blinking in the front window. "Um, tomorrow. Today— Now!"

Callie didn't appreciate the interruption or being chastised by Mark for doing her job. "You're interrupting police business, Mr. Dupree."

Mark glowered. "You're hurting my restaurant business, Chief Morgan."

Anxious at the tiff building between the police chief and his potential employer, Wesley took a half step back.

"He said someone gave him the sweater, Callie," Sophie said softly. "Let him keep it or just give it to you, but be done with this."

Several tables had quit eating to listen. Another couple entered, saw the bottleneck of people involving a uniform, and left.

Mark was right. This didn't have to take place here. "Wesley, come with me to the station."

"Callie!" Sophie exclaimed. "You're treating him like a suspect. You know Wesley. We all do."

But he *was* a suspect, in possession of stolen property. "Come on," Callie repeated, taking Wesley by the elbow.

"Job's waiting for you, son," Mark said as the two left, but as the door eased shut she felt his stare through her back.

Chapter 9

A DAMP, COLD rush of wind traveled up Murray Street, pushing a chill into the police station when Callie escorted Wesley inside. Marie raised her brow at his presence but had learned long ago never to ask questions in front of a civilian.

But everyone was familiar with Wesley. Born and raised on the island, he had fished, swum, and worked alongside most of the inhabitants at some time during their lives. Or they'd hired him for the unpleasant physical labor that they didn't want to do, but that he was always more than willing to take on for another paycheck. A good kid who lived with his mother and grandmother, with his other relatives nearby on several of the off-roads few tourists knew about. Roads looking like jungle roads that strangers were too afraid to venture down.

Callie itched to apologize to the kid, but if anyone had to follow procedure, it was she. Brice would have her hide if she didn't . . . which reminded her, she must touch base with him, too. On top of still needing to talk to Sophie, which might be a strained exercise.

Brice tucking himself away like this wasn't normal. If anyone wanted the criminal element squashed, it was Brice, and the thefts would have drawn him out big and ugly with a long list of demands on how to rectify the situation, with an equally long list about how they could've avoided the crime in the first place. *Anything to preserve tourism.*

"Want a Coke, Wesley?" Callie asked, sitting at her desk.

"No, ma'am." He held his arms out a few inches from his torso, studying the sweater. "Please let me take this thing off. I don't like wearing it anymore."

She buzzed Marie who soon brought in an Edisto Beach t-shirt and a windbreaker, and a Coke just in case the young man changed his mind. "It's a cool day," Callie said, as she stepped outside the room. "But it's all we have. Go ahead and change."

"Thank you, ma'am. I'm wearing an undershirt, so I oughta be okay."

Her back against the wall outside, she gave Wesley ample time, and a little extra to collect his wits. Several texts had come in. She flipped through them—Sophie calling her rude; Janet asking if the rumor was true that she'd caught the thief; Stan saying simply, *We have to talk.*

Funny how that last one sent trepidation through her, a throwback to her days under his oversight. Nobody could pin her ears back better than Stan . . . or steady her when she lost sight of the goal. Somehow she wasn't expecting an *atta-girl*, but she damn sure didn't deserve a tongue-lashing, either.

If it's not an emergency, will touch base later, she typed.

After sending, she entered her office. The sweater lay in a puddle in the middle of her blotter. She folded it neatly before setting it straight and centered on the edge of her desk in front of Wesley, who appeared twenty pounds thinner without it.

"The Edisto Santa gave me the sweater," he said. "You've heard of the Edisto Santa, right?"

She had. She hadn't, however, seen the gift-giving occur, had never given it much thought, and wasn't so sure the holiday tradition was more than a convenient excuse for Wesley. "Describe to me what happens with this Santa, and how you came to receive this."

"You see"—he shifted in his chair, not as though scrutinized under a light bulb, but more relieved to tell his side—"every year, some houses get a gift. Not all, but some. All done up with Christmas paper with a note from Edisto Santa."

"How do you know it's yours to open?" she asked. "And not something for your grandmother?" Maybe they opened the package, weighed who needed it most, and doled it out.

"Oh, they have names. This was the first in years for me. Last time I was a kid."

For some reason, the personal nature of the gift-giving bothered her. She knew little of the Edisto Santa details. Rumor had it that those who received gifts were the island's poor residents. There was no fanfare about the gifts. The privileged living on or visiting the beach wouldn't hear much about Edisto Santa.

But Edisto Santa himself, or herself as Arthur so aptly corrected back at Janet's, had to have deep roots on the island to be able to identify recipients and where they lived. Most likely *not* a tourist unless he or she was a hard-core repeat visitor who took the effort to educate themselves. Wesley would be easy enough to run across with his jobs in restaurants, but it would take a diligent individual to find his residence. He didn't live anywhere near the two-lane 174, the lone access across the island to the beach, the only road tourists usually dared travel.

"Was the tag handwritten? Do you still have it?" she asked.

"Typed, like on a computer. And we burned it in the barrel out back with the rest of the trash."

Convenient. "Who else received gifts this year?" Without a doubt these folks spread talk of their good fortune to their neighbors and friends, across the aisle at church, or over the produce at Bi-Lo.

He hesitated. "You gonna take theirs, too?"

"Wesley, I have a list of stolen goods, so yes, I will return them to their rightful owners. If your house was burgled, wouldn't you want me to find the missing item for you?"

But he ignored her question, instead revealing something he probably wished he'd done. "Some sell what they receive, getting a little something at the pawn shop to pay bills and such."

She'd have a specific gift list made up soon enough and distribute to her officers, Janet, Stan, and the business owners around town. "Who else received a gift?"

A sadness seemed to sweep over him. "Don't kill Edisto Santa, Chief."

Son of a biscuit. She felt like Scrooge. "Who else?" she asked again, with far less energy.

"My cousin got an Apple watch. A friend over on Jenkins Hill got purple sunglasses. And my mother's best friend's grandmother got a cross necklace." He stared into his lap. "All I can tell you. Besides, the presents just arrived last night, so I haven't heard of any others. That sweater made me think I could look better'n anybody else hunting a job. Never thought it could be stolen."

God, could she feel any lower?

CALLIE DROVE Wesley back to El Marko's, dropped him off, and headed out to the three addresses Wesley gave her. But she wasn't stupid. Phone calls traveled faster than cars, and therefore, she had doubts about locating Wesley's people, much less the gifts. Still, she had to try. Hopefully, by spreading the word that the gifts were stolen, and that anyone could drop them off at the police station without risk or blame, she would retrieve a couple by Christmas.

But in restoring some Christmas mornings, she ruined others. Others with a lot less Christmas to celebrate.

Her personal phone rang, and she pulled over.

"Hey, Soph. What's up?"

Callie yanked the phone back from her ear at the shrill *"You're canceling Edisto Santa?* Do you even try to see what the heck you're doing?"

Callie put the phone on speaker and resumed driving, passing the Edistonian convenience store on Highway 174. "I'm investigating burglaries, Sophie. That's all."

"Who cares if people with money lose one or two gifts? Edisto Santa tries to balance that. For heaven's sake, Callie, why can't you just look the other way?"

Because she was police to all.

Callie felt like a bug squashed under the woman's heel. Sophie shared her opinions openly, too, and the rumor mill would churn up and run full speed by the time Callie got back to the beach. Not that Sophie was malicious . . . just that she was talkative. And Edisto's business was everyone's business to her.

"You're off the beach. Not your jurisdiction," Sophie spouted. "I've heard you talk about that before."

"The crime took place *on* the beach," Callie replied, then recognized the foolishness in explaining to a person with no interest in the legalities. "Wesley get his job?"

"Yes, no thanks to you and a big, beautiful hearty thanks to Mark." Sophie's new hero.

Reaching Indigo Hill Road, Callie watched for the address that belonged to Wesley's cousin. "Glad to hear it, Soph. Tell Mark thanks."

But Sophie wasn't through. "Humph. Like that's going to help you. Girl, if anyone needs to sage their house at Christmas, it would be you."

Counting off mailboxes, Callie read 220, then 224, *there*. Box 230. "Gotta go. Sorry you're upset."

"I'm not the one who ought to feel sorry." She hung up.

So much for holiday spirit.

Callie left her patrol car. The residence before her, with the slightest lean to the east, couldn't hold more than two bedrooms. No sign of paint until she caught the barest remnants of brown. The gravel had long been mashed into a dirt drive. Though ten miles inland, the cold hung heavier here without the salt air of the beach to give it character.

The first step groaned with her weight then popped back up without it, the warped wood a potent warning of visitors. At the top, a man awaited her from behind the screen, caution in his stare. Who in his right mind ever welcomed an unannounced uniform?

Only she bet her arrival had been fully anticipated.

"Hey, Henry, is it?" Assuming this was Wesley's cousin. "Don't believe we've met. I'm Chief Callie Morgan from—"

"We all know who you are," he said. "And I lost the watch."

The cousin was in his thirties and hadn't held a job in a year, according to Wesley. Some mention of a car accident a year or two ago. He leaned on the door frame with the crook of a cane showing just above the screen's wooden cross-member. "Heard you tried to mess up Wesley's job."

She couldn't quickly think of a proper response to that.

"And you took his sweater," he quickly added. "He was proud of that sweater. Well, my watch disappeared. Not sure if it was stolen or misplaced, but ain't seen it since I went to bed last night."

She was worse than Scrooge. She was the Grinch.

"Mind if I help you hunt around for it?" she asked, reaching for the screen handle. It didn't budge, clasped on the inside.

"As a matter of fact, I do mind. Merry Christmas, Chief." The door closed.

Feeling mighty bah-humbug-ish, she walked back to the car and sank into the seat. Might as well check messages. Just one text. Stan. *We still have to talk.*

Dark could catch you unawares out here. Stan would have to wait.

On Jenkins Road, she found the grandmother of a friend of a . . . she wasn't sure, but the address matched the one Wesley gave. This residence had more pride of ownership. Brick, the old red kind from years past. Azaleas dormant all around the yard, some decades old, which in full bloom in the spring could make the poorest house Easter reverent.

A buxom middle-aged woman wearing three layers of sweaters answered the knock, and surprisingly, welcomed her in. "Come on in, Chief. We've been expecting you."

Callie entered immediately recognizing the scent of burning wood. A spindly woman in the realm of her eighties sat before a fireplace with barely enough wood to give warmth.

"Thanks for inviting me in. Which one of you is Miss Alberta?" Callie asked.

"That'd be her," the bigger woman said. "I'm Delores. Wesley said you'd be showing up. What's this about Edisto Santa being a thief?"

"May I?" Callie asked, motioning toward the sofa near Miss Alberta.

Delores nodded, and Callie sat. A standing uniform shouted authority, and she wasn't out to flaunt her badge. She just wanted to chat.

"I'm familiar with the legend about Edisto Santa," she started, tone humble, "but we've had burglaries on the beach. At least four. Someone is taking presents from under trees, and we believe based upon Wesley's sweater, that the gifts are being rewrapped and delivered as Edisto Santa presents."

The old woman continued to stare at the fire. Delores's head bobbed slowly, like she was taking in the message and making silent decisions. Callie couldn't detect overt signs she was being judged by these two women, but guilt filled her nonetheless.

Neither could she see any sign of the cross necklace Wesley connected to these people.

"Were all the Edisto Santa gifts over the years stolen stuff?" Delores asked.

"I honestly can't say, ma'am. Not sure we'd be able to tell this long after the fact."

More head bobbing.

Callie didn't want to tarnish past Edisto Santas. Taking back presents from the poor today to give back to the rich was harsh enough, and she suspected the harder she explained, the nastier the deed appeared.

"Here," Miss Alberta said, catching Callie by surprise. Her frail, stick-thin digits folded into a fist, shook as they reached out.

First the cross fell out, then the 18-karat strand snaked down, catching on the old woman's nail briefly before finally dropping into Callie's palm.

Callie's heart pounded, hurting, and though she'd done nothing wrong, she wanted to crawl into a dark hole. "I'm so sorry, ma'am."

"Stolen's stolen," Delores said. "And while I hope you catch the person, a part of me hopes you don't."

Callie heard that loud and clear.

Delores's chin jutted out a little higher. "But let's just say you don't."

And there was a strong chance she wouldn't.

"Yeah," the woman continued, a hint of defiance creeping in. "Let's say you never catch this man. Something tells me next year you'll never hear the name Edisto Santa. This island will protect a good soul, Chief Morgan. His methods might be off, but his heart is good. He ain't got money to do what he's doing or he'd of bought these gifts himself . . . not stolen them. We all liked to think a man of means was generously doing all this, but you done brought to light the fact he's not much more than one of us."

Callie took note of the wise deduction and tucked the necklace in her breast pocket, both women watching as she did.

Why *hadn't* anyone noted the theft-Santa Edisto connection before? Thomas spoke back at the station about there being only one or two minor thefts during the holidays. Had the officers never taken the thefts seriously before she became chief? Or was this a surge of crime by someone new, more courageous? Someone willing to go beyond the deeds of the Santas of old.

"I thank you both for allowing me in," she said. "I'm just so sorry things happened this way."

"Us, too," Delores said, standing.

Bending toward Miss Alberta, Callie tried to shake her hand, but the grandmother feigned that she didn't see, instead resting her attention back into the fire.

Callie respectfully took her leave, hating every damn instant of this horrible day. Mechanically she backed out of the drive, toward the highway, then headed left toward the beach.

It wasn't fair that the beach families were violated, but she considered these other families equally violated. She wanted to throttle the Edisto Santa. He'd blighted lives on both ends of the spectrum.

But nobody saw these crimes the way she did. No. Others saw the wealthy as able to file insurance, or forget about the loss and carry on as if little more than inconvenienced. But locals would cry for the poor as the unexpected and very welcome charity was ripped away.

If everyone was harmed because of a Robin Hood, that would make her akin to the Sheriff of Nottingham.

Her phone rang. The coroner. She sniffled and answered. "Chief Morgan." For a few hours, she'd almost forgotten about Ben and wondered if it had something to do with her distaste for him. Not a noble thought there either.

"Got your answers," Smith said. "Died of a brain hemorrhage caused by blunt impact to his head."

A knock to the head. But why on Brice's vacant lot? "Makes no sense," she said, not exactly talking to Smith, not really expecting the assistant coroner to care one way or the other.

"Might not have happened on scene," he said. "He died of an epidural hematoma. Could've hit his head, or been hit, someplace else and got up completely mobile. He'd have developed a nasty headache soon after, but he could've remained lucid. Bleeding continues, then the clotting, then pressure on the brain. If you don't deal with these hemorrhages within an hour or so after the incident, you drop dead like he did. Makes the exact time difficult. I'm guessing the afternoon of the day before you found him."

"Can you tell which?"

"Which?" he asked.

"Intentional or accidental?" she said. "A fall or a blow?"

"Can't tell, Chief Morgan. His skull was cracked, though. Upper right temporal area. Noted a small cut at the blow site. An uncanny sort of hit with just the right momentum and angle. A little bit off the speed or direction, and he'd be alive to tell you about it. Doubt he lasted the whole hour I mentioned; however, that's just a generalization," he said.

"Thanks, Dr. Smith. I appreciate—"

He hung up without a good-bye. Good thing he dealt with the dead, because his bedside manner sucked.

So Ben hit his head, or someone hit him on the head, then Ben felt inclined to walk to Dolphin Road a half block over from his place? Or was he dropped off there, and by whom?

Once she stopped off at the station for a check-in, to document all that had happened thus far in this oh-so-delightful day, she'd deliver the necklace to Mr. Young at the *Palms Up* house. In other situations, she'd have held onto the stolen items as evidence, but this was Christmas . . . and this was Edisto Beach where people came and went like the weather. After the quick stop with Young, she'd follow an overdue lead in what was looking more and more like a suspicious death.

Ben Rosewood was not a social person, nor a well-liked one, but he had at least the one pseudo-friend. A guy with similar behavior traits. Though not as extroverted, Ben still enjoyed the occasional lunch, even a round of golf with the councilman.

Time to revisit Brice LeGrand. He knew the deceased, and the deceased dropped on his property. Too much coincidence happening to be a coincidence.

Chapter 10

MARIE HELD THE phone to her ear when Callie walked into the station, another line ringing, but Marie juggled multiple lines like a corporate switchboard operator. It was after four, but Ike had drawn the town duty today. There'd been no new fires since the drunk guy Thomas had escorted off to jail.

Tomorrow was Christmas Eve, and another officer would replace Ike, leaving Thomas to man the town alone most of Christmas day. With Callie living a mile and a half from the station, she offered to serve as backup as necessary. Not that they expected anything other than quiet that day, but they hadn't expected Ben or a larcenous Edisto Santa, either. All bets were off this season.

After pushing a strand of straight black hair behind her ear, Marie held up a finger as Callie passed her desk, so Callie visited the coffee pot instead of her office. Watching the dark water drip steaming into her cup, she exhaled, trying to exorcise some of the blues. How quickly she'd become the town nemesis, particularly in a season of giving, peace, good will, and love. Finally, with the few last drops of her coffee done, she took her cup back to Marie's station to be instructed on whatever Marie deemed important enough to lift that finger.

The office manager served as keel, rudder, and sail some days, keeping them all afloat. Four years younger than Callie, Marie had entered the job straight out of high school, and what she didn't know about any person, event, or policy on the island, nobody needed to know. Name a family, and she could relay their ancestry, illicit affairs, accolades, and degrees. Every family's closet skeletons tucked away in her mental Rolodex. Invisible to most, she watched, listened, and took note of everything that ran through the government complex, to include the politics and gossip. Callie used the hell out of those skills.

Finally, Marie hung up, pursing her mouth with a long, tired outbreath. "We're going with voice mail for a few minutes, if you don't mind."

"Not at all," Callie said, and waited to be schooled.

Another sigh as her eyes settled on her boss. "Take a seat."

They'd all grown accustomed to the mother hen, and Callie did as told, but not before offering to get her clerk a coffee.

The phone rang once, and Marie ignored it. "Update me, please, on Wesley, El Marko's, and the burgled houses."

Callie did, but as she concluded, Marie reared back in her chair. "Don't get me wrong here . . . "

Damn, not Marie, too.

"It's not really anything you've done," her clerk continued. "Just call it the perfect storm."

Callie released a slow, dramatic shrug. "Perfect for whom?"

"Hmm, I guess everyone but you."

Callie scoffed. "I need more than that, Marie. Unless you've got something constructive, I really must see Brice."

Marie's eyes widened. "You're voluntarily going to see Brice? This *is* the season of miracles."

Callie glowered and motioned for Marie to cut to the chase.

"Gather around my children and let me tell you the tale of Edisto Santa," Marie started.

"Marie. It's been a long day."

"Fine," she said. "But you just stomped the hell out of an Edisto tradition. Not saying you meant to, and I'm not sure how you're going to fix it. I've been fielding calls ever since you took Wesley back to El Marko's. He's become their poster boy, and phones have been burning up the airwaves talking about how you made him cough up his Edisto Santa gift. That alone labeled you a villain."

"Grinch," Callie said.

Marie's eyes pinched a bit. "More like old man Potter. Like in *It's a Wonderful Life*? Jimmy Stewart?"

"Duly noted, Marie."

She nodded at her boss. "Though you visited here a lot with your parents, the whole Edisto Santa thing never entered your life, and unless you lived on the island, you wouldn't really understand. It goes back to before you and I were born, Callie. It's that old of a tradition."

Crap. Callie set her cup on the desk and sagged into a chair.

"Burglaries are the Edisto Christmas tradition, huh? And everyone's all right with that?"

"Nobody said anything about stealing."

Similar to what Delores just said back at that old brick house. "So since it's obvious that stealing is Edisto Santa's MO, wouldn't that make the guy a little less altruistic?"

The phone rang again, and Marie let it go to voice mail again. "One might logically think so, but this issue leans more to the emotional side. The poor receive gifts. The rich can afford it."

There was no winning this, which meant *stick to the law*. Favoring either side of this equation labeled her as almost crooked.

"Okay," Callie said. "But I can't do anything short of deal with the criminal element by the book."

"Just thought you needed the history before I let you know calls are coming in."

Callie squinted. "What sort of calls?"

"From folks who got Edisto Santa gifts, or are related to them. Asked if they gave back the gifts would they get dragged to the station like Wesley and arrested. They don't want stolen stuff, but they don't want to get nabbed, either."

Head back, Callie stared at the ceiling with a "Holy Jesus" under her breath. "I didn't arrest him."

Marie acted like a schoolteacher, reiterating a basic lesson. "But you hauled him in. And you did it in front of people. Same thing to a lot of them."

Rising and pacing toward the coffee machine and back, Callie raised arms in the air. "Mark was pushing me to get the whole issue out of his restaurant, Marie."

"I heard it was laced with a little spite. You said Wesley was in possession of stolen goods."

"He was." Damn it, Sophie and her chatter. *Son of a bitch.* "If their house was burgled, wouldn't they want me to retrieve *their* stuff?"

No response from Marie.

"Anyway," Callie said, willing herself to settle, "what are *you* telling them?"

Marie held a palm up. "Sort of took it upon myself, so I hope you don't mind."

Callie was afraid to ask.

"I've told them they can turn in the gifts here, no questions asked. If they still had the wrappings, we'd appreciate that, too. They could even send a surrogate if they didn't want us to put a name with a gift."

Callie sat back down. "Sounds like we're collecting firearms to get them off the street."

Marie lowered her voice to almost a whisper. "It's how they feel, Callie."

And feelings mattered. "If that's the way it's got to be done, then do it, Marie. The station must appear safe and approachable. These people are caught in the middle by something not of their doing. Everyone trusts you. Sugarcoat it or paint it any color you deem necessary, just give them peace of mind."

Marie gave a sympathetic smile. "I have, and thanks for seeing it that way. And I tell them you want to make it worth their while. Good idea, by the way."

Callie stiffened. "Refresh my memory?"

"An exchange token. Mark Dupree said we're giving each person a ten dollar gift certificate to El Marko's for their trouble. Said you'd agreed to cover the cost. That's really generous, Callie. Sophie's bringing the gift certificates over as soon as they can print them off."

The Mark and Sophie duo, getting even.

"Well, if that's the gist of the day's calamities, then I'm headed to Brice's place. Call me if things get weird . . . weirder . . . about those gifts." Callie went to leave. "Oh. Here's one to get you started." She retrieved the gold cross necklace. "This one goes to the Young family from *Palms Up*. Found it thanks to Wesley's info. A Miss Alberta had received it."

With an inhale, Marie slowly reached out. "You took a Christmas present back from Miss Alberta? That poor old lady."

"Marie!"

She shrugged. "First impressions, Callie. Sorry."

A BLUSTERY WIND, at least per Lowcountry's standards, made Callie rush to her patrol car and crank up the heat. She left the station and took Myrtle to Lybrand, which changed names to Dock Site Road.

Halfway down Dock Site, a skinny two-story house backed up to Big Bay Creek. This house was the last residential property owned by the LeGrands. Brice's family dated three generations back on the island, but his father had been the first to purchase rental income real estate on the beach. The rest had lived on acreage, like most of the old families did throughout Edisto's history.

At a young age, back in the early 70s before the beach was established, Brice inherited eight houses and ten lots, a respectable portfolio atop his father's mutual funds and stock. Never had to work a day in his life. But real estate values rose and Brice got greedy. He sold one, then another, banking on investment returns and interest rates continuing to fund his life. Then, when the economy tanked, he had to live off the principal. Since he hadn't curtailed his lifestyle, he'd had no choice but to sell a couple more. With predictable regularity.

Janet could prattle off who owned what on the small beach, and when Callie had moved permanently to Edisto, the Marine deemed it her responsibility to acquaint the green police chief with who was who and owned what, but Callie hadn't cared. Wasn't till Ben dropped dead that Callie remembered that Brice even owned a lot on Dolphin.

The sun shined lower in the sky, crisp and blinding, as Callie left the car. While sunsets were for Californians, from this site of the beachfront town, one caught more of the west, with the evening rays spinning needlerush, spartina, and cord grasses into reeds of brilliant gold and orange behind twinkling diamonds atop the tidal creek. Callie loved her beach, but the marsh held the most magic to her.

She knocked. No answer at first. She knocked harder.

The door whipped open, but Aberdeen gave a bonafide flinch at the sight of the chief. "Just great," she said, cheeks puffier, redder than usual. She hollered, "Brice? It's for you." And she left.

Had she been crying?

The grumbling started from the depth of the house, making its way to the front. "Who is it, Aberdeen? Oh."

The man who blustered his way in and out of the town's business, appeared deflated at the sight of her. Callie'd never seen the man be anything but flushed and ugly. Never calm, never civil. Ever on a mission to ruin her or her officers. She thought little about there being another side to him.

"Can we talk, Brice?" she asked.

"Where?" he said with a relinquishing sigh.

The sigh sort of touched her. "Um, here? Inside, outside, your living room? Doesn't really matter. With or without your wife. Your call."

His gaze darted to his left, toward where Aberdeen had retreated. "What's this about?"

"What's this about?" she said. "Maybe something to do with Ben Rosewood dying on your property?" She'd never seen him so nervous, much less express uncertainty to her.

"We'll take it to my study," he said, and widened the opening for her to step through.

Windows filled every wall. Wide, tall, uncurtained windows allowing the sun to saturate the interior, light reflecting off soft blues and whites. Touches of beige. Who'd have thought the dyed-red-headed, caftan-garbed Aberdeen had taste?

Pocket doors separated a corner room from the rest of the place near the back, windows letting the marsh view come in from two sides. Behind Callie, Brice slid the doors closed and flipped a little lock, heaving a hard breath. He didn't appear as if he'd been drinking—a first as far as she could recall.

"You're scared, Brice," she said. "Why don't we sit down and talk about it?" She made herself comfortable on a built-in window seat structure that wrapped two walls, setting three oversized pillows aside to make room.

He rolled over an upholstered chair on wheels, catching once on a throw rug, to confront her and that luscious marsh that stretched to St. Helena Sound. She figured the view might help him.

"You and Ben were familiar, right?" she said. "I assumed you were. I mean, more than business associates."

"He was my attorney," he said.

She tried not to smile, but then changed her mind, allowing a small one. He was frayed, not in touch with the old Brice. Maybe he had indeed considered Ben close, and as disgusting as Brice had been to Callie over the past year, she could manage to sympathize. She hoped she wouldn't regret it.

"I think Ben was more than that to you," she said. "I sense he was a friend. Am I right?"

"Used to be." He'd positioned himself upright, feet flat on the floor, shoulder-width apart, as if he established himself with some sort of foundation. In case something might throw him off balance.

Three modest words. *Used to be.* Words that could hold a wealth of meaning. She'd have to ease into that.

"There's nobody else here, Brice. No council, no public or reporters. Even your wife can't hear. Would you like to talk to me about what's going on?"

"Not particularly."

This was like leading a scared child. "Then let me start first. We received the coroner's report on Ben. Do you care to hear it?"

Instinctively, he threw his attention to the water outside. "Do I want to?"

Callie tried to show nonchalance. "I would think anybody would. How about you sit there and listen while I talk. You need something to drink?"

"That's the last damn thing I need."

While studying this grouse of a man, she went straight to the facts. "He died of an epidural hematoma. A hit on the head. Didn't die instantly."

He dropped his head into his hands. "Son of a bitch."

She watched him hard. "What happened, Brice?"

"We were friends. Closer than some might imagine. But we fell out," he said.

"When?"

"The day before he was found. I tried calling him back the next day, but he wouldn't pick up his phone."

"What did you argue about?"

He shook his head and appeared to sink deeper into himself. "Don't even remember. Something totally stupid. Had to be about his politics or my investments. He wouldn't advise about my money without badgering me about his political opinions, which often ended in some sort of tiff. Like his advice bought me as a captive audience."

Callie sat up, leaning forward, copying Brice with elbows on knees. They sat almost toe to toe. "Are you in financial trouble, Brice? Did he advise you about something you didn't care to hear?"

He jerked back. "Hell, I'm always juggling money." He jabbed toward the wall. "Try living with that woman in there. Thinks because my family goes back to the beginning of Adam out here that I'm rolling in hundreds of thousands of blue-blood dollars, but the recession about killed me. Rates are better, but I haven't come near to replacing the loss. And that damn woman wants to go to Paris?" His voice cracked on the end, but he continued.

"Actually, I went to ask Ben if I could afford the trip," he said. "He not only told me no, but laughed at the fact I'd even asked the question. Then told me I better put some rental houses on the lots I owned . . . while I owned them, to generate more self-sustaining income. Said I shouldn't have sold all my houses, but while I still owned Edisto dirt, I ought to convert it to something that made a buck."

Callie took all that in. "So what merited the fight?"

He shook his head, then shook it again, an internal debate going on.

"Brice. Better you tell me than someone else."

He glanced up, connected, then stared back down. "I honestly have nothing to hide, Callie."

By reaching out with her first name, the man made clear he really needed an ally.

They both heard the toilet flush in the next room, and some sort of thump. Callie barely noticed but Brice jerked and glanced at the door. Worried about Aberdeen hearing?

"So what is it you have no reason to hide, Brice?"

"Her," he said. "And him."

"Come again?"

"Ben. The son of a bitch told me he had feelings for my friggin' wife."

Chapter 11

CALLIE NEVER SAW that coming. Ben Rosewood and Aberdeen LeGrand. Her stunned impression must have shown, because Brice slapped palms on his legs with a loud, sarcastic guffaw. "Bet you love that, huh? The man who dated your momma, who could've been your daddy, who rides your ass about—"

"I get it," Callie said. "And no, it gives me no pleasure to hear your best friend and your wife may have had a fling."

Wait until her adopted mom heard about all this. Then the worst crossed Callie's mind. With Beverly a widow, and Brice possibly single in the foreseeable future . . . damn, she'd volunteer to work every holiday shift until she aged out in order to avoid sitting across the table from Brice at family events. The worst stepfather nightmare ever.

Still, she didn't love seeing anyone lose their spouse, however they lost them.

"No. There's no pleasure here, but Brice," she said, "this information prompts more questions. Like where you were the day he died. Cover your whereabouts on December twenty-first for me, along with witnesses or other corroboration."

He rose and tried to pace the small room, ultimately stopping to stare outside at the string of docks jutting to the back of each house between him and the marina. A killer view. Maybe in more ways than one.

"Ben and I met at SeaCow for a late breakfast. Ask anyone who works there. We talked finances, then he said to come by his house later, after I finished some work at town hall. Plenty of people can place me there, including Marie, because I went to ask her about anything amiss that you would've kept from me. Your flunky told me nothing, by the way."

Callie made no expression at the slur. Marie never liked to be anyone's source. She took in information, not gave it out, but she could confirm Brice's timeline. "Go on," Callie said.

"Then about 3:30 I went to Ben's house. We each had a scotch, picking up where we left off from the morning's conversation . . . talking some about you." He cut a gaze at Callie, still aiming to push her buttons.

No surprise at that. Those two hated her more than people she'd cited for violations.

"We discussed his wife since he'd been served papers, which pissed him off. Talked about how difficult he planned to make her life."

Just like that ass of an idiot to hate Sarah for making the first move to sever their marriage *while* staking a claim for another man's spouse.

But Brice had stopped talking.

"And then?"

"He told me he and Aberdeen had . . . once had . . . don't make me have to paint you a picture. Bet this thrills you seeing me taken advantage of."

"When did you leave Ben's house?" she asked.

"About four." He stared at the water.

She gave him a second. "Did you hit him?"

"Put nary a hand on him, Callie," he said. "Not my way. When he mentioned Aberdeen, I left. Couldn't stand to lay eyes on him and wanted to get the hell out of his house. Might not have even been there a whole hour."

Not my way. She tried not to express feelings about this man who held the long, engrained reputation of making threats, yelling, and cursing at his opposition whether political or simply some poor sap taking his parking space at the government complex. "A few might question how you would react to that kind of news," she said.

He released a long groan, half-exhale, the same noisy, opinionated mannerisms familiar across the island. Nothing discreet about him. If Brice was in the room, you heard him. "Believe what you want. I never touched Ben. I left angry, but he was alive and well when I did. What about the guy breaking into houses? Has he hurt anyone?"

"Hasn't even scared anyone," she said. "Diverting attention isn't helping your case. Let me do the investigating."

Then the old Brice reappeared. "Maybe you shouldn't *be* investigating this since you're prejudiced against me."

Fatigued by staring up at the paunchy, middle-aged man, she rose from her window seat. "What, you want me to call in SLED? Because that's who'd investigate you. Want your personal business spread across the state rather than the beach? Here people know what to expect from you, where even you have allies, though I fail to see how after all you've said and done over the years."

"That's low for you, *Chief*."

"Seems to be the only thing that you understand. Go get me your passport. Aberdeen's, too."

"I will not," he blustered.

"Or I can haul you in, Brice. And that means Walterboro since the council can't justify the cost of a lockup on the beach. But you've mentioned Paris repeatedly. You and your wife are on the outs, and I imagine you two are finding it difficult living under the same roof. That's called flight risks. So go get them."

Surprisingly, he left without further argument.

Demanding the passports wasn't wrong, but it wasn't the norm. He didn't have to comply, but Callie did have concerns.

His voice rose from another room, then Aberdeen's piercing shriek of resistance. "Let me talk to her." Stomps echoed across the planked flooring, louder with each approaching step.

Slamming the pocket door open, deep into the wall, she blew into the study, cheeks blotched and eyes raw. "Who the hell do you think you are?" Brice stood on the threshold watching behind her.

"I'm the person trying to solve a suspicious death," Callie said. "Your affair, your husband finding out, you trying to find the means to leave the country . . . what about that doesn't scream troubling? Are you trying to bail on us, Aberdeen?"

Aberdeen spun on Brice. "What the hell did you tell her?"

"Nothing," he shouted, moving into the room. "Ben told me. How long, Aberdeen? A month, a year? How damn long have you been banging the man?" He reached toward the nearest window seat, snatched a pillow and sling it. Aberdeen scrunched into herself, and it missed her by a couple feet, landing on the floor to slide against the wall.

They hadn't discussed the affair? Callie might not have spilled the indiscretion if she'd been aware they hadn't talked. But she had, so she chose to quietly stand ringside to hear who spewed what in retaliation.

Mouth wide, Aberdeen froze a second before yelling, "Oh my God, Brice, did you kill him?"

The furrows in Brice's forehead arched almost to his hairline. "How in hell can you even think that?"

The drama was on.

Aberdeen shifted her weight offering a sweeping hand through the air, as if on center stage. "How many rants have I endured, with you talking about wanting to kill this person, kill that person, kill anyone who got in your way?" Her hand stopped at Callie. "Like her?"

Callie only raised a brow, switching her focus from Aberdeen to Brice.

"I never said I'd kill anybody," he said to Callie.

"Like hell you didn't!" Aberdeen yelled. Her voice was stuck on high volume. "Shooting, drowning, electrocuting"—she turned to Callie, still counting—"and don't forget poisoning," she said.

"Real smart," Brice retorted. "You want to accuse me of killing? Ben probably wearied of your sorry nagging, and you flew off and hit him over the head. Otherwise, why the sudden desire for Paris? *Without* your lover?"

Aberdeen twirled toward Callie. "After all he's trash-talked about you across this island, you believe him over me?"

"I just believe facts," Callie replied.

Aberdeen inhaled deep. Callie suspected the rage wasn't about Brice hating the police chief, but was more about Ben being dead, and that reality short-circuited her temper. Tears poured, sloppy sobs behind them, so much worse than back at the empty lot.

But the husband was not inclined to soothe the wife. He reached into his back pocket and produced the passports.

"Don't!" Aberdeen cried, reaching to take them.

Easily avoiding her attempt, he gave Callie the two folios. "I don't have to give these to you, Chief, but I don't want to go anywhere anyway. And this'll keep her from traipsing off spending my money."

"Why would I even go anywhere after all this?" Aberdeen sniveled.

Callie tucked the passports away. "To get away from Brice? Or away from the scandal because to some you'd be considered a suspect. Love triangles can get messy. When did you last see Ben?"

Aberdeen's shoulders hitched with each erratic breath. She couldn't seem to grasp the question, no doubt finding it difficult to sift through today's revelation, yesterday's discovery of Ben, and most likely whatever intimate memories they'd shared and never would again.

The room hung still, Brice silent, just as eager for the answer.

"Three days ago," she finally said, and a wet sort of wistfulness crept into her voice. "At his place. Noon until three. He brought us lunch from Whaley's. Flounder sandwiches and stuffed shrimp." She trailed off realizing the threshold she crossed, sharing her last adulterous interlude with her husband and the law.

"Can anyone confirm you were with him?" Callie asked, making note to check with Whaley's.

Her stare was piercing through the moisture, her tone hard. "Sure. We had another couple over for an evening of bridge."

"So that's a no?"

Only the heave of her chest hinted what the woman was thinking.

Callie had a different direction to her investigation now. Whaley's records, or some waitress's memory, and Sophie Bianchi. Because to live next to Sophie like Ben did, put your life in her proverbial telescope.

"Sorry about ruining your holidays, Aberdeen, and I'm truly sorry about your loss. You hear? I mean it."

Aberdeen looked away.

"But please, please don't leave the beach."

A whine started deep in her throat, and as it rose to a loud wail, Aberdeen pushed Brice aside and fled, the sobs intensifying until she slammed her bedroom door shut, the cries muffled.

Brice remained wilted and no doubt emotionally spent. "I'm so sorry," Callie said to him. He appeared so impotent, more vulnerable than she'd ever seen him. "After all of that, though, are you sure there's nothing else you want to tell me, Brice? This is the opportunity."

Brice sat hard in his chair. "I'd say call my lawyer, but he's dead."

"There are plenty of others out there. You sure?"

His soft nod was enough.

"I'll be in touch," she said. "Remember what I said."

"Stay on the beach."

She started to wish more condolences but didn't. Seeing the island's biggest thorn-under-the-skin sitting there deflated, having lost his friend, his wife, and apparently his financial stability, she felt her words wouldn't make a damn bit of difference in assuaging how worthless he felt.

THE SUN THREW out its best display before shadows moved in, its last hurrah melting bold colors into the marsh. The sinking day reminded Callie she should have been off duty long before, and Marie was probably gone for the day.

In the car Callie checked her texts. Jeb said he'd be in from college tomorrow, Christmas Eve, around noon, and she hadn't cooked a darn thing for his arrival, much less thawed anything for Christmas dinner. Not that her culinary skills ranked high. She wondered if it was too rude to ask people to bring potluck.

Marie's text said in plain terms to get back in touch, and that she'd be waiting at the station.

The third came from Stan—coincidentally, his third of the day. *We still have to talk.*

But Marie beckoned. Callie drove out of the LeGrand drive with a heavy sense of having just delivered a death notice. Could Christmas get any worse?

In the few minutes it took her to reach the station, the day had given up its personality to the grays of early night, but the lights burned bright enough inside to tell her somebody remained at the helm. She walked in to find Marie taking notes at the counter, coping with a line of three people holding various shaped packages. A pile of other objects off to the side.

Marie glanced up, a hint of wariness in her expression, but before the warning registered with Callie, a middle-aged woman saw Callie, tossed a brown bag on the counter and bolted.

"Ms. Jenkins!" Marie called. "You forgot your gift certificate!"

"I'll give it to her," said the guy next in line. "She lives down the road from me."

Marie scribbled down something, gave him two coupons, and watched as he hustled out on the heels of his neighbor.

Not wanting to ruin anyone else's day, Callie strode to her office, not realizing how her heart beat a little faster at being considered the bad guy in the room. Ten minutes later, a gentle knock sounded in the hall. "Callie? It's me."

Marie peeked in. "I have somewhat of a list."

"Let's go out front," Callie said. "I want to see more than the list."

Marie led them to the counter and referred to a notepad she'd converted into a chart. "Initially tried to get more details, but when folks started back-pedaling, I went with what I could. I quit asking names, not that I didn't recognize them already. Required no addresses because I knew those, too. They only turned in an object, some mentioning the year, and asked for their free certificate."

Callie scanned the stack of boxes, bags both plastic and paper, several pieces of jewelry, and a few sweaters. "What do you mean the year?"

"We didn't specify this year," Marie said. "But we received sixteen items in the last two hours."

There were the lavender sunglasses from *Palms Up*, and Callie'd already collected the cross necklace and Nordic sweater. A nice silk scarf. She shuffled things around, opening boxes. No Apple watch. She didn't expect that one to show up soon, but quite the collection of upscale objects covered the counter.

She had no way of matching the goods to those burgled in previous years. Nor could she trust that all of them were part of the Edisto Santa caper. Gift certificates could entice people to turn over most anything for a free meal.

"I'll return the sweater, sunglasses, earrings, and necklace," she said. "Those I can identify. You wouldn't happen to have a birthstone bracelet in there, would you?" Figured that the piece still missing belonged to the most belligerent family vandalized.

Marie shook her head. "Not yet. Not that it can't still happen. I expect more of this tomorrow. Hopefully, you'll make some folks happy delivering these things."

"I guess," Callie said, collecting the four items. "I'll drop these off, then I'm headed to the grocery store."

Marie smiled, empathetic. "Good idea. Let everyone settle down. Besides, you've been going pretty strong since way early this morning. Give yourself the evening. Don't you have Jeb coming in?"

But instead of answering, Callie gave a once-over study of the pile before her, feeling worse than ever. Finally she said, "I'm fine, Marie. You've logged it all in. Leave everything as is, lock up, and go home."

She headed out, waiting for Marie while texting Stan. He quickly replied. *At Marko's. Come grab a bite.*

Why couldn't he be at home?

Chapter 12

AT *PALMS UP*, MRS. Young answered, the mistress of the red wrapping paper family, if Callie recalled correctly.

Callie passed over the paper bag, a last minute decision to hide the contents in case a kid appeared. "Here you go, Mrs. Young. We lucked up with your gifts."

"Oh my gosh. I'm not believing this. Langston!" She quickly ushered Callie inside. "Y'all, the police chief is here with our presents!"

Callie leaned in and whispered, "Except for the starfish earrings, I'm afraid."

"Oh, goodness gracious, that's fixable," the mother said. "I'm so impressed with the Edisto Police Department!" She seized Callie in a hug.

Mr. Young arrived, hand outstretched for a shake. "Impressive, Chief. Much appreciated. Goes far to cement our opinions about Edisto."

Callie could hardly get loose from the accolades, backing away to leave as more family appeared. "I hate to run, but I have another family to visit with their own good news, and it's getting late."

A cacophony of *yes, sure,* and *we understand,* traveled the group. The last comment she heard was *You're amazing* as she headed back to her car.

Taking a second, she breathed in and held it, basking in the balm of those words before cranking up and heading to the second address.

Two rows of houses inland, she knocked on the Anders rental, receiving equal praise once she delivered the Nordic sweater. "Not worse for wear," she said. "Meaning, I found it on a guy who was wearing it fresh out of the gift box. Might want to have it dry-cleaned."

"This is such a miracle," Mrs. Anders said, teary-eyed. "I thank you, and my sister who bought the sweater thanks you." Another hug. Another handshake from a husband. More fudge.

It only took her a half hour to cover both houses, but it was still after seven when she finally parked at El Marko's. Unlike most of the eateries on Edisto on Christmas Eve Eve, the restaurant was open and even had customers. Maybe Mark Dupree's research of the area had identified a sweet spot in the market. A food category and price that catered to the average palate might enable him to stay open year-round.

Aromas of cilantro and jalapenos reached her about the instant she saw Stan. He sat at the bar so as not to take up a table, though a third of the room remained vacant. Mark wasn't bartending, probably in the back.

Callie moseyed over, stepped on the foot bar and hiked her short stature up onto the stool. "Sorry, but I haven't been trying to ignore you," she said, rubbing her old friend on the back.

Mexican holiday carols filled the background, subtle enough for ambience but loud enough to hear the words. The same red and green lights strung all awry, like at her party. Had that only been yesterday during lunch?

"You had anything to eat?" he asked, beckoning to one of the waitresses.

"Nothing since seven a.m. and hadn't even thought about it until you asked." Stomach gurgling at the smells, she scanned the room, noting the absence of the owner but didn't comment. Sophie must've gone home. *Darn it*, because she'd wanted to touch base with her about Ben, tapping into whatever she'd noticed in her oversight of his house. Sophie wouldn't deny snooping, of course. It was more a matter of what she deemed interesting. She studied life more than most, often in detail others never thought of, but that meant she could miss the obvious, too.

"The day's special suit you?" Stan asked as a young girl in her twenties waited silently for confirmation.

Callie shrugged. "Sure, whatever. Thanks. And a tall iced tea, please." She smiled at the girl in appreciation, then once she left, Callie leaned elbows on the counter, hands on her face, and released a long soft moan from deep within. "God, what a day."

"Give me the highlights," he said.

She lowered her hands, leaning the side of her head on one as she abbreviated the last twelve hours to Stan. "We learned gifts were being stolen from renters, there's someone called Edisto Santa who's doing the stealing, the people who got the gifts weren't aware they were stolen, and I'm a piece of crap for sticking my nose into the whole mess. Returned four stolen presents to families who think I walk on water, but tenfold more people have labeled me Scrooge."

"And the body?" Never one to deliver long-winded talks, Stan had mastered the art of getting others to do the conversing. He claimed to have collected more intel that way back in the day.

"Yeah, coroner called," she said. "You'd think that burglaries would be enough news for one day on this beach." Her tea had arrived, and she took the opportunity to suck a third of it down. When had she last had anything to drink, either?

She wiped her mouth with a bar napkin. "Ben Rosewood, Stan. My birth mother's husband. An awful man, from my own personal experience, but regardless, his death comes with some suspicion."

Stan's expression carried only scant surprise. As Callie's Boston PD captain, he'd seen more than his share of murders, accidents, and the crazy situations that fell in between. "That the best the coroner could do, or he isn't done with his exam yet?"

"Died from an epidermal hematoma. Dealt with that before?" she asked.

"Don't think so," he said.

"Blow to the head, accidental or otherwise, and the coroner can't pinpoint which."

"Which falls on you," he added.

She nodded. "Yet Ben didn't immediately die. A person with that sort of injury can last a hour or two or more. He's pretty sure that's what happened here, just not how it happened."

She still thought of Brice, then Aberdeen, wondering if either delivered the blow, witnessed the accident, or walked off leaving the man sprawled in muck and poison ivy, and she wasn't sure she could prove a thing. "Would like to run it all by you, if you don't mind. The facts are too loose and scattered. Brice and Aberdeen stand front and center as suspects, but only because they knew Ben well and we have nobody else to consider."

"You ruled out Sarah?" he asked, wary.

"I believe so," she said. "She's bringing me proof of her whereabouts."

"Good, but we can talk later," he said as the waitress arrived. "First, eat."

Stan let her dive in and eat in peace, if she didn't count his off-tune humming to a Spanish version of *White Christmas*. Softer, slower carols for the evening. She rather liked it. The tempos took her down a notch.

Stan would help her pick through the details in a bit. Deaths didn't worry him, more like intrigued him, representing puzzles to solve, and once solved, those deaths remained the property of friends and kin of the deceased. He compartmentalized extremely well, almost too well. Good for crime solving, rather cold when considering the people left behind. She'd almost been like him back in Boston, trained in his shadow. But here on Edisto, Callie reversed the roles and tried teaching him. Policing a place as small and intimate as Edisto Beach meant the memory of anybody remained with them all.

Plate two-thirds clean, hunger pangs appeased, she interrupted Stan's off-key *Silent Night*. "Where's Mark?"

"Waiting until I talk to you," he said, and went back to humming.

She frowned hard at him, mouth full of refried beans. She swallowed, washed it down, and pushed the plate back. "If y'all orchestrated my being here, then one of you can pay for my dinner. What is this? Are you two BFFs now?"

"If that means friends, then yes. We hit it off. Someone to talk shop with," he said.

She flicked his arm. "Which you never told me about. Why didn't you tell me he was SLED?"

With a little shrug, he hummed another line then said, "Figured it was his tale to tell, Chicklet. Just like I haven't told him about you. Tell me how you would've felt if I'd relayed your colorful past to the stranger in town?"

A small scolding.

"Wasn't asking for his life's history," she said. "Just wondered if he had been an LEO." She drank the rest of her watered-down tea and set the empty on the moist napkin, then lifted to re-center it, avoiding Stan's eyes. She could feel that look. The one that told her she had a lesson to learn, and if she didn't figure it out, he was going to teach it in a manner that she'd remember.

He shifted over, bumping her. "He's just trying to fit in without shouting he'd been a cop. Sound familiar?"

"I never wanted to be a cop again," she said. "My case was different."

"How do you know that?" he asked. "Cut him some slack, why don't you?"

She blew out once through her nose, for his benefit, feeling a bit rebuked. He grunted with humor and tended his beer.

The waitress removed her plate and refilled her tea, and once she left, Callie swiveled her stool. "Okay, listen to what I have on Ben so far."

He twisted to hear.

"Ben and Brice fell out. I didn't even realize how close they were," she said softly, noting the nearest diners sat two tables off. "Brice and Aberdeen were seeing each other. Brice got mad and left Ben's house. The next day, Ben was dead on Brice's lot. The lot Aberdeen was trying to sell because she and Brice are low on cash. We also have someone breaking into houses, stealing, and it appears he might've done so while one house was occupied," she said, referencing *Palms Up*. "I refuse to call him Edisto Santa, because that gives him a cozy, holiday feel, and this has the potential of being anything but."

His mouth pinched, Stan gave a grunt. "Every break-in raises the odds of him being caught, and it appears he doesn't mind taking risks. He could get more daring, especially around here. None of these people expect bad stuff."

"Naïve is the word, Stan."

Another grunt.

"And we put out a call, word-of-mouth mind you, but still, we told people that they could surrender the stolen gifts and nobody would say a thing."

He laughed once. "That I already heard about."

"Because I ran it by him first," Mark said, sliding behind the bar in front of them. "When Wesley told me some of his people wanted to give gifts back, I called your office manager and suggested we sweeten the pot."

Callie stiffened straighter in her seat. "No, you told her I okayed gift certificates, which I did not, and depending on the volume that comes in, Edisto PD might not have the budget, which means it comes off my hip."

He gave a soft smirk. "How much can it be, Chief? A hundred?"

"When I left a little over an hour ago, we were up to sixteen items," she said.

Stan frowned. "Thought you only had four break-ins."

"Previous years, dude. Nobody set parameters, not that we'd tell the difference. Plus the mention of gift certificates probably had people going through closets, retrieving sweaters they no longer wanted."

Mark leaned stiff-armed on the bar, chewing the side of his mouth, apparently feeling the chastisement of not thinking things through. Or so Callie hoped.

"Oh, I'll cover it," she said before either man could speak. "I'll personally write the check. It's my name on the line, my department. Good thing Brice is sidelined or he'd be all over my butt. Oh, and I let Marie believe I had agreed to cover the gift certificates. Didn't want her to feel used, or feel disloyal to me."

Her pulse thrummed in her ears. This Mark person pushed her buttons, and she was almost ashamed to admit it. Not like Brice, but not totally unlike him either. Challenging.

With a glance at Stan, she couldn't read him. Sympathy, pity? Well, an apology for going along with Mark would be nice.

"Nobody saying anything?" she said to the long silence.

"I texted you three times," Stan said in long, even words. "When you didn't reply, I told Mark to go ahead. Told him to say it was your idea so you'd get the credit, Callie. Nobody expects you to pay a big tab. I'll own up to my share in this, and I'm sure Mark will own up to his."

"None of this had come about when you made the first two texts, boss, so don't BS me. Or try to shame me." She stared at one man, then the other. "Both of you ought to understand human nature better than this." Flatlining her mouth, she rapped a knuckle in front of Mark. "The family was happy to get their sweater, by the way. The wife cried in thanks. And there was fudge involved." With a smartly raised brow, she stared at them both, letting her words sink in, then flipped her phone on to check activity.

"Congrats," Mark said, his tone genuine. "I imagine they felt violated."

"They did," she said, still reading.

"But so did Wesley."

Oh, he'd damn sure pay for dinner now. She shut the phone off and stared up at the man. "You labeled me the bad guy." She tilted her head toward the front. "Standing right there."

"No, you did that yourself by approaching him in my place of business," he said. "If it had been me—"

"You do not get to go there," she said, bending in. "You are not the police here, regardless your experience. As a previous officer once told me, you wear the badge to work crime on this beach."

"And you're passing along this sage advice to me?" Mark tossed a look at Stan as if to say, *can you believe this?* "So what is this? Your effort to set me straight?"

Her patience fleeting, she glanced to the side at her old boss, daring him to choose a side. He didn't.

"So if this officer was so wise, why is he a *previous* officer?" Mark continued, a tightness in his voice though he kept the volume out of earshot of customers. "I imagine not much goes on here. Probably figured he best find a real PD."

"Mark," Stan warned while resting a hand on Callie's leg.

"Maybe he didn't like the idea of haranguing people like Wesley," Mark added.

"I think that's enough," Stan said firm.

To give him some credit, Mark glanced from Callie to Stan, suddenly reining himself in. "Was he your partner? Oh man, I'm sorry, Callie."

Stan gave a pat to Callie's leg, but inside she seethed, heart bouncing off her ribs. She didn't care if Mark heard her hard breathing or not.

Mark indeed sensed he'd royally sinned, his small apology insufficient. "Callie. I'm sincerely sorry if I crossed a line."

She squinted, a thousand words vying to be released, but she chose the most obvious since the man didn't seem to grasp nuance.

Her cheeks flushed as she delivered them. "He's a previous officer because he's a dead officer, Mr. Dupree. And his name was Michael Jenkins Seabrook. Ask around, just not while I'm present." She slid off the stool.

Skirting around the bar, Mark reached her before she took two steps. "My deepest apology, Callie. That was incredibly rude. God, I'm so so sorry." He gave a visual cry for help toward Stan, but the man just shook his head, holding one palm up, abstaining.

Mark started to reach toward Callie, then held back. "We got off on the wrong foot. Please, let me make it up to you."

But she wasn't up to talking transgressions, and she damn sure wasn't discussing Mike Seabrook with this stranger. Someone she didn't know well enough to trust, and after that demonstration she didn't care enough to try.

Shaking her keys at her side, she left, praying the crowd at Bi-Lo was thin this late at night.

Chapter 13

CALLIE TOSSED ONE of the last spiral hams into her shopping cart, the metal rattling enough to make someone peek around the end of the aisle. She smiled back at the elderly gentleman, like people threw hams every day. Green beans, cream of mushroom soup, and canned onion rings. Sweet potatoes. Butter, because she had none, and a block of cheddar, though what she'd use it for hadn't come to mind yet. Just felt right to have it. Crescent rolls. Premade pumpkin pie and a couple dozen eggs. Jeb ate them any way she fixed them, besides, she might make deviled eggs.

Fifteen minutes. Done and done. Nothing on the menu that took long to fix. Most of it could be made Christmas morning, especially if she boiled the eggs the night before.

She'd never shopped so fast in her life, but when someone threw gasoline on an emotional fire, the fury tended to spill into everything else. She ought to thank Mark for helping her crush her shopping.

She made one more pass through the aisles, remembering bread and at the last minute grabbing bananas. If Sophie came over, which was a big if considering how mad she'd been about Wesley, and then deemed the dinner not in her diet, her go-to was bananas.

Mark Dupree. Why couldn't she get the son-of-a-gun out of her head? Her temper wasn't quite dowsed. Retired or not, LEOs didn't challenge each other in front of civilians. Guess he embraced his new role as a restaurant owner first, and for a second she wondered what had altered his life so drastically to make that choice. Then she decided she didn't care.

Huzzah, no lines! The store was empty of customers. "I'd think someone would be cooking for you, Chief," said the chunky middle-aged woman up front. Dora had worked that register ever since Callie moved there. No telling how long before that.

"Once a mother . . . " Callie started.

"Always a mother," Dora finished. She reached over, grabbed a small box of chocolates on the rack and dropped them in one of Callie's bags. "Merry Christmas, Chief."

On the way out, Callie wrote off the moisture in her eyes to the biting temps coming off the water a block over.

Longest day she could remember in a while. But with the string of thefts and Ben's death still hanging between accident and homicide, and the fact that tenants rarely stayed more than six days, she had to play the hand she was dealt, running down interviews and addressing issues quickly. Cases in most cities could take weeks, but in a tourist environment, she and her officers leaped on crime in hopes of nailing them during those one-week interludes, before the beach's sea of unfamiliar souls went home on Saturday, replaced on Sunday. Thank God for cold weather and Christmas warmth inside, though. People remained inside and easily reached. She would continue asking questions, continue knocking, continue hoping someone saw something to help her gain traction on one or both of the cases.

Just after 8:30, she drove between the pylons under her house and parked. Arms filled with her three bags, she trudged up the first of twenty-four stairs. On the landing at mid-point, however, she glanced over at Sophie's house. Lights on, but Sophie's bedtime ran around 9:30 because of her early morning yoga classes. Something about yoga overlooking the ocean and the sound of rolling crashers kept her with four classes a week at eight a.m. Most mornings she rose earlier, for her own regimen of stretches and poses. Sophie worked for that body.

Then Callie noted the next house over. Sarah's. Lights on. She hadn't seen her mother since informing her about Ben's death, and guilt would keep Callie up tonight if she didn't check in.

She began putting groceries in the fridge and pantry, with phone to her ear as the number rang. Head in the pantry, Callie worried for a minute when she couldn't find aluminum foil to make the ham, then relaxed at the sign of two extra rolls on a lower shelf. "Hey," she said at the answer. "Care for a coffee with your daughter?"

"I'm already in my robe and slippers," Sarah said.

"I'll come to you. Just let me change real quick."

"I'll put the coffee on," Sarah replied and hung up.

Took Callie ten minutes to throw on the clothes she'd worn last night when Mark came over. A totally different man between then and this evening.

On her way to Sarah's, a text came through from Stan. *Um, dinner went well. Can you schedule me for breakfast? We still haven't talked.*

The only thing that made her want to agree, amidst all else on her plate, was his intuitive guidance . . . always appreciated. Plus he'd preserved his role as advisor by not taking Mark's side during the spat.

SeaCow at seven, she typed.

Damn early, he replied.

Take it or leave it.

See you there.

She trotted the final stairs of *Shore Thing* and rang the bell. Answering in fleecy muled slippers and a quilted baby blue robe, Sarah ushered Callie in. The fresh coffee smell made her crave a cup. She normally only took it black, splashing it in a go-cup to run, but tonight she'd splurge with sugar.

"How you holding up?" she asked, letting Sarah take them to the den instead of into the kitchen and their old routine of sitting at the kitchen table. Now Sarah could spread out. The house was all hers. Ben wouldn't unexpectedly descend from his upstairs office, ordering her to do some chore, or complaining about how she dressed. When they'd first met, Callie'd been seated at Sarah's table, still a civilian, and marveled at how much the damn idiot thought of himself in front of women.

She wouldn't miss him, and if she had to guess, Sarah wouldn't either. Their fifteen-month separation had prepared her for this life without him. To celebrate would be tasteless, but Callie could think it without compunction.

Sarah sank into a recliner. Callie bypassed the upholstered chair she remembered as Ben's favorite, choosing the deep, tufted, seven-foot cream leather sofa instead. She kicked off her shoes to stretch out, her short legs barely reaching the middle of the second cushion. A table-top ceramic Christmas tree about eighteen inches tall, its glass bulbs shining in contrast to the dark-green glaze, stood on a table between Sarah's chair and the one Callie avoided. Just enough Christmas glow. Of course no presents.

Callie almost said, "*Isn't this nice without Ben?*"

Instead, she asked for Sarah's proof she wasn't on Edisto on Callie's birthday and the two days before, like they'd discussed.

Sarah turned over a ripped-off notebook page and two printed off pages from her checking account. "Thank goodness Ben's study had good equipment and all his passwords written in an address book in the top drawer. I wrote my dates and stops then printed off copies of where my card hit the account. I have the motel receipt, but nothing for the gas other than where it cleared the bank."

Callie started to say, *"That'll make probate easier,"* and almost pinched herself again. Instead, she reached over hard, stretching, trying to avoid getting up, and took the three pieces of paper. Two women—one in sock feet and the other in pajamas. How easily she'd fallen into being comfortable with a mother she hadn't been told was hers until a little over a year ago.

She wanted Sarah to have the life of her own choosing, with creature comforts and peace of mind. After sacrificing a child, a lover, and personal freedom for over forty years, the woman deserved a better life.

The notepaper listed dates and places for the last week. Left Atlanta at three p.m. on December twenty-first, driving, with a gas receipt in Macon, Georgia. A little over halfway, she'd checked into a Wyndham Motel outside Savannah, where Interstate 16 met Interstate 95.

"You took the southern route instead of through Augusta," Callie said.

"It's all interstate," Sarah replied, blowing on her coffee. "Felt safer."

Callie lowered the papers and studied her mother. "Atlanta's five hours away. You could've driven it in one day."

Sarah lowered the cup, resting it on one leg that was already crossed over the other, the slipper flapping loose on her foot. "Didn't want to see Ben before I saw you. Was worried there'd be a . . . discussion, and I'd be late to your party. So I came in about an hour early and camped out at the restaurant. There's a receipt for that on my card, too."

Indeed her actions were all noted and documented, and while Callie didn't believe Sarah capable of hitting Ben, she breathed easy with the facts in black and white. Nobody else could place blame. It was all there. Laying the papers on the floor beside the sofa, beside her coffee cup, she scooched down and laid her head back on a pillow. A bright spot in her long and dreary day.

"So I'm good?" Sarah asked.

"You're good, hon," Callie replied.

With the remote, Sarah found Christmas music on the television with a burning Yule log emulating a fireplace. Callie sank her body into the couch.

"Funny, but I was rather surprised at the state of the place when I arrived," Sarah said. "Ben's standards dropped a bit in the year I was gone. He used to be finicky as hell."

Eyes closed, Callie gave a low giggle. "Listen at you dropping a curse word." But then the words registered, and she slowly sat up. "What was wrong with the house?"

With a brief pout of an expression, Sarah gave a tiny shrug. "The dirty glasses in the den. My wooden bowl from the entry credenza on the floor, like he knocked it off and forgot to pick it up. He hadn't vacuumed, because there were cigar ashes here and there."

"Was there scotch in the glasses? Maybe he was drunk," Callie said, not wanting to reveal Brice's story to Sarah quite yet. Nor the intel about Aberdeen.

"Yes," she said. "And I hate to say it, but I even wondered if he'd had another woman in here, and they'd gotten into a fight like we used to do. I've had to pick up that bowl after several of our more dramatic quarrels. As a matter of fact, that's one I bought to replace one that broke."

Callie rose to her feet, slipping her dock shoes back on. "Tell you what. Let's take you back to when you arrived home yesterday. Let's go out on the porch. I'll help walk you through it."

Callie'd had people recreate scenes in hundreds of instances. She preferred to do it as close to the moment of the crime as possible, but when she'd visited Sarah earlier, Callie had a coroner and a body waiting for her one block over. And she'd had no clue about Brice and Ben's disagreement. Best she help Sarah recall the images before they floated away.

They flipped on all the lights and walked out. The temperature had dropped into the upper forties.

"We have to do this now?" Sarah asked, arms tucked across each other.

"Should've done it sooner, so yes. Now. You came up the stairs. What did you have in your hand?"

"My purse on my shoulder, and one small carry-on size luggage bag."

"Which hand held the bag?"

She held up her left. "This one."

"What was in the other?"

Sarah held up her right. "My keys, but I didn't use them."

"Why?" Callie asked.

"The door was open. Not wide, but about two feet open."

Callie visually measured the threshold, the frame, cursing it being night, but envisioning Ben leaning on something for support, his head hurting.

"So you entered. What did you see? What caught your attention?"

Robe wrapped tightly, Sarah scanned the entry hall, remembering.

Callie took everything in as it stood, even noting the wooden bowl so smartly centered on a linen runner.

"I set my bag down here." Sarah modeled the move. "Oh, the rug. It was slid out of place. Angled like it had been moved. I put it back. The runner on the table was askew as well, and I straightened it. That's when I saw the bowl over in the corner. I put it back. So yeah, I wondered what I'd missed."

"What do you think happened?" Callie asked, feeding the energy of the story.

"Wasn't sure then. I shut the door and peered into the den, half-expecting to find Ben here. I mean, his car was in the drive. From the way I found the entryway, it appeared he might be mad, and that was the last thing I wanted to run into, Callie. I started to call you to get your read on it but didn't want to interrupt you in your work."

Callie really wished she had, so she could've seen the scene in its original state. Ironic. Sarah picking up the place, thinking Ben would be home soon, while Callie investigated his death.

"But when he didn't answer," Sarah continued, "I carried my bag toward the guest room."

"Stop and think," Callie said, moving them to where Sarah described. "What else was different?"

Her mother motioned to the table with the tree on it. "There were two glasses of Scotch right there, in his usual glasses. That's when I wondered if he had a woman in here. Then the entryway made more sense if he had. Oh, Callie." She gazed around the room as if revisiting a memory. "There have been moments in the past where my house was trashed just like that after he came after me for some stupid thing he thought I did. If he'd do it with me, he'd do it with another woman. Don't you think?"

"Maybe." The logic made sense. "Okay, since you mentioned someone else, was there lipstick on one of the glasses?"

Sarah thought. "No, I would've remembered washing it off. Maybe she didn't wear any."

But if Ben courted someone anywhere near his age, Callie'd expect lipstick, lip gloss, something. Especially if it was Aberdeen, noted for her bright reds and oranges. Which meant the extra glass more likely belonged to a male. "You mentioned ashes. Was there an ashtray?"

"Yes," Sarah exclaimed. "There, near the glasses. With cigar ashes."

"Didn't know he smoked a cigar."

With a scowl, Sarah wrinkled her mouth. "They bothered my

allergies. Ben had his nasty ways, but he preferred not listening to me sniffle and blow my nose, so he usually smoked outside, occasionally upstairs. With me gone, though, who says he didn't smoke wherever he liked?"

"One or two cigars?" Callie asked.

"Pardon?"

"How many cigars were in the ashtray?"

"Oh, one."

"Where'd you find the other ashes you mentioned?"

Sarah turned. "There, between here and the rug, across the hardwood floor. Not like he flipped the ashtray, but like he dropped a long ash before he made it outside."

Yet a cigar remained in the ashtray. Had he come back or were there two cigars?

By the elbow, she eased her mother around. "What else about the den? I assume you put up the little ceramic tree, right?"

"Oh, no," Sarah said. "It was there when I arrived. Right where you see it."

Callie couldn't see Ben putting up the tree, as meager as it was, just for himself. But no gifts. Maybe he already gave Aberdeen a gift? Or was he expecting his lady friend and had put up the tree for mood?

But something felt wrong about Ben so blatantly entertaining a woman in his house. Not on this small beach where nobody sneezed without someone two blocks over saying *Bless you.*

They covered the place from the upstairs study to the storage room beneath the house. Sarah claimed all else appeared normal. Even the refrigerator held nothing unusual.

A mantel clock chimed eleven. Callie had to meet Stan at seven in the morning, and she'd wanted to catch Sophie as she came out of yoga at 9:30. "Gotta go," she said, taking her cup to the sink and rinsing it out.

She left the kitchen and stood again in the entry hall, Sarah patiently waiting for Callie to finish her one-more-time analysis of the area. "Were any of these crooked?" she asked, referencing the mirror, the sconces, and a horizontal coat rack screwed to the wall.

Sarah shook her head, dark circles growing under her eyes.

"I'm sorry," Callie said, going to her mother. "I should've realized how much this might be doing to you."

"No." Sarah gently smiled. "I love watching how you work, and since I never saw Ben, it doesn't really hurt that badly." She went up and wrapped arms around her daughter. "Thanks for caring. That means so much."

But as Callie accepted the hug, she continued trying to put herself in that hallway, in the den, comparing Sarah's description of the abnormalities to Brice's rendition of his afternoon with Ben. Brice's version fell on the opposite end of the spectrum from Sarah's, unless after Brice left, someone else entered the picture. Like Sarah suggested, a woman might've triggered Ben's temper, or him trigger hers. Not Callie's choice of event, but a possibility.

"Hold on, Sarah." Callie let loose, eased her mother back, and took the two steps past her to the wall, to the coat rack. Wooden with bronze hooks, a metal ball on the end of each of the four hooks. More for decoration than use, she'd guess by the out-of-the-box freshness of the polished ends. Except for the one on the right.

She eased closer. "You have a flashlight?"

"Used to be one in the kitchen drawer." Sarah scampered into the next room, rummaged through junk by the clinks and thumps, then came back with a six-inch yellow light with a cord on the end. Like Callie often used jogging at night.

Shining the light on the end hook, Callie peered closer . . . at what appeared to be a slight trace of brown. No wider than a quarter-inch, no longer than a half, smeared from wide to narrow and just the right color of days-old blood.

Chapter 14

SARAH ALMOST WENT weak-kneed on Callie when the blood was noted on the coat rack, but a cup of coffee and Callie's soothing firmed her back up. Sarah had already changed into corduroy slacks and sweater and made a fresh pot of coffee when the three-man forensic team arrived in the drive. Once she learned her visitors would be around for a few hours, she whipped up brownies.

Callie recognized someone trying to keep busy and avoid thinking.

In just over an hour after Callie discovered the dried blood, the Colleton County Sheriff's team took up shop. Callie'd already taken pictures for her own use, shooting from all corners of several rooms, which she'd later use to question Brice. Better yet . . . maybe she'd get him over here once the team left.

Once hearing Sarah's first-hand view of the scene, the team went to work, and Sarah parked herself at her kitchen table, with Callie coming back frequently to sit and keep her mother occupied. Inside the house, a black light showed no blood except in the entry hall on the coat rack, with luminol confirming. Somehow the minimal blood proof lessened Sarah's tension. No blood bath.

"Check the front," Callie said, deducing that if Ben followed any-one to the door, he followed them out as well. On one of the larger posts at the top of the stairs, a bigger smudge of blood was found on the side facing west, not viewable from anyone coming up the stairs or standing in the entrance, unseen unless someone ventured to the far end of the porch. Upon further examination, it appeared he'd slid his hand down the railing after touching his head, faint thin blood markings on the outside edge, as he made his way to ground level, possibly in chase.

With the investigation spreading further than the coat rack, the team took extra caution, but the course of events began making more sense with how Sarah found the house when she came home.

The black of night softened to grays the closer it clicked toward dawn. With the coat rack in a large evidence bag and all Sarah's trash inside and out bagged, tagged, and loaded in a van, the team proceeded back to Walterboro, promising a report to Callie ASAP . . . but not until after Christmas.

But she had the gist of what they'd find. She expected confirmation of the blood being Ben's. She expected to find Brice and Aberdeen's prints, but she wasn't sure if theirs were in any kind of system, though she was sure she could arrange a way to collect them herself for comparison.

Seemed Ben had either scuffled with someone, fell pursuing someone, or been startled by someone. In other words, another person was involved. At the moment all arrows aimed at Brice, but the only way Callie would even suspect him was because he'd given himself motive and opportunity. But his accounting didn't include Ben's death.

A quarter to six. Seated on the porch, the occasional car going by with headlights still on, Callie finished one last cup of coffee with Sarah, choosing the cold weather to keep her head clear. She'd had no sleep and a solid day ahead of her, and that didn't even count prepping for Christmas.

Didn't feel like Christmas, though. Everybody's twinkling holiday lights were unplugged. No bustle for last minute gifts, and no traffic jams. Not on this tiny beach. Though she wholeheartedly preferred her South to the Boston she'd policed for fifteen years, there'd been something special about expecting snow every December.

She received a text. *What's going on? Sarah's lights on all night.*

Sophie. It was only a matter of seconds before she connected.

Callie typed. *We will talk. Later today.*

Sophie sent back a dazed, bug-eyed emoji to which Callie typed, *I'll find you.*

She pretended not to see Sophie slipping glances between blinds.

Sarah huddled under a blanket she'd dragged from her recliner. "You won't go home and get a few hours' sleep, will you?"

"Can't," Callie said, thinking of who she needed to speak to that day. Brice, Aberdeen, Stan, Sophie, and back to Marie regarding the Edisto Santa. Jeb would be in from college around noon. No way she'd be home to meet him, much less have anything homemade waiting for him. She hadn't even changed his sheets, last used over Thanksgiving.

Dampness weighted the air in this early part of the day when breezes weren't quite awake yet. Muted yellows began showing on the east side of palmetto trees, slowly riding up the trunks and changing to golds as the sun made its appearance.

Regrasping the blanket from where it slid and exposed a leg, Sarah worked to stay warm. "Wish there was something I could do to help."

Callie gazed fondly at this weary woman and wondered again how she would've turned out under Sarah's mothering instead of Beverly's. But no more sitting around thinking. She had daylight enough to call Brice. She dialed him, having already gotten Sarah's permission to let him come over.

He answered groggy, hungover sounding, though his persona hinted of drinking whether he had or not. A habit did that to a person. A habit she'd been intimately familiar with not so long ago.

"You up?" she asked. "I'd like to meet with you."

"Like the police chief demanding to meet doesn't wake a body up."

That was it. No fussing about his own daily demands or his lack of desire to waste words with her. No cranky belittling about some mishap her department hadn't prevented, or worse, may have caused due to their inabilities to keep the beach safe.

Sounded like Ol' Brice was cleaning up his act because he wasn't sure whether he was in the doghouse or aimed for the jailhouse.

"Meet me at the Rosewood place," Callie said.

He didn't try to hide the huge exhale. "When?"

"Now," she said. "A forensic team just left. You and I can talk about what they found."

No comeback. Not even his normal wheezy breathing.

"Let me put pants on," he said and hung up.

"He'll be here in a few minutes," she told Sarah, who rose, folded her blanket, and went inside.

Bless her, she offered to cook breakfast, but Callie had to meet Stan around seven at the SeaCow and was hell-bent on still making it. He made for better digestion than Brice.

Too rushed to change into a uniform and all the paraphernalia that came with it, she scooted home for her weapon and retrieved her paddle holster saved for civilian clothes, praying she'd squeeze in a shower once Brice left. She had her doubts.

Brice arrived promptly enough, but he parked beneath the house, not wanting his sedan spotted by natives. Callie was waiting for him at the top of the stairs, and he took a half-step of uncertainty when she spoke before he saw her. "Come on in before anyone sees you," she said.

As if waiting for him to appear, wind blew up behind, from the direction of the beach, tousling his thinning hair to uncover bare scalp. It gave him an older, more vulnerable image, stirring a sense of pity in

Callie. A far cry from Brice's normal formidable presence.

Inside, Sarah made a hostess's effort to put him at ease. "Brownie? They're warm." She'd nuked them last minute in the microwave.

Escorting him with his coffee and brownie on a napkin, Callie waved him into the den. Sarah disappeared.

"I believe you sat there," Callie said, deliberately taking the seat Ben would have, and motioned to Sarah's chair. "Did you enter the house with Ben or did he let you in?"

"Just tell me what the forensic people said," he groused.

"Answer the question, Brice. I promise, the truth is much easier to say."

"I knocked. He let me in. Do I need an attorney?"

"Only if you think you have something to hide," she replied.

He placed his coffee cup on the table between the chairs along with the brownie, apparently his appetite not keen. He wore a quilted vest buttoned tight across his middle over a flannel shirt, his khakis well-worn and thin on the cuffs. The attire made him look as weary as Callie felt.

There they sat, in an unwieldy silence, each waiting for the other to dole out the first thought, though they both knew she held the advantage.

"You talked with him," she prompted. "What about?"

"Finances to start with." He crossed a leg, and she was pleased to see him fall into his role. "He'd poured us both a scotch." He glanced at his coffee cup as if remembering. Good, he behaved as she'd hoped.

"He said inflation would bypass the interest I was making on the few investments I have left. Thought I ought to put rental houses on my lots. I told you that."

"So that's how y'all wound up on your empty lot a half-block over."

He twisted sharply. "We never went to the lot."

"Well, Ben sure as heck did," she said.

"Not while I was here." He was snipping his words.

"Fine," she said. "You were seated here in the two chairs, drinking scotch. He said to build houses. Then what?"

Brice gazed past the table, and Callie waited to see if he would come back around to spill those thoughts.

"Was the fireplace on?" she asked, following his current line of vision.

"No."

"Television on?"

"Cable, I think. Too low to really pay attention to."

She swung her focus back to the table. "You both had drinks. Guys having guy talk. How about cigars?"

He knew she knew, but he went along. "He offered me one. I took it. He always had good cigars."

She touched the Christmas tree. "Was this here?"

At first his nod seemed simply confirming, then he blinked with a pause and reached for his coffee.

"What else was there, Brice? Around Christmas, a lot of people keep small tokens under the tree for drop-in guests. Ben didn't have many friends, but he saw you more than anyone else, I imagine. Did he happen to have a gift for you?"

The man possessed an easy tell. When issues cut against his grain, his broken-capillary cheeks reddened as if his blood pressure raised the heat. Like now.

"No gift for me," he said. "No gifts under the tree, but I saw a bag on the end of the mantel. From Xavier's."

"The jeweler?" she asked.

He nodded. "Two weeks ago, he'd asked me who I considered the best jeweler in Charleston. I told him Xavier's, so when I spotted the gold bag, I asked what he'd decided to get. Even asked him if he was happy with their quality." Sarcasm sculpted the last sentence.

"He said he liked their work, so I got up and went to peek inside. 'I'd rather you didn't,' he said."

Brice's social graces often lacked polish.

"I sat back down," Brice continued, "feeling a little weird about his behavior, then I decided I required more information than that."

"Why on earth would you think that, Brice?" Callie asked. "What would make you dig deeper on something that wasn't any of your business? It could've been a peace offering for Sarah. She was on her way by then."

He laughed out loud. "No chance. He had plans to leave that woman broker than broke." He chewed his brownie, his crossed feet rocked him in his chair, a nervous sort of movement. "No, I'd had my suspicions for a few weeks, so I point-blank asked the bastard was he sleeping with my wife." He snorted. "Serves me right. He told me yes. Said Aberdeen was sick of me, tired of my money woes . . . disgusted with how I treated her."

"Ouch," she said, legitimately touched by his pain. Ben could be rude, but damn, that was harsh.

Another scoff from Brice with a meager grin. "Yeah. I think it hurt more than angered me. Instead of sitting, though, I headed toward the door. I mean, what do you say to that? 'How long? How is she in bed?' I know what I should've asked."

Callie waited.

"I should've asked if he was going to help her milk me dry. He could, too. After all, he understood my financial situation better than Aberdeen did. I felt so set up it just made me sick to my stomach. All I wanted was out of this damn house to find me a piece of water to sit at and think."

He wanted a drink was more like it. But it wasn't like the man to deflate and walk away. Curious. His reputation quite the opposite, Brice was noted for spouting off, cursing before he had facts, browbeating anyone to show he had generations of Edisto Island LeGrands behind him that made him wiser, nobler, and completely untouchable. He would've attempted to own Ben in some fashion, righteously protect his dominance on this beach.

Callie leaned on the chair arm. "You're telling me you stayed quiet, and he stayed seated while you walked out? Just like that?"

"No," he said. "He laughed at my back."

Admittedly, *that* sounded like Ben, but walking out without having the last word sounded nothing like Brice. "When did you hit him?"

Jumping out of his chair, he yelled, "I didn't touch him." With a shaking hand, he swept toward the entry hall. "I called him a son of a bitch and told him he could have my wife. If she didn't want me, I damn sure didn't want her. She's part of why I'm broke. Let her syphon off his bank account for a change."

That was more the Brice she'd expected.

"He got up and followed you, though," she said, standing and walking past him to where the action happened.

"He did, only I ignored him. Walked out and left. Never looked back," he said, growling with anger. "Was afraid of what I'd do if I didn't."

"I see." Callie walked to the hall, studying like she hunted for something. "You didn't shove him?"

"No."

"You didn't hit him?"

"No."

"You didn't struggle with him in any way at all?"

His rage flared up, fists before him as if he wished he could use them. "No, ma'am. Didn't touch him, and I'm sick of you trying to pin his death on me. Who says he didn't just have a heart attack?" Then in a release of temper, he punched the wall. "So damn sick of this! The son of a bitch is still taunting me from the grave."

"He's in a coroner's refrigerator, not the grave, and he didn't have a heart attack," she said, moving to where she could rub across the wall where two screw holes remained. "He lost his balance and hit his head on the coat rack that used to be here on this wall." She moved over and smoothed her palm over where Brice had punched, feeling the shallow impression in the sheetrock.

"But hitting the hook didn't kill him instantly," she said, staring him down. "Instead he wandered onto your lot. Want to tell me how that happened, and how you didn't see any of it? Cause any of it? You were here. He was seeing your wife. He died on your property. Tell me how you could *not* be a key player in all this, Brice? Your name's all over it."

He whirled on her, breathing heavy, and she braced to have to wrestle him down. He had a hundred pounds on her, but the reactions of a retired old man who'd done little more than lift a glass in fifteen years still gave her the edge.

"Don't even think about lashing out at me," she said. "You don't want to spend Christmas in jail."

But his red-spidery face enflamed with rage. "I don't give a damn about Christmas. Why is everyone blaming me for all this? I'm telling you, I didn't do it!" He started to hit the wall again.

"Stop it, Brice," Callie said, controlling her voice in hope to better settle his anger. "This is still Sarah's home."

"That's a thought. Why not blame her?" he growled back. "They hated each other, and she came back unexpectedly. Who's to say she didn't sneak in early to do him in before he financially ruined her? Slipped him something like arsenic with some sort of delayed reaction." His gaze roved back to the half-eaten brownie. "Just like she could've slipped me something in those brownies. You two could've called me in to set me up."

Sarah's gasp could be heard from the kitchen around the corner.

"Because she's already accounted for her whereabouts," Callie said. "The problem is you can't exactly account for yours."

"But would I tell you I'd been here if I killed him?" he asked. "You wouldn't have suspected me otherwise."

"Oh, Brice." She gently shook her head. "You keep underestimating me . . . and the science of forensics."

"You bitch. I trusted you. It's why I told the truth."

"Then tell me this," she said, opening the pictures she'd taken of the room from all its angles and flashing them in front of Brice. "Where's the jewelry bag you saw on the mantel?"

Chapter 15

UNCERTAIN HOW TO accomplish everything on her list, which didn't even include Christmas, Callie ordered breakfast without Stan. The waitress set the cheese, spinach, and bacon omelet before her just as Stan arrived at the SeaCow diner. She took her first bite as he stepped to the table.

"Merry Christmas Eve," he said, sliding out the straight-backed wooden chair. As he tugged himself up to the table, he jutted his chin at her food. "And sure, go right ahead . . . don't dream of waiting for me."

"Sorry," she said, mouth full. "I'm on my second wind, praying it'll carry me through the day. Didn't get any sleep last night."

He thanked the waitress for magically appearing with his coffee and double-checking that he wanted his regular order. He lifted the too-hot coffee, wincing with the first sip. "Too much crap in your head keeping you awake?"

"More like a forensics team at Sarah's house. Then an interview with Brice."

His dense brows raised high. "You get a break on what happened with Ben Rosewood?"

She filled him in on the blood on the coat rack. She was waiting for the forensics report, but the way the coroner described the head wound, she felt fairly solid about the hook on the rack doing the damage. "The question is who did it. Accident or otherwise."

"And you see Brice LeGrand as good for it? Uh, uh, uh. If your name wasn't muddied enough with the Edisto Santa deal."

She shook her fork at him. "We're still talking about Ben. And I didn't take this job to become everyone's buddy."

"Regardless why you took it, enough of these people have to love or respect you. Not saying you have to kiss all the butts, but a few puckers here and there matter. You can appreciate that . . . or you should."

His waffle and grits arrived.

"Since when do you eat grits?" she asked. "Thought you people from Boston ate Cream of Wheat?"

"Potatoes," he said. "But this grit stuff is growing on me." He ripped open a packet of sugar.

"Oh, no, that's not what you put on grits." She watched his faux pas while wolfing down the last of her omelet and tearing into her toast, a wash of milk in between. She'd enjoyed one too many coffees at Sarah's, and her nerves pinged.

"I take it you're in a rush then," he said. "What's happening with Brice?"

Callie began counting on her fingers. "One, he has no alibi during the estimated time of death. Second, he admitted Ben let him into the house during this same time period. Third, they got into an argument. Fourth, Ben was screwing Brice's wife. Fifth, Ben died on Brice's land."

"Hmm," Stan said, pausing between bites to take it in. "People have damn sure been hanged for less."

"The thing is," she said, hovering over her plate, "I never would've considered him if he hadn't told me he'd been there."

He drizzled syrup, flooding each of his waffle's tiny holes. Callie grimaced at the wealth of sugar going on that plate.

Pleased with his effort, he set the half-empty syrup container back on its saucer. "The thing is, Chicklet, and you realize this, that him giving up the info first is a good ploy to give the appearance of innocence. Especially when he lacks an alibi."

Callie let the waitress take her plate and asked for orange juice. There was a good chance this would be her only meal of the day. "But his story flaw is the jewelry bag. He inserted it in the story then couldn't account for it afterwards. It's missing."

"Like so many other gifts around here," Stan said, then thrust a huge bite in his mouth, chewing as he smiled at his joke. "Thought you hated Brice?"

Truth was Brice wasn't her favorite person, and he'd dogged her since the day she accepted the badge, but like the smelly uncle or the nagging cousin, Brice LeGrand was part of Edisto's family. Just as many enjoyed his influence as hated him for it. If a grand jury indicted him, there'd be as many fussing about him being railroaded as toasting his misfortune.

"I'm trying not to let that matter," she said. "This could seriously get him locked away, Stan. Between you and me, I lean toward him not doing it, or at the most, having shoved Ben and not realized the damage done. But murder? No."

"Doesn't he have a temper?" he asked.

"Sure he does, but it's always been bluster. Full of loud words laced with spit. That sort of thing. Interfering with the department doing its job but not causing crime for us. I'll wait until I get the report, but my gut's on the fence. Too much coincidence for me to say he didn't do it, but not enough for me to affirm he did."

"Chicklet," Stan said, question in his voice.

She never thought she'd find herself defending Brice, but if she didn't tackle this a thousand percent, to absolutely prove who did what and when, Brice could go down.

"Chicklet!" Stan repeated.

"Oh, sorry. What?"

"The Christmas heists. How're those going?"

She rubbed her face. "I'm basically a Santa killer. If I can fit it into my busy day, I'm gonna try shooting reindeer for Christmas dinner."

"No leads?" he asked.

She stared from between her hands. "I've been dealing with Brice and Sarah ever since I saw you over Mexican food last night, Stan. My superpowers are a little dulled from lack of sleep. The answer's no."

Judgment traveled down his wide nose. "Testy. However, I'm not Mark, who I actually want to talk to you about, by the way. He feels horrible about what he said."

And in those few seconds, her ire resurfaced as she relived the comments from the night before. An ex-badge telling the current badge how to behave. She was pretty damn sure he'd be pissed if the roles were reversed. Talking about Seabrook that way . . . . As much as she hated to admit it, Mark put a chink in the protective guard she'd carefully constructed over the last fifteen months.

"This is halfway your fault." She checked her watch. Sophie's yoga class would let out in a half hour, and Callie wanted to catch her as she left. The old bar where Sophie gave her lessons a block and half over, attracted a dozen people per class off season. Double that spilled out onto the pier in the summer.

"If you'll remember, I didn't side with either one of you last night," Stan said.

She finished the orange juice. "Instead of playing Switzerland, if you'd told me about his law enforcement past, and if you'd told him about my past, to include Seabrook, last night would not have happened like it did. So yes, accept it."

But his eyes clearly expressed he wasn't about to. "And you could've been more discreet about questioning Wesley," he said. "The kid wasn't guilty of more than opening a present, and Mark's been working himself silly to get El Marko's off the ground. You insulted both in public. Your sense of fair play might be shortsighted. I've seen you be more considerate of your residents before."

She tried not to let lack of sleep shade her reply. She'd done nothing wrong. Maybe she could've escorted Wesley outside, but would he have gotten the job if she had? Mark hired him out of spite because Callie had confronted him inside. A good thing Wesley had a strong work ethic and would prove himself regardless. "He possessed stolen property, Stan. You know better."

"Nope, not exaggerating in the least," he said, and honed in on the last of his waffle, like he ended the subject.

"I wanted to bounce these cases off you, not argue."

He wiped his mouth. "Whatever, Callie. You asked for my impression, and you got it."

He used her name instead of her nickname, meaning he stepped back into a formal relationship just like he had when he'd been her boss. Never good.

But she wasn't about to let him blow her off. Monotone, she asked, "Any suggestions on Brice?"

His reply wasn't much different in tone than hers. "Thought this case was about Ben? That's your focus. Next question."

Of course it was about Ben. How could it not be? Stan was being stubborn. "And what about the Edisto Santa?" she said.

Holding a stare on her, lips tight, he took a second to answer. "Put people on the beach on alert. Ask the people coming in to keep an eye out for anyone out of place. Keep offering the gift certificates to entice them to come forward. Interview as many as you can." Again, delivered flat and was nothing more than plain sense . . . and nothing she hadn't already thought of and done.

Callie suddenly felt the silence between her and Stan. "You coming over on Christmas?" she asked.

"I'll try to drop in," he said, waving for the waitress to refill his cup.

Oh. She had assumed he had no place else to be. "Was expecting you for Christmas dinner." Assuming she found a way to piece one together, but this was Stan. He'd eat pizza, if need be.

"Mark already invited me to his place," he said. "Sorry, but with him being new on the beach and having no family, I only felt it proper."

The shock of her old friend choosing someone else stunned her. She tried to rationalize that Stan was making a magnanimous gesture, but as soon as the thought crossed her mind, she realized her manners were sorely lacking.

She was the police chief. One of the town's leading figures. With Mark being LEO, and after he so generously hosted her birthday party, why hadn't she thought about extending an invitation?

But they hadn't actually been hitting it off, and how awkward would that have been? There was an edgy divide between them, and she wasn't sure she was going to manage Christmas for her son, much less a herd of others.

Stan got a text. "Mark asks that you come by today. He closes at three for Christmas Eve."

Elbows on the table, she rested her forehead on her hands and took a breath. "Stan," she said, looking up. "Yesterday was slammed, last night I got no sleep, and today I have no idea how I'll get half my to-do list done. Did he say what it was about?"

"Nope."

"Why didn't he text me?" she asked. "You didn't give him my number?"

With a droll expression he shook his head. "I don't ever give out your number, Callie. You choose who merits it. You've seen Mark twice and haven't given it to him yet, so he texted me."

But she read between the lines. Make amends. Make the effort to see Mark.

She wiped her mouth and stood. "Gotta run. I already caught your tab."

He nodded in appreciation. "You're spent. Go get a shower and catch twenty minutes of shuteye."

She shrugged into her jacket. "Oh, now he cares."

"I'll always care, Chicklet," he said. "If I didn't, why would I bother setting you straight?"

"So nobody else cares enough to bother, huh? Is that what you're saying?" She retrieved her cap.

"You tell me." He returned to his grits.

She hesitated, a tad stung . . . then left, nodding goodbye to the girl at the counter, trying not to think about Stan's last words.

She was in even more of a hurry to sniff out Sophie, if for no purpose other than to prove she had more than one person who cared . . . assuming Sophie wasn't still furious at her about Wesley.

Chapter 16

CALLIE TRAIPSED across the sand to the porch that wrapped around what used to be Finn's—that used to be a half dozen other names in the last ten years. The venue had been through a cadre of entrepreneurs, each adding their spin, each succumbing to the seasonal fluctuations of a beach town.

Following the wooden walkway toward the water, she made her way upstairs to the pier, the wind gently tousling her hair as she rounded the corner. Sophie had propped a window open, allowing the ocean noises to enter the old bar and enhance the mood, and Callie eased to the opening to peer inside.

Sophie's calming voice slid through the room, telling everyone to relax. "Surrender to the gravity. Welcome the act of nondoing. Breathe." Callie'd taken the class enough to recognize Child's Pose. Good. The class was about over.

Glancing through the window, Callie tried to catch the yogi's attention. Sophie sat cross-legged up front, studying her students, a dozen large candles flickering across tables. She gave Callie a wink in acknowledgement and reclosed her eyes.

Here they were on Christmas Eve and Sophie still attracted ten students. An off day, because Callie'd seen her spill a class of two dozen out onto the pier or even the beach. A decent, cash business.

Moving to the end of the short pier, Callie sat at one of the picnic tables. Still in her civilian clothes from last night at Sarah's, she hoped she'd be disregarded as the class streamed out.

One woman, however, waved and hollered. "Hey, Callie!"

She forgot how much this particular council woman loved yoga.

Callie waved back with a smile, praying the lady kept walking with her buddies, but with a touch on one of them, she said her goodbye and detoured toward Callie.

Callie pretended gulls caught her attention and twisted toward the water.

"Didn't expect to see you here," the councilwoman said, taking the opposite bench.

Temps weren't frigid, but the wind made it nippy. Hopefully Ms. Frank had sweated enough to feel it and would cut this greeting short.

"Thought you'd be investigating with all we've got going on," she said, a hint of judgment in her words.

Callie tried to keep a grin. "Glad to see you, too."

"Oh, sorry." The woman tugged her light jacket tighter. "Where are my manners? Merry Christmas, Chief."

Callie nodded, not wanting to fuel the conversation.

The woman mashed her yoga bag to her middle, squishing into herself for warmth. "What's going on about Ben Rosewood?"

"Still an ongoing investigation," Callie said. "Can't really say."

With an expression of consternation, the councilwoman seemed to rethink her approach. "How's Sarah taking it?"

"Okay, I believe."

Patricia waited, as if expecting more. "Well, I must drop in on her."

"I'm sure she'd appreciate that," Callie said, thinking the complete opposite. Then she crossed her arms. "It's getting nippy."

"Isn't it?" she said. "I really have to go shower. Why are you out here?"

With her best covert look around, she whispered, "Had plans to meet someone who really didn't want to be seen."

"Oh." The councilwoman glanced around. "Oh! Then I better go before I mess something up. That explains why you're not in uniform. Again, Merry Christmas."

"Much appreciated," Callie said, maintaining her Joe Friday demeanor as her company skittered off, not that she didn't scan the area, attempting to identify the secret person as she left.

Callie stood and moved inside, Sophie was rolling up mats and putting out candles. The room seemed to still hold a residual tranquility from the session, as well as the lavender and burnt carbon scent of extinguished candles. Sophie was darn good at what she did.

Callie collected the last two candles from a table and stored them in their box Sophie kept under the bar. "Told you I'd get with you today."

Sophie joined her, hopping up on a stool.

"Easy class?" Callie asked, noting no sweat on her friend.

Sophie rocked one shoulder, then the next. "It's the holidays, so I cut them some slack." Then she glanced sideways. "However, after the holidays, I tear these people up!"

Easily envisioning that setting, Callie smiled. "You've cut my butt a time or two, so I bet you will."

Dancing a hand, Sophie aimed it at her. "Might be good for you to start back. You've missed over a month's worth of classes. I'm not giving you your money back because you went AWOL."

"Give me until the first," Callie said, then as their conversation fell off she launched into her original mission. "I have a few questions to ask about Ben Rosewood."

Sophie waited for the questions, her sea-green contacts accenting eager eyes.

Callie started short and simple. "Do you see much of Ben?"

"Not since he died!"

This was how Sophie communicated. Darts and spits, tangents and off-topic. It was an effort to keep her on track, and Callie's patience wasn't on its best behavior after no sleep.

"Soph, when he was alive, did you see him come and go much?"

She shrugged. "Not really. He either worked from home or stayed gone. You knew that."

Callie did. "When he was in town, did he entertain much?"

"Entertain? No parties to speak of." She stopped and thought. "Brice on rare occasion. Aberdeen the same."

"Ever see both of them visit? Together?" Callie asked.

"Hmm." Curling a leg up on the stool in one of her pretzel moves, Sophie tapped her lips. "Come to think of it, no." But then her propensity for leaps took charge, and, mouth wide, she inhaled, those contacts about to pop out. "Were they having an affair?"

"Who?" Callie asked.

"Any of them!" she exclaimed. "Ben and Brice. Ben and Aberdeen."

Oh Lord, the unexpected image of Ben and Brice . . .

Sophie shook her head. "Not all three. Brice has visited three or four times in the last month. Aberdeen . . . maybe twice?"

"That you've seen."

Sophie huddled into herself, boobs and elbows on the bar. "Did one of them kill him?"

"Who says he was murdered?"

"Nobody said he wasn't, so what does that tell you?"

Okay, Callie had to bring her around again. "So not much activity?"

"No. *You* have more people come over than Ben did, if *that* tells you anything."

"Thanks so much, Soph."

Sophie delivered a soft pout.

"So where were you on December twenty-first?" Callie asked.

Sophie counted back using her coral-painted nails to tally. "Today, then yesterday, then your birthday . . . when Ben was found, right?"

Callie nodded.

"Then the day before . . . I assume that's when he died?"

Callie nodded again.

"Hmm, had a class in the morning. Coffee at the SeaCow with a student . . . who has done a remarkable job of losing weight with my yoga, by the way. Forty-seven pounds!" A gasp came with it. "If I needed more business, I'd capitalize on her, but I'm swamped as it is, plus, I don't like to take advantage of people. This is her private life, and—"

"Sophie. You had coffee. Then what?"

"I went home, finished decorating my tree. I only use seashells, and I'd found a few more down around Access Eleven, so they had to be washed off." She pondered a few seconds. "Then I went outside. It was a drab day, if you remember, but the wind had dropped some dead fronds off my palmetto trees, and I wanted the yard neat for when Sprite came home."

Callie did a windup motion with her hand to hurry her along, and Sophie bobbled her head only to stiffen.

"What?" Callie asked. "Any suspicious vehicles? Any unusual foot traffic?"

"No car but his all day. I hear them when they crunch his gravel," Sophie said. "I heard him though."

Okay, good thing she asked. "Did you speak to him?" A chat would be a Godsend. Maybe get a read on Ben. How he behaved . . . what was on his mind in his final hours.

Sophie's shag cut shivered. "No. I never talk to that idiot. But I was in the backyard and heard him yell something. I sort of slipped up to my carport, and saw Brice walking off the property and head off down Jungle Road."

Callie's heart leaped as she kicked herself for not having interviewed Sophie sooner. "Brice? Not Ben?"

"I'm positive. Brice."

"Where was his car?" Callie asked.

Sophie shrugged with her brows and a tilt of her head. "No idea. Never saw it. Funny, too, because I can't say I've ever seen him walk any farther than from his car to a place to eat. Not a bit of physical tone in *that* body."

Callie'd slipped a notepad out of her jeans back pocket and scribbled. "West or east from Ben's place?"

Sophie looked stunned.

"Did he walk right or left from Ben's driveway?" Callie said, simplifying.

"Right," she said.

Toward Brice's lot on Dolphin.

"Did you try to follow him?"

Puzzled, she questioned, "Why would I do that?"

Callie scoffed at the obvious. "No offense, but why do you do a lot of things, honey? You like keeping zoned in on the pulse of this beach. Did Ben follow him?"

Sophie relaxed at an explanation she couldn't argue with. "No, didn't see Ben. Just heard him yell that once."

"Anything else?" Callie had to get to Mark's, check in with Marie, revisit Aberdeen when she hopefully wasn't in one of her dramatic episodes. She started to close her pad.

"There was this jogger," Sophie said.

Except for hurricanes, the weather remained joggable almost year-round on Edisto. Joggers weren't that unusual.

Sophie was an odd bird, but she paid attention to details. "Did you recognize him?"

"Can't say who it was," she said. "He had a gray hoodie on, and baggy gray sweats, and when he passed Brice, he stopped and watched him for a moment."

"Did you see his face?"

"No. He faced away from me."

"Did Brice speak to him?"

"No."

"Did you shout out to him?"

"No, he never saw me, plus, I can't even say it was a *he*. But I was headed inside and hardly missed a step going in, so he didn't make too big of an impression."

"So what was different? What made you think of him? We get joggers all over this beach, Soph."

Sophie unraveled herself and eased off the stool. "Because I've only seen him jogging for the last week. On Jungle, on Jungle Shores, on Palmetto, and a bunch of other streets. Mainly on the beach side, not the sound. He just jogs up and down the roads," she said. "Like the tourists drive when they are studying the houses, wishing they lived here."

Or like someone casing houses, noting the lit Christmas trees with no cars in the driveways. Especially when the most remarkable thing about him was his unremarkability.

Callie's phone vibrated with a text. *Two more burglaries. Collected five new gifts. You coming in today?*

If Callie hadn't planned to, she darn sure would now. She texted Marie back. *On my way.* Dropping by to see Mark just got bumped back.

"Gotta go, Soph," she said. "But before I do, anything else about this jogger *jog* your memory?"

Sophie tucked away her yoga mats in a cabinet and closed the open window. "Nothing other than he was the most unidentifiable person I've ever seen jogging. If I could've seen their hands, I could've told you man or woman. I can read hands. "

"Height? See the brand on the shoes, maybe?"

"Oh," Sophie said, realizing there *was* something to note. "I can't tell shoe brands, but the person was shorter than Brice by about two to three inches. Jogged pretty effortlessly, which might mean on the younger side, but then I'm not exactly on the younger side and I can out-yoga anyone in Charleston, as well as this island."

But jogging was a different story. The youth had an easiness in their gait. And Brice was five foot nine or ten, making the jogger five foot eight or less. A shorter man or a taller woman. It was a start.

MARIE HAD TAGGED and locked away the turned-in gifts from the evening before, but she'd laid out the five recent gifts on the empty desk the officers alternated using when they had paperwork.

Clothing, accessories, and jewelry, with the clothing being on the large to extra-large size. Edisto Santa had a trend. Maybe he avoided any-thing too particular or that wasn't one-size-fits-all. Shoes had size issues too difficult to match, and electronics often came with added expenses like subscriptions and service memberships the recipient possibly couldn't afford. Guess the Apple watch was too good to pass, but she expected that to wind up pawned.

She was hungry for patterns, and her brain couldn't stop analyzing the type of gifts, how they were wrapped, how they were delivered, who received them . . . but nothing seemed carved in stone.

A long velvet box caught Callie's eye. The other jewelry had been in plain white boxes with cotton batting or in nothing at all. She opened the hinged lid to find a charm bracelet laying across the white satin base.

She removed the bracelet and held it up, tinkering with each charm. "Marie? Anyone report a charm bracelet?"

Marie didn't have to look. "No. One of the ones from today was a pearl ring, valued around three hundred dollars."

Callie kept analyzing the bracelet. "Easy to pocket."

"The other report mentioned a ladies' antique silver spoon ring. Make Gorham, pattern Medici."

"Am I that clueless or am I supposed to understand what you just said?" Callie asked, lowering the piece of jewelry and studying her office manager.

"I understood what it was," Marie replied.

"Hmm, answers that," Callie mumbled then rubbed one eye then the other.

"What's happened?" Marie asked. "You're in civvies, and you're kind of wilted."

Callie laughed, but not hard, too drained to invest in the effort. She updated Marie on the forensics team then generally mentioned breakfast with Stan and the chat with Sophie. "What are the addresses on the two recent reports?"

"Both on Jungle Shores," she said.

"Did you ask about them finding the wrappings in the trash?"

"Yes, but neither did."

Straying from his routine. The guy was bold to repeat himself on this small patch of real estate. Edisto Beach wasn't three miles long as the crow flew . . . Palmetto Boulevard four miles max. "Both renters?"

Marie rifled through papers and passed Callie the actual reports. "That's the difference. Residents."

Bolder indeed. Residents could label who was a visitor and who was not. She'd leave the station and head to the two addresses, hoping these residents had a different read on things. And Mark would have to wait a little while longer. It was going on 10:30. She could check these reports, stop and hug her son upon his arrival, and maybe only then make it to Mark's.

She held up the bracelet. "Who gave you this?"

Marie had already converted paper receipts into a spreadsheet. "Mrs. Isaacs out on Clark Road had her teenage daughter bring it in at eight this morning. Why?"

"Just came from a nice jeweler," she said. "No report of it missing yet?"

Marie shook her head. "They might not realize it until they go to open presents tonight or tomorrow. Sucks for you being right here on the beach, Callie. People can find where you live."

But Callie doubted strongly this charm bracelet would be claimed. A diamond on one charm, real, she bet, accenting the crescent on the South Carolina state logo. She touched a porcelain seashell and a half dozen others, each unique and expensive-looking, but the two that caught her attention most hung on the end. A replica of the Eiffel Tower and a graceful gull with *Abby* engraved on the back. Not to mention the name Xavier's scripted inside the top of the velvet box.

Chapter 17

THE BRACELET MEANT Edisto Santa had possibly escalated to murder. Ben Rosewood's murder. Instead of running to the recent reported burglaries, in spite of them being natives and outside the burglar's pattern, Callie made a bee-line to the Isaacs' home on Clark Road, the residence that received the bracelet, per Marie. Without a doubt this was the piece of jewelry Ben bought and Brice had questioned him about.

Callie wished Brice had been able to see the bracelet, to confirm. Not that the name *Abby* and the Eiffel Tower didn't shout Brice's wife. And it was easy enough to confirm Brice didn't buy it.

She drove off the beach onto the bigger island. The day had taken on a grayish aura with flat, discolored clouds. No feel of rain in the air but enough humidity to force the coolness into her skin. Christmas in the Carolinas could bring cold, bone-chilling rain or short-sleeve weather. This year the weather fit Callie's mood.

Just after eleven in the morning, she passed more cars than expected. Last minute guests, she figured, arriving to greet those who were already settled on the beach, primed for celebration.

She wouldn't be surprised to pass Jeb on the road in his effort to reach *Chelsea Morning* . . . probably expecting to arrive to smells of the season . . . fudge, peppermint, pine . . . none of which he'd find. She'd bought a balsam candle to flavor the air, but it sat in her pantry, waiting for her to get around to lighting it long enough to fill the house with its scent. The chocolate remained in its Bi-Lo bag, the butter and cream in the refrigerator. All the fixings of fudge, but she'd been unable to put them together. At least there was a carton of eggnog.

Eggnog. Not worth drinking without the spike, and not a soul in her world would dream of doing so in front of her. Jeb could drink it all as far as she was concerned.

Poor Jeb. She was tackling one of the weirdest, saddest, most disoriented Christmases of her life.

She should've called her mother. Either of them. Begged one of them to host the day, but it was too late to throw that on them. Beverly would chastise her royally. Sarah probably didn't know where to begin having never put together a family holiday for anyone other than Ben.

Enough. She compartmentalized her day, tucking away family thoughts. She had more urgent problems.

As her cruiser traveled slightly over the speed limit down the main highway, Callie pondered the odds of someone bringing in the very bracelet that could plant enough doubt in a jury about the killer's identity to keep Brice out of jail. Assuming all he said was the truth.

The jogger could be key. The jogger could be Edisto Santa. Santa maybe got bold enough to enter an occupied dwelling, making him beyond dangerous. Few crossed that line without expecting to meet someone and deal accordingly. Or he saw Brice leave thinking it was Ben, or that the house belonged to Brice . . . and he acted on opportunity. Not all of the six hundred residents knew each other . . . though they knew *of* each other, and Ben and Brice were of similar age.

Or the burglar peeked inside, saw an injured Ben maybe on the floor, and took advantage, running off with the bag. Could explain Ben's bloody prints on the post and stair railing. Might mean he chased the thief, ultimately collapsing the block over from his home . . . maybe.

A lot of maybes, but way more pieces to the puzzle than she'd had last night.

She glanced over at the bracelet resting on her front seat in a box from Xavier's. If Callie believed Brice's story about the bag on the mantel, this piece was clearly stolen the day Ben died.

But what made Edisto Santa start burgling residents instead of renters? Hell, what made him start burgling at all? Theft wasn't a part of his tradition, because Marie didn't recall that prior years involved extreme Robin Hood behavior, and if Marie didn't recall, nobody did. He was supposed to be a simple secret Santa, but he now seemed almost vengeful about the haves versus the have-nots. Ben's death could have marked a dark turn in Santa's deal.

God, she hoped with Christmas Eve being today, that he'd stolen his last gift. But the downside was once he stopped, once the crime spree was over, how would they identify him without waiting another year to the next holiday season? He could remain on the island, walking, working, and strolling the beach like everyone else. Unless he was a holiday visitor, but like she'd rationalized before, how would he personalize the secret gifts, and how would he find where they lived?

She took the right just past the Old Post Office on 174, then a mile and a half down and left onto Clark Road. The address Marie gave her led to a faded yellow single-wide trailer with at least twenty years of age resting on its axles. A makeshift wooden deck spread maybe twelve-by-twelve with a pergola affair over the top . . . webbed folding chairs to the left and right. *Isaacs* was burned into a wooden sign one could find at a county fair or bought off Etsy, and hung overhead at the steps.

Trying not to appear too hurried, Callie still walked faster than her norm and knocked. A cold wind slid up behind her, and she missed the warmth of her heavy uniform jacket.

A girl about driving age answered the knock. "Ma'am?"

Callie showed her credentials, and the teen gave a start at the badge. "Momma?" she called, her stare fixed on Callie, but her fear not allowing the stranger across the threshold.

A tall woman in her forties quickly appeared, and she eased her daughter to the side and stood in her place. "What can I do for you?"

Callie held up the box, opening it for confirmation. "I understand you returned this to the Edisto Beach police station this morning."

With switchblade speed, the woman pushed her daughter behind her and took a protective stance. "We did not steal that bracelet, you hear me?" She shoved her daughter. "Go to your room, and be prepared to make a call to your uncle when I tell you."

But the daughter hesitated.

"Go on like I told you!" the mother ordered, shoving the girl's shoulder. "Listen to me."

Not how Callie planned this meeting to occur. "Please, Ms. Isaacs, I'm here to thank you, not to come after you. I'm grateful to see this bracelet."

Ms. Isaacs watched, wary, her jaw tight.

"Ma'am," Callie continued, "I just wanted to hear how you found it."

"*Found* it? It was an Edisto Santa gift. My daughter was here when it arrived. Probably the most expensive present she's ever got, but with all the talk going round about this stuff being stolen, I didn't want her tied up in that business one bit."

Callie pushed the rise of guilt aside. She reminded herself that she wasn't destroying this tradition . . . Edisto Santa was.

"May I come in?" Callie asked, but the mother shook her head, lips mashed tight. Guess they were doing this in the open. "Do you still have the paper it was wrapped in?"

Another shake of the head. "Wasn't any paper. Was in a bag. Matched the box. Had a ribbon handle."

The others were wrapped per most of the people who turned in items. But why rewrap something so nicely packaged? Maybe an impromptu decision?

"Did it have a tag to your daughter?"

"No, ma'am. She's just the one who found it. Had a small piece of paper stuck in the top that said Merry Christmas from Edisto Santa. Wasn't for anybody in particular."

"Was it typed?" Callie asked.

Again with the negative. "Handwritten."

"Any chance you can find that paper . . . and the bag?"

"Shauna!" Ms. Isaacs hollered. "You got the stuff that came with that bracelet? If you do, bring it out here, please."

The please didn't sound optional.

The girl soon appeared with a gold bag, the name Xavier's scrolled across the front, and a piece of paper, as if torn from a pad, with the words as Ms. Isaacs said. Block lettering, like someone disguising their handwriting. The paper had been wadded, most likely retrieved from the trash, but it was addressed to nobody in particular.

Callie tried to seem pleading, desperate for their help. "Any chance at all you saw who this person was? We don't believe he's a very nice person," she said. "He's entering occupied homes and stealing, and we're concerned he's going to hurt someone. Anything you can remember might help us out."

She avoided describing the variances from the other Santa gifts. The bag, the note in lieu of a tag, the fact the gift wasn't targeted for a particular person. And she wasn't about to state Edisto Santa may have gone too far and killed a man.

"Chief, right?" Ms. Isaacs said. "Me and my daughter don't want to get swept up into anything. Not after what happened to Wesley. Just keep your gift, take the paper, and leave us alone."

But she hadn't answered Callie's question. "Did you see the gift get delivered? Can you establish a date and time?"

"No I can't," she said.

But the daughter piped up. "I can."

Softening her expression best she could, Callie slid attention to the girl, but the mother beat her to it. "Hush your mouth!"

"No, Momma. You taught me to be honest. And it isn't right for someone to steal. All this is his fault. What happened to Wesley is that man's fault, too."

With patience and a ray of hope, Callie listened, then asked, "What did you see or hear?"

"Footsteps," she said. "Those steps make noise. He knocked and ran."

Callie's heart beat faster. "You saw him?"

But the girl shook her head. "Was afraid to look. Heard him run, then when I peeked out the window, saw a hunter's ball cap as it got in the car, then I saw the car take off. Brown car."

"Camo cap?" Callie asked.

Shauna nodded yes.

"Make of the car? Model?" Callie asked.

"Bushes were in the way. Once he was gone, I went outside and found the bag."

"But he knocked?"

"Yes, ma'am. We haven't ever had Edisto Santa come to our house, so I didn't think nothing of it. Figured that was how it was done."

Ms. Isaacs' worry remained etched in her features, but she let her daughter talk. They were good people, and there was one comment that merited further explanation.

"Each of you mentioned Wesley. He received a gift and turned it in, just like you did, so when you talk about what happened to Wesley, what do you mean?"

But the daughter sought her mother before answering the question, and the mother stiffened. "We've said enough. You have yourself a good day." She pushed the girl farther inside and shut the door, the lock clicking before Callie rocked on her heel to leave.

She didn't blame them.

Just after noon. Just in case Jeb was late coming in, she'd delay checking on him until she was sure he'd be there. Too much going on.

This was as close as anyone had come to seeing Edisto Santa, and she wondered how many of the others had seen a car, a hair color, maybe noticed Santa's age. The Isaacs and, surprisingly Sophie, had shed different light on this case and accelerated the urge to dig deeper quicker. There was a possibility somebody saw Santa, and Callie bet he wasn't wearing red velvet trimmed in white fur, either. But these interviews would take way longer than she had. She needed her guys. Better to question folks on Christmas Eve than Christmas Day.

God, that would royally label her as a Grinch as well as the department, maybe even Edisto Beach as a whole. The sort of incident curious enough to draw state-level attention . . . national if social media went viral with it. If Brice wasn't a suspect in Ben's death, he'd be holding this bad publicity over her with a whip.

She hastily called Thomas and Ike, even placed a call to her often-borrowed deputy from the Colleton County Sheriff's Office, Don Raysor. Marie's list of Santa recipients numbered in the teens, and Callie couldn't hit them all. She jettisoned her three guys to the field interviewing those who'd given up gifts. They were ordered to collect details of the wrapping, something Marie hadn't noted, the specific date the gift was delivered since some of the returns were from previous years, and detections of a brown car or even Edisto Santa himself. Mention the camo cap. She'd hover on the beach, catching any local issues that came up while speaking again to Aberdeen, Brice, and the two latest burgled houses. Which meant she could run by Mark's as he'd been requesting, and check in with Wesley . . . or find out where he lived so she could pass his name and address to one of the guys to check out.

So stupid to not have Mark's number. She stopped on the side of the road to do a search for El Marko's, but before her search went through, the phone rang in her grip. "Chief Morgan."

"I demand a briefing, Chief. My renters still have questions."

Janet Wainwright. Frankly, Callie was surprised the old Marine hadn't called before.

"I'm headed back into town, so sure," Callie said, driving back onto the road. Wainwright Realty was practically across the street from El Marko's, so she could make a brief appearance before seeing Mark. "Will catch you in about ten minutes."

She started to hang up, then shouted, "Wait!"

"What?" Janet replied.

"You wouldn't happen to have the number for El Marko's, would you?"

Silence filled the call. "You dare stop for lunch first?" Janet retorted.

"I'm not interested in lunch. I want to call Mark Dupree."

"And I'm not interested in your social life."

"Janet, damn it, I just need the number."

"I'll have it for you when you arrive." The call went dead.

Callie sped up. She shouldn't let the holiday clock dictate an investigation, but when tourism, name recognition, and reputation drove the economy of your jurisdiction, such details mattered. Whether she liked it or not, she had an afternoon and evening to try and wrap up Edisto Santa, and the charm bracelet connection had unfortunately put a ticking clock on the Ben Rosewood murder as well.

After tonight, Edisto Santa would disappear back to his version of the North Pole. Ben's murder could drag into a cold case, and Callie'd be forced to wait another year for the culprit to make his appearance. Assuming this year's sudden interest in him hadn't scared him off for good.

Chapter 18

CALLIE TOOK Wainwright Realty's stairs in twos, her phone going off about halfway up. At the top, catching her breath, she noted caller ID.

"Can't chat, Stan."

"Mark said it's urgent," he said.

"Honest to God, Stan, I'm running as fast as I can, and he's on my to-do list. If it's that urgent, he'll call Marie, or 911." At the beach, one was as good as the other, and the residents knew it. "And for goodness sake, give him my phone number so he can text or call me direct, all right?"

"Where are you?" he asked.

"At Wainwright's," she said.

"When should I tell him you'll be over?"

As much as she loved the man, Stan was pushing too hard. While she cherished his guidance, he no longer gave her orders, and he damn sure wasn't managing her calendar. "He'll see me when he sees me. I have to go." Then she added, "Okay?" to soften the harshness creeping over her due to lack of sleep.

"Go take care of the world, Chicklet."

She hung up, telling herself she'd told her old Boston captain goodbye nicely enough. Her guilty feeling telling her she really hadn't.

Entering the building, the gatekeeper desk empty once again, she strode straight to Janet's inner sanctum . . . the office one usually waited to be invited into. But the Marine had called her directly and demanded she appear front and center ASAP.

Janet was on the phone, her nephew Arthur standing beside her, referencing something on her desk. Arthur wasn't so laid-back as before, and his aunt appeared more uptight than her standard rigid self. "I have the police chief on speed dial, sir, and I assure you that she's assured me, there will be a break in this case. You'll be satisfied one way or the other before your family checks out of *Purple Pelican.*"

Greg Anders, demanding his daughter's hundred-dollar birthstone bracelet.

Janet hung up but sassed her nephew first. "Tell me why that window's lock wasn't working."

He held out arms in his pleading. "Aunt Janet, the windows are old, painted over and over. I'd think that would stop a thief as good as any lock."

She leaned in his direction, and he reared ever so slightly. "Yet a thief got into their rental. And instead of them holding the police responsible for crime on this beach, they get mad at me. They feel less safe. Does any of this make sense to you, Arthur? Because if it doesn't, I've wasted years of investment in you. All it takes is one of these people to get hurt, or, or . . . killed like Ben Rosewood . . . for us to be out of business."

"But Mr. Rosewood was a resident," Arthur dared to say. "We ought to be good."

The tension thick enough to cut, Callie and Arthur stood awkward . . . the only sound being Janet's breathing . . . and it wasn't due to her age.

Taught by his aunt to not give up his ground . . . *improvise, adapt, overcome* . . . Arthur made another attempt. "Just pay him the hundred dollars for the bracelet, Aunt Janet."

Smart idea. Kid had a good head on his shoulders.

"And the owners of the houses ought to share some of the responsibility for lack of maintenance," he said. "We can't control—"

Her chair swiveled to focus her attention straight onto him, and he stepped back to avoid being scorched by the stare. "There are no excuses. While you are here, on duty, maintenance is your job, whether you wield the hammer or you direct Tate Jr. to do it. Don't care if Tate missed it before you got here, or you missed it after Tate." Her knuckle began pounding her desk blotter to the beat of each word. "Every single week we change renters, we check the locks and windows." The knuckle stopped. "And if there's a problem, we fix it and charge the owner up to a hundred dollars, or call the owner to get permission to fix it if it's over that. Basic contract clause. By our not informing the owner, and therefore jeopardizing the tenant, we expose ourselves. What about that is not clear to you, nephew?"

Arthur didn't come back to that.

"Janet," Callie said, moving closer and into the ring. "I hear you about the burglaries. I have been on this since we learned of it, to include no sleep last night. Just interviewed someone who may have spotted the car of the guy who delivered one of the gifts."

"Or girl," Arthur added.

The glares from both women sent him to the sofa.

"So what do I tell Mr. Anders?" Janet asked.

"You tell him that people are turning in Edisto Santa gifts thanks to Edisto PD," Callie said. "The department is offering gift certificates to El Marko's as inducement to turn the stolen articles in. Hopefully his daughter's bracelet will show, and when it does, you'll get it to him. Word is traveling around the island, but it hasn't reached everyone. I can't promise someone won't choose to keep an expensive bracelet rather than give it up for a ten-dollar Mexican meal, though. Arthur's idea to compensate your renters for the loss is actually pretty shrewd, Janet."

More silence . . . Janet processing and Arthur too afraid to speak.

"Good then." Callie stepped to leave. "I have a lot to do with way too many Mr. Anders-types expecting me to accomplish more than I can possibly manage."

Arthur rose. "Chief Morgan?"

Pitying him for having endured Janet's wrath, Callie gave him a moment. "Yes, Arthur."

"Are any of the burglaries happening in houses that are managed by other realtors on the island?"

Callie shook her head. "Afraid not."

"I could've told you that," Janet grumbled.

"And it's just rentals, not people who live out here?" he asked.

Janet appeared annoyed. "Nephew, yesterday the chief told us—"

But Callie interrupted. They deserved to know. "Actually, two burglaries were reported today by residents," she said. "I'll have more on those by this afternoon."

The relief was evident on both their faces. Arthur's especially.

"That's sort of a good thing, isn't it, Aunt Janet?" he said, eager for some sort of relief valve on Janet's pressure. "It's not all on us."

Janet's head fell to her chest, a resigned dejection in her expression. "Don't let me hold you up, Chief," she said. "Go do your job."

On Callie's way out, Janet's voice had reverted to Marine, and Callie hesitated beside the exit to hear.

"Call Tate Jr., Arthur. I don't care if it takes the two of you until midnight, I want our inventory records checked, and if any of them, occupied or not, haven't been cleared as secure, meaning you can actually sleep easy avowing those houses are safe, you'll be working through Christmas Day. Is that clear, soldier?"

"Thought we were Marines," he said.

Callie departed on that one, not wanting to feel the blister of what that young man was about to receive. *Nobody* called themselves Marine without having served under the globe and anchor.

Chapter 19

CALLIE DROVE across the road and down two addresses to El Marko's. Few cars in the parking lot, but upon entering, apparently there'd been enough foot traffic to justify Mark's decision to remain open part of Christmas Eve. A third of the tables were filled.

No Sophie though, probably because of the light day, and Callie considered that a good omen. She didn't need her yoga friend to go on the offensive again to protect Mark. This conversation had to be strictly between the current and the ex-cop, speaking the same language.

Mark appeared quickly upon hearing the subtle electronic bell that she assumed his ear was keenly attuned to. As he saw her, however, the energy in his walk came down a notch, but, to his credit, he approached hand out. "Chief," he said.

She accepted, attempting to judge his frame of mind . . . attempting to ignore the luscious smells her stomach suddenly somersaulted for.

After an uncomfortable breath, she waggled her phone. "What's so urgent? Stan has been on my butt about contacting you." She stopped short of telling him how busy she was or how many others commanded her day.

"Follow me," he said, adding, "If you don't mind."

"Something wrong?" she asked, not really up to guessing games, but she appreciated the accommodating behavior of the man and wanted to reciprocate. Behaving and going along would take her a lot further than confrontation.

They entered the small kitchen, light glinting off the stainless, fresh-out-of-the-box chip warmer, finishing oven, and sink. They stepped around boxes of foodstuffs, and off to the right a tall figure prepped orders.

"Wesley," Mark said. "Can I see you a second?"

The young man pushed plates back and removed the disposable gloves, which gave Callie a clear view of a splinted finger. As he approached, she took note of a shiner that added a puffiness along his cheekbone, almost to his jaw.

"Wesley?" she exclaimed, itching to reach up and stroke the wounds. "What the hell happened to you?"

Embarrassed, he studied the floor, then pretended to be interested in the clanging another worker made with utensils at the sink. "Nothing to worry about, ma'am."

No, this wasn't okay, and suddenly Ms. Isaacs's words were chilling. " . . . *what happened to Wesley.*"

"Who did it?" she asked. "And if it's off the beach and out of my reach, I'll have Charleston County come out here."

"No need," he replied, his head still ducked down. "A one-time thing."

Callie's senses clamored that the Edisto Santa ordeal had something to do with these bruises. "If you won't say who, then tell me when," she said.

"Last night after I got home," he replied.

Good, he inadvertently took care of the where, too. "You're not tiny, so I'm assuming you tagged a piece of the other guy. Care to share why? Is this some long-standing feud, or—"

"Wasn't no feud," he retorted.

"Or," she began again. "It had something to do with Edisto Santa."

His silence answered yes.

"Was it Edisto Santa?" she asked.

Wesley jerked around. "What? No! Don't even know who the guy is. Why would he do that?"

"Not sure," she said. "But another person who received a gift was afraid to keep hers for fear of getting some of what you got here." She motioned to his bruises.

His anger seemed to mingle with humiliation. "Wasn't no Santa. And I don't have to say who it was."

Mark laid an assuring hand on Wesley's shoulder. "I also heard it was because he gave that sweater to you, Chief. He's been accused of sucking the cops into this, which caused all these people to fear Santa and the gifts. If he hadn't worn that sweater to apply for a job, or if he hadn't spoken to you, nothing would've been stirred up. Or so that's the word."

Only half listening, Callie remained attentive to the injured man. "Wesley, you listen to me. We were all over these stolen objects before seeing you. You caused nothing, you hear? None of this is your fault."

It wasn't his fault, but truthfully, she'd had no threads to unravel, not a clue to go on before Wesley strolled in wearing that snowflake sweater. He wore stolen property, admitted it wasn't his other than by choice of Edisto Santa, and he had told her the names of others who'd enjoyed the same charity. He was a catalyst, but innocent nonetheless.

"None of this should've happened," Mark said, and when Callie peered at him she couldn't read the man. Instead he almost exuded sympathy. She wasn't sure whether his comment was critical of her or genuinely empathetic toward Wesley and his wounds.

She started to shake and recoiled at the broken finger until he shook with his left, and she gripped firmly. "My apologies," she said. "And I mean that, Wesley. If you change your mind about the person that did this, here's my card."

"Thanks, ma'am." He tucked the card in his hip pocket, though Callie expected it to find a home soon enough amongst the half-uneaten burritos in the outgoing trash. Regardless she had a strong suspicion about the culprit.

The supposedly crippled cousin who received the Apple watch. The one who'd never give up his Santa gift. To his mind, relatives shouldn't rat on each other, and he'd educated Wesley about family loyalty. She'd get nowhere trying to pin assault on him. And Charleston County SO wouldn't want to be bothered coming all the way out to the island for a family spat.

"Well, don't let me keep you," she said, and Mark smiled, okaying Wesley to resume his work.

"Can we talk somewhere else?" she said to Mark once Wesley left.

He escorted her to the same table on the edge of the dining room, outside the kitchen. Once Mark seated her and assumed his own place, a waitress slid an appetizer in front of them along with two glasses of tea.

"Hand signals?" she asked, holding off on the nachos though her stomach begged her to dig in. The SeaCow breakfast had come and gone some hours ago, but she couldn't scold and eat.

"Pardon?"

She held up a chip. "Food materializes out of thin air when we sit here . . . ." She got it then. When the boss took someone to that particular table, the wait staff had standing orders to bring an appetizer. Mystery solved.

He winked at her and snared a nacho, stacking two jalapenos atop the chip before inserting the whole thing in his mouth. "You figured it out, Chief," he mumbled, chewing until he swallowed. "Nothing gets past you."

"Who the heck was your training officer, because you apparently don't get it."

His smile melted. "Get what?"

"What's priority and what's not. Stan told me you wanted me to rush over here. For what? I get that Wesley got beat up, but it's well after the fact, and my bet is you already knew he wasn't giving up the name of who did it. In other words, it could've waited."

"We close at three today," he said, laying down his food. "Wanted you to see his injuries and have the chance to talk to him yourself."

His restaurant schedule wasn't dictating hers, though admittedly she was still sore over the incident yesterday. God, had it been only yesterday?

That was enough. Her energy lagging, she shook her head, tired. She noted her watch. "I really have to go. Two more burglaries reported this morning, and there's at least one more interview I'd like to take care of."

But he just sat. "If it makes you feel any better, I couldn't get him to say who pummeled him either."

She put her napkin on the table. "I feel so much more vindicated since your talent failed, too." Taking a big inhale, she started to redirect, only for Mark to beat her to it.

"I really did used to be good at my job, and word has it you're damn good at yours," he said. "Can we start over?"

She hadn't expected this, but nobody could say she didn't try to be fair. "I, um, sure."

"My apologies," he said. "For any of several comments on a list that's becoming too lengthy to specify. I do not question your abilities."

She guessed she could accept the apology in spite of the fact he indeed had questioned her abilities. "I can see why you care about Wesley," she said trying to meet him in the middle. "Maybe I could've taken him out of your dining room before questioning him about the sweater. You have a fledgling business to protect."

He smiled a smile that surprisingly warmed her.

"Well," he replied, "it didn't become an issue until I butted in, did it?"

"Um, Sophie sort of lit that match."

His grin showed he agreed.

She had places to be and people to see but sure could use a sounding board, if only for ten minutes. She hadn't vetted him through her contacts, but SLED didn't hire people lightly, and an ex-investigator of the agency would come with a wealth of experience. Plus Stan liked him.

"Show me your skills," she said. "Normally I go to Stan, but he's being particularly mulish these days."

Mark snared another nacho, doubling down on the jalapenos. She did the same, the burn kicking some life back into her. "And I could use another brain since mine is drained," she added.

"All ears," he said.

She went over the burglaries and gift interviews, all of which he hadn't heard of. Then she covered Ben Rosewood's death, and the coroner's conclusion.

"That type injury could go either way," he said. "Murder or accident. And ever thought that Edisto Santa accidentally caused this death? And once rattled about learning Ben died, is running scared?" He nodded back toward the kitchen. "Maybe took down Wesley for bringing more attention on Edisto Santa?"

He'd put the same pieces together she did, except she didn't think Edisto Santa would expose himself to Wesley like that. There they differed.

But with Mark having so easily connected the cases, she went ahead and added the intel about the bracelet.

"There you go," he said. "Brice is most likely out and Santa is in. There's your likely culprit."

"But Santa hits renters," she said.

"Maybe he knew about the bracelet," he replied.

She frowned at that. "Then that brings us back around to Brice. Or Aberdeen."

"Or someone saw a simple moment of opportunity and erred in his judgment finding Ben home."

"Which puts us back to Santa," she said.

He sat back. "Who do you think did it?"

"Did what? The Edisto Santa stealing or the Ben Rosewood

murder?" she replied.

"Let's just go with Ben first," he said.

"Brice is the most obvious but something feels off. While I need to speak to him again, to see if he had any idea what was in that Xavier's bag, I can't see him doing it. He's a lot of noise, but he's about as murderous as a loggerhead turtle."

"So remove him from the equation," Mark said. "What if the death was an unforeseen side effect of the burglary?"

The jogger, for instance. Or Edisto Santa himself.

"But don't let your history with Brice cloud your focus," Mark said. "If he lied about the bracelet, who says he isn't lying about shoving Ben? He hasn't merited a pass yet. Or rather, that's my opinion, for what it's worth."

Yeah, that's what she was afraid of. She kept thinking Brice incapable of shoving someone hard enough to warrant brain damage. Too much jelly in his spine. But when one's spouse is found cheating with one's close friend, who is one's attorney to boot, well, that can draw upon a power one might never think they had.

"Appreciate the feedback," she said. "I've really got to run. I'm interviewing the most recent burglary victims."

His face had softened in their exchange, and he reverted to the Mark she'd seen at her birthday party. Approachable and generous from beneath thick dark hair, gray up the sides. Back before he'd shown interest in Sophie, but Callie couldn't hold that against him. Sophie did that to men.

"I've been in your shoes, Chief," he said.

"Callie's fine." She wiped her mouth and stood before her waning energy got too comfortable not moving. He likewise rose, in a welcomed respectful nature.

"Callie, then." His grin widened at the use of her first name. "Ever want feedback again, call me." He slid out his phone. "Give me your number."

She did, and he called, putting his number in her phone, saving hers to his.

Then she pushed in her chair. "Thanks for the pick-me-up. Merry Christmas." She held out her hand, and he took it. She didn't squeeze as hard as she normally would, the usual overcompensation not feeling necessary. He held his grip for a half second longer than a regular good-bye.

But she hadn't the heart to tell him he told her nothing she hadn't already thought of.

This day was growing old way too fast.

Chapter 20

THREE IN THE afternoon on Christmas Eve, and Callie hadn't received a text from her son, much less a call, so she side-tracked by her house en route to the first of the two resident burglary scenes. Four houses before she reached her own, she spotted Jeb's Jeep. She parked parallel to the road rather than in her drive and texted Jeb before climbing those two dozen stairs to an empty house. *You home?*

But instead of a reply, the front door opened, and her son took the steps agile and quick like a college kid could. "Mom. Merry Christmas!"

How much of a man he seemed with a shadow of scruff around his jaw, the awkwardness of a teen replaced by toned muscle. Callie scurried around the cruiser, meeting him in a hug. She squeezed him hard, and he did so in kind, those long arms smothering the air out of her. She closed her eyes. She could breathe later.

"You didn't text me," she said, gripping the sides of his shirt, drinking in the familiar smell of his clothes.

With that half-grin of his deceased father's, he pivoted to the side, his butt resting on her car, but one arm still over her shoulder. "Sprite talks to her mom, like several times a day, and she learned you caught a couple cases. Ms. Sophie said you were going nuts chasing someone pretending to be Santa. Of course I also heard how you pissed her off, and how she would manage things differently, and so on and so on."

Callie playfully winced. "Not exactly the facts."

He shook his head. "Don't need them . . . don't care," he said. "I don't go up against Ms. Sophie, Mom. She might hex me."

They laughed easy together, but then his humor left. "She said she hadn't heard from you about Christmas dinner. So I called Mr. Stan, and he filled me in more on what you're into at work. After that, I didn't want to bother you," he said. "I figured you'd check on me soon enough . . . when you took a breath. I know you, Mom."

She squeezed him again in thanks. "Stan tell you about the murder?"

Letting her loose and crossing his arms, his expression darkened. "Death, yes. Murder, no."

The child had always possessed an older manner, but his maturity was born out of necessity. As a child of fifteen he stepped up to tend to his bereft mother through gin and tonic binges. At eighteen he delayed college a year until he trusted his mother to manage herself. He'd lost the father in Boston and a grandfather on his way home from Edisto, when she'd lost a husband and a dad, yet he'd held it together a hundred-fold better than she had. But when Callie lost Seabrook to a deranged killer and her youngest officer Francis to Scott Creek, Jeb stepped into the shoes of a full-grown man.

How grateful she was, though. She oozed with love for this boy God had somehow made the mistake of blessing her with.

"Should I be worried?" he asked.

Worried meaning, first, would she resume her drinking, and second, would she go all overprotective of him. Overprotective meaning hourly texts or regular calls. Cutting that umbilical cord had been damn difficult for her, but she'd seen more darkness in human beings than he'd seen.

"No, you don't have to worry," she said, addressing both his concerns. "But I'm not sure when I'll be home. Your presents are wrapped, and there's eggnog in the fridge, but—"

"Do your thing, Mom," and he pushed off the hood. "I can manage. My girlfriend is right next door, and I'll just go kick back with her. Let Ms. Sophie spoil me. But it's your turn."

Puzzled she asked, "My turn for what?"

"Checking in with me, okay?"

She gave him another bear hug, still marveling that he towered ten inches over her. "Will do."

He walked backwards toward the house. "Be extra careful," he said before going back inside.

Took her a second to put her police face back on and head toward the next burglary site, but she'd fueled up with enough Jeb-love to carry her a few hours into her evening.

Both burgled houses were on Jungle Shores. The eight-hundred and nine-hundred blocks, both backing up to the marsh. The first one, *Lowcountry Bribe*, was owned by the Clarks. Callie stopped there first.

The Clarks had lived on Edisto twelve years. They'd simply gotten up that Christmas Eve morning, the wife admiring her tree, going through the mental calculations of the finishing touches to make Christmas special for her husband and visiting grown sons. How she'd noticed that one tiny ring box gone from the myriad of gold, red, and green foil was beyond Callie.

"Have no idea when it might've been taken," the woman said, but her husband strongly asserted otherwise with a grunt and a laugh.

"She checks that tree every morning," he said. "If that ring had been missing yesterday, she'd have noticed."

"Description?" The report filed earlier held some details, but Callie liked to confirm.

"White gold. A saltwater pearl setting. Size seven," Mr. Clark said.

Callie took notes. "When was the house last empty?"

"Last night," he said. "I took the family out to the Waterfront Restaurant for seafood. From around 5:30 to . . . " He looked to his wife for the answer.

"We got home around 7:30," she said.

Callie tried to make connections to the other burglaries. What was the same. What was different. "You didn't happen to check your gifts when you got home, did you?"

The wife shook her head.

"Or find the wrapping paper in the trash?"

The couple sought each other for hints. "You think we accidentally tossed that ring in the trash?" Mr. Clark asked in disbelief.

Callie explained the pattern at the other houses.

Mrs. Clark appeared quizzical. "Why would someone unwrap such a gift small enough to tuck into a pocket and go?"

Why would Edisto Santa unwrap any gift, Callie thought, but patterns were patterns. "Have you taken the trash out today? Or last night after you got home?"

She sent the couple to the kitchen. After pilfering through egg shells, a milk carton, and assorted refuse, they found nothing. In an afterthought, they upended four other trash cans in bedrooms and baths. Nothing. Yet another difference between these two Jungle Shore burglaries and the others at the rentals.

"Do you leave your house unlocked by any chance? Not judging, mind you, just trying to decipher what to hunt for."

"I stay after her to lock up, but she doesn't always do so," the husband said.

"What about last night?" Callie asked.

"We were just going to dinner, so I didn't even think to look," the wife replied. "You could check all the locks, but I'm not sure that would help."

Smiling, Callie offered to check anyway, to ease the woman's chagrin. Front door had been locked behind her when she came in, but upon close examination showed no sign of disturbance. The back door, however, was unfastened. And upon close observation, Callie noted a small number of fine scratches on the plated lock.

Santa could pick locks.

Without telling the Clarks, she locked the door and thanked them, with a strong reminder to continue securing their exits.

Then after assurances and season's greetings, Callie left, uneasy about how skilled this burglar seemed to be. She thought briefly about Arthur, and how the poor guy was probably still checking houses under his Aunt Janet's orders when in actuality, the thief could've entered a house regardless how secure the locks were.

None of the other houses had appeared to have been picked, but then the rentals were more used and abused, locks coated with paint slathered from repainted surfaces, the lock sets years old and beaten. The Clarks' home was modern, well-maintained as a residence. A picked lock would be much more apparent.

Thank goodness, though, that it appeared the burglary took place when no one was home.

Maybe he was being more careful after what happened to Ben. If the two events were related at all.

So many random details. Like she was just starting to put a jigsaw puzzle together and realized a bunch of pieces were missing, hunted around and found a couple, added them to the pile and still had not a clue where they belonged in the overall design.

She left and eased past five houses to the second crime scene on the same street. *Anchors Away* was owned by a retired Navy captain and his wife. Captain and Mrs. McMillan.

Twenty-year residents, they'd noticed their packages all askew and out of sorts late last night . . . after coming back in from dinner, again, at the Waterfront.

"When were you there?" Callie asked.

"Got home around, what, eight?" he said, with a request for confirmation aimed at his wife. Funny how these older husbands deferred to their wives on matters of time.

"That's about right," she said. "We wanted to get home to watch *The Bishop's Wife*. The one with Cary Grant."

It had been a while since Callie'd heard someone actually run home to catch a television show with everything so easily recorded for later viewing, but there was a comforting feel to this simpler way of life.

"I haven't told her what the gift was," the white-haired captain said. "Can she be excused from this conversation?"

Ms. McMillan ran her hand over her husband's back. "But I noticed the gift missing, Captain."

Cute, she called him by his rank.

"It's not the gift. It's the thought," she added, then smiled through wrinkled lips at Callie. "Go ahead, Chief. Ask your questions."

Callie asked the same questions she'd asked the Clarks. Concern about wrappings in the trash proved fruitless, and Ms. McMillan repeated Ms. Clark's logic about pocketing a small package rather than unwrapping it. That and small boxes were harder to unwrap.

But Callie was almost positive about one thing. Edisto Santa had seen both families at dinner, in the same restaurant, and in recognizing them, took the opportunity to help himself to their presents. Confirmation that he was a local, able to place a person with an address. Armed with a lock pick set on both sites, because Captain McMillan spoke adamantly about keeping his place locked with them up in age.

Four thirty. She radioed her officers still interviewing the listed folks. Thomas, Ike, and Raysor replied, each having covered three to four homes, each with little to report. She ordered them in, telling them to wrap up their interviews since their presence was more needed on the beach. This was the last night that Edisto Santa could make another collection. While many families would be gathered around the pro-verbial fire awaiting the real Santa, others would be at one of the many church services on the island, ranging from dusk to midnight.

Callie wasn't sure how motivated this thief was. Hell, she had no idea what his motivation was, period. If he'd been the one to injure Ben, he was driven enough to take out someone in his way . . . or too nervous to think straight.

She even wondered if he acted on a schedule of some sort, with a deadline and a quota, but if she stopped searching, thinking he was done for the year, and he hit another house, she'd kick herself. She and her officers were the first and last defense on this beach, so to cease for something like a holiday would reflect badly.

She radioed her officers again, telling them to begin their on-the-beach grid searches reserved for situations similar to this . . . manhunts. She'd start without them.

Thomas radioed in when he'd reached the beach, then shortly thereafter, Ike did the same. Raysor had taken the addresses farthest away on the island but was on his way.

Then in their slow drives, they scanned different parts of the Edisto Beach community, scouting for anyone out of place. Any race, any gender, but Callie reminded the guys that on the day of Ben's murder, there'd been a questionable spotting of a jogger in a gray hoodie, gray pants, and sneakers that blended in. Five foot seven to ten. Most likely in his twenties or thirties.

Stop anyone who didn't belong, because who went out and about on a beach on the night before Christmas?

Didn't take ten minutes before Thomas called. "Chief, see a hooded guy who tried a door, peered in a window, then worked the lock and entered. On Sandpiper."

"Do your thing, Thomas," she said. "Be right there."

When she'd arrived, Thomas had Arthur Wainwright backed against the patrol car. "You understand why Thomas stopped you?" Callie asked.

He gave an exaggerated shrug. "I'm checking houses, like Aunt Janet said. Do you know how many I still have to go? You heard her. *Check them all before Christmas or work through Christmas.* I'm not messing with people on Christmas."

"Thought she said use Tate Jr. to help you do all this," Callie said.

He blew a hard breath. "No way I'm calling him off his vacation to do this crap for my crazy-assed aunt. I'll take care of it by myself. This kind of shit makes me wonder what the hell I'm getting into with her."

Thomas stepped closer, motioning at the house Arthur'd entered. "There are people renting there, man. I watched you let yourself in. Not cool at all. What if you'd run across someone in there, huh? Unclothed . . . having sex . . . do you realize the trouble you'd be in?"

"Or worse," Callie added. "The trouble your aunt would be in?"

The kid fidgeted as if fighting not to pee, eyes darting. "She's gonna gut me and feed me to the sharks, anyway," he said.

"Or worse, fire you then disown you." Callie suspected that while Janet considered this nephew her primary heir, she wasn't going to pass the mantle lightly. She'd liquidate it in her later years rather than give it to someone she couldn't see worthy of its Marine spit and polish. "Anyone could've mistaken you for this Santa thief."

His disgust came across with drama. "Edisto Santa's been doing his thing for twenty years, which makes me far too young."

But seeing Arthur desperate, noting how easily he could be considered the thief, made Callie think of something else. "Call your aunt," she said.

"Hell, no!"

"I can or you can," she said, "but either way she's getting here."

"I'm so dead," he grumbled, punching his phone. Wasn't five minutes before Janet's gold Hummer arrived.

"Chief," was all she said, expecting Callie to brief her accordingly.

The sun was dipping off in the west, and though those living on the Sound would enjoy it, those on Sandpiper and neighboring streets sat in shadows behind blocks of houses and palmettos. Callie tucked away her shades.

The temperature was falling, but the salt air pushed inland by the rollers of an incoming tide stabbed that chill through a person. Christmas lights popped on, a reminder she best hurry to get anything done. She told Thomas to continue his grid search.

Callie would have to take Janet on alone, well aware of the moves she danced with personalities on this beach. She updated Janet on Arthur, but when Janet started chewing out Arthur, Callie stopped her short.

"Put all that on hold, Janet. Answer me. Of all the burgled houses under your control, did anyone call you asking for assistance? A broken faucet, a key not working? Do you keep a log of such incidences?"

Repairs, housekeeping. Any of Janet's people could've had free rein to case these houses. What easier way for someone to gain access . . . or learn when someone would or would not be available?

"On second thought, both burgled and unburgled houses," Callie said. "A list of such calls over the last week."

Janet hesitated, building up steam, but before she could let loose, Callie threw more at her. "Are these houses keyed to a master?"

Janet slung her sunglasses off. "Absolutely not."

Callie kept going. "Who has access to the keys?"

"The office manager who's on vacation, our repair man, and each of our six agents." She snapped her head toward her nephew. "And, of course, Arthur."

"Do they check them out on a log?"

"Of course," Janet cracked back, but behind her, Arthur's expression told otherwise.

"Let me see that log as well," Callie asked anyway. "Any of these employees recent hires?"

Janet launched into a recitation of each name, their job, and how long they'd worked for her. The office manager had two years under her belt, and all but one real estate agent had worked for five or more, with the exception having worked for two and a half. Kudos to the Marine for low turnover, and those enduring Janet's tutelage that long would have pledged allegiance in blood.

"Anyone left in the last year?" Callie asked.

"No," Janet said.

"Wait," Arthur said. "What about Tate Sr.?" Compliments to the nephew for speaking up under duress.

Irritation bubbled up at her nephew's interruption. "He died, boy."

Callie hadn't made the connection about Tate Jr. versus Sr. Having lived on the beach for eighteen months, she'd heard of most everyone, but not necessarily met them all. Someone's handyman wouldn't usually be on her radar, and she wasn't sure she'd remember the Jr. or Sr. on the end.

"So Tate Jr. is a recent hire?" she asked.

"God, no, woman," Janet said. "That kid's worked with us since he was big enough to wield a hammer, and trust me, I wouldn't have hired him full-time when his daddy died if he wasn't trustworthy."

"He's solid," Arthur echoed, as if his validation carried any weight. When Callie got him alone, maybe later tonight since he still struggled with his Aunt Janet's to-do list, she'd delve into Tate's whereabouts.

"Tate drive a brown car?" Callie asked.

Janet's eyes about rolled out of her skinny, white buzz-cut head. "He's a repairman. He drives a pickup."

"And it's white," Arthur added.

The nephew was damn sure eager to please. Her phone rang. *Mark again?* She motioned to Janet then Arthur. "Any of your other employees drive a brown car? Be thinking about that." Then she took the call. "Callie Morgan."

"It's urgent," Mark said, voice hard but low. "I've got Brice over here about to shoot Aberdeen in the middle of my restaurant."

What the hell?

"Be right there," she replied, but then Mark was quick to say, "Don't hang up. I'm keeping the line open so you can hear."

She left Janet and Arthur standing at the Hummer. "Talk later," Callie said, leaping into her patrol car.

Then before she could radio Thomas, he radioed her. "You've probably been too busy to pay attention to social media, Chief, but you need to see Twitter."

"Screw Twitter," she said, cranking the engine. "Meet me at El Marko's. Brice has Aberdeen at gunpoint. Bring Ike and Raysor with you."

"On my way," he said, "but I'll bet my salary and yours that these tweets had a lot to do with where we're going."

But before Callie shifted into drive, Arthur rapped on the window.

She rolled it down. "Can't, Arthur," she said, and laid her foot on the gas.

"None of our employees drives a brown car," Arthur shouted as she left.

Chapter 21

MARK REMAINED on the phone, said he was hidden in the restaurant's kitchen, buying seconds before he made himself known to Brice, currently holding a gun on his wife.

"How many people?" Callie asked, in her cruiser, on her way. Damn if she hadn't underestimated Brice.

"Just Brice, Aberdeen, and me. Staff gone. Back's open for you to funnel in," he said. "Stay in the kitchen unless I call for breach. There are cameras. I'll find a way to lock the front so no innocents wander in. Going back to talk Brice down, but I'll leave this line open for you to hear."

"No, Mark," she ordered, her heart leaping at the man's ridiculous risk. "Just get out of there," but he didn't reply. And she was afraid to holler again for fear of Brice hearing.

"Son of a bitch," she grumbled, speeding up, lights bouncing bright off beach houses on a night with no moon, adding a bolster of blue to the red and green of the season, her siren causing porches to light up behind her.

Thank God for Christmas Eve and the roads being empty. Callie's cruiser sped up Dawhoo Road to Jungle, which gave her a straight shot to El Marko's. Adrenaline sharpened her focus and replaced her sleep-deprived headache.

"Brice, don't shoot me," Mark said next, and Callie's pulse kicked in along with her speed. "I'm not armed. Let's take this down a notch, okay, buddy?"

By moving the attention off Aberdeen, Mark attempted to slow things down, make Brice stop and think long enough to change his mind. At least set down his weapon.

"Talk to me," Mark continued. "Y'all are welcome to sit here and hash things out, but hey, let's put away the weapon."

Callie couldn't hear Brice, but she took it he wasn't cooperating, and a piece of her kept expecting to hear the blast.

One more block. With Aberdeen's high-pitched sobbing in the background, Mark continued explaining about how nothing warranted shooting anyone, and he was willing to listen to Brice's pain and help him through it. All couples hit rough patches.

Brice bellowed for the two to shut up.

Thomas beat Callie to the parking lot, stepping out as she nosed in at the restaurant end of the small strip mall. Phone still on speaker, she opened her door but remained seated, listening hard for Mark's next move.

"Brice, remain calm," he said, "while I lock the front. We can't afford company, don't you agree?"

Mark was doing as he'd said, and damned if he wasn't holding his crap together.

He smoothly kept Brice from escalating an argument. Callie soon recognized through Mark's coded speech roughly where the three were positioned in the dining room. Ike and Raysor had arrived. She leaped out of her cruiser, pulse pumping.

"Everyone wearing a vest?" she asked, shrugging into the one she kept in her trunk. "Thomas, you're with me," she said, taking her phone off speaker. "Brice and Aberdeen think better of you than the rest of us. Ike, you stand to the corner near the front."

The restaurant claimed the end of the strip mall, but due to its concrete block wall, they were hidden at the moment. Around the corner toward the front, however, eight feet of painted, decorated glass stretched across the storefront to the restaurant's entry.

"Raysor, where do you think?" Her most experienced man was more familiar with the logistics of the building than she and the two others put together.

"The outside tiki bar." He nodded to a rough-hewn wooden bar just off the walkway and surrounded by staggered shake planks, usually reserved for summer events. Good concealment for the deputy and shotgun he was so proud of.

Only two other cars in the parking lot and not a soul in terms of foot traffic . . . as though the scene occurred in a bubble ordained by providence. And as Callie and Thomas skirted to the back, Raysor and

Ike assumed their positions in front, and all that could be heard was the breaking waves of an incoming tide.

Weapon drawn, heartbeats uncomfortably filling her ears, Callie found the back door propped open with the head of a mop. She had fleeting protective second thoughts about Thomas . . . and a momentary flashback of Seabrook. Willing them away, she eased the door aside. She and Thomas entered, grateful for the lights being on, and the swinging door to the dining room closed.

She could hear some of their words, meaning they would be able to hear her.

The kitchen wasn't large but packed tightly with equipment and goods. To their far right directly off the kitchen was an office, and if her memory served, the bathroom sat tucked between the office and the dining room, its entrance near the end of the bar.

Mark had mentioned cameras.

"Check the office for a monitor," she whispered, able to hear a muffled Mark. She shut off the phone.

Thomas moved quick and with stealth, another reason she chose the younger officer, and as he disappeared, she maneuvered toward the swinging door.

"You need a refill, Brice?" Mark was saying. "And Aberdeen, drink more of your tea. It'll make you feel better."

"Who gives a shit if she feels better," Brice said, as thick a venom in his voice as Callie'd ever heard, and she immediately suspected he'd had a few before building the courage to pack a gun. "Are you aware what you did to me?" Yelling, no doubt at Aberdeen.

With blubbering snuffles she said, "But I loved him."

Not exactly the thing to say to the armed husband you cheated on.

Brice exploded. "You selfish whore!"

Mark's baritone voice rose in a crescendo. "Whoa, Brice. Let's tone it back down."

Aberdeen continued to wail from what sounded like a seat at the table Mark had used twice with Callie. The owner's table, which would put it through the swinging door to Callie's immediate left.

"Shhh," Mark said. "Come on, Aberdeen. Hush and let me talk to Brice. Just a chat between him and me, right Brice?"

Only a grunt from the husband.

"Tell you what," Mark added. "How about a beer, fella'? I'll have one with you. On the house."

"Quit conning me," Brice said, but he didn't decline the offer. Mark was making headway.

Thomas tapped on Callie's shoulder then motioned back toward the office, mouthing *cameras*.

Slipping the ten-foot distance, they entered the office, Thomas pivoting the computer screen.

Four camera views. Two exterior and two interior.

The exterior cams covered the exits, panned strategically and smart. Inside, one hung in the corner at the entrance, the other in the back corner on the same side, the two of them providing complete coverage of every table and the bar . . . and the three stars of the show.

As Callie suspected, Aberdeen huddled in a chair at Mark's special table. Mark sat at the bar, on a stool nearest the kitchen, probably putting him no more than six or seven feet from her and slightly to the right.

Brice continued to pace. From between Mark and Aberdeen toward a space about ten feet into the room, stopping most often at the farthest spot, he kept his wife and Mark in clear view.

Callie motioned for Thomas to follow her back to the kitchen entrance.

"You never said what was wrong," Mark said. "Maybe I can help. As an unbiased third-party."

"How the hell can you help?" Brice argued. "You don't have a damn clue about me." He must've waved the gun because Aberdeen squealed and Mark asked him to be careful with it.

"I'm a man," Mark said. "I've been married, and I've been cheated on. Plus, everyone confides in their bartender." Silence. "So," he continued. "What did she do?"

"What *didn't* she do?" Brice hammered those words. "She chewed up my reputation before the whole God-damned world on social media." He tried to recite some posts from memory, choking with tears after three.

Thomas held his phone in front of Callie showing a string of tweets on Aberdeen's Twitter account.

My SOB husband killed Ben Rosewood, and he's getting away with it.

The love of my life is dead thanks to my alcoholic, spendthrift, demeaning, condescending, abusive bastard of a husband named Brice LeGrand.

My husband drank away all our money and when I tried to leave him, he shot my best friend.

Brice LeGrand's daddy and granddaddy would roll in their graves at what a cheap, lush of a moron their offspring turned out to be.

Your town councilman, Brice LeGrand, has cheated me out of my life's savings. Who says he hasn't done the same to the Edisto Beach coffers?

The list was endless, as if Aberdeen went on a binge wording and rewording tweets over the course of hours, filling the Twitterverse with derogatory messages about her husband from every angle she could. Callie quit reading at ten tweets. The Twitterverse snagged them and ran, however, because the posts had been retweeted repeatedly, comments added. Some for Brice, some against, some just marveling at how two people would shamelessly post their marital strife.

"Brice." Mark sounded empathetic as Brice's emotions started to get the best of him. "Anyone will see this as just Aberdeen going nuts over the loss of a friend. I don't believe all this, why would they?"

Callie heard Brice's pacing recommence, his voice getting louder as he came toward her, then softer as he moved away. "She painted me the fool," he said. "Town council will impeach me, then what have I got left?"

"Hey, hold still," Mark commanded.

Brice's steps stopped.

Good job, Mark. No longer a moving target.

"You're an icon on this beach," he said. "Don't discount these people, and don't discount yourself. If you get killed over this, she wins. If you kill her, you lose. See what I mean? Put the gun down on the bar."

"No," Brice answered. "Quit telling me what to do with my gun!"

"Okay, okay." Mark's voice carried more wary. "At least stop waving it around."

Callie signaled to Thomas how to position himself and where she'd be. On her count, they'd roll through and into the room.

Mark remained on the bar stool, his voice stable. No doubt he'd done this before. "I suspect the police are outside. Can't have them shooting us, can we?"

Brice laughed, and Thomas frowned at Callie. She shook her head at him to ignore chatter aimed at defusing the situation by encouraging Brice to think about something other than Aberdeen and that damned gun.

"What cops?" Brice asked through a derisive grunt of humor. "Callie Morgan? Little Thomas? That fat idiot Raysor?"

Thomas frowned a second time, Callie again shaking her head for him to get over the insults of a deranged man who'd lost most if not all of his self-respect.

"Don't underestimate trained officers," Mark warned. "What do you say? Can we put that weapon down? Can't have SWAT pouring in here and tearing up my place, and we don't want to read your name in the obituaries of the *Post and Courier*."

Callie was counting down to enter when Brice started up again. "I didn't kill him. I really didn't. He was my closest friend."

Yeah, but his closest friend had stolen the world from him. How could anyone not want to kill after that? She was geared up, pumped to pour into the scene, praying to God she didn't have to empty her weapon into one of Edisto Island's family legacies.

"Can I get that beer now?" Brice asked.

"Sure," Mark replied. "I'll join you with one. How about a draft? Dos Equis all right?"

Callie let out a slow deep exhale and took it back in, trying to find a rhythm. What was Mark about to do?

His form moved past the inch-wide opening, and steps told Callie he'd moved behind the bar. The gush of the first beer sounded, then the thump as he served it. Callie held her breath, realizing that at Mark's beckoning, Brice would come seriously close to her, and become easier to disarm. She heard the second draft gurgle up in the glass, then a heavy clunk.

Brice sighed, apparently having taken a long draw on the draft. "God, I needed that."

They were really sharing beers?

But then Mark said, "How about I take this? Good." and Callie took the cue.

She and Thomas rolled through and into the room, her to the left and Thomas to the right, smooth and quiet, weapons drawn. "Stay where you are, Brice. Hands up."

Brice's beer sloshed as he deliberated what to do with gun sights beading down on him. Thrusting his mug onto the bar, he raised shaking hands. "I didn't mean it," he said in a panic.

Whether he didn't mean what he said about her and her officers or his intentions toward Aberdeen, Callie didn't care. Brice's gun rested in Mark's possession.

"We're all good here, guys," Mark said, sucking down a third of his beer. Yeah, she'd do the same after that kind of show-down.

The restaurateur was receiving quite the indoctrination to Edisto Beach. He'd been tested hard and aced the challenge . . . but he could've just as easily wound up dead.

If he'd wanted to remain a cop he should've kept the badge with SLED.

Brice reached for his beer. "I'm finishing this, and don't you try and stop me."

"Whatever," she said, holstering her weapon. "You packing any other guns? Knives?"

He sneered, like she had no right to even think the thought, making her yell at him all the harder. "Hold your arms out," she said, and she patted him down.

"Don't touch me," he ordered, dancing and dodging some of her touches.

Finding nothing, she spun him back around. "Sit on that stool right there and don't move."

"What if I—"

"Don't you frickin' move, Brice!" she ordered, then motioned for Thomas. "Radio the all-clear to Raysor and Ike then go sit with Aberdeen. See if you can settle her down." She peered around at Mark. "Can you unlock the front?"

Mark did a fast walk to let Ike and Raysor in, but as he passed Callie on the way back, she took his sleeve and leaned in. "What the hell were you thinking, Mark? He could've shot you just as easily as he took your beer, you realize that? *Jesus.*"

"Wasn't going to happen," he said, moving so she had to turn loose. "Come here," he said, and went behind the bar to withdraw a Sig Sauer P220 from underneath, just far enough for her to see.

"Oh, that makes me feel so much better," she said, shaking her head and going back to business.

About eight feet to Callie's left, Aberdeen sat like a soppy mess, a pile of tear-drenched napkins piled before her, and her tears had begun to seep anew as Thomas pulled his chair closer to try harder at stemming the flow.

Callie eyed Brice polishing off his brew to her right. "Stupid move, Brice."

He shrugged and tipped the mug for a finish, no longer angry . . . which angered her to hell and back. As hard as she'd tried to find an alternative to Brice LeGrand killing Ben Rosewood, as many times as she'd told Mark, Stan, Marie, and Thomas about how Brice couldn't possibly have done it, the son of a bitch holds his wife and a business owner hostage at gunpoint.

He set the empty down, licked his lip, then caught her glare. "What?"

"Raysor?" she called, waving him over. "Cuff him."

Brice's eyes stretched wide as saucers. "Nothing happened." He gestured at Mark. "Thanks to this guy I saw how stupid this was. And the beer . . . " He tapped the mug and sneered in appreciation.

Oh good Lord. "Raysor, since you'd head home to Walterboro anyway, he's yours. Am I ruining your Christmas Eve?"

He gave her a no-nonsense grimace. "I'd have just drunk too much eggnog. Planned to go to dinner at my aunt's around two tomorrow, so, nah, I'm good." He sneered at Brice. "Besides, this is about the best Christmas present you could've given me, Chief," he said, cuffs out in plain sight. He made a spin-around motion with two fingers, and with panic in Brice's eyes, he obliged while the deputy read him his rights.

Aberdeen's whimpers escalated seeing Brice in cuffs, and when Thomas tried to console her, she threw herself across the table, wailing and beating the surface with fists. Thomas leaped up, eyes pleading at Callie for an answer.

She mouthed *keep trying*, and he sat back down, easing Aberdeen to back off the table and into her chair. "Come on, Ms. LeGrand. Don't act like this. Can I get you some water?"

It was after eight o'clock, and what should've been a tranquil, family-oriented night on the beach had deteriorated into a damn three-ring circus. Callie ordered Ike to the streets, the officer on call for the night.

When he'd gone, she studied Aberdeen. Her cheeks blotched red and puffed up beyond recognition, Aberdeen sucked in erratic breaths like a child who'd cried themselves sick. Speaking in jabbering phrases, more mumble than talk, she made no sense.

Thomas came over to Callie, whispering. "We can't send her home like this," he said. "She's like . . . snapped."

"Is her purse with her?" Callie asked.

"Yeah, on the floor," he said.

"Then you have identification. Take her to Roper Hospital and put her on a psych hold."

He gave a glance over at Aberdeen. "Gonna be a long night, huh?"

"For all of us, Thomas, so you better get a move on. Call me if necessary. I'll see if LaRoache can watch the beach tomorrow."

"He has kids, Chief."

She motioned him toward Aberdeen. "And I suspect they're used to him getting called out. Go on. The night's not getting any younger."

Thomas departed with Aberdeen to the hospital in Charleston leaving Callie to walk out with Mark.

"Where's your car?" she asked, scanning the parking lot as he locked up the restaurant.

"I walked," he said. "My house is just over on Lily Street."

Two cars remained in the lot. One Aberdeen's white BMW. The other a dated Buick. She'd forgotten Brice LeGrand's car was brown.

With Brice tucked into his back seat, Raysor started to leave.

"Raysor," she shouted over at him. "Change of plans. Take Brice to the station. Afraid you've got to stick around, too."

Chapter 22

THE GOVERNMENT facility was quiet as a tomb when Callie flipped the switch and waited as the fluorescents popped on before leading the three of them to her office in the back. Then as in numerous instances in the past, burly Deputy Raysor parked his broad body in the corner chair of Callie's office, leaving Brice to sit directly across from Callie's desk. One of his sleeve cuffs on his flannel shirt had come undone, his collar askew. His comb-over having lost its way, he appeared balder than normal.

Jeb had texted her. *You all right?*

Then Stan. *Mark's over here. Everything okay?*

Sophie. *You'd think they'd leave you alone for Christmas. You coming over?*

Then Sarah. *When tomorrow? Not sure I ought to be doing Christmas on the heels of Ben's death.*

Other texts from two council women, inquiring on rumors about Brice.

And all of them could wait except Jeb, whom she answered only with a brief, *I'm fine.*

Weary, she laid out her recorder, read in the date, time, and bodies present, then stated, "I'm reminding you that we read you your rights." A notepad sat before her for scribbling thoughts as they went.

But Brice's first words were simply, "Damn, you really think I killed Ben."

"It's about the evidence," she said. "You talking to us or not?"

"I didn't do anything, so ask me your stupid questions," he said.

She slid a paper in front of him. "Sign this waiver first."

Too bad Ben was dead. He'd advise him otherwise.

With a script and an embellished underline he slid the form back around and pushed it at her. "There. Ask away."

Raysor's expression bordered cartoonish. Callie could almost read his mind, the words along the line of idiot, moron, short-sighted . . . and so on.

Surprisingly, Brice still had spunk in him, believing himself innocent because nobody got shot. "What am I being charged with? And you better have your ducks in a row, Chief, because I'll not only have your badge but own your house before it's all over."

Mouth open at Brice's gall, Raysor inhaled to bust out laughing, and Callie eyed him to stop. "I better get this right," she said. "Two counts of attempted murder to start."

His cheeks darkening, Brice started out of his chair. "I didn't try to murder anyone."

Raysor reached over and plopped him back onto the seat. "Stay put," he ordered. "Let her finish."

She continued. "Kidnapping, two counts. Aggravated assault. Possession of a firearm in the commission of a felony."

"What felony?" Brice bellowed.

How much more pitiful could this man get? "Felonies, plural. The attempted murder and kidnapping. There's also brandishing a firearm, disturbing the peace . . . on Christmas, no less." She took a pull on her water. "You didn't hit Aberdeen did you? Because if you did, we can add battery."

Brice got quiet.

Callie read that as a positive. "So I can add that, too, huh? Easy enough to confirm through Aberdeen, I'd think."

"No," he replied, then threw it at her again. "No! Of course I didn't hit her. I don't hit women." He watched for Callie's response, and she gave him none to see if he'd say more.

"I'd never hit a woman," he repeated, trailing off.

"And finally," she said, "there's the simple fact you f'ed up my holiday. You're spending Christmas in the Colleton County jail. Do you realize that?"

"You're lucky," Raysor added. That jail was in his neck of the woods, the uniforms his buddies. "They do up a pretty decent turkey dinner on Christmas."

But Brice still reverted to his old self. "You're just piling things on for the fun of it."

"No, I'm really not, Brice. This is not fun. I've gotta say, when you screw up, you go all the way," she said.

"I bet you're happy having your archnemesis cornered."

Raysor spit out a clipped laugh. Callie eyed him again.

Brice LeGrand had been the thorn in the PD's side ever since Seabrook died. A fair-haired Edisto favorite son, Mike Seabrook had maintained order on the beach in a gentile manner and hadn't even wanted to be chief. He charmed tourists and natives alike, to include Brice. He'd been the force in charming Callie to step to the plate and take the job.

Brice had oozed bastard ever since Callie'd accepted that badge. She'd yet to convince him and others that she had earned the badge, her position as chief. Seabrook had been better than she was in some ways, and she'd proven herself better in others, but her experience qualified her tenfold over the last three chiefs combined. However, it was up to her to prove her worth with actions, not argue with the Brices on the beach.

"Without a doubt you're a pain in my ass," she said, "but you're not quite the badass everyone thinks you are. You love Edisto. Work with me. Let's see if we can lighten that load I just gave you."

"Why should I talk to someone who'd love to see me go down?"

Admittedly, she'd thought of life without Brice too many instances to count. "I'm not out to get you, okay? But you've painted yourself in a corner with your theatrics and threats. We can stop, and Raysor can take you to jail. Or we can work on your facts. Let's start with the afternoon you went to Ben Rosewood's house. When was it?"

"Two thirty in the afternoon," he said with a pout, cheeks holding a blotchy redness. "I told you that."

"And you'll say it a lot more before you see the other side of this mess."

That was the timeframe Sophie said she saw Brice leave. Callie rubbed irritated eyes, feeling like sand had found its way in one of them. Her adrenaline had come down since the restaurant, and with it her energy. "Ben let you in. Take it from there."

She blinked hard. Raysor got up and left the room.

Brice managed to replay that afternoon's events in a way very much similar to his first recitation of the details. "When I found out the gift was for Aberdeen, and he'd been sleeping with her—"

"You didn't say they'd slept together when we first spoke about this."

He sat back, brows touching in the middle. "Jesus Christ, woman, what the hell do you think they were doing, holding hands?"

"How do you know they slept together?" she asked.

"Because she told me, damnit."

"But you said that afternoon, over scotches with Ben, you learned only then that he liked your wife. Sounds to me you knew before. Did Aberdeen tell you before your meeting with Ben?"

His head bobbled, dumbfounded. "What does it matter?"

Just goes to motive, Brice. She gave him a subtle wave. "Keep going. Tell your story."

Raysor reappeared and delivered each of them a water.

"Yeah," Brice said, twisting the cap, staring at the front of her desk in remembrance. "I went toward the gift bag, seeing it was from Xavier's, the jeweler I'd recommended. He asked me not to touch it, which triggered my suspicion. That's how we got into the discussion about Aberdeen. Then I left."

"Right," she said, taking a big swig of the water, wishing for almost all she was worth it was gin. Instinctively she glanced at her bottom drawer, where she hid a bottle for difficult days. She'd meant to dispose of it . . . and sort of hadn't gotten around to it.

Raysor leaned to see around Brice and make a connection with her. He was the only other person aware of what was in that drawer.

She massaged her right temple. A headache had started behind her eyes at El Marko's. Now her brain felt shrink-wrapped, fighting to explode free. She also had officers working overtime and her son home for Christmas. Homes had been violated and natives disappointed because she'd tarnished their holiday legend. She was double-axle loaded down with responsibility, her limbs almost limp with fatigue, but this was the job.

She had to handle Brice. She had a suspicion she needed confirmed. She might not be Seabrook, but she hadn't yet failed to come around in her duty to protect these people . . . to salvage their belief that Edisto was nirvana and nothing serious ever happened without her cleaning it up and leaving no residue.

Raysor spoke up. "Chief?"

"Let's go back to the Xavier's bag on the mantel," she said, her gaze on Brice. "You say you never touched it?"

"I never touched it."

She squinted as much to focus as to express her doubt. "Do you want to rethink that?"

"No."

She opened a non-gin drawer and lifted out the jewelry store bag. Methodically, she extracted the velvet box. With a deft touch, she stretched the bracelet across the desk directly in front of Brice, making all the charms lay out even.

"You recovered it," he said.

"It was never reported stolen," she said. "I didn't know this bracelet existed until you told me."

"How did you . . . how do you . . . " but he trailed off.

She leaned elbows on her desk and studied him hard enough to make him flinch.

"How can you tell it was a bracelet from Ben to Aberdeen?" Stiffening, he inhaled hard, nastily, then sniffed again. "What if it was a present from me to my wife?"

Gingerly Callie flipped over the engraved charm so that *Abby* appeared. Then she lightly flicked the Eiffel Tower. "Care to show me your plane tickets?"

He blanched, the obvious clear. All Callie had to do was ask Aberdeen who she had planned to boat down the Seine with.

"Let's clean up your story, Brice. You opened the bag anyway," she said. "Maybe with Ben attempting to take it from you."

But Brice shook his head. "No. That's not how it happened." He spoke low, beaten, and paused before explaining. "He let me see it. It was easier for him to just let me see the proof than tell me. He was a coward."

"Then what?"

"I decided to walk out with it," he said. "Ben started to rush me, but when I stared the son of a bitch down he hesitated. I left. He yelled at me from the porch. End of story." His attention remained glued to the bracelet.

"No, that wasn't the end of the story at all, Brice. I found where you disposed of the bracelet . . . whose house you dropped it off at. You didn't leave there fast enough, though. They caught the back of you getting into your brown sedan."

She scooped up the bracelet, repositioned it in its box, and dropped it into the bag that went back into her drawer. His eyes remain fixed on it until it disappeared.

"And we just added felony theft and obstruction of an investigation to your already long list of offenses. Why'd you take it?" she asked.

"Embarrassed. Hurt. Just a flash of a thought." Was that a tremor in his hands?

She scratched a brow. "Another issue. Where'd you park your car? It wasn't at Ben's that day. I have a witness."

His cursing began with broken emotion but grew quickly into fury. "Then you already know," he said, spittle flying. "You pride yourself on knowing everything."

"Cool your ass down," Raysor commanded.

Callie flashed a thank-you to the deputy. "For the recording, Brice. It goes better for you if you cooperate and say it. Where did you park?"

"The lot."

She almost couldn't hear him, so she asked him to repeat.

"The goddamn lot," he yelled. "The one Aberdeen tried to clear."

"Where they found Ben?"

He nodded first. "Yes. But you have to listen to me, Callie. I parked there so Aberdeen wouldn't spot my car. When I left Ben's, I walked, with the bracelet. Like I said, he yelled at me from the porch, a scotch still in his grip, mind you. Call it friendship or him deciding I wasn't worth his trouble, but he let me go. Next thing, it's the following day, I'm at your birthday party, and you get a call about a body. Wasn't till then I learned he'd died, and I have no damn clue how he got there, what happened, or who did it. But it damn sure wasn't me."

The more he spoke the guiltier he sounded. She almost pitied him in spite of the crap he'd doled out over the last couple of years, regardless the crap he'd tried to sabotage her career. No, she *did* pity him. He'd gotten swept up in a love triangle like some acned high school kid and let it get the best of him. No thinking whatsoever, except . . . "Why'd you pretend to be Edisto Santa and dispose of the bracelet?" she asked. Probably his most implicating behavior of all.

But to that he wouldn't answer.

Raysor used his own interrogation voice. "She asked you a question. Answer it."

Brice shook his head.

"Answer," the deputy ordered again.

Callie held up her hand. "That's okay, Don. I'll say it. Once Ben was found dead, he feared that piece of jewelry would place him at the residence and make us believe he killed him. That right, Brice?"

Wilted, his belly protruding below the length of his quilted vest, he slunk deeper into his seat, lost in the details of the carpet. His water bottle rested loose in his fingers.

"Is that right, Brice?"

He nodded.

"For clarity, let the recording show that Mr. LeGrand nodded in the affirmative," she said.

It bothered her when he didn't move, afraid he'd done an Aberdeen spiral in his own way, but he had to have a chance to say whatever he felt could clear him. At least help the situation go better for him. "Care to add anything else?" she asked.

"I swear I didn't kill him," he mumbled.

"The coroner says he wasn't killed instantly, Brice. Somehow, he hit his head on the coat rack in the entry hall. Death came later, after his brain bled. You might not have realized you did it."

"Damn you all," he cried, eyes reddening with real tears. "Are you not listening to me? I never touched him. Maybe if I'd stayed, he'd still be alive. Maybe if I hadn't been such a child, I wouldn't have taken that bracelet and left him to whatever happened."

He wiped the moisture away and let loose a sob he'd fought to contain. "My biggest concern was Ben having his hands all in my finances and helping Aberdeen take them. I'd already lost her. She wasn't the issue."

Callie listened. He was headed somewhere, covering ground they hadn't before.

"I always use attorneys to fight my fights." He held his arms wide, the bottle tremoring some. "Do I look like a physical person? The day we . . . after I left his house, I moved my money and found another attorney. Doesn't that tell you I still thought he was alive?"

Not really. "Anyone see you in the car? On the street? Speak to you?"

"No."

She drew upon Sophie's attention to details. "Not even a jogger?" Callie asked.

His eyes moved to the side as he thought, then down, then widened. "Yeah, on Jungle Road before I got to the corner of my lot." He livened up, desperate. "Have you interviewed him? Did he see me? Please say he did, Callie. He might've seen Ben, too."

He sounded desperate, especially using her given name.

"Maybe," she said, feeling only the slightest guilt at leading him on. "Black guy in a dark blue hoodie?"

"No," he said, worried his ray of hope was dashed. "White man in a light gray hoodie."

He *had* seen the jogger. "Red and white shoes?" she asked.

"No, no," he said, inching to the front of his seat. "Gray. He was, like, all gray."

"He speak to you?" she asked, hoping hard for more.

He shook his head, then in afterthought that he was being recorded, said, "No."

"Are you Edisto Santa?"

The abrupt shift stumped him. "What?"

"Are you Edisto Santa?" she repeated.

"No," he replied, lifting the word up on the end, like she was insane to ask.

"Did you beat up Wesley for talking about Edisto Santa?"

"What? No!"

"Do you know who Edisto Santa is?" she asked.

Blank and thunderstruck, he couldn't seem to make sense of her questioning. She let him think a second. "Brice?"

"He's a rumor. Somebody does it every year, like the Edisto mystery tree."

The mystery tree stuck up out of the marsh across 174 and down from the Botany Bay road entrance, decorated for every season with zany trinkets, blowups, hats and beads for years with no clear origin or idea of who maintained it. And nobody cared to expose the soul who did. Again, island tradition.

Suddenly eager to dig out of his hole he added, "I heard Edisto Santa was a rich guy. Someone living on the North Edisto River side. Others say Janet Wainwright."

Back in his corner, Raysor shook his head.

"But she'd tell everyone if it was her," Callie said.

"Yeah," Brice conceded. "She even probably *started* that rumor, but then she's never denied it either."

"Anything else on your mind?" she asked.

He shook his head.

She stopped the recording with the appropriate verbiage. "Then he's all yours, Deputy Raysor. Merry Christmas."

Brice stood. "You're really doing this?"

"No," Raysor said, freed with the recorder off. "You did this all by yourself, Brice. Stand up. Edisto Santa didn't take *these* bracelets." He brought out the cuffs.

She locked up the recorder and motioned for Raysor to take Brice out first. At the station door, Raysor paused a second, a slight tug on Brice's cuffs. "You coming?" the deputy asked her.

"Got to check something before I go. Won't take me ten minutes, tops, but I'll walk you out."

"You haven't even asked about Aberdeen," she said to Brice, their footsteps muted on the damp concrete walk toward Raysor's car.

Brice lumbered, stumbling once. "Why should I?"

Raysor put a hand on Brice's head, assisting him into the cruiser's back seat.

But he only stared ahead, as most criminals do when secured and confined to ride to jail.

She watched them drive off, unable to shake the feeling that Edisto Beach was about to change, maybe lose some of its fairy-tale glitter. There'd be enough blame spread around, because if this beach did anything right it was to give gossip a voice, and Brice had fed the beast enough to fuel whispers well into next summer.

Her phone had vibrated in her pocket throughout the interview, texts exploding across the screen like the headache hammering her skull. On her way back inside, she scrolled through the names. *Still fine*, she typed to Jeb. *Tell everyone else so they quit texting. Might be after midnight before you see me.*

Phone off and in her pocket. Inside, she settled at the closest computer and logged in, going through several files before locating reported burglaries for last December, and the two Decembers before that. Just as Marie said, this year's burglaries exceeded the last three years combined.

Callie rummaged around Marie's desk until she found the printed spreadsheet of the gifts. Twenty-one at last count. Marie hadn't noted the years received on all of them, since it hadn't become evident at first that these people were surrendering more than this year's Edisto Santa deliveries.

Burglaries on the screen . . . gifts on the sheet. And not a single stolen item from the last three years matched a return. So why had that changed? What was the catalyst that turned Edisto Santa from Samaritan to thief?

She shut it all down, shut off the lights, unplugged the blue wreath, and locked the station. With the station dark, another lit wreath suddenly shined more vividly over at the fire station. Her night wasn't over by a long shot. A comment here, an interview there. People who had no idea that what they said linked to someone else's words or deeds.

She headed out to see someone, and she didn't care whether it was Christmas or not.

Chapter 23

JUST AS CALLIE backed out of her Chief of EPD parking slot, Stan called. She threw the cruiser into park. He would be worried as much or more than Jeb about her late night absence, only Stan would envision all sorts of incidents that Jeb could not imagine.

"Jeb called me," he said. "Kid's anxious about his mom."

He would be. Way more than most sons. "Assure him for me, Stan."

Stan's grumbly gust of an exhale meant he'd been worried, too.

"I'm about to meet someone," she said. "Or tail then meet them. Depends." She wouldn't give him the chance to say she shouldn't be surveilling solo. "You interested in coming along for a ride?"

She had three officers already in three directions; one escorting Brice to jail, another carting Aberdeen to the psych ward, and Ike watching the beach. Her other officers were home with kids, at least one of them being yanked off his leave to cover tomorrow. She wasn't about to drag them out tonight, too. Stan hadn't been retired much over a year from the Boston PD. He had skills she could still trust.

"Wish I could," he said. "Already had more than a couple holiday spirits, so to speak."

And probably still imbibed since he wasn't smacking his usual cinnamon gum. "You drinking alone?" she asked.

His gravelly chuckle slid out far too loose for him to be sober. Yep, he'd had a few.

"Nope. Got my favorite bartender over here, filling me in on the action at El Marko's. Brice. Ha. Who'd have guessed he'd fall so far and so hard."

"We can catch up later, boss. Go back to your party. It's late and I have miles to go before I sleep."

His voice went down an octave. "You missed sleep last night, and you're pulling another all-nighter? Not safe, Chicklet. Tell you what—" He spoke aside from the phone. "You wanna take a ride with Callie on a surveillance?"

She inhaled sharply. "No, no, Stan. Not necessary—"

"Sure," Mark said in the background.

Stan came back. "Okay, it's settled. You can pick him up at my place. How long?"

"I'm just leaving the station," she said, not up to the argument.

The streets were pitch, half the holiday lights unplugged as people bedded down awaiting Santa. She reached Stan's house on Pompano in under three minutes. Mark waited on the street. Stan stood on his high-rise deck, waving down like a parent seeing kids off on a date.

Damn him.

At least her date could supposedly shoot.

"What's the plan?" Mark said, buckling in.

She waited before leaving, noting the piece on his belt under the shirttail he'd probably untucked once he got all social with Stan. "You don't have to come," she said, giving him the chance to opt out. "I'm in a hurry, so make it quick."

He waved toward the road. "I'm game."

She rubbed an eye, blinked wide to regain vision. "Onward then."

But before she shifted into gear, he touched her forearm, shooting a surge of something she couldn't read through her. "Let me drive?" he asked. "You seem awful beat."

"Not driving my patrol car," she said and eased away from Stan's, her head throbbing.

"Where we going? Didn't exactly bring along a vest," he joked, which made her realize she still wore hers. Vests were a sensitive topic to her after Seabrook's death, him having refused to make the effort to retrieve his, too excited about the fateful tip that got him killed. Her guys sensed it, too, and they felt the chill of her gaze when hot summer days tempted comfort over safety.

"Hopefully to see Edisto Santa," she said, almost to Palmetto Boulevard, hoping Arthur still hopped to Janet's orders, checking security on rentals.

"Oh? Got a name for him?"

"Have a starting point," she replied, cruising the speed limit, headed toward the main beach stretch. No shadows with a moonless night, after eleven, and she hoped Stan had called Jeb and settled him enough to finally go to bed and dream about reindeer.

She was reaching with this half-cobbled semblance of a plan, but she had to pursue it if for no other goal than to check her suspicion off the list. "Keep your eyes peeled open for a blue, two-door Ford Ranger. Four years old," she said. "South Carolina license EBEACH2."

So many shadows of clues and half-truths floated in her fuzzy brain . . . from Sophie, Wesley, Brice, Marie, even Janet. Practically everyone she'd spoken to in the last three days supplied a piece of intel on Edisto Santa, with none of them able to relay the full tale. Edisto Santa was a quasi-legend, unfounded, never seen, but he'd crossed a line this year. The benevolent native, which she'd decided he had to be, had altered his course or been forced to change his ways. Too broke himself to keep going, maybe? Angry at some unfairness in his or someone else's life? She sensed a desperation in this person, which might be why the break-ins weren't consistent . . . straying from the pattern of the first day's burglaries. But why?

Starting where she left Janet a few hours ago, Callie cruised the streets, scouting for the pick-up. "On the right. That it?" Mark asked, noting a sport truck parked at a Palmetto Boulevard house.

"Sure is," she said, continuing past then taking the next street. She came back out and parked beneath a vacant house on the beachfront, four houses away. She shut off her lights.

"Be quiet while I make this call," she told Mark, who made no move.

She put the phone on speaker. "Arthur? Chief Morgan."

With a hint of breathlessness Arthur replied. "What's wrong? My aunt okay?"

"She's fine. I called to apologize for running off on you like I did earlier. Got hauled away to some domestic thing, but still, was a pretty ugly move calling your aunt out like I did then leaving you to weather her wrath. She didn't go all hurricane on you, did she?"

"Ha," he said, laughing. "She stays in Category Four mode regardless."

Callie laughed back. "She's a trip, that's for sure."

Mark sat still, elbow on the armrest, rubbing slowly over a chin that carried a solid five-o'clock shadow.

"I'm at the station, and with Jeb and a few others in town, thought you could use help checking the rest of your houses," she said. "They're rowdy and awake and I thought I'd give them to you to keep busy. What do you say?"

"Um, that's awful nice of you, Chief, but I've about got this."

"Hmm, well, to be truthful, I needed them out of my way for some quiet time to sort out a few new leads today about the burglaries."

Callie cut a glance at Mark, who patiently listened. Arthur didn't say anything.

"You still there? Arthur?"

"Yes, ma'am, still here. Wasn't sure I caught that last part. There were more burglaries?" The lights went out at the house where he was parked.

"Oh, sorry," she said. "No. No more burglaries. Some folks gave me a few leads on Edisto Santa though. It could involve more of your properties, but we have a sense of who he is."

"He?" he asked.

"Yeah, we're sure of that much," she replied. "But Janet'll go all ballistic on us for getting her up, and since I'm talking to you, you might help me sift through these notices. Plus you're familiar with your aunt's staff. She'd be more inclined to protect them."

"You think it's one of our people?" he asked, incredulous. "Unh, unh. I'm not going behind her back, Chief. She'd eat me alive." Arthur locked the house's door.

"I'll tell her I dragged you in, if you like," she continued. "We can meet at the station since you stay with her. Plus, someone might report her office lights going on without her Hummer there if we met there. See you at mine in, say, ten minutes?" she said.

"I'm awful beat," he said. "Can't it wait until the day after Christmas?"

She sighed into the phone. "All right, Arthur. I'll be straight with you. Tomorrow I expect to be picking up Edisto Santa. Not my favorite holiday happening, but crime takes no holiday. Would like your confirmation about a few details, though. We can't afford for him to catch wind that we're onto him then boogie off the island."

Arthur's car lights went on. "Well, to be frank, I already ditched Aunt Janet's assignment, and I'm halfway to Charleston, headed to catch the end of my roommate's party at the college. Just crossed the Ashley River," he said.

He backed out into Palmetto Boulevard and nosed his Jeep in the direction of the beach's town limits. Callie gave him a second to drive past her and move a few houses down before cranking up her vehicle.

"Guess you'll have to read about it in the papers after Christmas," she said.

"Sorry," he said. "I'd help if I were there, but you see how it is."

"Oh yeah." She drove onto the road. "Have fun, but be safe."

"Merry Christmas, Chief," he said.

"Merry Christmas, Arthur."

The Jeep crossed Scott Creek, accelerating. Letting him get some distance, allowing a car between them, she then sped up, lights back on.

"Not sure I would've guessed him," Mark said, watching the taillights ahead.

Callie kept the Jeep just in view. "Not sure it is him. But there's the issue of picked locks and a gray hoodie that tell me Arthur knows more than he lets on."

"Not to mention he just lied his butt off to you," Mark said.

"Yes." She nodded, eyes steady on the car a dozen lengths ahead. "There is that."

They drove five miles, then another couple. Past Zion Church, then First Baptist. The island amply represented Christianity, and on this, the night most holy, services ran into the wee hours. Some services had broken up, leaving buildings stark and empty, some still entertained stragglers sharing holiday wishes on the steps before heading home. But in between, the curving road ran black, mysterious, with every bit the shadowy, secretive disposition of Edisto Island.

"Maybe Arthur meant it when he said he had a party in Charleston," Mark said, then added, "Damn, it's dark."

Callie's heart pumped a bit faster. "You could get lost out here, for sure," she said, only making conversation. Past Jane Edwards School up ahead stood the Presbyterian Church where Seabrook lay at rest. For a very long second, her gaze fixed on the spot she knew by heart before they passed it by.

"What?" Mark asked, trying to see what she did. "You think he went in there?"

"No," she replied. "Just remembering somebody buried there. Sorry. Tired, I guess."

"Hey, why not let me—" but he stopped when Callie slowed, redirecting his attention to the road ahead.

She eased into the closed Edisto EZ Shop parking lot in front of the gas pumps but left the motor running. "He took Maxie Road. Give him a second."

"Is there a way for him to slip out without us seeing him?"

She didn't immediately answer, but instead slowly drove back onto the road, not accelerating. "Only if he goes all the way down and circles back up Cedar Hall." She passed the Maxie entrance and went right onto Cedar Hall Road.

There weren't many houses on either of the two roads, jungle dominant on both sides, the landscape dense. An occasional trailer peered out from cleared pockets as they crept north, toward the tributaries off Russell Creek, cheap wreaths on the outside of the homes and meager trees propped in narrow windows.

At the t-bone spot where Maxie came into Cedar Hall from their right, she hesitated. Then she kept moving forward.

"You sure?" he asked.

"Not really," she said, "but I believe I've heard of most the folks on Maxie. Just call it my gut."

Then headlights off, a tiny breath hitch of surprise from Mark, she crept forward.

"There," he said, just as she spotted taillights. The lights went out. The rear-end of that Ranger pickup was too coincidental to not be Arthur's. The edges of Edisto roads consisted of wet bogs or silty patches, either of which sucked vehicles into surrender, so Callie parked where she was, shutting down quickly. The desolation on these roads made car engines discernible. Midnight on these roads made them downright noisy.

They sat together in the containment of the car, chilly with the windows down. She even tried hearing Mark breathe, to read him, and not hearing him, she glanced over at his silhouette. He seemed steady, patient.

"Let's go," she said, putting her phone on mute.

"We walk?" Mark whispered.

"We walk." She reached up to shut off the interior lights. Both softly rested their doors closed, avoiding the latch.

She slid a small LED flashlight into her pocket, a backup from her glovebox. Best to scout the area, catch some conversation, determine what was up before making themselves known. Assuming they even did.

Thank the stars they hadn't had rain in over a week. Mark stayed on her six, letting her lead, and Callie appreciated his silence.

Up ahead, a dog barked, and Callie hoped it wasn't loose.

She'd been down Cedar Hall but only out of curiosity in her earlier days of learning the turf. This road, like so many others, dead-ended into marsh, or if the owner was lucky, deep water. This was one of those in-between sites, where the tide dictated the length of your dock and the ability to put a boat in, but regardless the views were million-dollar values.

They hugged the wild vegetation, Callie still very much aware that snakes didn't necessarily hibernate in this region. A snake could bask in a seventy-degree day then hunker down in the forties, their temperament nasty at best when disturbed from a half-sleep. She kept touch on her weapon as much for them as the human they pursued.

They neared a house and its clearing, catching the sound of voices. They stooped behind a tightly woven thicket of green briar and myrtle growing in and around the pines and cabbage palms.

The house was eighty years old if a day, with decades of attentive upkeep by someone familiar with what they were doing. Nothing worth the cover of *Southern Living*, but certainly preserved to be livable and sturdy. The siding had been painted a light color, the exact hue not discernible in the dark. No lights other than the screened porch facing a low tide marsh thick with cordgrass.

"I barely got away," Arthur was saying. "The police chief said she's identified who you are, dude." He peered around, as if afraid of someone hearing, if not storming the place.

"City boy, you ain't got a phone?" asked the other party, his voice young like Arthur's though without the social culture.

Callie was pretty sure she recognized Arthur's buddy, but scanned the area for confirmation.

In a shed/garage/carport compilation thirty feet off from the house, Callie spotted a dated white Chevy pick-up mentioned by Janet only hours ago. And just as far to their left on the edge of the fanned dirt drive was a black mailbox. The worn, reflective lettering read TATE.

Chapter 24

THANK GOD IT wasn't miserable and wet, but the temp still dipped enough to wish for gloves. The middle of night took the chill deeper.

On the porch, Arthur and Tate Jr. no longer spoke loud enough to hear. People from the water understood that voices carried, and only snippets of phrasing reached where Callie and Mark crouched behind brush. Repeatedly she'd missed her uniform and all the gear that came with it, today . . . last night . . . and the day before. Ever since she visited Sarah and found Ben's blood on the coat hook and kicked off a shit-storm of forensics and interviews. Eons ago.

Hell, when was the last she'd slept? Hours ran together, and her head throbbed dully.

"Who's that with Arthur?" Mark whispered.

"Tate Jr.," she said, whispering back close in his ear, catching a whiff of the remnants of his day-old cologne. "He's the handyman for Janet Wainwright."

She'd not personally met the twenty-something young man, but she'd seen him working decks and on boats and would recognize the tanned skin and kinky dark-red hair, both colors deepened from a life of fishing, swimming, and working in the weather.

"We armed for *him*?" Mark whispered.

"We're armed for whatever," she said. "Shhh, let me listen."

"Could hear better with a directional mic."

She remained still.

"They're cheap. I'll buy you one."

"Hush. No need."

"You have a need for one now," he said.

"Shut up, Mark." She left her spot, hunkered, then made her way back toward the carport, then up along the house to where she squatted between wild-growing nandina bushes and the whitewashed cement foundation of the house. Mark joined her, quite stealthy after all his jabber. Their position put them not ten feet from the two men though below their foot level. A sixty-watt bulb in an overhead fan gave the faintest of light ten feet up above Tate and Arthur.

The dog growled behind the porch screen. Some breed large enough to be a concern.

"He isn't growling at me, is he?" Arthur asked.

"Nope. S'pect something's crawling around close he don't like." Then Tate's dialog shifted edgy. "What do ya' mean I gotta leave? I ain't going nowhere. Besides, ain't done nothing they can catch me at."

The dog's nails tapped on the plank floor, as he sniffed his way to their direction. There was nothing to do about the animal except hope he didn't—

The dog barked once, then clawed at the screen above Callie's head.

"Shut up, Crock," Tate ordered. "Get back over here."

The dog whoofed once more in defiance then honored his owner though continuing to make threatening low whines.

Tate switched his attention from his nervous dog to the fretting frat-boy. "Quit worrying, man. Ain't no problem."

"She said she's arresting you tomorrow." Arthur sounded like a thirteen-year-old caught breaking a window.

"Trust me, she ain't," his buddy replied. "Go on back to your people, dude. Keep your mouth shut and nothing'll happen. Ol' Edisto Santa's history for another year . . . maybe forever after the trouble caused."

"*You* caused," Arthur said in a tone Callie would've heard back in the brush.

"No, dude. I was doing just fine till you panicked."

Arthur spoke in a higher pitch. "You son of a bitch, you came to me and I did all I did for you. To cover your ass."

"Did what?" Tate asked and chuckled. "Besides, told you. Didn't want your help."

But Arthur obviously wasn't feeling the humor nor peace of mind. "Then why'd you come to me? I could turn you in."

Outright laughter erupted from the young handyman. "Not without cutting your own head off. Quit fussing. Each tide buries deeper."

"What?" Arthur said, almost girlish.

Callie could picture Tate's backwoods marsh self-assurance that came with fending for one's self. Arthur's confidence came from money, structure, and rules, completely worthless in a world of callouses and survival instincts.

Like Ben deceived Brice, Callie sensed Tate had some sort of betrayal going on with Arthur. And while Arthur missed the message, the tide reference meant that secrets would be hidden with the passage of time.

Edisto Santa was done this year.

But she needed to talk to him . . . them . . . before their North Pole went dormant for the year. She had a seed of a thought she had to address, or rather, get them to address.

Flicking on her flashlight, she strode out of the bushes, aiming her light through the screen, the porch floor eye level to her. "Arthur Wainwright. Tate Junior." She'd never heard his first name. "Police Chief Callie Morgan. I have questions for the both of you."

Tate bolted into the house. Crock barked once at the intrusion then followed on the heels of his master. Mark took off around the house toward the back.

By instinct, Arthur almost followed Tate, panicked gaze hung on the heels of his buddy.

Callie shined her light in Arthur's eyes, changing his mind. "Don't do it, Mr. Wainwright," she said firmly, hand on the butt of the weapon on her hip. "Unless you want to land in deeper trouble than you already are."

Arthur's legs almost gave way, and he reached around to settle in a rusted metal chair.

"You armed?" she asked hard.

"Armed . . . what?" Then he understood. "No. Oh, God, no, ma'am." And he raised his hands.

"Don't you dare move from there," Callie ordered. "I can find you." She took off after Mark, hunting for him in the beam of her flashlight, halfway expecting to find him corralling Tate at the back steps.

"Stop," Mark yelled, and Callie hustled faster, her light bouncing, arriving to see Tate darting side-to-side before Mark dove to take him to the ground.

The two rolled as one at first, grunting and cursing, until one got in a hit, then the other. Amidst the flailing arms and legs the hound dog scrambled for all he was worth to land a bite.

"Give it up, Tate," Callie yelled to no avail, her light and weapon held in sync this way, then that as the two tussled. Adrenaline dumped into her system, her biggest fear being Tate having grabbed a weapon in the house, or somehow getting a hold of Mark's.

The only other light came dim from a kitchen window muted by cheap cotton curtains. Nothing overflowing into the yard to help, but they soon wrangled out of its range anyway. Callie moved with them in big steps, small stutter steps, gun at the ready. She couldn't throw herself in the midst of them, and couldn't shoot safely.

The tangled pair gravitated across the open yard toward the black of the jungle, the goals clear . . . one attempting to reach an escape, the other to block. But with an opportune punch and a kick from Tate, Mark landed on his back, the whump whooshing breath out of him.

Relishing the chance, Crock pounced on Mark as Tate disappeared amongst the oaks and pines.

Callie shined her flashlight after the escapee, the light swallowed up like a firefly in the dense woods. She popped a warning shot in the guy's general direction. "Stop where you are, Tate," but he was gone.

However, the gurgling snarls of the relentless dog wheeled her around.

Arm in the dog's teeth, Mark pummeled and fought to break free from his disabled position, the dog atop him.

Again, Callie aimed, unable to take a safe shot.

Mark landed a punch upside the dog's muzzle, sending a high-pitched yelp into the sky.

A whistle sounded from the inkiness of the woods. The dog cut around on cue and darted into the gloom of trees, brush and vines.

"Son of a bitch!" Mark yelled, shaking his arm. Callie trotted to him and held out to assist. He refused and rose on his own, doing a bit of an off-balance side-step as he righted himself, massaging his left arm.

"You hurt?" she asked, shining her light. Cuff flapping, sleeve torn in literally shreds, blood darkened the flannel in several places. She put the end of the flashlight in her mouth and shoved back the material. Several punctures. Smears and oozing trickles of blood. "Move your fingers," she said.

"I'm all right," he said, tugging the sleeve back down. "Just aggravated letting a damn punk get the best of me." He dusted himself off though he could be covered with dog crap for all they could tell in the dark.

"The leg?" she asked when he shifted weight.

"Fine, too. Let's get back to business."

She resisted the urge to check him closer, sensing embarrassment coming off the man. "Let's go get Arthur, then," she said. "I parked his ass on the porch."

"He hasn't run?" Mark said, fighting not to show his limp as they made their way back to the front.

"He hasn't the wild, feral nature of Tate," she said, her own pulse trying to level out.

Mark glanced behind him, as if Tate might reappear. "What're we doing about him?"

"Tate?" she asked, anger thick in her voice. "We aren't chasing him into his own woods at night, that's for sure. He'll skip over the bogs and gator spots we'd never see. No, we'll catch up to him some other way, and instead we take that white-bread kid we got and milk him dry. And we aren't calling his damn aunt before we do it."

Her thoughts pinged about how much of the burglaries had been orchestrated by Arthur. Or performed by Tate. Because without a doubt they'd both been involved. Both had access via Janet's realty. Arthur had lied to Callie, and Tate took off like the guilty party she assumed him to be.

But the reasoning for it all escaped her.

"Arthur?" she shouted, striding around the house, her temper rising back to the surface at the opportunity to go after somebody. Unfortunately for Arthur, he was it. "Get your sorry ass out here."

For a second she thought he might've absconded, but the screen door creaked, Arthur peering out.

Callie moved closer and took a stance. "Get down here, I said."

Mark held a couple yards back as the kid gingerly approached the chief. "All I did was stop to invite Tate to the party. Figured after all Aunt Janet dumped on us, we were entitled to enjoy ourselves." Each word tumbled faster. "Whenever I come down here, I try to do something for him. It's not like he's got much. Not sure he even passed high school. Surely you heard his daddy died last year, and it's not like he's got much family around here. He was telling me how he doesn't have the clothes, so I just thought—"

She aimed the beam in his eyes and enjoyed his cringe. "Speak only when I ask you a question."

He flashed obstinance, and she lowered the blinding beam and gave him a dose of her own pig-headed, *bring-it* stare. His melted first.

"Turn around," she said.

He froze instead, stunned.

She leaned closer, jaw tight. "I said turn around, Arthur! You'd think you barely graduated middle school instead of college." She harshly motioned in a circular manner, and he obliged.

The cuffs drew a whimper out of him. The first cuff made him flinch. She recited Miranda rights while securing the second. "Do you understand these rights as I have explained them to you?" she asked.

"Call my aunt," he said.

"Is that a yes or a no?" she asked.

"Yes. Call my aunt," only he yelled, the panic cracking in his speech.

She shoved him toward her car. "Don't think so. Frankly, if you cared anything about her, you'd leave her good name out of all this . . . but then, I don't see you and Tate being too magnanimous in your gestures these days, so I'll do it for you. We're not calling Janet. Your attorney, maybe, but not your aunt. At least until I say so."

"But I don't know any attorneys," he said.

"Another lie." She pushed him forward. "In your business you'd have run up against any number of attorneys."

He tilted his awkward stance to see her. "Real estate attorneys. That doesn't count."

She quickened her pace, making him do the same. "Any one of them can find you a criminal attorney, I'm sure."

Wide-eyed, Arthur stumbled once and Mark gripped the cuffs to help rebalance him. Callie led the way and let Mark direct Arthur as they commenced walking, while she lit up the woods.

Tate was no dummy. As sure as he was in these waters, he recognized Arthur as the weak link. Whether burglary charges were worth coming after law enforcement, Callie had no clue. But if there were more than tourist burglaries involved, he just might.

He'd be worried about how much his wimp of a friend was about to say in the control of a cop, but what he'd do about it was the wild card. The ease with which he talked to Arthur about their escapades spoke volumes. In other words, she wasn't sure how deep Tate's criminal activities went.

Still no moon, and for the seventy yards or so back to the patrol car, Callie kept an eye on both sides of the one-lane road. Mark did the same. One couldn't assume anything except that Tate could probably see better in the dark.

She didn't rest easy until they'd loaded Arthur in the back, properly buckled and trussed. She and Mark got in the front and drove slowly back up Cedar Hall Road.

"First aid kit is in there. Use it," she said to Mark, pointing to the glovebox, then she keyed her radio mic. "Edisto One—Charleston SO."

"Charleston SO—go ahead."

"BOLO on subject to follow." She waited for dispatch, glancing in her mirror at a wide-eyed Arthur listening for all he was worth. "What's Tate's first name, Arthur?"

"Um, John," he said.

Callie raised the mic. "Subject John Tate, Junior. White male. Twenty to thirty years. Five nine to six foot. One-sixty to one-seventy pounds. Dark red hair, tanned complexion. Last seen end of Cedar Hall Road on Edisto Island around midnight. Might be traveling with a dog. Considered armed and dangerous. Suspect in a homicide investigation."

Charleston SO acknowledged, and Callie signed out.

Arthur screamed, "Homicide! I have not killed anyone, Chief. And neither has Tate. You're wrong. Awful wrong." Then to himself, he mumbled incessantly, "Jesus, Jesus, this isn't right. This isn't right."

Good. Let him agonize. She said that for his ears. He'd be begging to spill anything back to stealing crayons in second grade once they reached the station.

But instead of retreating all the way back up Cedar Hall, she veered left on to Maxie Road. Mark scouted the scenery for movement with the assistance of the cruiser's spotlight. If they could snare Tate before dealing with Arthur, that'd be the best Christmas present they could wish for.

For a change, Arthur was too afraid to ask questions.

She switched the radio to a car-to-car channel and called Raysor. She repeated the BOLO to him.

"Need me there?" he said.

"First, what's the status on Brice?" she asked.

"Dropped him off to the hospitality of the Colleton jail. Said I'd be back the day after Christmas."

He said something else, but she missed it. "Come back?"

"En route to you," he said.

"Don't you have Christmas plans?"

"I'd only eat too much and sleep the day on my aunt's sofa," he said. "Lots more fun catching this little bastard."

Hopefully Tate didn't hitch a ride, even as sparse as they would be this deep of night. And once they went back to the station, Tate could circle back and grab his truck. "One more thing, Don."

"Go ahead."

"Before you leave, can you tell one of your deputies over there to man the McKinley Washington Bridge in case Tate attempts to leave the island?"

Only one road reached Edisto Island, and she'd blocked it before for worse than Tate.

"I'll keep an eye on the roads until you arrive, but just in case he gets by me, watch for that white truck on your way here," she said.

"Roger that," he answered. "En route. Colleton Twelve out."

She'd gone left on Maxie to its end, lights out for a minute, then drove back to 174. Up to the highway, then down Cedar Hall circling again.

"How's your arm?" she asked, as Mark put away the first aid kit.

"Might call for a stitch or two," he replied. "Used up all your bandages and most of your tape."

"The leg—"

"I said it was fine," he answered, all too anxious to move past that subject.

So he hated to be doted on. Okay with her. This wasn't the moment to unearth the quirks of the new guy in town. Instead, she focused more on Tate.

Junior was born and raised out here as was his daddy. Edisto was all he knew, all he owned, all he understood. Leaving the island would be like relocating to Mars, so she didn't expect him to run far. Grew up without a mother, from what little she'd heard, and per Janet, his daddy died earlier this year.

"So Arthur," she started, slowly covering aged asphalt toward the road's end to the Tate place again. "What do you think about your ol' buddy now?"

Even in the night his pallor glowed. "We're just friends, Chief. I'm . . . I'm not sure what you think we've done. I think this has blown up way out of proportion."

"You lied to me for starters," she said.

He dredged up a smidge of sarcasm. "That's not a crime."

"Actually it is a crime," Mark said, talking back at him.

"Whatever," Arthur said and faced the window.

Callie decided they'd scour the area a while longer, at least until Raysor arrived. Might as well mess with Arthur while hoping to run across Tate. The clock read 12:10 in the morning. "Well, how about that," she said. "It's Christmas Day. Merry Christmas, Mark!"

"How about that," he replied. "Merry Christmas, Chief."

She peered into her mirror. "And if you don't want to spend your next twenty Christmases behind bars, I suggest you start talking, Arthur. Prison isn't kind to spoiled soft college boys like you, although you'll make a lot of friends."

"Real close friends," Mark echoed.

Arthur's words came out choked. "I was trying to do the right thing."

"The right thing for who?" Mark asked.

Callie could only guess at the scheme between these two, but she could absolutely predict one thing about the Arthur and Tate team. The scales tipped heavily toward Tate in terms of street savvy with Arthur too naïve to recognize the manipulation. But Arthur came from privilege, with money to afford an attorney smart enough to plea down to probation.

Trouble was, Tate understood that, too. He was in the wind, but for how long? He had no other home, and friends could hide him for only so long. He'd lose his job with Janet if Arthur went down for the burglaries.

Either way, she'd use them both, starting with whoever she could grab . . . ending with the one not smart enough to turn first on the other.

Chapter 25

BY ALMOST ONE, Raysor's headlights reached Callie at the EZ Go. Once briefed, he replaced her, hunting Tate, taking up where she left off in scouring each spidering road off Highway 174. He had more familiarity with whose house to knock on. His knowledge of the island was as good as Marie's, only he could eye-to-eye recognize folks . . . recalling who'd been picked up for what when . . . and who he'd helped. His history went far and wide, and he could make better time as boots on the ground than Callie.

Arthur had wilted, uncertain how to behave, and with him worn down, Callie felt it opportune to cart him to the station before she wilted too far herself. But first she asked Mark if he needed the one local family doctor on Edisto Island. Mark's tough act was stupid if that dog had done some serious damage . . . if the fall had injured his leg.

"I'm pretty sure the doc stayed on the island for the holidays." Callie approached the road of the small practice. "She usually sticks around because of the surge in holiday tourists."

Mark held up his bandaged arm, sleeve dangling. "Peroxide on this and a couple naproxen for the leg. I'm not waking up some poor one-room doc on Christmas for this."

"Those things can fester ugly," she said.

"And if it does, I'll seek your doc out. Move on."

She hoped he did. Dogs in the marsh didn't make regular visits to a vet . . . didn't have shots. "So—take you home?" she asked.

He shook his head. "I told Stan I would partner with you tonight. For better for worse. I won't be that guy who ditches you just when you might need him."

Callie drove past the lane leading to the doc, glancing over at Mark again for his second chance, then with his head shake, she sped toward the beach, too weary to take up the topic of men protecting women. Not up to confirming that Stan wanted her watched, guarded, whatever he called it. Not that she didn't appreciate Mark's backup. And she especially appreciated his not mentioning her lack of sleep in front of Arthur, who'd considerably quieted in the back.

Leaning a little, she could view him in her mirror. Head against the window, Arthur appeared to study the scenery, but Callie bet his mind focused more on his future than the flora and fauna invisible in the dark. The occasional Christmas light in sleeping homes only accented the fact he'd been yanked from his comfortable world and thrust into trouble he might never completely recover from. The darkness would make him feel alone.

Good. She hoped he'd worried himself sick.

Before long, they reached the office, and she took the trouble to flip on the blue-light wreath as they entered, a tiny taken-for-granted reminder of what Arthur could lose in his life. She grabbed three bottles of water from a short refrigerator in the corner before she ushered the two men into her office. She acknowledged the déjà vu; however, Arthur instead of Brice sat in the hot seat before her desk . . . and Mark instead of Raysor warmed the backup chair behind the perp.

Five hours short of working a forty-eight-hour shift and two meals away from her last. Her stomach churned . . . loud enough, she was sure, to be heard on the recorder.

Setting out an assortment of energy bars, she offered them to each man. "Want one?"

Both declined, but she made them sit there while she wolfed down the better part of a bar in three bites while switching on the recorder, swallowing hard between sentences.

"When I called you, Arthur," she began, after all the perfunctory intro. "When I offered to help you finish securing your aunt's rentals, you flat-out lied."

Arthur bent forward in his chair, still cuffed. "Can you take off these things? My hands are asleep, and I'm getting a cramp in my shoulder. Isn't this abuse?"

Without thinking that he was not active LEO, she motioned for Mark to release the cuffs before catching herself and going for her own key. Surprisingly, Mark had one at the ready, and set Arthur loose.

Arthur rubbed his wrists, raising them to study close. "Excessive, Chief."

"They go back on real easy," she said. "You lied to me. Why?"

"I was already on my way to Charleston," he said. "Not a lie."

Mark gave a mild quick muffle of a laugh.

She gave Arthur a flat-line grin of her own. "I was parked four houses down from you on Palmetto, watching throughout the whole call. My witness is right over there in the corner." She motioned to Mark. "You weren't where you said you were, so again, why lie?"

"Like I told you, I didn't want your help with the houses."

She frowned at his headstrong behavior she'd hoped he'd lost in her cruiser's back seat. "If you expect me to believe that, then you must believe in Santa." Sitting taller in her seat, she proclaimed, "I, too, believe in Santa . . . Edisto Santa. A tradition around here for longer than you've been alive, from what I hear." She gave him a second. "Have *you* heard of Edisto Santa?"

He glared at her from narrow eyes, not welcoming the performance.

"Of *course* you have," she said, as though speaking to a child unsure of Santa's existence. "You were speaking to him just this evening, weren't you?"

"I'm not playing your games," he said.

Elbows on her desk, she inched forward. "But you've been playing games for several days," she said, the singsong of her voice gone. "As a matter of fact, you're Santa's elf, aren't you?" She scowled, more irritated than acting anymore. He'd broken the law. Several of them, and he wasn't owning up to it . . . or didn't understand the seriousness. As Janet Wainwright's kin, he should definitely know better, and his spoiled nature was pissing Callie off.

Her mouth drew tight. "This Santa steals from people. Breaks into their homes and removes their Christmas presents. Disappointing children. Not a very nice Santa, in my opinion, what do you think?"

"Have no idea what you're talking about," he said. "I've been friends with Tate for years, since we were kids. We were just getting together tonight."

Arthur apparently thought that he could find a way out of this mess because of who he was . . . or because Callie had nothing on him. Nothing he knew about, at least.

Mark spoke up, in a hard tone. "What do you think Santa's leaving under your tree, Arthur? No, wait, your Christmas morning will be in the, what is it . . . Colleton County jail?"

Callie confirmed with a nod.

He continued with a tip of his chin for thanks, " . . . with those new friends we mentioned back in the patrol car. Your holiday dinner might consist of a bologna sandwich, no condiments, mind you, with Kool-Aid to drink. No ice. Budgets are lean."

Arthur gave a cock of his head. "Oh, quit with the drama." Then he leaned forward as if to stand, only for Mark to shove him back in his chair.

"Stop it!" Arthur yelled. "I've got to stand a minute." He tried again.

Mark shoved harder, scooting the chair a few inches in the effort. "You sit or the cuffs go back on."

"My aunt is going to be all over both your asses, you got that?" the boy growled. "I have nothing to tell you."

Callie hadn't budged during Mark's show of authority. "Arthur," she said, "you keep saying I won't learn anything from you."

"You won't," he replied, with a smirk.

"But regardless what you think, this is the way statements and interrogations work, Arthur. You'll be asked the same thing many times and many ways," she said.

"To trip me up." He spit on the floor and glared back, as though hoping for a response.

Instead, Callie leaned and peered around him to Mark. "Did you see what he just did?"

The adjunct officer for the night tsked, then released a "Hmm, hmm. I sure did. How many more is that? One year? Two?"

"You're out of your f-in minds," Arthur said through his teeth. "Wait until my aunt gets here."

"Tell you what," Callie said, surprised her brain could creatively function on a granola bar and two days without sleep. More than one person could throw Janet's name around. "Call your aunt. We just might read her her rights as well. You worked under her umbrella. Broke into houses while on her clock, using keys managed by Wainwright Realty." Again, a notable aside at Mark. "What do you think?"

"Without a doubt," he said. "I've used conduits from one perp to another like that before. He worked for her . . . makes her a definite person of interest. Might be guilty."

Eyes widening, Callie aimed her pen at him. "You might be right. He might've been following her instructions. Maybe she's . . . "

"Edisto Santa!" Mark exclaimed. "Yes!"

Arthur lost his color. "She had nothing to do with anything we did."

"I thought you didn't do anything. Maybe you're just trying to cover up for her." Callie laid his phone on the desk before him. "Call her."

"No," he said.

She took out her own phone. "Then I will. Imagine waking up at two a.m. to my caller ID rather than yours."

"Don't." He snatched up his phone. "I'll do it."

"Good," she said. "Then before she gets here, maybe you can tell me what happened with those houses, because once she's here, we'll be questioning her, too. Adding her to this recording. Because you can't convince me that a woman of her intelligence, a decorated Marine, no less, didn't suspect anything."

He lowered his phone, staring at it.

Mark raised a brow at her, a silent affirmation of Callie's ploy.

Callie noted the wall clock, giving Arthur a half minute to decide which option to go with. This was important to him. If he called Janet, no doubt Callie'd interrogate the Marine as mentioned, because Janet's ignorance was at question. But if he didn't dial her, Arthur was choosing the right side of things.

He needed to commit . . . on his own.

"Can I talk to you first?" he finally asked.

"Once you call her," she said. "And I'm reminding you about your right to an attorney."

Mark made an expression she easily read. He wouldn't have referenced the attorney, wouldn't have given their suspect an out.

But Arthur, outside his immature arrogance and braggadocio, had led a straightforward life laced with lessons pumped with moral codes. He possessed an intense allegiance to Janet regardless his mouthiness about her overbearing nature, and when it came to choosing Tate or Janet, Callie hoped she'd predicted right.

Furthermore, if she speculated correctly, Arthur's sense of loyalty may have even been taken advantage of by Tate. Or Arthur had overestimated his young friend's fidelity.

He absentmindedly ran his thumb across the back of his phone. "What happens to Tate?"

"That depends on Tate," she said, no longer demanding. "Best you be concerned about your own fate."

He gave a slight nod into his lap.

"Call her."

He did. "Aunt Janet. I'm sorry to wake you."

Some chatter in between, most likely Janet asking questions of his whereabouts and health.

"Yes, ma'am. I'm at the Edisto Police station. I think I've been arrested. Yes. About the burglaries."

More questions, more of his nods, and a lot of "Yes, ma'ams." Callie could imagine the staccato snapping of words that indicated some serious Wainwright orders.

Then a final "Yes, ma'am." He hung up. "She told me not to talk to you."

Callie sat back. "I rather expected that. Then we'll interrogate her first. We can sit right here and wait. Sure you don't want one of my granola bars?"

His head shaking, he continued talking in spite of his aunt's directives. "Ask me your questions," he said. "I'd rather you hear what happened from me. And I'd rather not talk in front of her."

Guess the nephew had a good core after all.

"Is your aunt involved? Does she have intimate knowledge of the burglaries?" Callie asked.

His brows knotted, and Arthur's words backed up on each other before he could put them together. "Why the hell would you still think that?"

"Like I said. She has the keys, has the means—"

His nose wrinkled like assaulted with a stench. "No! You've got to believe me. She had nothing to do with any of this."

"Any of what, Arthur?" Callie said, and aimed a conscious glare at the wall clock. "Janet's probably getting in her car right about now."

His leg bobbed, the heel up and down fast, almost mechanical. "Tate worked for Wainwright Realty since he could walk. His daddy came to work for Aunt Janet not long after she arrived on Edisto . . . twenty-five years, I guess?"

"Why is that important?" Callie asked.

His butt left the seat. He was nervous and eager to pace, but he self-corrected, recalling Mark with a glance around. "Just let me talk, Chief. It's recorded. It doesn't have to make sense till it does, and I don't have but a few minutes to say what's on my mind, okay? Okay?" he repeated, prodding her to understand fast.

She calmly nodded. "Go ahead then."

"Tate Sr. had been barely getting by when my aunt hired him, and in the beginning he didn't make much. Not till Aunt Janet got going in the business. Tate's momma got frustrated with living so poor, and she left when Tate was maybe five, I think. But a year later, Wainwright Realty took root, and things got better."

Callie nodded toward his water on the edge of her desk as a reminder, and he took a swig. He seemed to be taking a long while to get where he wanted to go, but damn if his heart wasn't in the storytelling. She peeked at the recorder. All good.

"Tate Sr. would do anything for my aunt, and she'd do anything for him. Somewhere along the line, Edisto Santa got started."

Callie held up a hand. "Sorry to interrupt you, son, but I already asked once. Is your aunt Edisto Santa?"

"I already told you . . . no, ma'am."

With a wave, Callie gave him the go ahead to continue.

He rocked in his seat. "Tate Sr. wanted to give back for his good fortune. There wasn't anything he could give my aunt, so he started tithing into what he named his Edisto Santa fund. Then every Christmas, after keeping his ear to the ground as to who needed help or who had a dry run of luck that year, he bought and delivered anonymous gifts. Not a lot, but enough. Tate Jr. used to help him. He only told me a week ago."

Callie peered up at the clock again. The story had gone on long enough for Janet to arrive, that Hummer breaking all the speed laws to do so, but she hadn't appeared.

"Want to call and see where she is?" Callie asked.

Arthur shook his head, his eyes reddening. "Let me finish first. Please! This is hard enough as it is."

She stilled with a quick look to Mark. He gave the mildest shrug that she interpreted to mean he couldn't disagree.

Arthur methodically struck up a steady rhythm with his palm on his knee, a dull patting sound. He set his stare on the empty granola wrapper on her desk. "Then Mr. Tate died last spring," he said. "I came to Edisto on spring break, as usual, mostly repairing houses with Tate. He was lost and trying not to show it, and my aunt thought it best he have some company. We went through a lot of beers that week."

He thought a second. "When I went back to school, Aunt Janet kept him busy. Gave him jobs all summer long, jobs probably not worth doing, but she didn't like him rambling around that old house by himself."

He groaned softly. "But then Thanksgiving came around. He told me he hadn't the money to do Edisto Santa like his daddy did." Arthur's distant gaze came back to hone in on Callie. "Frankly, that's when I first learned that Tate's daddy had been Edisto Santa for all those years.

Damn fine secret, if you ask me."

"Sounds like a fine man," Mark said.

Arthur stiffened toward Mark. "He was. And Tate felt the pressure to honor his daddy. So when he found himself unable to continue Edisto Santa, he came up with what he did."

"Which was?" Callie asked, her headache making a return climb behind her eyes, sinking into her skull. And she was beginning to worry why Janet wasn't on site yet.

Another sigh from Arthur. "The renters. And I had no idea he was doing this at first," he quickly injected. "But he thought if he could take one present from each house, just one, it would be a proper balance. The renters paying a couple grand a week to rent on the beach could afford to lose one gift, several in that big house, and the needy on Edisto could continue receiving Edisto Santa."

"I see," she said.

But when she didn't welcome his explanation, he jumped to his feet. Mark leaped up and gripped an arm, but Arthur tugged forward, tears pooling. "You don't see. I can tell you don't see. He made a mistake. One sorry-assed mistake. That's when he came to me . . . "

He full-on cried and sank back to his chair, shoulders bouncing with the sobs. No longer trusting his behavior, Mark stood inches close rather than sit.

Callie came around the desk and stooped before the distraught young man. Touching his knee, she let the surge of sobs ease before questioning him again. "What did he do, Arthur?"

His cheeks blotched and eyelids swollen, he sniffled hard. "What he did . . . what I did . . . it just got all screwed up," he cried.

Pounding sounded on the station's front door. Incessant. Demanding. Callie motioned for Mark to welcome the arrival, whom she assumed would be Janet. She wanted to keep the recorder running, the interviewee talking while he felt the urge to get worries off his chest.

Arthur spoke openly with Mark gone, with just Callie squatted before him. Before he finished, she kicked herself for not putting all the pieces together sooner. What a mess. What a stupid mess.

Even from her office, Callie could hear the exacerbated knocks, imagining the blue-lit wreath shaking on its hook. Mark's voice rose, then Janet's. Then banging sounded on her office. Callie let the Marine in, keeping the recorder going, but instead of any sort of gracious thanks or apology for what might be going down with her nephew, the woman stormed past Callie to Arthur.

"Shut up, boy!" she ordered. "What have you told them?"

"Enough," he said, with starch surprising them all. He rose to his feet. "You always taught me to rely on the truth, so that's what this is . . . airing the truth. There's no other way around it."

"I'm not letting you tarnish the Tate name, nephew."

To that he stiffened, dumbfounded. "The Tate name? What about our name?"

Mark was primed, ready to follow whatever lead Callie directed. Callie, however, watched Janet's vexation, wondering just how much Janet *was* involved in a tradition gone awry.

First, the Edisto Police Chief locks up Brice LeGrand, sullying that old Edisto heritage. Second, she disrupts Edisto Santa. And if she understood Arthur correctly, Callie might be locking up the son of a revered island native. Son of a bitch.

She didn't really suspect Janet, but God help her if on the outside chance she was wrong. In that case, Callie might wind up taking down the real estate broker who'd spent over two decades ushering Edisto Beach into its lucrative tourist era.

If Callie didn't manage this smartly, she and her job might go down with the whole bloody lot of them.

Chapter 26

JANET BACKED ARTHUR against Callie's office wall with a strength uncanny in contrast to the age and white hair. Her leathered throat bulged, teeth clenched. "It doesn't matter whose name I'm talking about. Tate . . . Wainwright. What have you done, nephew?"

Arthur hesitated to respond, and her brows jerked up. "Never mind. Don't say a thing." She whipped around to Callie. "Nothing he said can be used without an attorney, and mine is on his way from Charleston."

Smoothly inserting herself between the aunt and the nephew, Callie calmly said, "He's twenty-two, Janet. He speaks for himself."

"*My* attorney," the older woman barked. "*My* nephew."

"And *my* choice to speak up," Arthur said, straightening his clothes from his aunt's assault.

Unaccustomed to being bested, Janet sought for better footing in a quick study of her adversaries. "He wasn't aware of what he was saying," she said. "And I want proof you Mirandized him."

Callie lifted the recorder and spoke into it. "Let the recording show that the additional person in the room is Janet Wainwright, resident of Edisto Beach, aunt and employer to said Arthur Wainwright. She entered the room at approximately . . . 2:15 a.m."

Then before Janet could build herself into too huge of a lather, Callie asked her to sit, with Mark silently offering and moving his chair beside Arthur's. Callie returned to her desk chair, and thank goodness Arthur followed suit to his.

Still standing, the aunt eyed each of them, prepared for a fight.

Callie's headache fought to explode out her ears.

"Janet," she said. "Your nephew divulged what happened with the burglaries, on the record. Are you willing to hear it? It's already on tape, but I think it best you hear it from him."

The old woman sat, but she was leery. Not accustomed to doing anything but confronting fear and sending it packing, she seemed more alarmed showing weakness than facing whatever Arthur had done. She preferred sizing up her enemy, but right now she couldn't tell what was coming at her.

"Aunt Janet," Arthur started and instinctively peered down, ashamed. But then he appeared to force himself to man up and proceed, and he held onto Janet's hand for assurance . . . his and hers.

He began with the rental burglaries. How Tate hadn't saved his money and found himself in December wanting to continue his daddy's gift deliveries with no dollars in his pockets. With access to Janet's rental inventory and knowledge of which were occupied for the holidays, he convinced himself into taking one, just one, present from under Christmas trees so abundantly bedecked for the wealthy. No one would notice. How could people who already owned so much, miss one small present, probably something they didn't even need. And how the bigger rental, the one with four families, had tempted him to shortcut and steal more.

"Arthur didn't realize that Tate unwrapped them," Callie said, "to make sure he stole something useful. After all, his daddy bought his gifts, with specific individuals in mind. Tate had to fumble, hope he could locate gifts that halfway matched the wishes of people on his list. He shoved the ripped-off gift wrap to the bottom of trash cans."

More deeply saddened with each addition to the story, Janet rubbed her chin, trying not to cover her mouth as would most people hurt with disappointment. "Poor Junior." But then she stiffened. "I'll make good with every one of those people, Chief. And then some. I'll cover half their stay on the beach."

But when neither Callie nor Arthur agreed with her offer, when neither of her allies seemed pleased with a plan to make the people whole, she stalled. "What else did he do?" But she pleaded to the chief instead of her nephew.

"Aunt Janet—"

Without taking her gaze off Callie, she firmly said, "Shut up. You had your chance to come to me earlier . . . and didn't."

Callie's heart hurt for Arthur as his aunt's clipped words horse-whipped him into submission. Janet recognized the urgency to absorb all this mess, but Callie also read this woman well enough to see her preparing for the worst. And she wanted it from someone who could deliver it pragmatically, stripped of the disgrace and humiliation.

"What stupid line did Tate Jr. cross that can't be undone?" Janet asked. "We wouldn't be sitting here in the early morning hours of Christmas about some stolen presents when restitution could make it right."

So Callie spoke. "We're guessing that Tate found breaking and entering simpler than he expected . . . maybe developed a taste for it. Our police records routinely show one or two burglaries around the holidays, but not as many as this year. One or two became six, then eight, and I suspect we'll hear of more once folks go to open presents this morning and find more missing. But unfortunately, Tate told Arthur that he took advantage of a resident when the opportunity dropped into his lap, and that's the issue. A damn big issue, Janet."

The aunt stole a hard stare at her nephew, then gave attention to Callie. "Proceed."

"On December twenty-first, Tate was jogging east on Jungle Road, probably casing houses to judge which families had left to enjoy the beach, or shop, or dine out. Tate told Arthur, and we have a witness who placed a man of his general description at the scene. The weather was colder than usual, meaning people remained inside more than in the warmer months. He was short of gifts for Edisto Santa."

Janet's pursed, wrinkled lips held their own. "He was familiar with these houses through my company."

"And living here his whole life, but yes," Callie said for the recording.

"Well, shit," said the Marine. "So go on, December twenty-first . . ."

Waiting to see if the woman caught the importance of that date, but seeing she didn't, Callie continued.

"He noted a door open to a resident's house, leaped at the prospect, and entered, hoping to snare a gift without breaking in. Only the resident appeared before he could leave. Somehow the resident apparently was shoved, and Tate ran away. No witnesses." She waited again for the recognition in their eyes, but they were too caught up in their own exposure, like all suspects.

"It was Ben, Janet."

The revelation drew a hard gasp from the old woman. "Oh my Lord." She spun on Arthur, and landed a hard palm smack against his cheek. "I have to hear about this now? That man died!" She stared fire-hot rivets through him.

"But it was an accident." Then to Callie, he said, "Isn't that right, Chief? Isn't that what you said? Tell her."

"While it may have been an accident," she said, "his burglary resulted in a death, whether he meant to or not. Tate can still be charged with murder."

"But, but . . . " and he stopped his stuttering to put words in order. "Tate came to me. The first thing that crossed my mind was the fallout against Wainwright Realty," he explained. "Since he'd only taken gifts from rentals, I changed the pattern to residents . . . hoping it would just go away. The fact he went into the Rosewood house gave me the idea, then at the Waterfront that night I saw the Clarks and McMillans there for dinner . . . remembered they lived close together . . . and I just did it."

"What?" yelled Janet.

When nobody spoke, she moved to the wall, hands on hips and her back to Arthur.

"I was thinking of you," Arthur cried again.

She rolled back around, steely eyes tinged with hurt. "You broke into the houses of locals to cover up Tate's deeds? What image does *that* present? A man died. We don't hurt our own . . . we don't hurt anyone," she said. "I'm so damn disappointed in you."

His tears rolled freely now.

Callie interpreted clearly the underlying message in Janet's outburst. Nobody on the island would dare weigh the value of a tourist over a resident, but the residents had roots. Businesses gave unofficial discounts to natives, and natives took up for one another.

Natives weren't as affluent as the tourists, but they lived a lifestyle the tourists paid thousands to emulate. The residents were envied. They had sacrificed to come live on the island. Residents committed to Edisto and to each other. Part of why Callie felt horribly about Brice, though they'd clashed from the start.

Nobody crapped in their own sandbox. And when they did, they attempted to police and protect each other. Which led Arthur to do what he did, or so Callie wanted to assume.

"I still have the stolen gifts from the Clarks and McMillans," he said. "I'll give them to you, Chief."

Like that mattered at this juncture.

So much pent-up exhausted emotion in the room, and memories that would alter everyone's Christmas for years to come. But despite the night's confessional, Janet and Arthur were about to learn that crime doesn't pay. And that often honesty doesn't pay either. As frantic as they were, they were about to be crushed.

Arthur had shown his prowess at breaking into houses and fessed up to his lockpicking skills. He'd owned up to breaking into residents' homes to alter the impression of Tate's MO . . . to not only hide Tate's participation in the break-ins, but to also help cover up Ben's death.

Another knock sounded on the station door, and without being told, Mark rose to greet the newcomer, who would most likely be the attorney. Callie had to say this fast.

"I'm sorry, Janet . . . Arthur, but we still have a serious problem."

Janet's forehead furrowed deeper wrinkles than already resided there. "You have the facts, Chief. Your task is to round up Tate. Once he talks, it's down to negotiations between attorneys . . . with recommendations from you, of course. I doubt the Clarks and McMillans will file charges when they learn it's Arthur."

This had gotten complicated. Callie heard Mark talking with the attorney in the lobby, possibly delaying him, so Callie took advantage of the brief opportunity, while she could.

"We'll eventually round up Tate," she said. "But all he's got to do is find an attorney that tells him to shut up, not confess, and play dumb."

Shaking his head, Arthur wouldn't accept the thought. "But we already know what he did, because of what he said."

"What we think and what we can prove are two different things," Callie said. "You've admitted to breaking and entering, stealing. You've admitted doing so in light of Ben's death. Tate, however, can deny every bit of this and pretend he had no part in any of it. You're of similar age. You own a gray hoodie like his."

"I gave him that hoodie," Arthur blurted.

"Noted," Callie said. "But let's say we round Tate up tonight. He can spin off of your story and say you tried to incorporate him in *your* deeds, only he declined, not wanting to break the law. Or he can state he has no idea what you're talking about."

Arthur blanched snow white, a lone word tumbling off his lips. "What?"

Janet hung her head and lowered to her chair, reaching over to her nephew. "There's no proof against Tate," she said, and took a long slow exhale.

"Janet?" called a tinny voice trying to sound empowered. A man came through primed to own the show. "Janet. Don't say a word." He addressed Callie with his well-practiced lines. "I'm Attorney Madison Gibbes, Chief, and I represent Arthur Wainwright. My client has nothing to say."

Callie reached over and spoke into the recorder: "Upon arrival of Mr. Madison Gibbes, Mr. Wainwright's attorney, the interview of Arthur Wainwright is terminated at 2:40 a.m."

Then she clicked off the recorder. Her brain muddled, she hunted for options. The attorney wouldn't let Arthur speak anymore, but he might be enticed to allow Janet to do so. Or wait, maybe do more than speak. Whatever Callie did, she had to think quickly before Janet left.

Chapter 27

WHEN THE ATTORNEY didn't attempt to lead him out, Arthur surveyed the room as if lost in a sea of strangers. He pleaded silently for direction, even at Mark propped in the corner.

"We can go, right?" Arthur asked. "We meet someplace after Christmas and try to find Tate?"

Mark studied the carpet. Janet's veined hand rested on her nephew's back, thin lips flat. A soft sheen reflective in her eyes.

Never seeing Janet show more emotion than a curt dip of her chin, this display tugged at Callie's soul. The old Marine actually had a heart deep down in there, and the one person who could draw it out was about to get yanked from her . . . his young, naïve life about to be diced and dismantled.

And since Janet couldn't quite piece the words, Callie spoke on her behalf. "Afraid you're headed to Colleton County jail, Arthur," she said. "You've committed a felony or two, more if Tate doesn't corroborate your story. We're not done working this case, and Tate won't get far on my watch, but I'm so sorry. They have to take you in." She gently motioned for his attorney to take up where she left off.

"What?" Arthur fussed, then with a higher pitch wailed, "Wait, I can't be going to jail."

"Listen to me, son," attorney Gibbes began, and Callie stepped out into the hall and phoned Raysor.

His calm gruffness was a welcome from her office steeped in stress. "Was able to put out a lot of feelers and woke up a lot of folks, but haven't run that guy down yet," he said.

Not surprising. A person that well-versed in the saltwater marshes and jungle growth of Edisto had a dozen places to hide that most people wouldn't foresee, and after Callie and Mark left his house with Arthur in tow, Tate probably tracked back and packed up enough food and water to last him for days. "He might be hunkered down someplace right under our noses," she said. "And we don't have enough people to roust him out. Not without calling in Charleston County SO."

"Which means Colleton County SO," Raysor added. "One of Colleton's uniforms is still on the bridge, by the way. You're fully aware of how those Charleston boys hate coming out here."

"Well, Don, rein it in. You get to cart another prisoner to your beloved Walterboro lockup," she said.

"Thought you said Tate was—"

"It's not Tate," she said. "It's Arthur Wainwright."

Road noise sounded under his cruiser's tires, and Callie imagined him already redirected toward the beach. She filled him in on the interview.

Raysor gave her a growling *hunh, hunh, hunh* at the update. "Stupid little bastard."

"Don't put him anywhere near Brice, okay?"

"Yeah. Wouldn't want to do that to the poor kid."

"Or in any kind of general population, you hear me? He's scared out of his mind, and he'll be in there for at least two nights until we can find a judge that'll hold an arraignment on the other side of Christmas."

"You mean like tomorrow? It's already Christmas Day, doll."

His personal nickname for her, derisive to some women, carried a history they both could laugh over in a moment other than this one, but it still warmed her. On what should be the most relaxed week of the year, she felt as if she'd polluted the holiday cheer. It was the job, she told herself, like she mulled over alone in bed at night. It was her lot in life to upset people's lives as she attempted to put others right. "Just come on," she told Raysor. "I imagine the attorney will follow you there. His name is Madison Gibbes."

"She brought in a high-priced Charleston shyster, huh?"

"Yeah," Callie said, though relieved Janet chose this man. He was sharp. As sincere as most of Colleton County's attorneys were, they were small-town experienced. Janet had instead grabbed a top shelf one from the Holy City for her nephew.

Callie hung up and went to her office. With aunt on one side and lawyer on the other, Arthur appeared about to faint. She explained how Raysor would escort him in, the others could follow, and he'd be isolated from inmates until a judge could be found.

"We appreciate it, Chief," the attorney said. "That means a lot."

Callie wanted to say that these were Edisto people; therefore, they meant a lot to her as well, but she had to maintain her professional stance. Didn't mean her heart wasn't bleeding for how the holidays were treating the Wainwrights.

An idea about involving Janet remained foremost in her mind, though. Wouldn't take Raysor more than fifteen minutes to arrive, probably less with him driving hard on an empty highway, so she got to her idea quickly. "Janet, I've got a way for you to help me, and maybe simultaneously help Arthur . . . in a big way. If you're willing."

Janet seemed a tad stunned, but that was Janet. A tad was usually the most off-kilter indication you'd get out of her.

"Your attorney's right here," Callie said. "Hear me out and run it by him."

Janet's counselor gave a nod to hear the offer.

"Does Tate use a company phone provided by Wainwright Realty?" Callie asked.

"Ha," the woman said. "Wouldn't get a hold of him any other way. Had to threaten to take the damn thing away to convince him he had to be twenty-four ready for me."

Good. Just as Callie expected, but she wasn't so sure about the next. "You ever use the locater on it?"

"Damn right I do," she answered. "To see if he cuts out early, or to judge where he is so I can see how soon he can get to an emergency repair."

Even better. Janet was a smart old bird.

"Does he know you use it?"

The Marine got it. With a sly grin she shook her head. "Why would I go telling him what I deem as need-to-know?"

Even Arthur showed surprise, with a reflex glance down at his own phone.

"Let's call him in," Callie said.

The attorney paused, though, not giving immediate sanction.

"Arthur was forthcoming, Mr. Gibbes," Callie prodded, "and I believe him, but the reality is he committed several felonies, albeit to help a friend. But the friend was the one who engaged in a higher level of criminal activity to include the possibility of murder. Unfortunately all evidence links to your client. I don't feel you have anything to lose by helping me bring Tate in."

"Be glad to," Janet said, not waiting for permission from counsel.

The attorney winced at her quick agreement. "Can you guarantee her safety?"

"Absolutely," Callie said. "Care to try it, Janet?"

With a few buttons, Janet waited for the signal, pinching the screen for adjustment, waiting for the satellite to settle on Tate. "What's he doing there?" Then something clicked enough to make sense. "That's on Manse Road where we have a couple low-end rentals. He just did some work on one two weeks ago where a live oak dropped a limb on the roof. Never gets rented in the winter."

Manse Road. Silted and not conducive to a herd of patrol cars. Only five houses on the road. One way in and one way out. Callie had to think about this a minute.

Keys sounded from the lobby. Raysor had made the trip quickly.

She called him back, and he appeared in her doorway. "Y'all ready?"

With jelly in his knees, Arthur stood, and with the beckon of his attorney, he moved to leave, then stopped. "Aunt Janet?" he asked, sounding ten years younger. "I thought you would come . . . " but he couldn't finish his sentence.

In a vise of an embrace, the Marine hugged her nephew. "You'll be fine, Arthur. I'll be along, but we have to see what I can do to help us out of this shit. You be strong. You hear?"

He nodded into her narrow shoulder. "Yes, ma'am."

"Good," she said, pushing him from her to see his face. "Go nicely with Mr. Gibbes and the deputy. I'll be along soon as I can."

The attorney reached for Arthur's arm, but not before he leaped for his aunt again, and she crushed him against her.

Callie had to look away.

Janet was different with Arthur, and watching them Callie had a better sense that Arthur's logic, though flawed, was to protect Wainwright Realty from the burglaries. Deeper down these two shared a love neither gave the world a chance to see, and Callie could assume Janet loved as hard as she fought.

Raysor spoke. "Got to go, Mr. Wainwright."

The threesome left, lawyer, cop, and culprit. Callie returned to business. "Call Tate, Janet. He's out and about, uncertain what to do, and you're probably his most trusted person on Edisto. Or am I reading your relationship wrong?"

Emotion tucked away and no more sign of rattle, the Marine had regained her composure. Mission-oriented. "I've treated Tate decent," she said. "His father served me well, and I tried to pave the way for the son, knowing he could stray without a tight rein on him. His momma leaving when he was five might've influenced that. But Tate appreciated who buttered his bread . . . or at least I thought he did."

Janet Wainwright was one of the toughest, most formidable people Callie'd ever met, her durability instilled by the Corps. But such stiff and unrelenting management didn't always work when things got personal. She had to accept the dilemma that tending to her nephew could pit her against Tate.

Mark sat back down, taking it all in and waiting to be needed. Callie appreciated his contribution to the night's events and might use him again.

"Go ahead," she repeated to Janet. "Call Tate and I'll monitor. Express concern for him. Say they took Arthur, you're sort of lost as to what's going on, and because of Tate Sr., you feel beholden to help. If you can't help Arthur, you can at least help Tate."

Her mouth pruned, Janet pondered the instructions. "How am I supposed to help him?"

Callie shrugged. "Ask him if he needs a ride off the island until things blow over. If he needs money. If he needs a place to stay."

"He has a truck," she said.

Callie nodded, glad to see Janet engaging. "And this way we'll learn whether he has it with him." If Tate went back home to collect some belongings, he might've taken the truck, too, but he remained on the island per the tracker. He might easily jump at the offer of financial aid.

"Can't see Junior wanting to live anywhere else," Janet said. "Most young people itch to leave a place so confining, but Tate breathes Edisto. His father left him that house, and he's smart enough to realize its value on that marsh. Houses on water are a limited commodity. Hell, I taught him that much. When he reaches thirty, that land'll be worth a million."

She was stalling. In the middle of Callie's small office, the two women studied Janet's phone. "The sooner you do this, the sooner we can help Arthur," Callie said.

But Janet had to choose to violate Tate's trust in favor of Arthur. Trust meant a lot to a Marine.

She breathed in once more, deeper. "Let's do this."

Quickly going over some conversation options, Callie prepped her. "And I'm right here if he goes off script, okay?"

"Got it," Janet said, and before Callie could tell her to go, Janet dialed. Callie grabbed the recorder, speaking a fast introduction into the machine.

Tate didn't answer, and the call rolled to voice mail. Janet left no message.

"Again," Callie said.

Janet redialed, and five rings in, a familiar but leery voice answered. "Miss Janet?"

"What the hell's going on, Tate?"

She sounded just like herself.

"Um, why you calling in the middle of the night?" Tate wasn't taking the bait that easy.

"Why do you think I'm calling? They took Arthur to jail." An arm flailed as she spoke, and she started to pace. Callie motioned for her to stand still for the recorder.

"Tate? You hearing me, son?"

"Yes, ma'am."

"They won't tell me a damn thing because Arthur's technically an adult. But I at least heard they arrested him at your place. Why didn't you call me? Arthur wouldn't be there for his health. He had to be seeing you."

Mark eyed Callie, nodding, impressed at Janet's role-play.

"Tate?" she asked into the hesitation.

"Um, I got away," he mumbled.

"Speak up, son," Janet ordered.

"I ran," he said louder.

"Why?" she asked. "What have you and Arthur gone and done?"

Callie gestured, petting the air for Janet to take it down a notch. They couldn't afford to lose the guy because of Janet's anger.

But Tate's nerves were already on edge. "Because that bitch police chief accused us of all them burglaries."

Janet gave the conversation a second, then softened her delivery, though remaining in charge. "Did you burgle those houses? Did Arthur? I can't help without the truth."

"No, ma'am. I didn't. And I swear Arthur probably didn't either. Not his way."

Her jaw line hardened. She'd been deceived by Arthur and now lied to by Tate.

Mark moved so he could watch her reactions, watch how she talked. Callie made hard eye contact with her to keep her on task, but from the Marine's jawline and cocked brow, she was thinking. Thinking hard. Tate had crossed a line. Worried before about whether Janet could deceive this kid she'd half raised, Callie had confidence Janet would cooperate now.

"I've got lawyers, Tate, but I've got to hear what this is about first. Where are you?" she asked.

"I got this, Miss Janet."

Releasing a *humph*, Janet held her shoulders further back. "You telling me you've got transportation? Gas money? *Any* money? And if they catch you, you think you have any damn idea what kind of attorney to call?"

"They give you attorneys," he said, not feeling her reeling him in.

"Last thing you want is some half-wit public defender. You get what you pay for. With my okay, you might even get the one Arthur has since he's already on the ground."

Tate had a lot on his mind, and Janet had only added to it. But she was the known quantity in his life. He didn't have to weigh her merits, and he didn't have a contact list of folks willing to help when cops got involved.

"Don't come to the house," he finally said.

"Where then?"

"The Mullet place on Manse. Where I did those repairs."

Then *she* let the call get quiet. The old woman was rocking this.

"Miss Janet?"

"Anybody see you go there?"

"No, ma'am."

Callie wrote on a pad and held it up. *Meet around 8.*

Puzzled, Janet threw a frustrated glance before snatching the pen from Callie's hand to write, *Why?*

"Miss Janet?"

"I'm thinking, boy. Hold on."

Callie scribbled *Got to see Arthur in Walterboro first.*

"I told the attorney I'd head over to Walterboro, to the jail," Janet said. "Arthur needs clothes, and the attorney wants a retainer. Damn bottom feeder."

"I'm worried, Miss Janet," and he sounded like it. "I thought you controlled everybody."

"Hold on," she said. "I can't draw attention to myself, can I? While I'm out, I'll go by the ATM and get you some money. I can meet you around, say, eight? Will you be all right till then?"

He exhaled loud enough for all of them to hear. "I'll be fine. Tell

Arthur . . . never mind. Don't want anyone suspicious."

"That's right, Tate," Janet said. "You catch you some sleep. See you in a few hours. Want me to make you an egg sandwich and bring it? I'd pick something up, but nothing's open."

"No, I'm good," he said. "Sorry I messed up your Christmas, Miss Janet."

"We'll get through this, Tate." Her face froze steely hard. "I promise. We'll all get through this."

Chapter 28

TATE HUNG UP, the plan in place for Janet to meet him at the *Mullet House* on Manse Road around eight a.m. It was just past three.

"What the hell, Chief," Janet fumed. "There's no time for delay. My nephew's future is at stake, and—"

Callie heaved a hard exhale. "Janet—"

But Mark stepped up from his silent vigil, the older woman giving him an up and down stare like he didn't belong. "Cool your heels, Ms. Wainwright," he said. "Callie's had no sleep in forty-eight hours. She's been dogging this case hard, much of it to do with protecting your reputation, in case you hadn't noticed."

Just his mention of no sleep put added weight on Callie's limbs. Regardless Janet's demand for urgency, without a couple or three hours of rest, Callie'd make mistakes. Tate might be easier to retrieve using Janet, but then he could also go wild on them, too. Desperation changed the meekest of people.

"I'll meet you at your house at seven," Callie said.

But Janet didn't say anything.

Callie peered straight into the woman's gaze. "You still up for this? If not, tell me. I have other people to coordinate, and if you're not involved, their plans change."

Janet clicked her attention onto the police chief. "Of course I'm game. My house at seven." And she left.

The door closed with a muted whump at the realtor's departure. "Let me drive you home for a nap," Mark said.

"Gotta call the guys, first." She reached for her cell. In under thirty minutes, she'd spoken to Raysor, Thomas, and Ike, with Raysor insuring another Colleton County deputy still blocked the McKinley Washington Bridge, the only road egress from the island.

Though Manse Road ran through Charleston County, this was Christmas . . . this was an Edisto Beach case . . . Charleston County wouldn't be eager to jump into what might be a simple run out to pick up a burglar. As expected, they said call if she needed them. Like they could travel forty miles instantly if she did.

"It's 3:30," Mark said.

Almost too weary to stand, she rose, putting weight on her desk as she did. "I'm not going home." She led Mark out of her office and into the lobby. An aged leather sofa took up a corner, used more for the officers to kick back on than the public. Phone out, she lowered herself to the center cushion, the two end cushions worn thin and cupped. A homemade pillow with a sprinkling of shells embroidered across its front, rested on one end, made by a grateful resident.

"Three hours," she said, setting her alarm, then texting Stan as to her status. He'd tell Jeb. "If I go home my worried son will keep me up talking, and if I lay on my bed I might not wake up. This suits me fine." She halted, sighing up at Mark. "Well, damn. I can't exactly give you the keys to the patrol car and let you drive it home, can I?" With effort, she lifted fatigued bones upright.

"No, no," Mark said, just enough pressure on her shoulders for Callie not to fight him. She relaxed back down on the middle cushion.

She went to reach in her uniform pocket for the car keys and realized she still had on her civilian clothes. Two-day-old civvies. "Screw rules," she said, finding the keys in a different pocket than accustomed. "Take the car. Just be back by 6:30. I'll run home, shower, and put on the uniform." *And change underwear.*

"I'll take care of myself," he said, walking to shut off the lobby light. He left the blue wreath lit on the door. "You just sit there . . . "

But she'd already rested her head on the pillow without a worry about how many other heads and hands had left remnants of skin cells and germs, her breathing immediately regular and deep.

HER DREAM TOOK her on a dark road overhung with Spanish moss, ankle-thick poison ivy vines draped Tarzan-like conjoining massive oaks, the air thick with exhalations of the forest. A common place for her nightmares. And as always, time ran out for whoever she pursued. She'd run for miles, and her legs quivered, fighting her effort.

She chased a genuine person, a friend, she guessed, and she was moving too slow, fearing she'd be unable to save him from whatever lay in wait. It was a him, that much she knew.

The man called, and she dug in her heels and kicked up silt, passing trees and bushes, trying to guess where to veer off the sandy road and into the jungle growth . . . into the blackness where sound and smell, feral and natural instincts would have to direct her. If she misjudged where to venture into the thicket it would aid her enemy, and slow down the rescue.

The victim kept calling. Too far off to see without sunlight able to breach the canopy. She couldn't decide where to leave the road. Where to dive in.

"Callie." A voice struggled to penetrate the deep well of her unconsciousness.

Then movement under her thrust her back to the surface. She peered from beneath puffy eyelids to Mark rubbing his own sleep-deprived eyes . . . her feet in his lap. He patted her legs and slid his way out from under them. "How can you not hear that?"

While she grappled on and then beside the sofa, hunting the racket, he reached it first, her phone shouting irritation in a repeated jackhammer noise from the edge of a chair he'd moved close.

"Damn!" he yelled when he finally shut it off.

Damn was right. She struggled up, the noise still an echo in her brain. "Sorry," she said. Jeb had put that awful ringtone on her cell over Thanksgiving when she'd overslept, made her promise not to take it off . . . the unspoken being a hangover might make her late to work.

Six thirty per the alarm. She willed energy back into her limbs. Then she felt her sock feet.

Mark had napped sitting up, removing her shoes and making room on the too-short sofa for himself beneath her feet. A stunned feeling she had no time to interpret. Thirty minutes to shower and meet Janet at her house.

"You coming or am I dropping you off at home?" Callie asked, tying her laces then jumping up. She ran back to her office without an answer, retrieving keys and purse, weapon in the paddle holster at her waist.

"Coming," he said, tucking his shirt back in on the side. "Feel like a new man after that nap."

Yet after she locked up and strode to catch up, ahead of her he nursed that limp en route to the car.

On her way to her house, she radioed Raysor. "You on island yet?"

"Sitting at the Tate house," he came back. "Nothing I can see."

"His truck still there?"

"Yup."

Janet was right. Tate might be fearful of leaving his homeplace, but while he might appreciate the woods and water like his own skin, he couldn't stay hidden for long. Surely he sensed his job was history.

"Your guy still at the bridge?" she asked.

"Yup again. Been keeping each other awake," he said. "Still on for eight?"

"Yes, sir. Edisto One out."

At her drive, she'd confirmed Thomas's location at the EZ Go, and Ike hidden at the Presbyterian Church, on either side of the Manse Road entrance off Highway 174. Tate shouldn't have gotten past any of them, but assuming he had, he'd be coming to her on the beach or headed to the bridge where the Colleton deputy would be waiting.

Nope. Tate was still at *Mullet House.*

She reached *Chelsea Morning* and raced up her steps, for a change cursing her home alarm system for eating up minutes. Mark said he'd wait in the car, and she hoped he'd catch a nap.

"Mom," Jeb shouted as the alarm shut off, his hair disheveled, pajama bottoms puddled across the tops of his feet. "What's the deal?"

She hugged him deep and drew his head down to kiss the top. It pained her to treat his Christmas like this. He'd come home mostly for her sake, and he always put the deepest thought into his gift for her.

"I'm still on that case. Have to meet someone at seven."

"On Christmas?"

"Can't help it," she hollered, touching him once more before dashing into her bedroom, clothes shed across the floor and bed. In the shower, she soaped up, and after a couple spins under the spray leaped out.

Jeb hung outside her bedroom. "Where've you been sleeping?" Always the parent, never the child.

"Haven't," she said. "Grabbed a couple hours at the station."

He'd accepted her job long ago after a longer spell of hating her for it, but he held her accountable. To him. To her health.

"I hate it when you act like this," he shouted.

"Like what?" she said, though she understood. "And I can hear you without the shouting."

"Pushed, frantic, agitated. . . . I can't describe it."

"I'm not drinking," she said, running out with uniform mostly on, the one she'd left on the bed when she'd gone to visit Sarah.

He studied her straightening, buckling, fastening every aspect of her being a cop. "You're wearing your vest."

"I'm supposed to wear a vest," she said finishing up, telling herself not to be concerned about straightening the insignia but doing it anyway passing the hall mirror. "You ought to be glad I wear a vest."

"I'd be gladder if you were going to a meeting where you didn't *have* to wear it." His sweetness no longer in his eyes, he took a hold of her arm. "What aren't you telling me, Mom? Mr. Stan talks in a dozen versions of *everything's okay, Jeb.*"

She withdrew from under him grip, then threw on her uniform jacket to fend off the December cold. "It's all good. Really, it is. This thing is just . . . time-sensitive." What other words would fit without giving him more to worry about? "Tell Sophie I have no idea about dinner."

"Seriously?"

Leaving him in the hallway, the coolness no doubt prickling his naked chest and arms, she spoke over her shoulder, "I'll check in. Promise. Love you, Jeb. Keep the place locked." Her best effort at sounding routine, though she knew he knew better. But at ten minutes to seven, she had no seconds to spare.

She leaped into the driver's seat, waking Mark in the process.

"That was fast," he said, coming to. "We late?"

"Hope not. One is never late to meet the Marine." Callie drove the four blocks over to see Janet. A black case rested on the seat beside her. She hoped Wainwright was willing.

Beach Head's lights were on, the winter dawn keeping seven a.m. gray and drowsy, even the surf sounding sleepy from a block over. Janet opened the door before Callie and Mark reached the top step.

Having changed into dark brown corduroys and a khaki, lined hunting jacket, Janet stood ready with a rested appearance, when in fact Callie worried she hadn't slept at all. The old woman's mind would probably have been churning the facts, words, and deeds that had led them to this hour. Anyone who'd been in danger, who'd stood on the sideline worried about someone else's plan falling into place . . . fathomed the endless mind games that came with the waiting. Janet Wainwright was primed.

"We're taking my Hummer," she said, giving an order.

"Yes, ma'am, we are," Callie replied. She held out the case. "Would you mind wearing this?"

"A wire?" Janet asked.

Callie nodded.

Janet took the case. "Be glad to."

Callie followed her into the bedroom and helped her rig the device. When they reached Mark, it was 7:20.

After a few words of explanation about the wire, and instructions for Janet to lead Tate out but not pick a fight, they left.

"Guess you're driving the patrol car after all," Callie said, tossing the keys to Mark. "We'll head to Tate's, and you'll relieve Raysor. He'll need to come block Manse Road."

All exits covered.

They left Janet's with the two women in the Hummer, and Mark following in the car. At the EZ Go, the ladies waited for Mark to take Raysor's place monitoring Tate's house, and for Raysor to follow them to Manse where he'd guard that road's entrance.

Once alone, Janet driving and Callie tucked low in the back seat, the two took the silt thoroughfare, barely a half mile in, past an ancient multi-level treehouse in the woods, and came on to a low, split-rail fence. During their brief idle, Callie put the preamble into the recorder and checked yet again the reception on Janet's mic, then they took their respective deep breaths and eased headlights first into the twin-rutted drive.

In contrast to the beach houses, *Mullet House* sat flush, with only an eight-inch step inside. The tiny one bedroom, one bath, rustic unit served as a retreat for two at most. Without water frontage, the bungalow was tucked under an intense canopy overhead, the trees seemingly endless, disappearing in the back until they all ran together into a gray-green mass. A falling limb had necessitated Tate's recent repair job, which left the place fresh in his mind when he needed a hideaway. Years of leaves and pine straw covered the grounds. A natural-stain siding on the front made the place blend into the setting. Only the window trims painted white declared the house hadn't surrendered to the elements completely.

"You can do this," Callie said.

"Of course I can," came the reply, and Janet left the Hummer. But as Janet slid out of the seat, her coat flipped up and Callie caught a glimpse of the weapon on her hip.

Son of a bitch. When had she managed that?

She bit her words, frustrated, torn between calling out to Janet to leave the gun in the vehicle which would blow the op or letting her continue. Nothing good could come of her being armed. Nothing.

The woman traipsed up an old brick walkway. Her transmitter fed signal one way—to the recorder in the Hummer.

Callie could only watch and listen.

Janet knocked on the screen after finding it latched. The wooden door eased back, the person not discernible, but Janet was then able to open the screen. However, no sooner than she widened it, the person snatched her by the sleeve, jerking her off balance, and she fell forward.

"Damn it," Callie whispered, checking the receiver, her heart kicking into a higher pace.

Nothing. For a long minute, Callie struggled not to breathe too heavily, listening for the slightest of sounds and simultaneously watching the closed door, suspended in the agony of waiting, worried her wire had gone wrong . . . or been discovered.

Chapter 29

SCRATCHING. STATIC. Then silence in Callie's earpiece. *Give it a moment. Tate's sizing her up.* At least she hoped it was Tate . . . and that's all he was doing.

"What are we doing here?" Finally, Janet broke the ice.

"Losing my shit," he said. "You're all I've got, Miss Janet."

"I understand that," she said, stable and level, like a father to a son who'd had his first fender bender. "And that's why I'm here. First, before we plan anything, you have to tell me what happened. And tell me the damn truth, you understand me?"

Callie could imagine the Marine's stiff stance, elbows sharp.

But Tate wasn't Arthur. "What have they told you?"

"That someone burgled a lot of houses. No break-ins, just easy access. Like someone had keys . . . except for the ones lock-picked."

Janet kept to the burglaries, discussing them in elementary terms. Good. Few details. Talk of murder sent most people off their rocker.

"Where's Arthur?" he asked.

"In jail. They're trying to decide whether to believe him. Trying to determine how you fit into all this."

Tate got silent.

No interior lights despite the cloudy skies. They'd be in the semi-dark, Tate afraid to bring attention to the small house. Callie envisioned Janet trying to read Tate, and him doing the same though his younger eyes would have the advantage.

She prayed Tate wasn't armed.

"Care to come in and tell authorities the truth?" Janet asked. "I'll be right there with you."

"What, confess to the burglaries?" he asked back.

"Confess anything, Tate. You're not a criminal, and you don't have the skills to make this disappear."

"I did before Arthur got involved."

He was right. A lot of crimes went unsolved because the culprit kept his mouth shut and drew no attention. Tate's problem was talking to Arthur. Arthur's problem was not going to the police.

"What if I said I didn't do anything?" He wasn't so quick to trust.

"But you did," she said. "I'll supply the attorney, like I said."

"About that . . . why would you pay that kind of money for me?" His voice hardened sooner than Callie expected, given that Janet painted the junior as innocent, raised by a good father who'd taught him well with Janet's assistance.

"Why would you ever ask that, boy?"

"Quit calling me that! *Boy*. Like I wasn't grown."

Cramped, Callie changed positions, daring to leave the floor and sit on the seat, hunkering down. *Bring him around, Janet. You're all he's got. Use it.*

"I'll always think of you as a boy, Tate. You weren't quite six when you started coming around my office, hovering behind your daddy, thinking I ate children for breakfast."

He laughed. Thank God. "I did think that, didn't I? You were my daddy's boss, but more than that, you had military stuff everywhere, and I imagined you killing a hundred people. That white hair of yours covered in blood as you waded through rifles and bayonets all camouflaged up." He laughed harder. "A hard-assed bitch taking out three-hundred-pound men."

Janet's snort came through, making Callie give a half-grin at Tate envisioning a young Janet with white hair. "You have no idea what I was like . . . " and Callie could feel the woman avoid using the term *boy*.

The day remained cloud-covered and stifling in spite of the coolness. No breeze, especially tucked this far back on the island. Humidity started building in the Hummer. Callie readjusted the bud in her ear.

"I was seen," he finally said.

"Who saw you?" Janet asked, matter of factly.

But the kid didn't answer the question.

"You tried to keep your daddy's legacy alive, didn't you, Tate?"

No doubt with age came wisdom, and this moment Callie respected everything about Janet Wainwright. Her purpose, her strength. With nothing more than a prod and a wire, she'd plowed masterfully into this situation as if this had been her plan from the beginning.

"Yes, ma'am, I was thinking about my daddy," Tate replied. "Didn't think about what he used to do until December crept up on me. Then I didn't have no money. Wasn't till I went to fix the faucet in a rental, after the family was checked in, did I see their tree and come up with my plan. Not like they'd miss one present, right, Miss Janet?"

"What went wrong?" she asked.

"Oh," he said, animation kicking in. "It went great, frickin' great, until . . . until it didn't. Until I was seen."

"A renter?"

Smart, Janet kept him talking, covering all the bases she could to get intel on the record. *Go, Marine.*

"No, not a renter," he said, disgusted. "And you get what I'm saying without me giving an instant replay. Quit with the con, Miss Janet."

"I'm not conning you." And she said it like she meant it. "You don't even have to tell me what you did or who saw you. I'll get you off this island, put money in your pocket and nobody'll be the wiser."

Silence.

Callie would give a thousand dollars to be able to read Tate's expression and body movements. Wires were good . . . to a point, but she worried how strung out Tate was . . . how much he'd pondered his future through the dark, early morning.

"No, you won't help me escape," he said, as if insulted. "You may throw a few dollars at me, but your real blood's in jail. You'd use me to get him out. They'll believe that college degree more than me, so he'll come out smelling good regardless. The question is what to do with you."

"No, it's how to save you," she said.

Callie agreed with that.

Raysor radioed in. "Update please."

She reached for her walkie. "Ongoing, Don. Continue to stand by."

Eagerly she clicked off, listening hard for Janet.

Tate was starting to sass back. "Miss Janet—"

"Man up to what happened." Out came the drill sergeant mode. "Did you go into Ben Rosewood's house? Answer me."

"What if I did?"

"Did you kill him?"

He laughed, but a thread of queasiness ran through it. "Guy was found dead on Dolphin Road, so how could I have killed him?"

"You tell me. And tell me now!" Janet barked like she missed those days drilling recruits on Parris Island. "You say you didn't do it. Did you follow him to the lot and drop him there? Did you bash him over the head, load him in the truck, and cart him there? What the hell did you do!"

His voice exploded. "I did not touch the man!"

"But they can prove you were in the house," she lied.

"The door was open, okay? Saw a man leave it all open and walk down the street. I can't name all these residents cause I never fix their houses, but thinking fate was telling me something, I went to check out an easy Christmas tree. Instead, I run into this other guy. Arthur told me later who this Ben guy was. But there I go, expecting to dart in and out, and he's standing there around the corner in the living room, rich and fine, drinking his liquor."

"Why didn't you run?" she asked.

"I did!" he yelled. "But he ran after me. He was a big man. Spun me around, but I only shoved him against the wall and took off. No way I killed him, because he chased me, Miss Janet. For half a block."

The kid was saying all the things they needed to hear, but Callie's nerves jittered a warning at the emotion beginning to pour out. She watched the cottage's entrance hard and tried to judge whether she should intervene. Once someone spilled their feelings, they either felt exorcised . . . or wished they hadn't.

"It had to be someone else, Miss Janet. Had to be. Is that why they arrested Arthur? Someone thinks it's him?" A different level of emotion. Grasping for options, Tate sought excuses to use as an alibi.

Callie slid the recorder to the floor and lifted softly up on the door handle. Tate was quickly realizing the limitations of his choices. Janet had discreetly started backing him into a mental corner, hoping to convince him to surrender.

"Well, there you go," Janet said. "Couldn't have been you or Arthur."

Tate wasn't one to give in, though, and he'd forfeit Arthur in a heartbeat. Callie could hear it in his words. He sought a way out, and if Janet didn't provide him with one . . .

"Arthur will stand by you," she said, still fighting for the young Tate she'd supported for so long. "And so will I."

"And why would I believe you'd side with me over Arthur?"

She attempted to come off more as the cherished aunt, taking her tone down. "Doesn't have to be one or the other."

"But he's in jail, and I'm not," he said, escalating. "With me in the wind . . . they'll likely stick with what they've got. Hear what I'm saying . . . ma'am?" Sarcasm dripped on the end.

He wasn't as naïve as Janet said. As with any animal, self-preservation kicks in, and Tate had endured a long enough night of retrospection to sense his existence was threatened six ways from Sunday. He probably listened to Janet to insure he'd ruled out all his alternatives.

"Just had to hear what you knew . . . and what Arthur knew . . . so I could decide what to do," he said. "Heard they arrested Mr. Brice, and they done locked up Arthur. Sounds like they got plenty of suspects to go around without adding me. And I imagine your Hummer would take me off this island way sooner than my old pickup. So head out, Marine. March!"

Callie lifted the walkie to call in the guys. Tate had said enough in her opinion, but then noises of scuffle and a bump replaced conversation. Alarmed, Callie heard a half-grunt, half-groan that could only be Janet, low and distant.

"Tables are turned," Tate said. "I'm the drill sergeant. Get your ass off the floor and head to the Hummer"—*grunt*—"wait a minute . . . what's this?"

Oh Jesus. Callie's blood chilled. He quickly confirmed what she feared as she slid out of the Hummer and moved around its tailgate toward the driver's side, walkie close to her mouth. Weapon drawn.

"A nine mil?" He'd found Janet's gun. "Thought you loved me, Miss Janet. Thought I was your favorite when Arthur was off at school."

"I go armed most places," she said.

"The hell you do," he replied.

"You ought to be surprised if I *wasn't* armed. You said yourself I killed three-hundred-pound men in my day. So you have my weapon. What do you intend to do with it?"

"Take you and your Hummer and haul ass off this island," he said.

Callie hesitated to call in the breach signal if they were coming out. The last thing they wanted was for Tate to hole up in the *Mullet House* with a hostage . . . or worse. If they could get him outside, and Janet outside . . .

Callie thought the door moved, but nobody appeared, maybe some second-guessing going on.

"Give me the gun, Tate." Janet sounded stronger. She was too tough to stay down.

"How about give me your keys instead?" he replied.

"They're in the vehicle."

"Good enough," he said. "Go on, move."

The door opened for real.

Callie spoke low into the walkie. "Here comes Santa Claus." The prearranged breach signal, indicating Tate was armed. "Hostage situation. Move."

Suddenly Janet shook his grip loose. "You're pissing off the wrong Marine, boy."

But Tate only gave a deep chuckle, unconvinced of the threat. "You trying to intimidate me, you old crow? Get on over there."

Tate shoved Janet toward the vehicle, but she peeled to the passenger side. *Good job, Janet.*

Callie aimed her pistol around the driver's side of the vehicle, using the Hummer for cover best she could. Tate's head pivoted left and right, from Janet to Callie.

"Freeze right there, Tate," Callie yelled. "Put the weapon down slowly."

Raysor's cruiser arrived, sliding on the silt to a few yards behind the Hummer, angled some to the left. He rolled out and crouched, his aim in the crack between his door and the car's interior, the engine block additional cover.

Holding the nine mil on Janet, Tate opened the Hummer's door to hide behind. Callie'd hoped a twenty-two-year-old islander would have a greater fear of a fire fight. He wasn't much older than Jeb; she couldn't imagine a boy this age throwing away his life so recklessly.

Was this brashness taught to him by his daddy, or a foolishness of his own? By association with Janet? Who could tell, but his stubborn reliance on himself as his savior was about to work to his disadvantage.

"Tate," Callie said. "Put the gun down." Then she noticed Janet wasn't exactly cowering on the other side.

"No need to shoot," Janet told her. "His weapon's not loaded."

Then why the hell didn't she drop down and run? She had the bulk of the Hummer's engine as protection.

Tate snapped a glance at Janet. "That's lame, Janet. What Marine goes out with an unloaded weapon?"

Indeed, Callie thought, making her completely uncertain whether Janet told the truth. Might explain her not running.

"And you, Chief," Tate yelled, jerking the weapon once for emphasis. "Shoot me and I shoot her."

Callie adjusted her grip, sniffed a cold runny nose, and spoke to him down the barrel and through her sights. "Afraid you got that reversed,

Tate. Shoot Ms. Wainwright, and I shoot you. Of course, you're assuming I don't shoot you first. Lay the weapon on the hood of the Hummer and back off while there's still a clean way out of this for you."

Thomas's vehicle arrived, Ike's on his tail. Thomas drove around Raysor and stopped, lights flashing, as he threw his door open and assumed a similar position, only with a broader, better bead on the target. Ike assumed a spot behind Raysor, a much clearer view of Janet. A lot of firepower on such a scrawny, sad, mixed-up confusion of a young man.

An insignificant one-lane road without much breathing room. Tate wasn't leaving, at least in the Hummer. Callie's bigger concern was him dropping the weapon and bolting for the jungle, where he had the advantage.

But he showed no signs of dropping that gun.

"Tate?" Callie tried to speak just loud enough for all to hear, but without yelling. He'd threatened, assaulted, and kidnapped an older woman. Atop stealing the gun itself. Additional felonies for which he'd have to answer. No attorney, including any of Janet's acquaintances, would get Tate out of a jail sentence. "This is getting serious," Callie said. "Slow down and think. Surely you don't see your way out of this standoff, and we really don't want to hurt you."

"Kill me, you mean," he said.

"Yes, you're absolutely right," she answered. "Glad to hear you recognize that."

"Stop it. Everybody," Janet hollered. "The gun is not loaded."

Didn't she see it was too late for that? Callie's exhaled breath hung white in the cold morning. "Hush, Janet. Can't afford to believe you. You might just be trying to keep me from killing Tate. I see an armed and dangerous individual, who's committed a lot of felonies in my presence. He has to comply or land in the morgue. You hearing that, Tate?"

But Janet shook her head, and yelled, "No. I'm telling the truth." Then at Tate said, "Aim up and fire, Tate. Squeeze the trigger. Show them before they hurt you."

Callie eased herself out into the open a little more. "Don't, Tate."

Left hand holding the weapon on Janet, Tate eyed Callie, anger radiating from his shivering body. Brow creased deep, he opened his mouth . . .

Raysor's Model 66 S&W erupted, spinning Tate around then to the ground. The echo took off through the trees, sending birds to flight.

Janet rushed to Tate. Callie collected the weapon where it landed a dozen feet from the Hummer, then squatted beside Janet. The Marine put pressure on the wound, maroon already staining her lap and chest where she'd maneuvered Tate to better stem the blood flow.

Damn this stupid kid. "Thomas? Call 911," Callie said, a tightness in her throat watching the agony in Tate's expression, no longer the bad boy he tried to be.

Leaving the nursing to Janet, she called to Raysor. No doubt in her mind he'd placed that shot where he wanted in lieu of center mass . . . in lieu of killing someone who'd barely begun his life. "And cancel the BOLO. Suspect in custody," she said, then in afterthought, she checked the pistol. "Damn," she whispered. "It really wasn't loaded."

Holstering weapons, Thomas did as told, and Ike closed in, for his own peace of mind insuring Tate wasn't mobile enough for a run for the jungle.

They went over him for more weapons, and finding none, left him in Janet's arms.

Tate writhed in pain, caring little who held him, his eyes shut, his good arm crossed to protect the damage. But Janet murmured assurances to the young man she'd maneuvered to her lap, a slight rock to her thin body.

Regardless of the audacity of the little bastard, he was damn lucky he still lived. All because of his misdirected loyalty for his daddy's Edisto Santa tradition. Stupid, stupid kid.

Saddened and ready to fall exhausted in her tracks, Callie walked back behind the Hummer . . . not wanting to see Marine tears.

Chapter 30

REGARDLESS OF everyone's effort, Tate lost a lot of blood by the time an ambulance reached Manse Road. Edisto Island was remote, and most emergencies took patience and creative use of a first aid kit until medical personnel could make the trek. Janet never left his side and would've accompanied him to the hospital except he was under arrest. Instead, she left for the jail where Arthur anxiously awaited his beloved aunt. Regardless how anyone cut this, Janet's obligation would tilt to Arthur, and it tore at Callie to see the woman so divided.

Callie didn't think she'd ever see Janet in the same light again. Devoted, loving . . . yet vulnerable. Tate and Arthur pulled off their stunts under her purview, and not only would Janet see that as a flaw on her part, but so would some parts of Edisto.

With Thomas having missed one night's sleep already, Callie sent Ike to stand guard over Tate in the hospital, but she placed a call to the Charleston Sheriff's Office after the ambulance left, calling in a long-due favor from Sheriff Mosier. Which meant he'd gladly assign a deputy to Tate's bedside until he was well enough to be transported to the jail. Edisto Beach Police Department didn't have the manpower to spare. Four of the six officers had missed a lot of sleep of late.

The Hummer was gone, the ambulance and Ike on their way to the hospital. Raysor and Callie sat on the hood of his cruiser, while Thomas took notes, bagged Janet's and Raysor's guns, and performed the beginning of all the necessary paperwork required by the shooting of the soon-to-be-infamous Edisto Santa.

Callie's brain, shoulders, thighs, every inch of her body threatened to give out. She'd managed three hours sleep over a long, grueling forty-eight hours chasing Brice, Arthur, and Tate, but she had to assist in wrapping this up. The work wouldn't complete itself, and it definitely wasn't happening if she continued leaning against Raysor's car, a spot she couldn't seem to leave.

Mark drove up in her patrol car.

"Oh, crap," she whispered. "I forgot to call him off Tate's house." With serious effort, she pushed her way to her feet and walked to meet the restauranteur, who'd become more the ex-SLED agent in her eyes.

She held out her arms, giving him a dramatic groan. "I'm so damn sorry, Mark. I should've called you sooner. The ambulance just left—"

He directed her back to Raysor's hood, glancing around the scene. "I assume Janet's all right?"

"On her way to see Arthur. Things got touch and go for a while. Janet threw us for a loop by hiding a weapon under her coat . . . that Tate got his hands on."

Mark frowned. "I hope Tate's in the ambulance."

With a slow wave, Callie nodded, her head felt oddly off-center and like it weighed fifty pounds. "Yes, but don't make me rehash it. Not now."

She bent over, leaning on her knees, the world suddenly trying to spin, but she wasn't going to be the damsel, so she pointed to Raysor. "That man did the deed. Shot Tate in the shoulder, removing the threat." She peered up at her deputy. "Damn you and that old style wheel gun. About burst my eardrums, dude."

The deputy belly-laughed. "Yeah, but my old-school gun got the job done, didn't it?"

"That it did," she said, grinning at the ground, letting the landscape settle. Taking in a deep breath, she held the cold air, seeking rejuvenation. "Anybody got a candy bar or something?"

"Tell you what," Mark said, eying her. "Go sit in your car—"

But she interrupted with a limp wave. "No. We still have to clear this place."

"Guy's right, doll," Raysor said. "You look like hell."

"Love you, too, Don," but her voice tried to disappear on her.

"Twenty-minute power nap," Raysor added, standing as if he'd just had one himself. "Isn't that what they say is supposed to work for corporate types?"

Their talk of naps and sleep increased the heaviness in her bones, so she stood in attempt to shake it off. Maybe moving around would help.

Mark took her by the shoulders, his six-foot height winning the day in redirecting her to the car. He opened the passenger rear and helped her inside. Twenty minutes, she thought, and for a second she worried about being chilled, calling Jeb, maybe Stan. Then her world went black.

SHE AWOKE IN her underwear, head so fuzzy she wasn't sure where she was, what day it was, and for a long, disjointed moment, where her nightshirt was.

But she didn't raise her head or move her body. They were perfectly comfortable where they were, like rocks embedded in sand at low tide. No real need to shift until the next tide rolled in, and even then, some other force would have to take over.

Events sifted back in, pieces at a time . . . at first all out of place until slowly they found order in her mind.

Poor Janet. Then pity for Brice bubbled up as well. He'd been taken advantage of by his wife and his friend, but worse, he'd spent his life strutting around Edisto professing to be nobody's fool only to be proven the biggest fool anyone had seen in ages. Would he step down from town council of his own volition? Or would he puff up and dare anyone to take him down? Either way, he'd have to adapt to how people treated him, and his own behavior would dictate how well he endured. A plus for his future was Edisto's usual willingness to ignore anyone's past before they came to Edisto. Hopefully, that passive island forgiveness would spill onto Brice once he arrived home. Assuming he didn't land behind bars.

She couldn't believe she felt so sorry for him sitting in jail without a soul on his side.

She rolled her head to the side, toward the window. Dark. Then to the clock. Nine fifteen. Listening, she expected to hear Jeb, or at least the television show he had on, maybe even Sophie bouncing around. Her yoga friend often switched to nursemaid when Callie was down, whether flu, exhaustion, or hangover, and she couldn't stay quiet to save her soul.

A quiet house meant an empty house. Good.

Sluggishly she left the bed, happy for the solitude. She could drink a glass of tea as big as she was, and yawning, she padded barefoot toward the door.

"Merry Christ . . . mas . . .uh, oh."

"Damn it," she yelled and darted back in, slamming the door.

Laughter erupted in the living room, the squeal coming from Sophie's pitchy giggle . . . a room also filled with both her moms, Sarah and Beverly, Jeb, Stan, and Mark.

Heart thumping and back against the bedroom wall, Callie's first thought was thank the heavens Thomas hadn't come as promised for dinner.

She made them wait for her to shower, but she soon emerged in jeans and her annual Christmas sweater flaunting a gingerbread man in uniform, a gag gift Jeb bought her years ago. "I guess I'm back in the world of the living," she said. "Where's the eggnog? I think I deserve . . ."

"Virgin eggnog," Sophie said, slipping a crystal cup into Callie's hand. "I'm calling the others. Damn, girl, I thought you'd be sleeping through the night. We've been dying to open gifts."

Callie took a sip, hugged her mothers, then made her way to the men, each with a variety of smirk. With Mark more than double her size and the one possessing her patrol car keys, she could guess how she'd been deposited in her bedroom. "So now that you've seen my Walmart underwear, you can get over yourselves. But the biggest question is which of you stripped me down to see it?"

Jeb held up palms in surrender and pivoted away. Stan stood fast and winked. Mark, however, took a sudden interest in the Christmas tree.

"Noooo," she said, drawing it out, embarrassed too deep to hide. "You?"

Sophie sashayed in and smacked her on the butt. "He did the police stuff and shoes, but I did the rest."

With an exhale, Callie added, "Thank God."

It didn't take long for Sophie's two grown kids to appear, and in a half hour, they had a Christmas dinner on the table. Less than that and the food was gone, the younger people in Jeb's room, the two moms in the kitchen cleaning up while the rest of the adults lazed around on sofa and recliners.

"I ought to check in," Callie said, setting a coffee on the end table.

"Hold on," Mark said. "One, Arthur's still in jail, and Janet got home this afternoon. She's probably sleeping. Two, Tate required surgery, but he's recovering cuffed to a hospital bed. Expected to be released in three days. Ike was relieved"—he glanced at a clock on the mantel—"about two hours ago by a Charleston deputy. Raysor's at home, eating, sleeping, whatever. Thomas, good man that one, by the way, took a partial shift then went home to sleep, apologizing for missing your Christmas. And LaRoache is on duty."

Unaccustomed to a civilian other than Marie filling her in, she still reached for her phone. "But we were expecting a lot of calls about missing gifts once families started opening presents," she said.

"Isn't that what voice mail is for?" he said. "They aren't emergencies since you've already solved the crime."

Callie sank back into her sofa cushion, studying the El Marko's owner, remaining as unimpressed as she could appear about how seamlessly he'd maneuvered himself into her law enforcement. "What happened to you being retired?"

"Hey, you invited me along," he said, and laid back in the recliner. "Guess the guys considered me a part of the team today. They wanted you informed so why not through me?"

She scowled at Stan.

"Don't get pissed; they called me, too," he said. "It's not like they had many choices."

She couldn't disagree, so she let it go and noted Mark's bandaged arm instead. "Hurt?" she asked, touching her own arm to emphasize his.

"Like a b—, um, yes," he corrected, noting the mothers an earshot nearby. "Called your doc, by the way."

"Thought peroxide and gauze served your purpose?" she said, droll with a grin.

Stan gave a short *hah*. "And tell her who had to remind you of it, too."

"Your boss over there," Mark began.

"Ex-boss," she corrected.

He flipped a wave at Stan. "Yes, well, he mentioned that Tate might not have vaccinated his dog. We'd never find that beast in this jungle, so it appears I'll be taking rabies shots for a few weeks."

Oh my goodness. "I'm so sorry, Mark."

He just shrugged.

"Well, a very deep, very sincere thank-you's in order. You didn't have to stick by me for Arthur's interview, Janet, and the Tate pursuit." She tipped her chin in his direction. "But your services were appreciated, kind sir."

"No problem." His attention strayed to his coffee. "Felt good to engage again."

Then she recalled the limp. "How's your leg?"

"Fine. I'm used to it."

Oh, he hadn't injured it at Tate's house? Was this more of an old wound flaring up? She almost asked him the story behind his periodic hobble, but then, the story might not be one best shared in a room full of others. Maybe not even be hers to hear.

Though she wouldn't mind talking to him more about it . . . about his past life.

The silence raised her awareness. Other than Stan's aside, she and Mark had been the only ones talking. Sophie being uncharacteristically mute; Stan unusually passive. Winks slipping between them.

The room suddenly awkward, Mark excused himself to the restroom, and Callie retrieved her cup, craving amaretto in it so badly.

Chapter 31

WITH NO SURPRISE, the New Year's Eve celebration wound up at El Marko's, and Callie could see a tradition taking shape on Edisto Beach. If Mark kept advertising the restaurant as the go-to place for birthdays and celebrations, the happy-go-lucky locale available for impromptu festivities, his name would crop up first in people's thoughts no matter the season.

The dining room filled to capacity, Mark tended bar as usual, with Callie and Stan claiming the familiar owner's table near the back, a selection of appetizers between them. Sophie dolled up in heels, pencil pants and a white faux-fur top, hair freshly frosted and a Happy New Year tiara in her pixie. She'd ceased welcoming folks and flitted table-to-table meeting partiers' requests. Callie heard her squealing laugh at least every five minutes.

Mark, Sophie . . . someone had hung mistletoe in several strategic spots throughout the place, and the revelers took ample advantage of the opportunities. Everybody kissing everybody. The music oscillated between Mexican and American, both throwing out enough beat to keep bodies bouncing. The big clock, hung on the wall just for this occasion, read just after eleven.

"I can't hear myself think," Callie spoke up, the bass of the present song clashing with the patrons shouting to hear each other. Sophie squealed again.

Stan just shook his head and ate a mini-quesadilla.

Mark arrived, setting another beer before Stan and a tonic and lime before Callie then snatching up their empties. "Y'all need anything?" he yelled.

"No thanks," she yelled back, happy to just sit and not be needed.

Natives had already spoken to her, their stories about Edisto Santa running rampant and no two alike. Many of them had asked her for confirmation of specific facts—lurid details really—about Brice and Janet, Arthur and Tate, but she stuck to the facts. The case was solved, suspects were in custody, and everyone was safe. Gossip already churned.

Nothing to be done about that until all the Edisto Santa facts were presented in court. She'd said her piece as the chief law enforcement officer. She had to leave the rest to the judge and jury.

Sarah made her way to the table and grabbed the empty chair Mark had occupied three hours earlier before the business consumed him.

Funny how nobody'd inquired of Callie about Ben.

Callie leaned over and gave a finger wave for her mother to move in closer. "How are you doing?" she asked, trying not to shout.

Her mother smiled in the sweet manner she always had, then motioned for Callie to lean over and listen, too. "Ben's ceremony is Wednesday," she said. "Cremation."

Raising a brow, Callie mouthed "Where? When?"

"I'll send it to you," Sarah replied. "We're renting a boat through Botany Bay and scattering his ashes on the water."

Callie smiled, then caught herself. Ben hated Edisto and just about everything affiliated with it . . . except for Aberdeen. He never went on the water, never fished. Visually querying her mother only prompted another smile from Sarah, with a dose of cool self-assurance behind it.

With an approving tip of her chin, Callie figured enough said. She'd delivered the bracelet Ben purchased to Sarah, for her to do with what she wanted. No way Callie'd ask what that plan would be. It would take a mighty magnanimous woman to fulfill Ben's wishes and deliver the piece of jewelry to its intended, but Callie suspected Sarah would do so.

"Where's Jeb?" her mother asked.

Of course the grandmother would ask about her grandson. They'd conversed some on Christmas, but Jeb had dodged her since. He grew up with Beverly as his grandmother, and out of the blue he learned she wasn't. And he wasn't accepting that change in his life as easily as Callie had in hers.

"He's in Middleton with Beverly," Callie said. "As the mayor, she has to appear at some high-brow function, and she asked Jeb to be her date."

Sarah gave an approving nod, the environment not conducive to too much discussion. This lady had endured a lot yet chose to believe all would be fine. Callie hoped she'd inherited a piece of that gene. With the noise escalating, they ceased attempts at conversation that were best had in another setting, and they watched the frisky New Year's celebrators.

"Too much noise," she shouted to Stan when the long hand on the massive clock ticked to 11:20. "I'm done." When he didn't hear, she made a cutting motion across her throat.

He swallowed the last of his beer, then rose and mannerly pulled out her chair.

"Bye, Sarah," she said in her mother's ear, a hug following. "Happy New Year."

Holding Callie's hand, Stan parted the people, his barrel-chested presence convenient when Callie's diminutive stature squared off with a horde of half-juiced merrymakers. Just past the bar, he stopped, and she almost ran into him.

"What?" she said, but he peeked up, and before she could follow his gaze, he stooped down and laid a kiss flush on her mouth. She withdrew laughing at the slick mistletoe move. "You old bear," she said, and he hugged her against him.

Their relationship had covered the gamut from boss and disciplinarian to mentor, from friend to almost lover and back to friend, but regardless, he deserved to steal a kiss on New Year's Eve. She loved this big guy. Both smiling, they went to leave, but a touch on Callie's shoulder stopped her.

Expecting yet another holiday well-wisher, she pivoted to return the good cheer only for another kiss to find its aim. A kiss longer than Stan's. Then a second peck after the first before Mark backed up.

She had no words, but when he grinned big, she couldn't help but grin back, though with puzzlement. "Um, Happy New Year?"

"Had to do that," he said. "You're leaving before midnight."

"Sorry." She tried to yell over the noise. "I'm just not a big crowd person."

He drew her to him, though stopping short of a hug. "I get it. Thanks for coming. I'll see you." Then he slipped a small envelope in her front pants pocket . . . and winked.

Still watching Mark, she reached for Stan behind her. He found her hand and started to leave. "Thanks again," she said clumsily to Mark as Stan led her outside.

The night sounded like a tomb after the racket, and Callie took a deep breath of relief at the peace . . . and tried to interpret that last kiss. Stan continued walking her to her car.

Once inside her SUV, she warmly grinned up at him holding her door. "Want to come?"

He did a little back up move. "Only if you want me to."

"Sure," she said. "Hop in."

He didn't have to ask where she drove. He read her that well. And about five blocks over, she nosed into the drive of the Seabrook beach house, grateful it wasn't rented. They left the car reverently and took the stairs to the porch. Without words, they relaxed on the wide red swing anchored into the high ceiling, and with her legs folded under her, she let Stan start the sway.

"You're a good kisser," she said, feeling comfortable in the dark with one of the few friends she could say almost anything to.

"Of course I am," he said.

Both stared across the street, past the empty lot that gave them the deep, dark vista of the Atlantic. The weather had warmed after Christmas, no surprise since South Carolina weather proved fickle in the winter holidays. The tide was out leaving a wide expanse of beach, but the low rollers still held enough splash to reflect diamonds from the three-quarter moon. Low breezes and muted noises. The peace she'd wanted in order to greet the New Year as close to Mike Seabrook as she could get.

But she wasn't as sad as last year on this swing. At least not about Seabrook.

"Brice owes you," Stan said. "How'd court go yesterday? The guy better count his blessings that all his crap went down in Colleton County."

"And not Charleston. Or a city like Boston," she said, referring to their past work as detectives. "Brice is out on bond, but damn if he doesn't owe Mark a monster favor. If this goes to trial, which I don't think it will, Mark's told the attorneys that he voluntarily stayed in the restaurant that night and that Brice never held him against his will. Aberdeen's coming off as a flake and was told Brice could file adultery charges against her in this state. Parties will probably come to an agreement of one or two years' probation and loss of right to own a firearm."

"Divorce is definitely in their future," Stan said.

She outright laughed. "Aberdeen has no place to go with Ben dead. Brice isn't wealthy, but with adultery on the table, I wouldn't be surprised if she begged forgiveness."

His sighed deep. "They're idiots."

They hadn't behaved well, that was for sure. She wondered how all this would change her relationship with Brice. Would he hold anything against her or understand she was simply solving a crime in which he'd stood front and center as the most likely culprit? Few people got over an accusation of murder, even if found innocent. If only he hadn't lost his frickin' mind in El Marko's they could've made all this go away.

"Your mother doing okay?"

Funny how "your mother" had come to mean Sarah in the last year in lieu of Beverly, though her adoptive mother had been a fixture on Edisto for fifty years. "She's fine."

"Ben's case concluded?"

"Yeah, I'm closing it," she said. "Though there are no witnesses, the pieces seem to fit. Tate slipped in to take a gift, saw Ben, shoved him, then ran. Ben chased Tate, but of course Tate out-maneuvered him. Ben most likely knew Brice clandestinely parked on Dolphin Road, so without a phone, and being closer to Dolphin than home, he went to find his friend. By then his head had to be throbbing, maybe his judgment off. Brice was gone, but Ben hadn't the steam to go home. So there he fell. Can't prove it, but it makes the most sense."

She swung a bit more, shifting her thoughts toward Janet. "Arthur's out on bond, too. Haven't seen him or Janet since. This has got to be a lot for them to absorb. Kid just made wrong choices, Stan, then lied about it. He gave back the stolen rings, and the two families, luckily, don't want him charged."

"Yeah," Stan said, "while those two families don't have a say-so, their opinions influence. He's lucky his aunt is sticking by him which means money and attorneys worth a damn. He'll have a record and considerable probation but likely come out okay."

Not like Tate, though, which went unsaid between them. No way those two boys would remain friends. Resuming a friendship might not even be an issue with the length of sentence Tate would likely receive.

His getaway into the jungle then the ordeal at the *Mullet House* removed any chance for bond. And regardless what Janet did, said, or paid for on his behalf, Tate would become a long-term resident of state prison. She'd mentioned taking care of his assets, namely, the marsh house, but unfortunately, she was a victim in the crime and wouldn't be allowed his power of attorney. Worse, the prosecution against Arthur would without a doubt demand Janet's and Arthur's testimony and cooperation against Tate . . . in order to get Arthur off lightly.

Janet's heart had to be broken.

Callie'd gone by Janet's house once, the Hummer in the drive, but no one had answered her knock.

God, her world had changed this year, and only fate would tell how these changes would impact the next one.

Stan clicked his phone and showed it to her. "Two minutes to midnight." Together they watched the countdown, then the little explosive cartoon fireworks as the fresh year ticked in. Then they watched the ocean again.

"You're much better, Chicklet," he said.

She peered over. "What, because I'm not sitting on Seabrook's porch bawling?"

He gave a dismissive shake of his head. "That's not you, gal. You're tough. Too tough. You don't let people in, but I've been keeping watch on you."

She scooched closer to him and he put an arm across the back of the swing. "Yes, you have," she said. "It helps."

"This beach wouldn't function without you," he continued, "and I hope you see that . . . now that . . . " But he seemed to find it difficult to finish.

She peered up at him. "Now that Edisto Beach has gotten over their favorite son Michael J. Seabrook being gone and finally accepted that I took his place? Go ahead, say it, because I can. It's okay, Stan."

But he shook his head. "No, Chicklet. Not what I'm saying at all."

"What then?"

"Edisto Beach's accepted you because you've accepted yourself, Callie. Which allows them to respect you."

She watched the water again. "I'll have to ponder that."

"Well, before you do, what's on that paper Mark passed off to you?"

She lightly slapped his leg. "If you know about it, then I assume you had a part of whatever it's about."

"Nope, not at all," he said.

Reaching into her pocket, she retrieved the note. "Shine your phone light over here," she said, opening the paper.

"Here's to the future, Callie. Your future service, your future friendship, and my future on Edisto Beach. Signed, Your future Edisto Santa."

"Told you he was a good guy," Stan said, after a *humph*.

Callie tucked away the paper, and he shut off his light. And as he rocked his feet on the floor, giving the swing renewed sway, they enjoyed the beach for a while longer . . . hidden in the dark. Because some thoughts you kept to yourself.

The End

About the Author

C. HOPE CLARK holds a fascination with the mystery genre and is author of the Carolina Slade Mystery Series as well as the Edisto Island Series, both set in her home state of South Carolina. In her previous federal life, she performed administrative investigations and married the agent she met on a bribery investigation. She enjoys nothing more than editing her books on the back porch with him, overlooking the lake with bourbons in hand. She can be found either on the banks of Lake Murray or Edisto Beach with one or two dachshunds in her lap. Hope is also editor of the award-winning FundsforWriters.com.

C. Hope Clark

Website: chopeclark.com

Twitter: twitter.com/hopeclark

Facebook: facebook.com/chopeclark

Goodreads: goodreads.com/hopeclark

Bookbub: bookbub.com/authors/c-hope-clark

Editor, FundsforWriters: fundsforwriters.com

CPSIA information can be obtained
at www.ICGtesting.com
Printed in the USA
JSHW041440011022
31121JS00003B/116